6/21

GIRL, 11

GIRL, 11

AMY SUITER CLARKE

Houghton Mifflin Harcourt
BOSTON   NEW YORK
2021

For information about permission to reproduce selections from this book, write to trade.permissions@hmhco.com or to Permissions, Houghton Mifflin Harcourt Publishing Company, 3 Park Avenue, 19th Floor, New York, New York 10016.

hmhbooks.com

Library of Congress Cataloging-in-Publication Data
Names: Clarke, Amy Suiter, author.
Title: Girl, 11 / Amy Suiter Clarke.
Other titles: Girl, eleven
Description: Boston : Houghton Mifflin Harcourt, 2021.
Identifiers: LCCN 2020034220 (print) | LCCN 2020034221 (ebook) |
ISBN 9780358418931 (hardcover) | ISBN 9780358449027 | ISBN 9780358449386 |
ISBN 9780358494935 (ebook)
Subjects: GSAFD: Suspense fiction.
Classification: LCC PS3603.L3699 G57 2021 (print) | LCC PS3603.L3699 (ebook) |
DDC 813/.6—dc23
LC record available at https://lccn.loc.gov/2020034220
LC ebook record available at https://lccn.loc.gov/2020034221

Book design by Margaret Rosewitz

Printed in the United States of America
DOC 10 9 8 7 6 5 4 3 2 1

To my mom,
who read thousands of my words before a sentence was published;
and to my dad,
who encouraged me to tell the truth even in fiction.

I need to see his face.
He loses his power when we know his face.

— MICHELLE McNAMARA

Part I

THE COUNTDOWN

1

Justice Delayed podcast

December 5, 2019

Transcript: Season 5, Episode 1

ELLE VOICE-OVER:

Minnesota is known for the cold. Frigid winters and stoic Nordic sensibilities. On this bright November morning, as I drive southwest in the land of ten thousand lakes, drifts of snow gust over the highway, aloft and swirling like phantoms. One minute I'm winding my way through flat expanses of prairie and farmland, the next I've arrived in the city—all concrete and lights and neat, modest lawns. Like many Midwest American states, there's a separation that runs along the invisible but impenetrable borders between rural and urban. Just a few miles is all it takes for demographics, ideologies, cultures, and customs to change.

But every now and then, something happens that shakes a whole state. Its impact is felt by everyone, uniting people in grief and a common purpose.

Just under twenty-four years ago, in the lively college student community of Dinkytown, a young woman named Beverly Anderson disappeared.

[THEME MUSIC]

ELLE INTRO:

The cases have gone cold. The perpetrators think they're safe. But with your help, I'll make sure that even though justice has been delayed, it will no longer be denied. I'm Elle Castillo, and this is *Justice Delayed*.

[*SOUND BREAK: Snow crunching underfoot; the echoes of "I'll Make Love to You" by Boyz II Men playing in the distance; the laughter of young adults.*]

ELLE VOICE-OVER:

In February 1996, twenty-year-old Beverly left a party she was at with her boyfriend and several other fellow juniors from the University of Minnesota. When the group walked out of the party, Beverly's boyfriend tried to convince her to come with them up to Annie's Parlour for late-night burgers and milkshakes. But Beverly had to get up early the next morning, so she insisted on going home. She was three months away from finishing her psychology degree and had already started an internship with a local clinic. They had an argument about it—nothing serious, just a spat like college lovers do. Eventually, he gave up and followed his friends alone. It was only five blocks to her apartment—a short walk she had made alone a hundred times before. Beverly zipped up her black wool coat, dipped her chin into her scarf, and waved goodbye to her friends.

It was the last time any of them saw her alive.

When she didn't show up for her internship the next day, Beverly's supervisor phoned her apartment. Her roommate, Samantha Williams, answered.

SAMANTHA:

I don't know how to explain it. As soon as I got the call, I had a feeling that something was wrong. I went up to her room to check, just to make sure, and yeah. Her bed wasn't slept in. None of her stuff was there, like her bag and keys and everything. I could tell she had never come home.

ELLE VOICE-OVER:

I'm sitting with Samantha Williams, now Carlsson, in her kitchen. She lives about an hour outside Minneapolis with her husband and two beagles, who sounded the warning before I even made it up to her front door.

SAMANTHA:

[Over the sound of two dogs barking.] Hush! Go to your crate. I said *crate*. Good girls. You see, they're well trained when they want to be.

ELLE:

So, what happened when you realized Beverly hadn't come home?

SAMANTHA:

Well, I told her supervisor, and he said we should call the police, so that's what I did. At first, they didn't want to investigate — you know, it hadn't been long enough or whatever. But once her boyfriend and me told them she was seen walking home alone, and that she was a dedicated student who had just started an internship, they started getting more worried. I know they interviewed [redaction tone], but his friends gave him a solid alibi. Other than that two or three minutes when they argued about her coming up to the restaurant with him, he was with them the whole rest of the night. The police came and talked to me that day, I think in the afternoon. You could find out in their report, if you have it.

ELLE VOICE-OVER:

I do. According to Detective Harold Sykes, Samantha was interviewed on February 5, 1996, at 3:42 p.m. — approximately seventeen hours after Beverly was last seen.

ELLE:

And from what you remember, what happened next?

SAMANTHA:

Nothing, really. All her close friends had been with her that night, and they were at Annie's Parlour for at least two hours after she left. Her family lived hours away, in Pelican Rapids. They figured there was no way the boyfriend did it, because he was only out of their friends' sight for a couple minutes. She just . . . vanished. Everyone thought she might have gotten lost or disoriented, maybe she was drunker than her friends thought and fell into the Mississippi River and drowned. It's happened before. But they searched the banks and snowdrifts for days, and there was no sign of her. Not until a week later.

ELLE VOICE-OVER:
Seven days after Beverly went missing, the manager of Annie's Parlour was locking up for the night when he noticed someone huddled up against the outside wall. He thought it was a homeless person and bent over to offer to take them to a shelter. When they didn't respond, the manager pulled the scarf away from their head and discovered the lifeless face of Beverly Anderson.

SAMANTHA:
[Through tears.] All anyone could focus on then was Beverly. Everyone was horrified, you know. This sweet, innocent, smart girl— dead. I couldn't believe it. I barely left our apartment for weeks after that, I was so afraid. Turns out, I had good reason to be.

ELLE:
Do you remember when you found out about the other victims?

SAMANTHA:
They didn't say anything on the news until they realized that second girl, Jillian Thompson, died the same way Beverly had. And she was missing for the same length of time—seven days. I think they found something on Jillian's body that linked her to Beverly, some DNA or something.

ELLE VOICE-OVER:
It was skin cells on her jacket. The police figured Jillian must

have offered it to Beverly when she got cold, wherever they were kept together. Jillian Thompson disappeared from a parking lot at Bethel University three days after Beverly did. Her family thought she had run off with a boyfriend they disapproved of. He was the primary suspect until the cases were finally connected.

[SOUND BREAK: A chair squeaking; a man clearing his throat.]

ELLE:
Can I ask you to introduce yourself for new listeners?

MARTÍN:
Uh, yes, I'm Dr. Martín Castillo, and I'm a medical examiner, an ME, for Hennepin County.

ELLE:
And?

MARTÍN:
And, full disclosure, I'm Elle's husband.

ELLE:
Regular listeners might remember Martín from seasons one and three, where he provided expert insight about the autopsies of Grace Cunningham and Jair Brown, respectively. His identification of an oddly shaped lividity mark on Jair's back helped us make a connection to a sofa in his uncle's house, which was key to helping the Minneapolis Crimes Against Children Division solve that case. I've brought him back into the studio to discuss the other way the cases of these murdered girls were connected, before the DNA test from Jillian's body even came back.

MARTÍN:
The simplest answer is that they were killed in the same way. The same, unusual way.

ELLE:

Explain that.

MARTÍN:

While Beverly Anderson showed signs of trauma on the right side of her head, her autopsy revealed that she had been struck several days before she died—likely on the day she was kidnapped. She passed away after suffering gastrointestinal distress, dehydration, and multiple organ failures. Those symptoms are consistent with a huge variety of poisons, and the pathologist might never have narrowed it down if it weren't for her stomach contents. It took a few weeks, but eventually tests determined she had eaten castor beans—likely several. Ricin poison takes days to work, and often people survive ingesting it, but it was clear the killer fed the toxin to her multiple times. She had also been whipped on her back shortly before death. Twenty-one lashes.

ELLE:

How could you tell it was shortly before death?

MARTÍN:

The way the scabs formed indicated that her blood stopped flowing soon after the wounds were inflicted. Her heartbeat was probably already slowing when she was beaten—meaning she was already dying, which led the ME to determine that the whipping was part of a ritual, not an attempt to kill her faster. This was confirmed when they found Jillian's body and she had been killed in exactly the same way. Organ failure due to castor bean poisoning, and exactly twenty-one lashes across the back, made with a switch.

ELLE:

What do you mean by "switch"?

MARTÍN:

A stick or branch of some kind—thin but sturdy. There was evidence both bodies had been in the woods or the country somewhere.

Leaf particles in their clothing, dirt under their nails. They figure the killer found a branch wherever he took them and completed the ritual then.

ELLE VOICE-OVER:

Jillian's body was also found seven days after she was taken, but not in the same place she'd disappeared from like Beverly. That would have been too easy. Instead, she was left on the lawn of Northwestern College—now called the University of Northwestern–St. Paul—a rival to her own Christian university, Bethel. However, despite the fact that both young women were college students, held for the same length of time, killed in the same manner, and left in a public space, their deaths were not immediately connected. Two different homicide squads worked on the cases, and while there were centralized police databases for things like DNA and fingerprint collection, there was no modus operandi database—nothing that collected the way victims were killed and analyzed whether cases might be connected based on the method of killing.

Police investigated for months, even arrested Jillian's boyfriend, but the charges were eventually dropped and both cases went cold. There were no similar murders, no new leads. Not until the following year.

[SOUND BREAK: A waterfall roaring.]

ELLE VOICE-OVER:

This is Minnehaha Falls, fifty-three feet of limestone and cascading water rushing on its way from Lake Minnetonka to the Mississippi River. The famous *Song of Hiawatha* poem by Henry Wadsworth Longfellow solidified its name, Minnehaha, which Longfellow interpreted as "laughing water." The Dakota name would be better translated as "curling water" or simply "waterfall," both of which are more apt. The intense, almost violent noise of charging water belies the idea of laughter. It was here, beneath the controversial bronze *Hiawatha and Minnehaha* statue, that the body of eighteen-year-old Isabelle Kemp was found.

The recording you heard was taken last spring, when the falls were swollen with melted snow. But when Isabelle was found, the water was frozen—a thick, rough mass of ice stuck in the act of falling, as if enchanted. She almost wasn't seen; a fresh blanket of snow was halfway finished covering her body before a tourist couple who came to view the falls noticed her red jacket peeking through the powder.

[SOUND BREAK: Background noise from a diner.]

ELLE:
When Isabelle Kemp's body was found in January 1997, police quickly connected her murder with the cases in 1996. She had been missing for seven days and was whipped shortly before death. That's also when you came up with the killer's moniker, isn't it?

DETECTIVE HAROLD SYKES:
Yes, although indirectly. It certainly wasn't my intent.

ELLE VOICE-OVER:
That's the lead detective on the case, Detective Harold Sykes. I met up with him at his favorite diner in Minneapolis.

ELLE:
But you noticed something that no one else had picked up on. Tell me about that.

SYKES:
Yes, well, we had already noticed that the killer seemed obsessed with certain numbers. He kidnapped the first two women three days apart, he kept them for seven days, and he whipped them twenty-one times. So, we figured those numbers meant something to him. The pattern was consistent. Which meant my team immediately scoured the missing persons records, looking for someone who might have been kidnapped three days after Isabelle was. But then when I was going through the cases, I noticed another pattern. Beverly Anderson

was twenty years old. Jillian Thompson was nineteen. And Isabelle was eighteen.

ELLE:

They were each a year younger than the last.

SYKES:

Yes. It was just a hunch at that time, but I thought there was a good chance his next victim would be seventeen. It also fit with his number obsession. If the ages weren't a coincidence, I knew that was bad news. It meant he probably had a plan. And that's what I told them, when the reporters interviewed me. I regretted it at the time, but I suppose it doesn't matter now. Someone would have thought of it eventually. I just told them: I think this guy has started some kind of twisted countdown.

ELLE VOICE-OVER:

It was a simple observation, but it stuck in the minds of Minnesotans across the state, filling everyone with a sense of impending doom. The killer was far from finished. Every girl knew she couldn't let her guard down—as much as any girl ever does. A catchy name is all it takes to turn a local case into a national sensation.

Within hours, all the channels were calling him the same thing: the Countdown Killer.

2

Elle

January 9, 2020

Elle pulled her car up outside Ms. Turner's house and paused the podcast on her stereo. It was one of her favorite true crime pods, more focused on the psychology of convicted criminals rather than investigating cold cases like hers. They were just getting to the good stuff, behavioral analysis of a legendary serial rapist in the Pacific Northwest, but it wasn't exactly child-appropriate, and her best friend's daughter was already making the half run between Ms. Turner's front door and the warmth of Elle's car.

The passenger door swung open, letting in a gust of frigid, dry air tinged with the smell of snow. Natalie jumped in and slammed the door, letting out a dramatic "Brr!"

Cranking up the heat, Elle asked, "How were piano lessons, kiddo?"

"Good." Natalie buckled her seat belt and tugged her scarf away from her neck. Even in the dim late-afternoon light, her usually pale face was ruddy from the slap of winter air. "I mean, I'm still just doing scales all the time. I don't think Ms. Turner knows how to teach more than that."

Elle chuckled as she pulled back onto the road. "You've only been taking lessons for four months."

"Yeah, I know, but it's boring. I can do it in my sleep."

"Be patient. Scales are the foundation. You have to learn to do the basic stuff well before you can tackle a whole composition." Elle smiled at how quickly she could snap into mom mode, teaching life wisdom and doing piano lesson pickup like Natalie was her own kid.

"I guess she did teach me the happy birthday song today, too."

"Oh, really? How come?"

Natalie laughed. "Aunt Elle, you know why."

At a stoplight, Elle looked at her and gave an exaggerated shrug. "What do you mean?"

The girl giggled and rolled her eyes. "Because it's my birthday, nerd."

"Nerd!" Elle put her hand to her chest, as if mortally wounded. "You only ever call Martin that."

"That's 'cause he's usually the only one being a nerd."

"All right, all right, no more games. Happy birthday, sweetheart." She couldn't quite believe that Natalie was ten. So close to the age of the youngest victim in the TCK case, which had been absorbing every minute of her life since she started doing interviews for the latest season of *Justice Delayed* six months ago. She could barely close her eyes without seeing the faces of those girls, the ones that lined the wall in her recording studio. Natalie was the closest thing Elle had to a daughter—imagining her in the place of TCK's youngest victim caused a surge of rage that made Elle dizzy. If it wasn't for Natalie, Elle probably wouldn't have started the podcast. If she hadn't known what it was like to love a child enough to kill, she might never have started hunting the monsters who hurt them.

Elle leaned across the console and gave Natalie a loud kiss on the forehead just as the light turned green. "Did you do anything fun for your birthday?"

"I got sung to in class, and they let me bring in cookies for everyone," Natalie said, fiddling with one of her dark blond braids. "And I came in third in freestyle."

"You couldn't pay me to put on a bathing suit in this weather."

"If we stopped swimming when it got cold, we'd only swim three months out of the year," Natalie said as they pulled up to Elle's house. "Besides, it's, like, eighty degrees in there."

"I'll stick to lakes in the summer, but I'm proud of you for doing so well," Elle said. The wind bit into her skin as she got out of the car and checked to make sure Natalie was walking carefully on their slick driveway. She made a mental note to ask Martín to put more salt down later.

"Yum!" Natalie said as soon as they walked through the front door. Elle's mouth watered in agreement, taking in the warm, spicy fragrance. They followed their noses to the kitchen, where Martín was wearing his favorite floral apron and twisting a salt grinder over a pot simmering on the stove. He was making his take on spaghetti and meatballs: the meat a blend of beef and minced chorizo, with a dash of chili pepper in the sauce. It was Natalie's favorite.

"Hey, birthday girl!" Martín dropped the spoon into the pot and reached his arms out to catch Natalie, who ran into them and squealed when he lifted her up into his signature bear hug. They spun around once, and he set her down on the counter, pulling the spoon out of the pot and blowing on it before he offered it to her. "For your inspection, señorita?"

Natalie gave it a taste, and her eyes lit up. "I believe that's your best work, señor."

When Martín set her back on her feet, he pointed at the silverware drawer. "I know it's your birthday, but would you mind setting the table? Your mom should be here soon." As soon as the girl gathered the cutlery and left, Martín turned to Elle with a smile. His wavy black hair stuck out in a few random angles; he was always running his hands through it when it wasn't covered by his surgical cap at work. Still stirring the pot, he leaned away from the stove and gave her a warm kiss.

"Smells delicious." Elle turned to pour herself a glass of red wine.

"Thanks. How are you, mi vida?" Martín asked.

Elle remembered the first time he called her that in front of Natalie after she started Spanish classes last year. Elle hadn't learned any until high school, and Martín spoke fluent English by the time they met, but she'd dug out her old college Spanish textbook the day after their first date anyway. She didn't want to miss out on conversations when she met his family in Monterrey, and with Minnesota's high population of Mexican and Central American immigrants, it had come in handy on the job too. But the fancy prep school Natalie attended let kids start from third grade, so she knew what it meant when he called Elle *mi vida*.

"Why do you call her your life?" Natalie had asked. "Is it because you can't live without her?"

Elle had expected him to tell her it was a common term of endearment where he was from in Mexico, particularly between men and their wives, but instead he looked at Elle while he answered: "No, it's because when I met Elle, she reminded me I spend too much time around death. She helps me remember to enjoy my life."

He was being extra romantic that day, and Martín gave most men a run for their money in the romance department.

"Elle?" His voice brought her back to the present.

"I'm fine," she said, knowing that her forced smile wouldn't fool him. "I can't believe Natalie is ten. Seems like just yesterday she was that skinny four-year-old knocking on my door out of the blue." Elle blinked away tears and took a drink of wine.

Martín set the spoon down and pulled her into his arms. "This investigation is getting to you, isn't it?" he asked, rubbing circles on her back.

Elle tensed. "I'm fine," she said again.

He pulled away, meeting her gaze. "I know you are." He looked like he wanted to say something else, but instead, he just nodded and turned back to the stove.

The doorbell rang as Natalie returned to the kitchen for plates. "I've got it," Elle said.

"Geez, it's cold," Sash said, shivering as Elle shut the door behind her. Sash stamped her boots on the entryway rug and slipped them off, careful to avoid the melting slush on the carpet with her stockinged feet.

"My dad used to call this tongue-gluing weather," Elle said, surprised by the sudden recollection. She hadn't thought about her dad in ages. "You know, because of all the dumb kids who used to dare each other to lick something metal in the winter and then got their tongues stuck."

Sash's big bangle earrings caught the light when she laughed, her head tilted back. After unwinding her scarf, she pulled the purple knit cap off her head and set them both on the bench by the door. She'd shaved her hair off again sometime in the last couple days, leaving only a short fuzz that highlighted her elfin features. It was an odd look for a corporate lawyer and often led people to underestimate her, which made it all the more delicious when she decimated them in court.

"That's great. I'm using that one."

Elle led the way to the dining room, past the hallway mirror that reminded her she hadn't showered or done anything with her hair today. She'd been locked away in her studio right up until she had to go pick up Natalie.

"Any new leads on TCK?" Sash whispered.

Elle paused. Aside from investigation, she didn't get out of the house much, and most of the family members and witnesses she'd interviewed never said his name. It was unsettling to hear someone say the initials that had been running through her head for months, like a fading echo becoming loud again.

"Nothing new," she said, glancing back at her friend. "It's a little early yet."

Sash smiled. "A couple of the associates were talking about the case in my meeting today. This is going to be your biggest season yet, for sure."

Nodding, Elle tried to keep her expression neutral. She had felt pressure to solve the cold cases she investigated in earlier seasons on the podcast, but nothing compared to this. It had only been a few weeks since she launched episode one, but she already knew this case was going to be different. Her inbox was full of comments, theories, and criticism—not just from listeners in the Midwest, but Australia, Indonesia, England, the Netherlands. It felt like the whole world was watching her.

But she could do this. All the cases she'd worked before, the troubled children in CPS and the previous four seasons of the podcast, they had been the foundation—the scales she practiced as she built toward something more complex. TCK was her magnum opus.

"You look pale." Sash took her arm gently, stopping her before they could enter the dining room. "Shit, I'm sorry, Elle. You're probably already nervous enough without me telling you how big this case is."

"No, it's okay. I mean, I've always known it was going to put a huge spotlight on the podcast. I just didn't anticipate how much." Elle met her best friend's gaze as she pressed her fingernails into her own palm. "My producer and I are seeing lots of chatter online, ideas floated on our social media, but nothing concrete yet. I know it's only been a few weeks, but I feel like I'm failing them."

"The girls on the wall," Sash said. Besides Martín, Sash was the only one Elle ever allowed into her studio upstairs. "You're not failing them, Elle. You're *honoring* them. You're telling their stories and trying to get justice. You're too hard on yourself."

Before Elle could respond, the door to the dining room swung open and Natalie peeked her head out. "You guys going to come in or what? I'm starving."

Sash smiled at Elle, gave her arm one more squeeze, and then they followed Natalie into the room where Martín was dishing up.

\\\\\\\\\\

"How's your birthday been, sweet?" Sash asked, giving her daughter a hug.

"Good. Thanks for leaving work early," Natalie said.

"Of course! You think I'd miss this?" If Elle didn't know Sash better, she might have missed the shadow that crossed her best friend's face. It was a sore subject between her and Natalie, how late Sash worked some nights. But she always made it to the events that counted, and now that Elle worked from home full-time, she was able to help fill in the gaps. Swim meets, piano lesson pickups, even the occasional field trip chaperone gig. At this point, she was somewhere between a very involved aunt and a glorified babysitter, although Sash insisted she was more like a second parent Natalie had adopted herself. Either way, she loved it.

Pulling out the chair next to Natalie, Sash lifted her hands like an MC announcing the next act. "Ladies, gentleman, and gender-ambivalent: ten years ago today, a remarkable event happened." The sleeves of her draped blouse swept the top of the table, narrowly avoiding the spaghetti sauce. "My daughter, the one and only Natalie Hunter, came into this world the size of a Chipotle burrito and squawking like a crow."

Natalie giggled and covered her face with her hands.

"I know things weren't always easy, the first few years of your life, when we moved around so much. But I'm glad we're here now, and I'm glad you get to celebrate turning ten with your family." Sash looked in Elle's direction, but it was hard to see her expression through the sudden blur of tears. It still got her whenever Sash referred to Elle as family. Besides Martín and her in-laws, Sash and Natalie were the only family Elle had.

Natalie leaned forward, looking at the plate of cooling food in front of her. "C'mon, Mom, I'm hungry."

They all laughed, and Sash raised her glass. "All right, all right. Sue a mom for giving a speech on her daughter's tenth birthday. To Natalie!"

"To Natalie," Martín and Elle echoed, raising their wineglasses. They clinked with Natalie's glass of cola and then they all dug in.

"How was your day, Sash?" Elle asked as she twirled pasta onto her fork.

Sash took a sip of wine. "Not bad. This merger I've been working on is soul-destroying, though. The CEOs both insist on pretending everything's rosy at their board meetings, but I can't even get them to sit at the same table to negotiate anymore. One guy said something about the other guy's golf swing, and suddenly a multimillion dollar deal is on the line. And they say women are emotional."

Martín snorted around a mouthful of pasta.

"How about you, Martín? How's life with the stiffs?" Sash asked. She pronounced his name correctly, Mar-teen, rather than the anglicized way their lazier acquaintances tried to get away with.

He held up his fork with a speared cherry tomato. "Oh, you know, pretty busy. This time of year I can't clear the bodies fast enough."

"Martín!" Elle said.

He held up his hands, palms out in the classic I'm-innocent stance. "Sorry! It's not like they don't know what I do."

"Yeah, Elle, it's not like I don't know what he does." Natalie took a sip of her water and grinned. "I want to be a medical examiner someday."

Elle shook her head and cut her eyes at her best friend. Sash confided in her a few weeks ago that Natalie had developed an innocent crush on Martín, although by that time it had been obvious. She'd abruptly stopped calling Martín "tío" about a month ago, insisted on using his first name, and clung to every word he had to say. Sash blamed it on puberty. It had been a few years since Elle did her master's in child psychology, but developmentally speaking, a ten-year-old girl falling in love with the only close adult man in her life was pretty standard stuff.

Even though he must have known they were watching in amusement, Martín ignored Sash and Elle and made eager conversation with Natalie about how to pursue a career in forensic pathology.

"I think you'd make a great medical examiner," he said. "You're going to have to improve your knife skills, though. I'm still scarred from the last time you helped me chop peppers for fajitas." He held up his thumb, showing her the small pink crescent that marred his medium-brown skin.

She shoved him on the arm, her face turning red. "That was two years ago, and I apologized like a thousand times. You're such a baby."

Martín cradled his hand to his chest, his mouth dropping open in fake offense. "Cómo te atreves. But I suppose you're right. In my line of work, no one risks bleeding to death if your blade misses the mark now and then. I'm sure you'll be fine."

Elle laughed, but there was a layer of sadness underneath as she watched her husband interact with Natalie. It was hard not to wonder what kind of father Martín would have been. Sash and Elle met during the time that Elle and Martín were trying hardest to get pregnant, when they had moved into the new house across the street to make space for what they were sure would be at least a couple children. All the dewy, fertile girls Elle went to high school with seemed to get pregnant just by thinking about it, so it was a relief when Sash was so transparent about her own experience with IVF. She'd never been interested in sex or romance, but she always wanted to be a parent, so she had gone the test tubes and injections route. When Elle told her about her own fertility treatments, they commiserated about the anxious nightmare of trying to get pregnant through science (although Sash liked to joke that the idea of getting pregnant the other way was much more anxiety-inducing for her).

After years of trying, though, Elle couldn't keep putting her body through the stress and hormones anymore. She and Martín finally agreed they weren't meant to be parents, but by that time, they were so close to Natalie that it eased the ache of that decision—at least a little.

"You know you're going to have to do a lot of science to be a medical examiner, right, sweet?" Sash said. "And you might need to get over your fear of needles."

Natalie lifted her chin. "I can do that."

Elle took a bite of food to hide her smile. Natalie was the kind of kid who was always getting excited about something new. Six months ago, she was into animal rights—she found a video on YouTube and swore off eating meat for the rest of her life. Not a day went by that she wasn't talking about cages or cattle prods. And then one day, Elle went over to her house and she was eating a hamburger and ranting about climate change. Most of the time, she moved on after a few months or so, but one of the things she'd stuck with was religion. Natalie's school friend gave her a Bible a couple years ago, and since then the girls had been going to church together almost every Sunday. To Sash's credit, she never tried to convince Natalie to stay home, even though she had no interest in religion herself.

Elle loved the girl's passion. She knew better than anyone: the thing that pisses you off the most in life can make a pretty good career. Natalie was still too young to settle on one thing yet, but she would. Elle had been only a year older than Natalie when her life was set on fire, blazing an unmistakable path in front of her.

That thought reminded her of the faces on her studio wall upstairs, all those young futures that had been snuffed out, and suddenly Elle sat back in her chair, blinking hard against the images branded on her mind. Taking a sip of wine, she glanced around the table. Sash and Natalie didn't seem to have noticed, but Martín was watching her, one eyebrow raised in a silent question. She nodded once and picked up her fork again.

When they finished eating, Sash stood and started to pick up the empty plates.

"Oh, Sash, you don't have to do that." Martín got up too, trying to take the dishes from her.

"Relax, Martín, I'm not going to wash them or anything. Natalie can do that—consider it payment for the gas money you spend carting her around everywhere while I'm at work."

"Hey, the pleasure of my company is payment enough," Natalie said as she tossed a braid over her shoulder.

Martín burst out laughing, and Sash hollered her daughter's name from the kitchen. Pushing aside the pictures in her head, Elle chuckled too.

As she stood to help Sash clean up, her phone buzzed in her pocket. Elle stepped into the hall and looked at the screen. There were dozens of email notifications from her show account. She ignored the alerts on her social media; she'd deal with those later. Most of the subject lines were the standard fare, but one jumped out like a typo on a billboard:

I know who he is.

3

Justice Delayed podcast

December 5, 2019

Transcript: Season 5, Episode 1

ELLE:
What happened after the press went wild with the TCK moniker?

SYKES:
We had almost nothing to go on, no physical evidence. You didn't have shows like *CSI* or *Law & Order: SVU* back then, so the awareness of what could be done with DNA wasn't there for most people. Yet somehow, this guy avoided leaving any trace of himself behind. Which led us to think he might have some sort of science or medical training.

ELLE:
Or that he was a cop.

SYKES:
That was also an option, yes. Either way, we weren't able to find anything that could help us stop the inevitable from happening. Within hours of connecting Isabelle's murder to the 1996 killings, we figured out who his next victim likely was: a seventeen-year-old girl, Vanessa Childs, who'd gone missing three days prior while taking out the

trash at her fast food job. When we told her parents our suspicions, they were understandably distraught.

ELLE VOICE-OVER:

There is a special kind of helplessness, waiting for someone to turn up dead. Vanessa's family hoped police were wrong about the connection, but the timing was so precise. And then, late in the afternoon on the day Isabelle's body was found, another girl went missing. Sixteen-year-old Tamera Smith, a promising basketball player and straight-A student, vanished on the short walk between her school and the gym.

Detectives continued to search for suspects. Lab results were rushed, but no male DNA was found on Isabelle's body. They had nothing to go on. The story was all over the news by then, and sales of mace and handguns shot up. Everyone was waiting for the next girl to disappear; everyone was determined not to be that girl. The mayor of Minneapolis reportedly considered instating a curfew, but was told it would send the wrong message that the women were to blame.

Vanessa's family organized searches in the parks and wooded areas around the suburb of Roseville, where she was last seen, but it was fruitless. Three days later, a week after she had been taken, her body was found in some shrubs on the shore of Bde Maka Ska. There was barely time for the city to breathe before Tamera's parents went to the media, convinced their daughter would be next and the police weren't doing enough to stop it.

[SOUND BREAK: A phone ringing three times.]

ANONYMOUS:
Hello?

ELLE:
Hello, is this [redaction tone]?

ANONYMOUS:
Who's calling?

ELLE:
Hi, my name is Elle Castillo, and I'm an investigator looking into the Countdown Killer case. I was hoping I could talk to you about—

ANONYMOUS:
Are you a detective?

ELLE:
No.

ANONYMOUS:
I don't talk to you journalists.

ELLE:
Well, I'm not really a journalist either.

ANONYMOUS:
Then who the hell are you?

ELLE:
I'm an independent investigator specializing in cold cases of crimes against children. I share my work on a podcast.

ANONYMOUS:
A what?

ELLE VOICE-OVER:
It took some time to explain the concept of a podcast, especially an investigative podcast, but eventually I got her to come around. I'm keeping her anonymous, because it was clear she didn't want to be associated with this case. For the purposes of clarity, I asked if I could call her Susan, and she agreed.

ELLE:
So, can you tell me how you came to be involved with the Countdown Killer case?

SUSAN:

I came to be involved by sticking my nose where it didn't belong, and I have regretted that decision for about twenty years.

ELLE:

Can you explain what you mean by that?

SUSAN:

It was in 1997, after the second girl turned up dead. For days, I'd noticed my husband acting strangely: coming home disheveled and skittish hours after I expected him. At first, I thought it was an affair, but that didn't explain the dirt.

ELLE:

Dirt?

SUSAN:

Yes, his pants were filthy, like he'd been kneeling in a garden or something, only it was the dead of winter. It took me two washes to get his jeans clean. Then one night we were watching TV together, and they were talking about this serial killer on the news, how they thought he had killed two girls the year before, and now it seemed like he was back. And Jimmy, he'd been half asleep, but as soon as that segment came on, he sat up like he'd just been shocked by a bad outlet. He didn't say anything, just stared at the TV until they moved on. It made my hair stand on end.

So that night, I started thinking and looking at my old calendar, and I realized that Jimmy had told me he was on a work trip a year before. Right at the same time those poor girls got killed. I just couldn't shake the feeling it could be him.

ELLE:

What did you do?

SUSAN:

If you can believe it, at first I considered not saying anything. I mean,

I was only twenty-three. My husband was twenty-seven. We were young, and I was in love. I didn't think he could do something like that, but the timing was just . . . uncanny. So eventually, I put all my notes together and visited the detective who was running the case.

ELLE VOICE-OVER:

Detective Sykes was in that blurry stage of having too many leads and not enough time, so when Susan walked in with all the reasons why the killer had to be her husband, he initially brushed her off. She was halfway to her car by the time he scanned her notes and ran after her into the parking lot. Susan's husband, Jimmy, became the first major suspect Detective Sykes had—a solid lead, after all this time.

SYKES:

You know in Greek mythology when they talk about the sirens, those beautiful women that lure sailors to the rocks and kill them? Well, [redaction tone] was a nice girl, but deep down, I think she had some siren in her. Of course, it's mostly my fault. By the time Tamera went missing, I was so desperate to have something to tell these girls' parents that I wanted to listen to her. And she wasn't wrong—the time-frame of the murders did line up with her husband's unexplained absences. But that was it. So, I got together a detail to follow this guy 24/7 for the next two days, to see if he would lead us to wherever the girl was being kept. We figured TCK visited his victims during the seven days he held them. He may even have kept them in his home—there was evidence on Isabelle's and Vanessa's bodies that they had been forced to do some domestic labor while they were held captive.

ELLE VOICE-OVER:

This was an escalation. Beverly and Isabelle showed no physical signs of abuse other than the effects of poison and lashes on their backs, but TCK's triad of victims in 1997 was different. Their hands were dried and cracking, and harsh cleaning chemicals were found on their skin. Their knees were bruised and their palms blistered. In addition to the lashings, TCK had clearly forced them to clean, probably for hours on end, but it was impossible to know what or where. Or, more importantly, why.

Also, while I think Detective Sykes is entitled to his view of her as a siren, nothing about my interview with Susan led me to believe she was being intentionally manipulative or distracting when she accused her husband. Even though she later divorced him, she clearly loved him at the time and agonized over the decision to come forward. And she wasn't completely off base. The tail Detective Sykes put on Jimmy turned up a reasonable explanation for his odd behavior — although not an innocent one.

ELLE:
Tell me about what you found out after surveilling Jimmy.

SYKES:
She was right about one thing: he was committing a crime. Jimmy worked as a county commissioner, and he'd been accepting cash bribes in exchange for granting government contracts to certain businesses. He'd been burying money on a property out in the country that he'd bought with cash, without telling her. He thought once he had enough saved up, he could surprise her with their dream house and tell her he won the lottery or something.

ELLE:
What about the way he reacted to the news story about the murdered girls? [redaction tone] said he sat up like he'd been shocked and couldn't stop staring at the screen.

SYKES:
Ah right, yeah, we asked him about that. Apparently, he was looking at the moving chyron on the bottom of the newscast, where they show the stock market numbers. One of the companies he had invested in with some of his illicit cash had taken a dive. He lost a huge chunk of his investment. He told us he kept watching for the numbers to come around again, hoping he had imagined them, and he hadn't realized his wife had noticed his reaction.

ELLE:

So, you never found any reason to believe he was involved in the murders?

SYKES:

None whatsoever, and I want to make that clear. I'm not excusing political bribery, but what Jimmy did, he's paid for. He lost his job, his wife left him after he was convicted, and he spent eight years in prison. There's no way he could be TCK.

ELLE VOICE-OVER:

It might seem like such an obvious thing that it doesn't need to be stated, but suspicion of Jimmy has continued to circulate in online forums and the popular culture references of this case for two decades. Some online sleuths believe that he was the original Countdown Killer and then a copycat took over, or that he was partnered with someone else from the beginning who continued the work after he was in prison. They say this is why there were only two girls that first year, and also why there was a difference in the way they were treated. I want to make this clear: in my years of investigating this case, I have looked into Jimmy's life extensively, and I can say with absolute certainty that he is not TCK. You don't have to believe me, but if you want to save yourself hours of trying to pin these gruesome murders on an innocent man, rest assured that I have tried and failed.

What is true is this: while Detective Sykes and his team were reasonable in listening to Susan's suspicion of her husband, their investigation took them off course. And while officers followed Jimmy from his work to his property and watched him bury stolen money, Tamera Smith's body was found under the Stone Arch Bridge. Like Isabelle and Vanessa, she showed signs of manual labor.

ELLE:

I'm wondering if you can clear something up about the timeline for me. A lot of people interested in this case find it confusing. If TCK took the girls three days apart, wouldn't he have had them all together for at least one day? One girl on day one, two girls on day three, and three girls on day six?

SYKES:
Yes, that was commonly misreported at the time, and you still see it pop up now and then. Especially in online forums, where people want to dispute the patterns and numbers. There will always be people out there who don't want to admit the existence of an active serial killer. The girls were taken no less than seventy-two hours apart —three full days. Some people find it easier to think of it in terms of nights, though. He had each girl for three nights before he took another.

ELLE:
So, they were there six nights, not seven, before he killed them?

SYKES:
That's right. They were usually dead before noon on the seventh day.

ELLE:
Okay, that helps, thank you. I think it's important to be clear about the pattern, and with a case this huge that has had so much information put out already, it's good to make sure it's accurate.

SYKES:
I'm all for accuracy, yes. Don't see a lot of that in media these days.

ELLE:
I only aim to tell the truth on my show, Detective. Now, despite the lead on Jimmy not panning out, you did get something when you found Tamera's body—a clue that, despite TCK's obsessive attention to detail, seemed to be a mistake.

SYKES:
Yes, on her pant cuff, there was a stain the lab later determined to be tea.

ELLE:

Tell me more about that. Your department has said that it's a special kind of Darjeeling tea, but there are people who have expressed doubts that you could tell what specific tea a stain comes from. What do you say to those people?

SYKES:

Well, first of all, it's not my department saying it; all we did was pass on what the forensics lab told us. And our knowledge of this tea sample has evolved over time, as the lab technology has improved. Back in 1997, they were only able to tell us it was an oolong tea, because of the way the leaves were oxidized. Based on the flecks of tea in the stain, they were reasonably confident it was brewed loose-leaf, rather than from a sachet. But they did more testing on the sample last year, using a newer technique called direct analysis in real time, or DART, which they can do without diminishing the sample. That's good because it was small to begin with, and now it's almost gone. Several local teahouses donated boxes of all their teas, and a few of them made lists of signature ingredients for the lab techs to look for when examining the sample. This helped the lab identify markers they could compare the stain to.

ELLE:

Yes, she didn't want to be recorded, but the forensic biologist I spoke to, Dr. Forage, said they combined the DART process with something called a High-Resolution Accurate-Mass mass spectrometer. They were able to identify the specific tea the stain most likely came from, an expensive loose-leaf Darjeeling imported from India that uses a patented fermentation process. Something called Majestic Sterling.

ELLE VOICE-OVER:

Quick listener note: A local tea expert I interviewed talked to me for over thirty minutes about Majestic Sterling, and I'm sure he'll be disappointed to know that I didn't use any of the audio. I'm sorry, but I just couldn't do that to you, although I'm deeply grateful for his time. I think the most important information he relayed boils down to this (pardon the pun): this is not your run-of-the-mill Celestial Seasonings Darjeeling. Majestic Sterling sells for almost a dollar a gram.

SYKES:

I'm a coffee guy myself, and the science always went over my head, but if you talked to Dr. Forage, you have the best information available. She's the foremost expert in Hennepin and did the latest round of testing herself. Hates being on any sort of media, but she knows her stuff.

ELLE:

As I understand it, the identification of the substance as oolong tea led to the first major debate within the investigative team over what information should be released to the public, and what should be kept secret. Ultimately, you decided to let the public know, hoping it might push someone who was already suspicious of their neighbor or family member into coming forward, isn't that right?

SYKES:

Yes, that's right. That was the first moment I can point to in this case where I can say, "That was a mistake." We should not have done that.

ELLE VOICE-OVER:

Next time, on *Justice Delayed* . . .

4

Elle

January 9, 2020

At the kitchen door, Elle told Martín and Sash she'd come right back, and then she raced up to her studio.

She opened the email on her desktop. It contained only one line of text besides the subject — a phone number. She dialed it on her cell and held her breath. On the fourth ring, a man with a Mexican accent said, "Hello?"

"Yeah, hi, this is Elle Castillo from the *Justice Delayed* podcast." She glanced at the name on his email. "Is this Leo Toca?"

For a moment, there was no response. She looked down at her phone to see if they got disconnected, but no — the call was still active. "You emailed me a few minutes ago?"

"I know who he is."

It got hard for Elle to breathe. *Is.* Both in the email and now on the phone, the man had used the present tense. She tried to keep her voice steady. "How do you know?"

His words spilled out, urgency making them all jumble together. "I knew something was off about him, and then I started listening to your newest season a few days ago, and I realized there were connections with your case. He was in the areas the girls were killed. He has that fancy tea in his house they found on that one girl's clothes.

I'm sure of it. I have the evidence, but I knew no one would believe me. That's why I called you—you've got to help before it's too late for her."

"Leo, please, slow down. Too late for who?"

Another few seconds of silence went by, and then: "When can you meet me?"

Elle's voice was hoarse. "Now. Right now. Do you live in the Cities? Let's meet at a Perkins or something."

"No, I . . . Please, you need to come to me. My apartment's in St. Paul. It's not safe for me to leave my house."

Her brain did a quick calculation, weighing the risk of meeting a strange man at his home against not getting what could be a critical lead.

"Why don't you feel safe? Tell me what's happening. This is serious; you had better not be fucking with me." She bit her lower lip, regretting how aggressive the last sentence sounded. Dealing with fake tips was part of this job. So was dealing with nervous informants.

"In an hour. Meet me in an hour, and I'll give you everything you need to know to catch him." He rattled off an address on Hamline Avenue and hung up.

For a moment, Elle sat at her desk with the phone still clutched to her ear. Then she set it down and opened her internet browser.

There were a few social media accounts for guys named Leo Toca in the Twin Cities area, but only two who had loose enough privacy settings for her to get a look at their profiles. One was an abuelo with a brood of grandkids surrounding him in his profile picture—definitely not the guy on the phone. The other was thirty-five years old and worked two part-time jobs, one as a janitor at a local university, the other as a mechanic in a shop on Snelling. Moving on to Google, a news report from last year caught her eye: Leo's name alongside his business partner's, Duane Grove, from when they appeared in court accused of running a chop shop. They were acquitted; the only reason it made the news was because one of the cars they were accused of stripping for parts belonged to a local politician. Since that trial, it seemed like he had kept a low profile.

Someone knocked on her studio door. Elle stood up, flicked off the light to hide the crime scene photos on the wall, and opened the door.

Natalie stood in the hall, one braid threaded through her fingers. "Mom said to tell you it's time for cake." She tried to look past Elle into the dark room. "Are you working on your podcast?"

"Sort of, yes. Sorry, I know I shouldn't on your birthday." Elle put her hand on top of Natalie's head, smoothing her perfect part. They started back down the hall.

"Doesn't it make you sad, working on cases where people hurt kids?"

Elle winced. Natalie was aware of what Elle did, just like she knew the fascinatingly macabre information about Martín's job. But just as she would never be allowed in the morgue, Elle did her best to keep the girl out of the podcast studio where all her crime scene photos and case notes were stuck to the walls. Still, there wasn't much Sash could do to keep Natalie from listening to *Justice Delayed*; her generation had no issue navigating parental controls and erasing browser history. Elle was pretty sure the girl had heard at least a few episodes.

"Yes, it makes me sad. I know the families of those kids loved them just as much as I love you, and I can't stand what people did to them. But if I can help find those bad people and make them pay, then I think that's a good thing. And that's what I try to do."

As they got to the bottom of the stairs, Natalie looked back at her. There was a somber depth to her eyes that had no business in a ten-year-old. "Are you good at it?"

"I think so. Yeah, I am." Elle nodded.

"Okay, then you should keep doing it, even if it's hard. That's what Mom's always telling me when I complain about swimming."

Elle put an arm around the girl's slight shoulders and pulled her in close.

They walked into the dining room where the light from birthday candles flickered on the table. Beaming, Sash started "Happy Birthday" about three keys too high, and they did their best to get through it. Everyone clapped as all ten candles extinguished with a whoosh of the girl's breath.

Trying not to be obvious, Elle glanced at her watch every few minutes until finally, Sash announced it was time to go, since Natalie would be up late tomorrow. They had moved her usual Friday piano lesson to today so they could do dinner and a musical downtown.

By the time they bundled out the door, there was just enough time to get to Leo's.

She ran up to her studio and opened the small safe under her desk, pulling out her handgun. She had gotten a permit to carry after a run-in with the angry father of the suspect in her season two case. She had evidence his son had been collecting and disseminating child porn for eight years, but the man chose to threaten Elle instead of directing his anger where it belonged. That was the only case she'd covered that still wasn't resolved. She'd been sure she assembled enough evidence alongside the police in Alexandria to arrest the guy, but so far, nothing had been done. Still, there'd been enough public outcry that she hoped the guy's life would be unbearable in a small city like that. The threats had slowed down now that a few years had passed, but she kept a gun nearby when she was out investigating.

"Hey, I've got to run an errand," she said as soon as she was back downstairs.

Martin glanced away from the baking show he'd sat down in front of. "Where you going?"

Elle wrapped her arms around him from behind the couch and dropped a kiss on the back of his neck. "Just something I've got to check out for the podcast. I should be back in an hour."

"Want some company?"

"Nah, you've worked all day. Thanks, though."

"All right," he said, blinking lazily at her. He already looked half asleep. By the time she got home, he'd be crashed out right where he sat.

She smiled and kissed him again. After bundling up, she walked out into the freezing night air.

It took about fifteen minutes to get to Leo's apartment in Falcon Heights. He lived in an old three-story without an elevator, and she was panting by the time she got to the top of the stairs, coat unzipped. Her fitness routine had taken a turn for the worse since she started working from home. After regaining her breath, she knocked on Leo's door, and it creaked inward an inch or two. It wasn't latched.

"Hello?" Elle called out, and knocked again. "Leo Toca?"

"Are you the police? Don't shoot!" someone shouted inside.

Elle gripped the gun at her hip, but didn't draw it. "I'm not the police!" she shouted, then realized it might be unwise to let him know that. But it was too late now. Taking a deep breath, she pushed the door open the rest of the way.

There was a man kneeling on the floor, his hands covered in blood as he leaned over a body.

Elle froze, her mouth open. The kneeling man looked up at her, his face white with shock. She recognized him then, from his picture in that news article: Duane Grove, Leo Toca's suspected chop shop associate.

Finally, she found her voice. "Did you kill him?"

"No!" the man shouted; then, more quietly, "No . . . I—I just came over to borrow something, and I found him like this."

"I'm coming inside." Elle's fingers were wrapped tightly around her Ruger, her eyes wide and unblinking as she stared at Duane, waiting for any sudden movements. "Is he breathing?"

Duane took a shaky breath, arms stretching overhead at the sight of her gun. "No, I don't think so. I just found him like this, I swear."

On the floor, the victim was flat on his back, wide brown eyes staring at the ceiling. Elle didn't really need to check for a pulse, but when she did and felt the stillness under her fingertips, she cursed.

The shots were at point-blank range, leaving a scorch mark around the hole on his forehead. Elle had never seen a murder victim in person—only in crime scene photos—so it was hard to know if they all looked like this. But the expression on his face was undeniable.

Leo Toca looked like he saw his attacker coming and he couldn't believe who it was.

\\\\\\\

"He's dead."

As soon as Elle said the words, Duane Grove hightailed it out of the apartment before she could stop him. She sat back, staring at the body for a few minutes before she could will her limbs to move.

Finally, her fingers stopped trembling enough that she could dial 911. Once they had the details and an officer dispatched, she texted her old friend, Ayaan Bishar. Being in Crimes Against Children, Ayaan would probably have nothing to do with investigating Leo's murder, but it was best she knew Elle had inadvertently gotten wrapped up in another Minneapolis PD case.

Then Elle clutched her phone, unable to take her eyes off Leo's slowly graying face.

It sounds like every choice in your life until now has been made for you.

Dr. Swedberg's words from nearly a year ago echoed in Elle's head as she stared at the body. She had seen five therapists in her life, but for some reason, Dr. Swedberg was able to cut through her distrust and shine a light on a part of her mind that had long been hidden in shadows. That was the day her blurry future snapped into focus. That was the day she decided she had to stop hoping other people would fix the broken pieces inside her.

That was the day Elle decided her next case would be TCK.

Now, sprawled out on the floor in front of her was another unmade choice, another of someone else's bad decisions screwing up her plans—and taking Leo Toca's life.

Knowing the first responders would be at the apartment any minute, Elle snapped into motion. Leo's apartment was starkly furnished: one sofa that folded out into a bed, a wobbly dining table with two mismatched chairs, a bare kitchen with paper plates and plastic cutlery and an empty trash can. There was no sign of a computer or printer, and no backpack in sight. That left one place to search, and it could get her arrested. But if Leo actually did have a clue about who TCK could be and had some evidence to prove it, she had to know.

Looking over her shoulder at the partially ajar apartment door, Elle crouched next to Leo's body and pulled a pen out of her laptop bag. She inserted it in his left jeans pocket and gently lifted at the fabric, bending to peer inside. Nothing. The sound of a distant siren made her pulse pick up; she scurried around to his right side and did the same. A dark bit of plastic stood out against the white interior of his pocket. Her fingertips were clumsy and numb as she used the pen to slowly nudge it up and dislodge it onto the floor. Elle looked around. She couldn't steal the flash drive. That would be too much, even for her. She'd been building up a trust with Minneapolis PD for two years; she couldn't break it now. The siren was getting closer.

She stood up and ran into the bedroom, looking for a computer. There was a small desk against the window across from a twin bed, but no computer or laptop on it. She opened the desk drawers, slid her hands under the pillow, checked in the closet—nothing.

"Shit," she spat. Back in the main room, she rushed to Leo's side. Pounding footsteps were coming up the stairs. Using a clean tissue from the box on the counter, she picked up the flash drive and put it back in Leo's pocket with trembling hands.

She was standing, flushed, with her hands in the air when a detective with dark brown curly hair burst through the door. His weapon was drawn but not aimed at her.

"I'm Elle Castillo," she said. "I called it in."

"Detective Sam Hyde. Are you the only one here?" he asked as another officer, a white woman with a slick blond ponytail, walked into the room. She went straight to Leo's body to examine it.

"I am now. When I arrived, there was another man here, right next to the body. I think it was the victim's business partner, Duane Grove." Elle quickly explained their limited conversation, including the fact that Duane said Leo was already shot when he arrived and seemed distraught when she confirmed he was dead. She did not mention the flash drive in his pocket. Ayaan might not charge her with disturbing a crime scene, but she wasn't so sure about Detective Hyde.

"Are you armed?" he asked when she was finished.

Elle nodded at her right hip. "Yes, I have a carry permit for my Ruger LCP II. You can take it off me if that'll make you more comfortable."

He nodded, a slight tint coming into his cheeks as he swept her coat aside and pulled the handgun out of its holster. Without ceremony, he released the magazine and shoved both it and the gun into his coat pocket. "Sorry, it's policy. You can have it back later. Commander Bishar vouched for you; she called when I was en route."

"Yes, she and I met when I was in CPS. And I've worked a case with her before as an independent investigator."

Sam's lip curled up at that, and Elle had to fight to keep from rolling her eyes. It wasn't like she was some teenager researching cases from their mom's basement — and even if she was, she'd seen internet sleuths crack cases that had stumped law enforcement for decades. It was kind of the whole reason she'd been able to make this podcast her career. But she could always tell when someone on the force immediately disregarded her work because she wasn't a *real* cop.

"I'm supposed to bring you back to the station so Commander Bishar and I can ask you some questions. That okay?" The way he asked, Elle could tell she didn't have much choice. She nodded and picked up her bag.

Sam looked past her at the other officer. "I'm going to have Ms. Castillo follow me back to the station. Forensics will be here in five. You good?"

The female officer nodded, and Sam walked out the door with Elle following close behind.

I-35W was a cluster of red brake lights and swirling snowflakes. There were three inches of fresh powder on the ground, and as usual, people were driving like assholes. Elle drummed on her steering wheel as she stared at the cars, at people cutting in and out of lanes, horns blaring. The longer she sat, the more she wanted to scream. She should be talking with Leo about the Countdown Killer. She should be in her studio, preparing for next week's episode. She should have a name, a direction, a lead. Instead, she was stuck here in traffic — and stuck on this case.

Thirty minutes later, they finally got to the station. Elle pulled in next to Sam's sedan. Sam had about a foot on her, so she had to rush to keep up. He brought her through the familiar double glass doors and down the hall to an interview room.

"Take a seat. Want anything to drink?"

Elle shook her head, but then changed her mind and said, "Yeah, some water."

Sam left the room, shutting the door behind him. She looked at it and wondered for a moment if it was locked. She wasn't under arrest, but she also wasn't used to being the only one in a room like this. When she'd been here in the past, she was sitting next to an officer across from a suspect or a neglectful parent.

After a moment, Commander Ayaan Bishar entered the room and sat across from Elle, facing the direction of the hidden camera. Seeing her in the seat Elle associated with the suspect was oddly unsettling, like running into your dentist at the bar.

Ayaan led the Crimes Against Children division, but before she made detective, she used to accompany Elle on protective custody calls for CPS. They also worked the Jair Brown case together a couple years ago—the five-year-old boy who had gone missing from his home and turned up buried in a shallow grave less than a mile away two days later. Ayaan had made the arrest after Elle, Martin, and her podcast listeners finally put together the evidence on the boy's uncle.

"Hey, Ayaan," Elle said.

She looked exactly the same—round face framed by a soft purple hijab, tied up in a turban style; deep brown eyes sharp and probing under perfectly penciled eyebrows. "Hi, Elle," she said. "It's nice to see you, although I wish it were under better circumstances. I meant to call and tell you I'm enjoying your new season."

"Thank you."

Sam returned with a bottle of water and sat next to Ayaan, across from Elle. She wondered if they did this on purpose, putting her on the side where they normally sat, like that would make her more comfortable. Elle fidgeted, feeling ridiculous. She wasn't a suspect here.

"You briefly said on the phone, but can you tell me why you were at Leo Toca's apartment?" Ayaan asked.

"He emailed my podcast account, said he had a tip for me. So, I went to meet him."

"Why didn't you meet somewhere public?"

"I wanted to, but he asked me to come to his house."

"Do you often go to strangers' houses alone at night because they ask you to?" Sam asked.

Elle fought to not roll her eyes. "No, but I don't often get someone claiming they know who Minnesota's most notorious serial killer is."

Sam's eyes widened a little. "You're doing the Countdown Killer case?"

She lifted her chin. "Yes, I started releasing episodes in December. I've gotten a lot of tips since then, but Leo seemed especially credible to me."

"Why is that?"

"Because he mentioned having seen this special tea from one of the crime scenes in the man's house. And he sounded scared, like he was sure someone was after him." As she said the words, Elle sat back in her chair. In all the chaos, she'd almost forgotten about that. Leo had sounded terrified.

Ayaan leaned forward, steepled her hands under her chin. "I'm sorry. You must be very frustrated."

"He . . . he sounded genuinely scared on the phone. That's why he wouldn't meet me at a restaurant. I thought maybe he was being paranoid, but apparently he had reason to be afraid." If he really did know who TCK was, that information could have gotten him into trouble. "Could someone have been tapping his phone? How would they know he'd reached out to me?"

Sam wrote something down on the pad in front of him and then looked up at her again. "I highly doubt Leo was killed for saying he had a tip for your podcast investigation. You saw Duane Grove next to the body moments after Leo was killed. I just spoke to the landlord, who said he overheard Leo and Duane fighting about their business at the mechanic's last night. Right now, his partner is a strong person of interest. Do you remember what he said when you got there?"

"Just that he had found Leo like that. I think he said he'd come over to borrow something, and Leo was dead when he got there." Elle clenched her hands. If Leo really did get shot over a business dispute just minutes before she arrived, she must have the worst luck in the world. "I can't believe this."

"What did you do after you arrived and found Leo murdered?"

"I took his pulse to make sure, and I told Duane he was dead. Then Duane ran off, and I called 911, then texted Ayaan to let her know."

"And you didn't find or touch anything at the scene before I arrived? You didn't see what Leo was supposedly going to show you?"

Elle grew very still, her eyes focused on his. "No, nothing. That's why I'm so pissed."

Ayaan nodded and stood up. "Well, I think that's enough for tonight. Detective Hyde or I will be in touch if we have any other questions. Are you feeling distressed at all? We have a liaison you can speak to if you want to get some numbers for counseling. Discovery of a body can be traumatic."

"I've seen worse things," Elle said, then winced at how flippant it sounded. But it was true. Death was by no means the worst thing that could happen to a person; surely Sam and Ayaan knew that. She stood and followed Ayaan out.

After collecting her gun and saying goodbye, Elle headed to her car on autopilot. Maybe Sam was right. Duane was the obvious suspect, and if he and Leo had fought the night before, it didn't look good for him. But she couldn't shake the memory of the fear in Leo's voice. He had known someone was after him, and it didn't make sense that he'd be that scared of someone he still worked with. If Leo knew he had key evidence against a serial killer, though, that would certainly be cause for fear.

She wished she had a way to find out what was on that flash drive. But if Leo protected his files, it might take the police lab weeks to get access to it, and that was if they made it a priority. Even if they did, they wouldn't share that information with her. The only way she might be able to find out what he knew was by looking into him herself.

Back in her car, Elle turned up the heat and sped off into the night toward home.

5

Justice Delayed podcast

December 12, 2019

Transcript: Season 5, Episode 2

ELLE VOICE-OVER:

The history of tea has deep roots in colonization and stolen land. White settlers are responsible for the experimentation and exploitation of the tea planting process all across the continent of Asia, and Darjeeling is a classic example of this. A British doctor named Archibald Campbell is the person credited with planting the first tea in the Darjeeling region of India, using Chinese tea leaves. Similar to Champagne, which is a sparkling wine from a specific region in France, Darjeeling is prone to bastardization by companies wanting to leverage the name to sell a substandard product. Only teas from the Darjeeling region are meant to bear the name, but identifying and stopping the fakes from selling is a nearly impossible task. As with so many things in life, people are willing to accept a fraud if it saves them money. But that was not the case with the tea found on Tamera's clothing. While they didn't have the technology to show it at the time, it would turn out that tea was one of the most expensive of its kind, imported from the region itself. But all they knew in 1997 was that it was an oolong, and that's what police told the media.

[THEME MUSIC + INTRO]

ELLE:

Can you explain why you feel you shouldn't have released the information about the tea to the public?

SYKES:

Let's just say, it led to the community exhibiting . . . suspicion of a certain group of people.

ELLE:

Asian people, specifically, right?

SYKES:

That's right. As soon as we told the media about the tea stain, our office was inundated. Oolong tea isn't all that exotic, but at the time, it wasn't a common household drink for the majority of the population in the area, who were mostly descended from Scandinavian and German immigrants. Which meant the suspicion laser-focused on marginalized communities, even though that was completely illogical. But, as I'm sure you know, racism isn't logical.

Under the guise of being good citizens, every Tom, Dick, and Harry in the state who didn't like brown people seemed to find a reason to call us. For all we knew, the killer was some snobby white guy who liked imported tea, but this was the biggest case in the city at the time. We had to vet every tip, no matter how ridiculous.

ELLE:

And a lot of them were ridiculous, weren't they? I have information that you received tips about Pakistanis, Koreans, Chinese people, even one Saudi. Did any of those result in arrest?

SYKES:

No.

ELLE:

Did you bring any of them in for questioning?

SYKES:

No, there was no need.

ELLE:

You have to understand, I'm not trying to berate you about this. I know you made the best decision you thought you could at the time, but the resulting chaos led to a spike in hate crimes in the city. Indian and Chinese restaurants were targeted with vandalism and bomb threats. Minneapolis PD wasted some five hundred hours of police resources over the following weeks as you tried to sort through the thousand or so tips you got.

SYKES:

That's correct. Of course, I'm not excusing it. As a Black man on the force in the eighties and nineties, I certainly faced my share of dis-crimination—both within and outside the department. Now I can see that I was too hasty, releasing that information without thinking about the possible consequences. But I still think that information is important. The tea, I mean. I still think it will matter, especially now that we have the specific kind down to the brand.

ELLE:

I hope you're right.

ELLE VOICE-OVER:

The tea is a clue, but it could also be a needle in a haystack. My best estimate, based on the historical records I've been given access to, is that approximately five thousand tins of Majestic Sterling tea were ordered by individuals in the USA in the three years preceding the Countdown murders. A further seventy-five thousand had been or-dered by specialty tea sellers throughout the Midwest. Trying to nar-row down a list of suspects, even if police could get subpoenas for all of the vendors' records, would be next to impossible—and then there's always the chance TCK just walked in and bought it from a store with cash. The clue was important, but it didn't solve the case.

ELLE:

Now, can you talk to me about how the case changed after Tamera was found? There were no more bodies until a year later, but of course no one knew at the time how long the reprieve would be. Tell me about that gap.

SYKES:

The public moved on after a while, started to calm down, but my work never slowed. I knew that unless he'd been caught, he was just biding his time, waiting to strike again and continue his spree. For months, every time a fifteen-year-old girl was reported missing anywhere in Minnesota or Wisconsin, I asked the local squad if I could review the case notes. Police departments get a bum rap for bad cross-departmental communication, much of which is justified, but I never had much issue. I chased down a few of the missing girls myself, but no one fit the profile. Thankfully, most of them turned up eventually.

ELLE:

What was that time like for you?

SYKES:

I . . . huh. No one's ever asked me that . . . It was pretty tough. I once stayed up three days straight, just researching all the possible meanings behind the numbers three, seven, and twenty-one until I finally got sent home after I vomited into the trash can by my desk. When you've been a detective for as long as I have, you start to put the cases you've worked into categories. There are the ones that blur together, but you remember bits and pieces from over time. There are the ones that you forget entirely, either because they didn't stick out or because you've forced the memories down. And then there are cases that stick with you no matter what—the ones that wake you up in the middle of the night like a spider crawling across your face, even decades later. I guess I don't have to explain that to you, of all people. I was only six years into my career when I got the TCK murders, but I knew right away that I wouldn't be able to let that case go until we found the guy.

ELLE VOICE-OVER:

But they didn't find the guy. Detective Sykes worked the case on top of his other caseload, but nothing panned out. And then, after a year of chasing fruitless leads and vetting wildly unsubstantiated tips, he was called to the scene of yet another girl's murder.

[SOUND BREAK: Orchestra instruments tuning up, with a particularly sour note from a violin.]

ELLE:

Can you say your name and your job title, please?

TERRI:

I'm Terri Rather, and I'm the music teacher at Hillview Academy.

ELLE VOICE-OVER:

Hillview is one of the most expensive private schools in the Minneapolis area. Its student body ranges from first to twelfth grade. While it's technically a Christian school, approximately 20 percent of their student body is non-Christian. In 1998, that number was probably slightly lower, but fifteen-year-old Lilian Davies was one of the secular attendees whose parents enrolled her for the excellent music education. Lilian played clarinet—she was something of a prodigy, in fact. She had her heart set on applying to the New England Conservatory of Music. On February 2, 1998, she was walking to the main road from the school's music hall after rehearsal when she disappeared.

TERRI:

Back then, there was no road up to the entrance of the music hall—it was set back a couple hundred yards, and it was a pain for parents to drive all the way around campus to the parking lot at the back. So, a lot of students who needed to get picked up would walk across the big lawn and through a cluster of trees to get to the sidewalk next to Hamline Avenue. There was a path over the lawn which the school kept shoveled all winter. Usually, the kids all walked up together, so we didn't worry about their safety. But Lilian had to leave a little early that day for a doctor's appointment, so she was by herself.

ELLE:

When did you know something was wrong?

TERRI:

I was packing up after rehearsals finished, and her dad came rushing in, ready to give her a talking-to for making them miss her appointment, I think. He thought she'd just forgotten. When we both realized the other didn't know where she was, we started to panic. We called the police right away. One witness thought he saw a girl that looked like her getting into an unmarked van, but she wore a gray stocking cap and a black coat. There was no guarantee the person he'd actually seen was Lilian. Other than that one possible witness, it was like she'd just vanished into thin air. But then . . . then a few days later . . .

   [A nose blowing.] I was . . . I was close to Lilian and her father, Darren. He and I had been seeing each other. So, I was with him when the detective showed up at his house and let him know another girl had disappeared. He told us they couldn't be certain, but he was fairly confident Lilian and this other girl, Carissa, had been taken by the Countdown Killer.

ELLE:

That must have been devastating.

TERRI:

It was like if someone strapped a bomb to your chest and handed you the timer: you know exactly how long until everything explodes. Darren and I went on the news, tried to talk directly to the killer. We told him we knew he had Lilian. We . . . we begged him not to hurt her. We begged him to change his mind, even though some people told us that seeing our pain might have been part of the thrill for him. What choice did we have? She was going to die anyway. We had to try. By the time it got to day seven, Darren was going out of his mind with terror, knowing any moment the police would call and say they had found Lilian's body. In the end, he had to be sedated. I was the one who answered the phone when they found her.

ELLE VOICE-OVER:

A tattoo artist in St. Paul discovered the body of Lilian Davies lying on a dirty piece of cardboard in front of the door to his shop seven days after she was taken. Detective Sykes was the second cop on the scene, but as usual, there was nothing to be found. No physical evidence, no unidentified DNA. Lilian's young future had been snuffed out in the same way as all the other girls'—with poison and twenty-one lashes.

ELLE:

I appreciate that this isn't an easy conversation for you to have.

SYKES:

In all my decades doing this job, I've never seen the spirit leave a man's eyes the way it did when Darren Davies found out his daughter was no longer in this world. When I saw that, I was more determined than ever to get justice for her—for all these girls. I left his house believing I could save the next one. I had to. She only had three days left, but she was just a child.

ELLE VOICE-OVER:

Carissa Jacobs was fourteen. A talented young gymnast who loved riding horses and visiting her grandparents' California vineyard during the winter holidays. In fact, she had just returned to Minnesota two weeks before the day she went missing. Carissa spent every weekday afternoon at her aunt's house while she waited for her parents to get home from work. It had been more than thirty minutes since Carissa left for the six-block walk between her school and her aunt's when her cousin asked why she wasn't there yet. They went out searching, and after calling around to her other friends and her parents, they finally reported her missing. By the time police were notified, she had likely been gone for more than two hours.

I wasn't able to get any of Carissa's family or friends to speak to me on the podcast about her murder, and I respect their desire for privacy. As you know, one thing I always try to do is focus on the victims. As in every case, the victims extend well beyond those who were killed. Their families, friends, and communities were damaged irreparably. I know what it is to experience trauma, to live and breathe it every day. I know what it's like when grief embeds itself in your skin, rushes through your bloodstream, leaks out in your sweat. And I know what it's like to have people ask you to relive it, rehash it, until it feels like you're enduring every second of it all over again.

Nothing will undo the damage TCK did to people. I want to bring him to justice, make him pay for the lives he ruined, but I will never knowingly cause more harm to any of his victims on the way to doing so. That being said, if you're listening and you knew Carissa Jacobs, I would love to hear from you—on the record or off. I would love to be able to honor her memory more fully.

ELLE:

Is it true you didn't get confirmation there was an eighth victim until she'd already been missing for nearly four days? That must have caused confusion. The records I have indicate Katrina Connelly didn't show up in your police file until just hours before Carissa's body was found. What did you think had happened—that TCK broke his pattern?

SYKES:

To be honest, it was chaos. The media was in a frenzy, with Lilian's body having been discovered and Carissa just hours away from the time we knew she would die, and we still had no idea if TCK had taken his third victim of the set. She should have gone missing the day Lilian was killed, but we had no new reports. I remember the spark of hope I felt, that maybe he had died or been arrested, and there would be no more missing girls. But then we got the call. Katrina had been missing for a full three days before her parents realized what happened. They were recently divorced and she had lied to both of them about going to the other's house in order to spend the weekend with her friend. Classic kid stuff, you know. She was thirteen, angry about her parents' separation, all the rest of it. Just wanted to go blow off some steam.

ELLE:

Most of the girls were taken doing something routine, right? Or at least, something the killer could have learned about by listening in on phone calls or outside the girls' houses. But this was different. This was something even her parents didn't know she was doing.

SYKES:

That's right. Which means he was likely stalking her, following her and waiting for an opportunity.

ELLE:

So, he takes Katrina when she's catching the bus to her friend's house, and both her parents don't realize she's missing until three days later?

SYKES:

Yes. They weren't on speaking terms at that point, so they each assumed the other had her. Meanwhile, I abandoned my hope that TCK had stopped and tried everything I could to make sure Katrina didn't end up dead too—but by that point, I think we all knew it was too late.

I always felt like I was running out of time, and also that the days were dragging by before the inevitable conclusion. In the Child Abduction Response Training, they tell us that of the children who are abducted and killed, 44 percent are dead within the first hour. Almost three quarters are killed within the first three hours, and 99 percent are dead within the first day. Every one of TCK's murders were in the one percent, the cases that defied the odds—but the time-frame was still rigid. He didn't budge. And even though it seemed he had the ricin poisoning down to an exact science, he messed up when it came to Katrina.

[SOUND BREAK: Shuffling papers, tapping fingers on a desk.]

ELLE:
Martín, what can you tell me about Katrina's autopsy?

MARTÍN:
While she did suffer the effects of ricin poisoning and twenty-one lashes on her back, there were a couple key differences in her death when compared to the other TCK victims. First, she was not dying as she was whipped; she bled much longer than the other girls had. Second, her cause of death was not organ failure due to poisoning. She died from blunt force trauma to the head, which caused a cerebral hemorrhage.

ELLE:
What do you think that means?

MARTÍN:
Well, the medical examiner on her case thought it was due to a fit of rage. Essentially, that the killer became furious with her because she fought back—there were defensive wounds on her arms—and he killed her for defying him.

ELLE:
Do you agree with that assessment?

MARTÍN:
I think it's possible.

ELLE:
Are there any other possible explanations?

MARTÍN:

Yes. I think it's clear that he was angry with her. Blunt force trauma is usually a spontaneous method of killing, generally brought on by sudden passion or rage. But I'm not convinced it was because she fought back. The autopsy showed that her systems were shutting down at the time she died. It's impossible to know for sure, but if I had to speculate, I would guess that she had mere hours to live. But the poison hadn't acted as fast in her as it did in other girls. As I've mentioned before, ricin isn't like cyanide; it usually takes days to kill when it's ingested in castor beans. With the other girls, it might have worked to his timeline, but my hypothesis based on the autopsy results is that Katrina metabolized it more slowly than the others. I think he was angry with her for not dying when he wanted her to. It was more important to him that she died *when* he wanted, even if she wouldn't die the *way* that he wanted.

ELLE:

Explain what you mean by "might have worked." All of his victims were found dead on the seventh day, so presumably that means it did work, except in Katrina's case.

MARTÍN:

That's how it's always been reported by police and the media. But I've always wondered why TCK waited a year in between killings, and why he always killed in the winter. It could just be part of his pattern. But it might also be for convenience. In the winter, Minnesota is one big outdoor freezer. If any of his victims succumbed to the castor beans before the seventh day, he could easily keep their bodies outside or in an unheated outbuilding where they would be preserved. It would be very difficult for a medical examiner to determine their time of death, especially since the victims were almost always discovered hours after they'd been placed in the public space, so they were usually frozen solid anyway.

ELLE:

That's an interesting theory. And it answers one of my other questions, which was about how Katrina could be the only victim who didn't seem to die on time. My understanding is that ricin poisoning is relatively predictable, but the timeline leading up to death has a lot of variables.

MARTÍN:

That's true. I've always struggled to believe that all the rest of the girls simply died at the exact right time. It would be a remarkable stroke of luck for him, let's just say. I think it's more likely that some died earlier, but he just waited until day seven to "present" them to the public, because that was the most important part to him.

ELLE VOICE-OVER:

Over the decades, criminal behavior analysts, detectives, internet sleuths, and journalists alike have tried to figure out what the numbers mean. Why TCK was so obsessed with them, and why—if Martín is correct—the time of his victims' deaths was even more important than the method. This is an anomaly among serial killers, as far as I can tell. Much of the time, the physical act of torture and murder is how they get their release. Psychopaths and compulsive killers can literally spend months planning it ahead of time and then reliving it afterward.

According to John Douglas, the former FBI special agent who made his name interviewing and analyzing serial killers, there is a difference between the modus operandi—the way a crime is committed—and the signature. The signature is what the killer does to achieve fulfillment. The way they kill might change over time, and it won't necessarily impact the killer's satisfaction. But every killer has a signature, something they *have* to do, or the kill won't give them the release they're after. Based on what we know, the numbers are his signature. The three girls, three days apart; the seven days of captivity; the twenty-one lashes.

The numbers mattered more than anything else. And that tells us something.

It tells us sticking to them was nonnegotiable, that death by poison was preferable but not essential. If Martín is right, it tells us that even if they died too soon, it was still critical to wait until the seventh day to reveal their bodies. I think the evidence shows that the act of killing probably wasn't what gave TCK pleasure—it was the satisfaction of doing it within his constructed pattern. This is important when classifying him into a category of serial killers.

Katrina's violent death proves that the timeline was inflexible. On the seventh day, a girl had to die. And yet, detectives would continue to be too late.

Next time, on *Justice Delayed* . . .

6

Elle

January 9, 2020

Just as Elle suspected, Martín was sound asleep on the couch when she got home a little after midnight. She crept over and pulled the fleece throw off the recliner next to him. Little sparks of static electricity leapt through the dark, prickling her fingers as she flicked the blanket open and laid it across him. Satisfied she hadn't woken him, Elle poured herself a glass of wine in the kitchen and went upstairs.

A night of research stretched out ahead of her. Even with the bullet wound in his face, she could tell she had found the right Leo on social media. She went through his profile again, more carefully this time. Last year, he'd changed his status from "married" to "single," but his ex-wife's name wasn't tagged. The people he'd connected with as family on Facebook were all listed as living in various cities in Mexico. It wouldn't be the first time she had to travel for a case, but she wasn't sure she could justify an international flight for a tip she wasn't even sure was legit. Plus, if they lived in Mexico, odds were none of them was the person Leo suspected of being TCK.

Just to be sure, she sent off a couple messages to people she could see he'd interacted with recently on the timeline: photo comments, status likes, et cetera. *Your son/brother/cousin told me he had information on a cold case. Do you know anything about that?*

It was in poor taste to message about him on the very day of his untimely death, but this was the job she'd made for herself. She was here to get the truth, not make friends. In case they hadn't heard the news yet, she kept condolences out of it.

She looked at the time on her computer. Five hours ago, she'd been singing and eating cake with her family. Four hours ago, she'd gone to get what could have been the biggest lead on the TCK case to come out in twenty years. Or maybe it was nothing; maybe the tea was a red herring, or Leo had been making it up to get her to come to his house. Maybe he had plans to hurt her, and whoever killed him first had done her a favor.

It had only been a month since she started her season on the Countdown Killer, but already the levels of online harassment she dealt with had reached new heights. Instead of just the mindless trolls in her mentions—who loved to offer stupid takes on every picture she posted of her sound setup or the mass of multicolored sticky notes around her desk—now there was outright aggression. Vicious emails mocking her for daring to think she could solve a case this big that no one, including some of the best detectives in the world, had been able to. Warnings to not bring back the decades of hurt the TCK murders had caused. Twitter DMs so sexually violent they made her skin crawl; those she reported instantly.

If Leo was one of those, maybe he had a different plan altogether. Maybe he was going to set her up with a false tip that she'd go chasing, in order to discredit her. She did a quick search through the threatening emails she'd filed just in case, but none of them contained variations of Leo's name. It was a small relief, but it didn't really mean anything.

Elle took another drink of wine. None of the family members had responded. It was after midnight, and her eyes prickled with exhaustion, but her brain was too wired for sleep. Scrolling through Leo's friend list, she found the name she was after.

Duane Grove's profile was relatively locked down, but there were a few posts and status updates he'd made public. The latest photo was a cross-post from Instagram dated two weeks ago: him in a backwards baseball cap and sunglasses, throwing the peace sign at the lens like a tool. She considered sending him a message, but it would have been a waste of time. If he was on the run from police, there was no way he'd be checking social media; if he wasn't, he was probably in a jail cell by now anyway.

A box popped up on her screen—a video call coming in from Tina.

Tina Nguyen was a former fan-turned-producer of *Justice Delayed* who lived in Chicago. She was also a crack online researcher and had helped Elle track down a lot of records that other organizations had assured her were permanently lost.

When Elle answered the call, Tina was sitting in her usual spot: surrounded by other monitors, her face bathed in a bluish white glow. "How's it going, Elle?" she asked, typing as she spoke. "You seen all the reactions to today's episode? Molly won't stop texting me every time we pass another ten thousand downloads."

"I haven't had a chance."

Tina glanced at the camera, her black irises reflecting the screen. Something in Elle's expression made her sit back in her wheelchair, take her hands off the keyboard. "What's wrong?"

Elle hid her face by taking another drink of wine. "What makes you think something is wrong?"

"Come on, don't do that pretend shit with me."

"Fine."

Tina listened with her arms folded over her Paramore T-shirt as Elle told her about Leo's email, their phone call, finding him dead. She finished with a rundown of all the research she'd done into Leo's background so far. "I guess now I'm just wondering if it'll be a waste of time to keep trying to figure out the tip he was going to give me, if the tip even existed in the first place. Odds are, the guy I saw at the crime scene is the one who shot him. They supposedly ran a chop shop together, and from his profile, Duane seems like an asshole. There's every chance Leo had no idea what he was talking about and I should just keep going with our scheduled episodes as they are."

After Elle stopped talking, Tina stared to the right of the camera lens for a moment, tapping her finger against her lip. "What if you're wrong, though?"

"Then Leo really did have something, and it's probably on the flash drive that was in his pocket."

"Which you can't tell them you know about without getting in trouble. And you'll probably never hear what they find, because there's no reason for the police to give it to you."

"Right."

"Hmm." After a moment, Tina looked straight down the lens. "What if you're wrong about the business partner, though?"

"What do you mean?"

"What if he really was just in the wrong place at the wrong time, and the killer got away before you both got there? What if Leo was killed because someone knew he was about to give you key information about TCK?"

The thought had risen to the surface of Elle's mind a hundred times in the past several hours, but each time she had shoved it back down again. If Leo was killed because of the information, that was both the most terrifying and the most exciting thing that had ever happened since *Justice Delayed* started. It meant what he had was legitimate, and it also meant that she owed it to him to find his killer.

"Elle, cut it out. I can see you blaming yourself right through this screen."

"I'm not!"

"You are, and it's not your fault. No matter who killed Leo, it was their decision to do it—not yours."

Elle nodded, looking down at the tattoo on her right wrist—a semicolon. On Sash's suggestion, Elle had gotten it done two years ago, right around the time she gave up on getting pregnant and sank into a deep depression. It was her reminder, her promise, that even the worst moments in her life didn't have to be the end of the story. As much as she just wanted to crawl into bed right now and give up, she couldn't. Not when she might be closer than she'd ever been.

"I just . . . I have to know what he was going to tell me," Elle said. "I have to know if he actually knew something."

For a moment, Tina was quiet. Then she looked at the camera again. "I know this case means more to you than the others, Elle."

She met Tina's gaze through the lens, swallowing hard. "What do you mean?"

"I know about your childhood 'incident.'" Tina held up her hand when Elle opened her mouth to protest. "And before you get mad at me for digging into your background, you should know that I did it ages ago, back when I was just a fan of your show. And for what it's worth, your information was really tough to find. You did a good job hiding it."

When Elle didn't say anything, Tina continued. "It's okay, Elle. What happened to you was awful. I've read the news articles, the police reports. Those aren't on Google, but hey — you're not the only one who breaks the rules. I didn't mean to pry, honestly. And I want to help you. Anything I can do, really, you can ask."

Elle tapped a finger on her desk, fighting the urge to slam her laptop shut and end the video call. Whatever good that would do. Tina might as well have found a revenge porn site splashed with intimate pictures of Elle — it would have been no less violating. Angry questions about where she had looked, what she had seen, burned on Elle's lips. It didn't matter. If Tina knew about the abuse Elle had faced as a child that caused her to feel so much solidarity with TCK's victims, it was too late to do anything about it now. Elle swallowed her anger and looked back up at the camera.

"How can you help me?" The words sounded harsh, but Tina didn't look put off.

"Well, I'll start by trying to get ahold of any of Leo's coworkers, see if any of them knows anything. And I'll manage all the emails coming in about the show stuff for now, so you can focus on this. But I want you to promise you won't cut me out if you get new leads. I don't care about credit, but I want to help you nail that asshole." She smiled, her eyes twinkling even in the dim light of her computer screen.

As much as she felt betrayed by Tina's snooping, Elle needed her help. If anyone could convince Leo's reluctant family and friends to talk, it was Tina.

"All right, and I'll look into the girlfriend angle, while you're at it. See if he was close to anyone romantically since his separation last

year. But let's do this quietly, okay? I don't want to broadcast anything until I know whether Leo even had real information for me."

Pinching her fingers together, Tina mimed zipping them across
her tinted lips. "You got it."

Elle forced a smile, pushing down her anxiety. "Great," she said at
last. "Let me know as soon as you find anything, please."

7

Elle

January 10, 2020

She had tried to run from him as soon as he stopped the car at a light — opened the door and stumbled out into the frosty afternoon. It had been stupid to get into his car, even though he said he was friends with her parents. Stupid, stupid, stupid. The fear made her legs heavy and numb, and her steps were uncertain on the icy street. She ran and ran but went nowhere.

A thick glove that tasted of gasoline closed over her mouth. She bit down, but he lifted her off her feet and threw her into the backseat. He got in and locked the doors.

"There, now, don't you feel silly?" he said.

She did not. Warm, sad, angry, anxious. But not silly.

He started driving again, and she glared out the window, watching the black dead trees blur by. When they passed her house, she felt a hand squeeze inside her chest.

"You passed my house, mister."

There was no response.

"Hey! You passed my house!" She brought her feet against the back of his seat. "You. Passed. My. House." Each word punctuated with a sharp kick.

He turned around. All the concern and kindness that had been on his face when he picked her up had melted off like wax.

"Shut the fuck up."

When Elle woke up, her body ached—muscles sore from the tension of her nightmares. She rolled over, searching for the musky morning warmth of Martín's body, but he must have stayed asleep on the couch. She put her hand on the cool sheets where he should have been, hating his absence. They often went to bed at different times, but they usually woke up together, spent the first few moments of the morning wrapped in each other's arms.

She wondered who was missing Leo today, if there was a woman longing for the comfort of his embrace who would never get to experience it again. Sadness sliced through her as she thought about his body sprawled out on the floor. Since she'd started the podcast, hundreds of people had contacted her with tips and theories on the cases she investigated. As far as she knew, no one had ever ended up dead because of it. She hadn't pulled the trigger on Leo, but if he was killed because of the information he was going to give her, she couldn't help but feel some sense of responsibility.

But there was nothing she could do to change that. The best thing she could hope for was finding someone who knew Leo well enough to guess at the person he suspected.

Elle threw the covers off and put on sweatpants and one of Martín's hoodies. After tying her hair up in a ponytail and washing her face with cold water, she tramped down the stairs for coffee, which she could already smell brewing. Martín was at his usual place in the kitchen, sitting on a stool at their breakfast nook with a coffee in one hand and his cell phone in the other, reading the news.

"Buenos días," Elle said as she poured herself a cup of coffee.

"Morning."

"Late shift today?"

He nodded, not looking up from his phone. "I swapped with Dr. Phillips so she could get out of town early for the weekend. Blizzard's coming."

Elle pressed her lips to his temple and stroked the back of his head, fingers tangling in his curls. "Okay, no problem. Guess I'll fend for myself for dinner—been a while since I did my standard apple, cheese, and wine like in college." When he didn't laugh, she pulled her hand away. "Hope your neck doesn't hurt from the sofa cushions. You were so out I didn't want to wake you."

"It's fine."

She took a step back. "Everything okay?"

Martín set his phone down and looked up at her. "Where'd you go last night? I was worried."

She pulled out the stool next to him and sat down. "I got an email on my show account. This guy, Leo Toca, said he knew who TCK was. I talked to him on the phone, and he wanted me to come over so he could give me the information."

Martín's eyes widened. "You went over to some strange guy's house late at night because he said he had a clue about a serial killer?"

"I took my gun."

"Dios mío, Elle. That is so dangerous."

She took a drink of black coffee. "Well, obviously I'm fine."

"Just because you weren't hurt doesn't mean it was okay to go by yourself."

Her hands tightened on the mug. "This is my job, Martín, and I don't need a babysitter to do it. Nothing happened to me, see? You don't always have to imagine the worst-case scenario."

"Dealing with people who got caught in the worst-case scenario is *my* job," he snapped.

She knew that, of course. Martín had always maintained a sense of humor about his gruesome line of work, much like the cops and social workers Elle knew. It was the only way to keep their heads from exploding with all the pain they saw in the world.

But when it came to Elle's work, Martín's humor ran short, and since she'd started the TCK case, he had been more on edge than usual. It was understandable, but she wasn't going to stop putting herself in dangerous situations—it came with the territory, when you were trying to catch a child killer.

After a few moments of silence between them, he put a hand on her arm. His voice was soft as he said, "Elle, don't you understand how much it scares me to think of you getting hurt?"

"It was about TCK. I had to go."

He squeezed her arm. "Well, obviously you're in one piece. What did the man say?"

"Um." Elle took another long drink.

"Elle. What did he say?"

"He didn't say anything."

"Why not?"

She looked at the dark liquid swirling in her cup. "Because he was dead when I got there."

"What?!" Running his fingers through his hair, Martín let out a growl of frustration. "Pues, claro que sí estaba muerto en la casa. How? What happened? Who killed him?"

"I don't know, but it looks like probably the guy who ran off when I got there."

A vein above Martín's right eye bulged. Elle swallowed hard. When he spoke again, his voice was strained. "You went to a stranger's house in the middle of the night, found someone standing over a freshly murdered body, and you didn't call me? Didn't tell me when you got home?"

"I didn't want to wake you," she said.

He let out a bark of laughter and scrubbed his hands across his face. "You didn't want to wake me. ¡No manches!"

She pulled at his hands so she could look him in the eye. "Look, I get why you're upset, cariño, I do. But we've talked about this. You know I don't do anything half-assed. If I'm going to catch this guy, I'm going to have to take risks."

"Not stupid ones like this, you don't." When Elle bristled, his expression softened. "I'm sorry. That came out wrong."

"I know you're pissed, but I'm not stupid."

"I know you're not. And I'm not pissed, I'm worried." He put his hands on her shoulders, held her at arm's length as if to examine her for wounds. "You're sure you're not hurt? Carajo, mi amor, I can't believe this. So, you walk in and the guy's dead and the other one runs off. What happened next? You didn't try to stop him, did you?"

"No, I didn't. I called the police." Elle explained the rest, including the subsequent interview with Sam and Ayaan, although she left out the part where she searched Leo's corpse for evidence. She'd given Martín enough to deal with for today. By the time she finished, he was sitting across from her again, their knees touching and hands clasped, coffee growing cold on the counter.

"So, what are you going to do now?" he asked at last.

"I need to see if I can find someone who knew Leo well enough that he might have trusted them with the information he was going to give me. If I'm really lucky, I might be able to figure out who he suspected just by meeting them, but I'm not banking on that. Hundreds of people have thought their weird uncle or their abusive father was TCK over the years; it's possible Leo was just another one of those, but I have to investigate it."

He nodded and met Elle's gaze. Reaching out to cup the side of her face, he leaned forward and captured her lips with his. It was a deep kiss, stronger and more passionate than she expected. She let herself get lost in it for a moment.

When they broke away, Martín's eyes were bright with emotion. "Elle, you're good at your job. I know how important this case is to you. Just, please promise me you'll be more careful, okay?"

Elle took his face in her hands and kissed him one more time before pulling back to look into his eyes. "I promise."

8

Justice Delayed podcast

December 19, 2019

Transcript: Season 5, Episode 3

ELLE VOICE-OVER:

There is an event known in medical circles as agonal respiration. It often happens when a person is dying. They open their mouths and take a gulping, wheezing attempt at breath. You can hear the air get trapped in their throats, unable to pass through.

That's what investigating the Countdown Killer case is like: one final gasp of something that's near death, a last-ditch effort to get enough oxygen to survive.

[SOUND BREAK: Cars driving by on a highway; the blare of a semitruck horn.]

ELLE VOICE-OVER:

Twelve-year-old Jessica Elerson was the last known girl murdered by the Countdown Killer. She went missing just a few yards from where I'm standing outside a Super Target just off I-694.

[THEME MUSIC + INTRO]

[SOUND BREAK: A clip of theme music from SpongeBob SquarePants.*]*

ELLE VOICE-OVER:

Jessica loved SpongeBob. She was a bona fide nerd, spending her free time watching goofy cartoons and playing whatever video games she could buy or rent with her allowance. Jessica loved board games and science experiment kits, My Little Pony and microscopes. She kept her parents busy with all the school clubs she joined, but she always made time to help out with her little brother. She loved being an older sister more than anything in the world.

BONNIE:

If Jessica wasn't at school or one of her extracurricular activities, she was playing with Simon. She was seven when we found out we had another baby on the way, and she couldn't have been more excited. She was meant to be a big sister.

[SOUND BREAK: Steaming wand screeching as it foams milk; grinding coffee beans.]

ELLE VOICE-OVER:

This is Bonnie Elerson, Jessica's mother. We met in a café in her town, which I won't disclose for privacy reasons. Bonnie looks like most of the white, Midwestern mothers I grew up around: graying hair in short, loose curls; smooth hands with blunt, practical nails; straight teeth with a smattering of silver fillings that show when she laughs, which she does more than I expected. I like Bonnie. If you didn't know what she'd been through, you would probably never guess. The amount of pain a woman can bear with a smile on her face is astonishing.

ELLE:

Does Simon remember her?

BONNIE:

Yes. It's hard to tell, really, how many of his memories were formed independently, and how many have been created by us recounting them. He was five when she was . . . when she passed. But we talked about her all the time. Some of our friends said it might be better if we pretended with Simon like she had never been there, but we couldn't do that to him. All he did for weeks after was ask for his sister. For the first month or so, I couldn't stop worrying about how upset he was, how devastated that she wasn't coming home. Then, when he finally accepted it, I became terrified he would forget her entirely. Somehow, that broke my heart just as much. I had to make sure he remembered his sister, how much she loved him. So yes, we talked about her. We made sure he knew she didn't leave him on purpose.

ELLE:

You took care of your son, even when no one could have blamed you for falling apart about your daughter.

BONNIE:

Of course. We couldn't stop being parents.

ELLE:

I can't imagine the decision to speak to me was an easy one. I want you to know I'm really grateful for it. You're the first parent who's talked to me about their child, and even though I completely understand why no one else was able to, it's invaluable to hear from you. You knew Jessica better than anyone. If you don't mind, can you tell me what happened the day she was taken?

BONNIE:

We were at the store, getting groceries after her swimming lessons on Monday. We always did our weekly shop on that day, so we could have the weekends to relax as a family. Like she usually did, about halfway through my shopping she got bored and asked for some money to play the arcade games in the entryway. She liked the claw one where you try to pick up a stuffed animal. Wasn't very good at it, although I think those things are rigged. But the money went to charity, so I didn't mind.

Well, I finished up and went to get her, but she wasn't there. I searched the candy section, the bakery, called her name. I just remember being so embarrassed. I felt like one of those useless moms that lost her kid, and Jessica was twelve. It wasn't like she was a toddler. But finally, I had to give up and find security. They put it out over the PA system, telling her to come meet me by the service desk, and I remember thinking I was going to give her a piece of my mind once she came back from whatever silly shopping excursion she'd gone on. Only she never came back.

ELLE:
Do you remember what happened next?

BONNIE:
It took a while for it to hit me that something was wrong. That the delay in her coming back was far too long to be explained by her trying not to get into trouble. This was before most people had cell phones, so I used the phone in the security office to call Chris, my husband. After that, it's a blur. I don't remember who called the police, but they were there and asking questions, and I was just staring at that stupid claw machine, waiting for her to pop out from behind it and say it was just a big misunderstanding. I even entertained, for a moment, that she had somehow climbed inside to get the stuffed bird she'd been trying to snag for weeks. It was a parrot, Simon's favorite animal at the time. She wanted to win it for him.

ELLE:
It's okay. Take your time.

BONNIE:
[Through tears.] She had such a good heart. That's what I remember most of all. I'm sure every mother thinks this, but she would have done amazing things. I'm sorry for myself and my family, still, but I'm also sorry the world was robbed of her.

ELLE VOICE-OVER:

Renewed panic shot through the Minneapolis area when Jessica was kidnapped. Again, it was almost exactly a year after TCK's last murder spree, and by nature of the countdown, the girls were getting younger, more vulnerable. When a victim is killed, one of the first questions both police and the public tend to ask is why. Why them? Why would someone do this?

The public, via the media, wants to know for reasons both sensational and self-preservationist. Murder makes a good story — our national obsession with true crime podcasts like this one is proof enough of that. But there's more to it than just entertainment. If we know what the victim did before they were killed, we know what not to do, and in that way convince ourselves we can feel safer — regardless of whether the victim's actions had any bearing on their death.

The police want to know for other reasons. Victimology, the study of crime victims and their possible relationships with their attackers, plays a key role in solving homicides. The more investigators know about the victim, the better chance they have at finding the killer. What made the killer choose that victim at that time, in that place, to kill in that manner? This may sound close to victim blaming, but the intention is to point the spotlight on the perpetrator — not the person they hurt. People classified as high-risk by a victimology analysis can walk around every day without becoming victims. Someone classified as low-risk can go about their normal, safe routine and still be attacked by an opportunistic killer. What's important is learning who the victims are, and therefore who they spend their time around, in order to home in on a possible suspect. Answering the standard victimology questions can be the difference between catching a killer and letting them go free.

ELLE:

By the time Jessica Elerson was taken, you had gotten assistance from the FBI on the previous murders, is that right?

SYKES:

Yes, they set about creating well-developed profiles for each of TCK's victims, in the hopes there would be something in their victimology that linked them all together and helped us identify the killer. Unfortunately, they didn't find anything specific. They did conclude that none of them was particularly high-risk for becoming the victim of a crime. Although some engaged in moderately risky behaviors, such as walking alone at dusk or after dark, they were all in populated areas, and some were even taken in the middle of the day. This led the FBI to conclude that the killer must have stalked them, probably for weeks at a time, and either knew exactly when they would be alone or struck in a random moment of vulnerability. We know at least with Beverly Anderson and Lilian Davies, they were crimes of opportunity. Their normal routine was disrupted, but he was able to strike at the exact right moment, as if he'd been waiting for an opening. But others were captured doing something in their regular schedule, as if TCK had shown up knowing exactly where they would be at that specific time. And because his pattern and timeframe for each kidnapping was so critical, there was no room for error.

ELLE:

Speaking of his pattern, let's talk about that. We know the numbers three, seven, and twenty-one are important to him. He took the girls three days apart, but he also kidnapped most of them in threes. Isabelle, Vanessa, and Tamera were taken one after the other. Then Lilian, Carissa, and Katrina. But there are only two victims, Beverly and Jillian, from his first known murders in 1996. This is something that has been a source of speculation and conspiracy over the years. We know those murders were different; Beverly and Jillian did not show evidence of being forced to clean like the others, for example. And as we discussed previously, this has led some people to theorize that Jimmy killed the first two girls and then a copycat took over. But, Detective Sykes, after two decades working on this case, what do *you* think about the disparity?

SYKES:

First of all, I'm going to say that I don't know for sure. This is only my opinion. But like you said, it's based on twenty-three years of living and breathing this case. I think that Beverly Anderson wasn't TCK's first victim.

ELLE:

You look hesitant, but I'm going to ask you to expand on that.

SYKES:

I'm retired now — what the hell. Once I had some breathing room, I spent months looking into unsolved homicides all across the country that fit the Countdown Killer's MO. It didn't make sense for him to start with a twenty-year-old girl when we know twenty-one was one of his trigger numbers. If the 1996 murders were really his first, then it made sense they would be less organized. Maybe he'd killed her a few weeks, a few months before the others. Maybe holding them for seven days was an escalation and the first girl was killed right away. But try as I might, I couldn't find anything that came close. I even searched for other twenty-one-year-old women who were killed in different ways: strangulation, gunshot, different kinds of poison. Nothing. The answer is probably in some cold case file box in some police storage unit in the state, but even though I still look now and then when I'm bored, I have never been able to find it.

ELLE:

Seems like finding that first victim could be a pretty big clue.

SYKES:

I certainly think so. Serial killers often make mistakes with their first victims. Even someone as meticulous as TCK could have been triggered to kill in a rage, dispose of the body hastily. Maybe he even left DNA behind. Thousands have tried, but if you were able to figure out who that person was, I think it could be a huge turning point in the case.

ELLE:

Well, sir, we'll certainly do everything we can. Getting back to the pattern, though. He'd established in all the murders since you joined the case that he was taking three girls three days apart and holding them for seven days before murdering them. This would have required intense studying and planning on his part, which was likely why it took him a year in between each trio of killings to prepare for the next group. What did this tell you about the killer's profile?

SYKES:

We all agreed that he was *meticulous*. That was evident from the state he left the bodies in: not a stray skin cell or eyelash to be found. The only way we figured he could have had a girl available to kidnap on each day in his countdown sequence was if he had dossiers about each of them, and if there were others he had ready as backups if one failed. There were likely dozens more potential victims of each age that he considered and decided not to pursue for a variety of reasons. He must have had girls of each age with different days of the week where they were open to victimization. Suzie walks home alone on Tuesday afternoon, Bess goes to church alone on Sunday, et cetera. He would have to, because all the circumstances had to line up precisely for him to take each girl, and his pattern for taking the other two after he had kidnapped one was inflexible. It had to happen three days apart. Jessica's kidnapping was a mix of both opportunity and planning. Her mother's gaze was probably only off her for ten, maybe fifteen minutes, and she was gone. He had to have known their habit of shopping every week, because he'd scoped out all the areas there were security cameras, and he knew exactly how to avoid them. But it was incredibly risky. He had to get her out of a busy store without a trace in a narrow window of time. Taking her in that way, it was cocky. He knew it was a challenge that he was ready for.

The only time we saw him create his own luck was with the last victim. Her routine usually left her exposed on that day, but she deviated from it, so he had to force the opening.

ELLE:

How did he do that?

SYKES:

Eleanor Watson, known to everyone as Nora, was sometimes home alone for an hour in the afternoon, between school and her parents coming home from work. She was a classic latchkey kid, which was getting rarer by then but hadn't completely gone out of fashion in 1999—especially not for kids her age. Most days, Nora stayed at a friend's house and her mom came to pick her up around dinner. She had been going home more and more, though, in a bid to prove her independence. TCK must have been banking on her being home alone that day, but she went to her friend's house instead. That's when he took his biggest risk yet. He went up to their door and knocked.

ELLE:

Who answered?

SYKES:

Nora's friend. Her mom worked from home in a study at the back of the house, and she was not to be disturbed during business hours, so her daughter answered the door. TCK was apparently wearing a paisley knit scarf and a red hat. It's a trick, wearing something intentionally distinctive if you think you might be witnessed so when you discard them, you blend into the crowd. He told Nora's friend that he had been sent to pick her up because her mom had been taken to the hospital. Nora didn't think twice about it. She was so worried about her mom, she got in the man's car. It was more than an hour before her friend's mom came out of her study and learned that Nora was gone.

ELLE VOICE-OVER:

And that could have been the end of it. If everything had gone to TCK's plan, there would have been two more murders after Jessica's, and then three the next year, and then the next. All police knew was that he took a new girl every three days and killed her a week later, like clockwork. They had no reason to believe he'd ever stop—and they had no idea how to stop him.

It might have gone on forever, TCK changing his chosen victims after his countdown was complete, starting a new ritual entirely. A man like that doesn't just stop killing after he gets a taste for it.

But that isn't how this story ends. Because Nora Watson wasn't killed by the Countdown Killer. She escaped.

9

Elle

January 13, 2020

A blizzard swept through the Twin Cities, leaving roads impassable for the whole weekend. Martín's sister, Angelica, called on Saturday morning. She was the only family he had in the Midwest; most of the rest still lived in and around Monterrey. Her kids stole the phone and took it outside to show them the snowman they had made in their backyard in Eau Claire. The nephews clearly loved the snow and cold, but when they handed the phone back to Angelica, she and Martín managed to fill nearly an hour complaining and joking about the winter weather until Elle was in tears laughing.

After they hung up with Angelica, Elle and Martín invited Sash and Natalie over, and they spent the rest of the weekend watching movies and drinking copious amounts of Abuelita hot chocolate. Besides sneaking a few hours to put together an episode outline for the upcoming week, Elle tried her best to relax and not think about the case. There would be plenty of time for that once the roads were drivable again.

Sash and Natalie left once the snow finally let up on Sunday afternoon, and Elle spent the night recording the remaining script for the week. Tina would tie everything together and make it sound flawless over the next few days. Episode six would feature their bombshell discussion with a woman Elle had tracked down just last week. She couldn't wait to reveal their findings to the world.

After she sent the audio files to Tina, she collapsed into bed in the middle of the night and was asleep within minutes.

Monday morning dawned sharp and white through the cracks in their bedroom curtains. Martín pulled her close, slipped a warm hand under her shirt and caressed her back. Elle blinked awake and smiled up at him.

"Morning," she murmured, throat still raw from last night's recording.

"Hi, there," he whispered before pressing his lips to hers. He rolled into her, covering her upper body with his. "You were up late."

"Episode six." She kissed his neck, inhaling the faint smell of yesterday's cologne. "All wrapped up and sent to Tina."

"This is the big one?" His hand slipped between her legs, and her eyes fluttered shut.

"Mm, yes. Probably still a letdown after last week's, but it'll be hard to top that." Her breath caught in her throat as he stroked her. Fumbling under the sheet, she smiled when she found him already naked.

He chuckled. "If I didn't know you better, I would swear you did that on purpose."

She opened her eyes to study his face. "Did what?"

His other hand worked her pajamas down her legs and then they were together, skin on skin. Mouth next to her ear, he whispered as he moved, "'It'll be *hard* to *top that*.'"

Laughter burst from her lips, cut short by a moan as he pressed himself even closer. His body vibrated with another chuckle as he kissed her neck. And then they stopped talking altogether.

An hour later, after Martín left for work, Elle logged in to her computer to check her messages. There were several emails from her executive producer at the podcast network, exclaiming over the ratings from the episode that had dropped on Thursday. Her marketing coordinator was planning to up their radio advertising and pay for the drive-time slot to lure new Gen-X listeners who'd been teens or young adults when TCK was active. There were hundreds of unread emails, but she could see that Tina had been through thousands more and tagged them based on their filing system. The thick scattering of red was concerning.

Red was for messages that were threatening enough to consider reporting.

Not in the mood to deal with those at the moment, she flipped over to Leo's profile on Facebook again. None of his family members had responded to her queries, although several messages had been left on *read*. Disappointing, but not surprising. She started going through his profile pictures, searching for a woman's face in the year since he'd separated from his wife. He obviously wasn't Facebook official with anyone, but he might still have a girlfriend.

No luck. Every picture was of him alone stretching back nearly three years, before she finally saw him cheek to cheek with a Latina woman wearing her thick straight hair in a high ponytail. Elle clicked on the photo and did a little victory dance in her chair when she saw the woman was tagged. Luisa Toca. This must be the ex-wife. Elle went to her profile.

Luisa's profile picture was the Guatemalan flag, a section of white with a coat of arms surrounded on either side by strips of pure, bright blue. Her status updates oscillated between English and Spanish. One from three months before caught Elle's eye: it announced that Luisa's mother was moving in with her. A look through her pictures revealed the back and side views of dozens of women's hair in various styles and colors with a downtown salon tagged in each one. Elle called the salon, but the manager said Luisa hadn't showed up for her shifts in the last few days and wasn't answering her phone.

Elle clicked over to the section about Luisa's family and sent up a silent prayer of thanks — her mom's account was basically empty, but she had one. And now Elle had a new name.

\\\\\\\\\

After sending Luisa a private message, Elle set about finding her address. Since starting an investigative podcast, she had learned that people had no idea how much of their private information was easily accessible online to those who know where to look. Current and former addresses, phone numbers, places of work, even social security numbers are publicly available if you go to the right site. Scrubbing the information is possible, but expensive. Eight years ago, Elle had paid a lot of money to get rid of that information about herself, but it was worth it. A new married name, a new future—no more being asked to rehash the worst time of her life. Definitely worth it.

She hit a dead end looking for Luisa's information, but she struck gold with the mother. After an hour, Elle found Maria Alvarez's address and got in the car, heading toward Fridley.

Most of the roads were cleared of the previous night's snowfall, but the ground still sparkled with the fresh, gauzy layer. As much as she hated winter, there was something magical about the way a blizzard transformed the city into something brand-new. The day felt unblemished, unsullied—too pure to exist in the same universe where she had walked in to find Leo's dead body. Whatever had happened before, this was a new start.

On the way, she fastened her microphone and headset over her stocking cap. Over the years, she had found it was always better to record a thought even if she never used it on the podcast, rather than find herself with a gap in the episode and no monologue to fill it.

"Three days ago, I received an email from someone claiming to have a tip about TCK. I went to meet him, to find out what information he had, but when I arrived at his house, he had been murdered." Elle paused, blinked away the sight of Leo's bloody body. "I don't know what information he had, if any. There's a chance none of this will be relevant to the case, and I'll archive this recording like I've done with thousands of others. But for right now, I'm still trying to figure out what he might have known. I'm going to his ex-wife's house, to see if she had been in touch with him recently. It's obviously a long shot, but I have to try. I . . . I still can't believe that it was a coincidence, the timing of when he was killed, even though it seems apparent that it was. I have been running this podcast for four years, and I've never had any of my listeners end up in danger because of a tip they gave me. Not that I know of, anyway. I want to remind all of you to be mindful of your own safety first. If you feel that you're in danger, call the police immediately. I'll report back once I have more." She pressed stop and pulled the headset off.

The early cramps of an anxiety attack started building in her chest. As she pulled into the parking lot of a tan-bricked apartment complex, Elle took a deep breath through her nose, held it for ten seconds, and blew it out through her lips. She did this twice more before the stitches came apart inside her, letting her breath flow naturally again. She turned off the car, grabbed her bag full of recording equipment—in case Luisa was willing to do an interview—and opened the door to the crisp winter afternoon.

According to the research Elle had done at home, Luisa and Leo had been married for five years before separating last year. Now, she apparently lived with her mother in an old apartment building next to the highway. Elle lugged her bag up two flights of stairs that smelled like mildew and knocked on number 207. Inside, slow footsteps creaked toward the door, followed by the sound of the peephole cover being lifted.

"¿Quién es?" a hoarse voice asked.

"Señora, me llamo Elle Castillo. Estoy buscando a Luisa Toca—"

"¿Sabe dónde está mi Luisa?" The woman's voice pitched a little higher with anticipation.

Elle's shoulders slumped. The woman was looking for Luisa too. "No, estoy buscándola."

A chain rattled inside and then the door swung open, revealing a stooped, elderly woman who leaned heavily on a mobile oxygen tank. Cannulas rested inside her narrow nostrils. Her deep brown skin was carved with wrinkles from age and worry. Upon seeing Elle, the woman's jaw tensed, her chin raised. "I can speak English, you know."

"Oh, I'm sorry. I shouldn't have assumed; we can speak whichever language you're most comfortable with."

After a moment, Maria nodded. "It's okay. You speak Spanish well, but I'm fine in English. Are you police?"

"No, I'm an independent investigator." Elle held up her microphone. "It's not recording, don't worry. But I look into cold cases for a podcast—it's like a radio show. I was hoping Luisa might be able to help me find someone."

"I don't know who she could help you find. But please, come in."

With shuffling steps, Maria turned and led Elle through the little hallway in her apartment, to a kitchen that smelled of cilantro and onions. Elle settled into a wooden chair, inhaling the spicy air.

With slow, deliberate movements, Maria filled a kettle with water and put it on the stove. She twisted a dial, and the ring grew orange with heat.

"Mijita," Maria whispered, almost too low for Elle to hear. Then she turned away from the stove to look at Elle. "I haven't heard from her in days. Almost a week. She was supposed to call last weekend, but she didn't. I tried and tried. Who sent you here?"

Elle leaned forward in her seat, itching to help the woman to a chair. But it wasn't her place to do so. "I found Luisa on social media and saw you were her mother. I tracked down your address from there. Her work hasn't heard from her in a few days either, so I was hoping I'd find her here."

"So, you don't know where she is." Maria pulled two brown mugs out of a wood-paneled cupboard and set them on the counter. She opened a bright yellow Therbal box and dropped a tea bag in each cup.

"I'm sorry, no," Elle said. "She doesn't live here anymore?"

"This is still where she gets mail, but she spends her nights with a man."

"A boyfriend?" Elle hadn't considered that Luisa might have anything to do with Leo's death, but if there was a new man in the picture, that made things more interesting. New lovers always complicated old relationships.

Maria's wizened face screwed up in distaste. "He is too old for a boyfriend. This man, he is twenty, twenty-five years older than my Luisa. She is still young; she could still find a good man and marry again. But she doesn't try. She wants only this old man."

"What's his name?"

"I don't know," the woman said, shaking her head. "She knows I hate him, so she does not bring him here. He is a white man, blue eyes, with . . . Cómo se dice . . . está perdiendo su pelo."

"Losing his hair? Balding?"

The kettle started to whistle and Maria turned to fill their mugs with water. "Right. Luisa is so beautiful! She could have any man she wants, and she chooses this . . . this viejo feo."

Elle bit her lip. Luisa was lucky to have a mother like Maria—doting and complimentary, convinced no one was good enough for her daughter. That must be nice.

Maria started to pick up the mugs of tea, trying to navigate two in one hand so she could still move her oxygen tank.

Elle stood. "Please, Señora, can I help you with the tea?"

The older woman met Elle's gaze for a moment and then nodded. "Thank you."

Once they were settled back at the table together, Elle held up her tea and smiled. "Thank you for this. It's my husband's favorite brand."

"Your husband is Mexican?" Maria's eyes lit up. "No wonder your Spanish is good. It's the language of romance, you know."

"It certainly worked on me." Elle laughed. Maria seemed to be letting her guard down. It was never an easy thing to do with a stranger, but in her experience, between a woman of color and a white woman —even less so. As a Mexican woman in America, Maria would have a million reasons not to trust someone like Elle. She would try not to give her another one.

A few moments passed in silence. In between sips, Maria stared at the swirling liquid in her mug. Finally, she looked up at Elle again. "You never really explained why you're looking for Luisa. Is she in trouble?"

"No, she's not in trouble, but her ex-husband is . . . was."

"Leo? Oh, I love Leo. She should never have left him." Maria's eyes glowed, stabbing Elle with guilt. Maybe she should just leave without telling Maria about what happened. Let her find out from police or her daughter when the time was right. But she couldn't let her go on believing Leo was alive when he wasn't. That didn't seem fair.

"Señora Alvarez, I'm afraid I have some terrible news. Leo was killed a couple days ago. He was shot in his apartment."

The old woman's face froze, and the warmth in her eyes was replaced with a sudden flood of tears. "¿Qué?"

"I'm so sorry. He's dead."

Suddenly, Maria's jaw clenched, bringing all her wrinkles into straight lines leading down to her pursed lips. "It was that hijo de puta. That pelado Luisa is with. I am sure of it. He stole her from Leo, but it wasn't enough. He was always jealous of her marriage to him, to a real man who loved her." The woman slumped in her chair, resting her elbow on the table and leaning her face into her hand.

Elle looked down at her lap, trying to give her privacy in her grief. Another possibility to add to the mix. If Leo really was killed by his ex's jealous new boyfriend on the day he was trying to give Elle a tip about TCK, that was the worst possible timing.

After a few moments, she tried to speak to Maria again. "Señora, is there anyone I can call to come be with you? I'm so sorry, but I really need to keep looking for your daughter. If you're right about the man she's with, then Luisa could be in danger too."

Wiping her eyes, Maria stood up and shuffled to one of her kitchen drawers, opened it, and took out a sticky note. She wrote two lines and then handed it to Elle. "This is the address where she stays with that man. I never go there. She knows I do not support."

Elle took the note and started to pull away, but Maria clasped her hand, meeting her gaze. "You find him. Find him and keep him away from my daughter. Please."

She nodded, bringing her other hand up to squeeze Maria's. "I'll do my best."

\\\\\\\\

Outside Maria Alvarez's apartment, Elle turned the car on to warm it up. While she waited, she took out her phone and visited Luisa's social media profiles again, scrolling through her recent activity. A scan of her pictures revealed no older man that matched her mother's description; all of her photos were either selfies or the finished product of her clients' hairstyles. She hadn't posted or interacted with anything in more than a week. Her last status update simply said, *No Matter What,* with a prayer-hands emoji. Cryptic, but not exactly ominous. Hopefully Luisa was staying with this guy Maria had pointed her to in Falcon Heights so Elle could at least see what she knew about Leo's suspicions. Although if she was in a relationship with another man, odds were she wouldn't have anything helpful to say about her ex. Not to mention the possibility one of them might have had something to do with his murder.

The air pouring through the vents finally started turning hot, and she shifted her car into gear.

After swinging through a Dunn Bros. drive-through for a mocha, Elle drove toward Falcon Heights, taking sips of strong, sweet coffee at the stoplights. The afternoon light was fading into evening, giving her a twist of longing for the days when the sun didn't start giving up at half past three. Even though Elle had lived in Minnesota her whole life, she'd never been able to reconcile herself to the cold, dark winters.

Just before the exit off I-694, a familiar logo caught Elle's eye. It had been over a year since her podcast network started putting up billboards promoting *Justice Delayed,* but she still wasn't used to seeing her silver-on-black branding blown up on a roadside advertisement. The marketing team had mercifully let her reject their original request to feature a picture of her on the ads. People knew what her face looked like from the local news shows she occasionally dialed in to for commentary on a case, but she didn't need to be splashed all over the Twin Cities billboards. Having her name out there was risky enough. She took the exit and let out a breath.

The address Señora Alvarez gave her was a modest two-story brick house with an attached double garage and a neatly shoveled driveway. On closer inspection, it had to be a heated drive—even the best shoveling job wouldn't get rid of every scrap of snow and ice, but the pavement was wet and completely clean. She left her half-drunk coffee in the car and braced herself for the cold wind before she got out.

As she walked up the path, Elle examined the house: slate-gray bricks and white trim with a series of spotless cottage windows, darkened from the inside by heavy drapes. A flower garden sat beneath the windows next to the path, every part covered in snow except for a few dry branches of a large shrub peeking through the powder.

Remembering that Maria was convinced this guy killed Leo, Elle rested her hand on the Ruger strapped under her coat. Using her free hand, she pressed and held the doorbell until it chimed inside.

There was no answer. She stepped back and looked at the closed garage door. No way to tell if someone was actually home. The windows carved into the front door were frosted, and there was no light behind them, but she rang the bell again anyway.

After a moment, Elle heard footsteps inside. It sounded like someone coming down the stairs. She shuffled in place and breathed into her cupped hands. Finally, the front door opened into the house, just a few inches until a chain stopped it. Appearing above the chain was the face of a man in his fifties. He wore blue-tinted glasses like Bono, and his graying stubble met up with the thinning hair around the bottom of his faded Twins cap. The creased skin around his mouth had the texture of dried-out leather. For a moment, his expression went from confused to tense, but then he pasted on a polite, Minnesota Nice smile. He was probably expecting someone he knew.

"Yes?" he said.

"Hello, Mr.—" Elle waited for him to finish her sentence, but he just stood there, examining her. She cleared her throat when the silence stretched on, then finally gave in and continued speaking. "I'm looking for a young woman named Luisa. I've been told she lives here."

He shifted his weight. "You must have the wrong house," he said, starting to shut the door.

"No, wait." On instinct, Elle reached out and put her hand against the door. He paused. "Please, I really need to find this woman. Are you sure you don't know anyone by that name? Luisa's mom, Maria Alvarez, gave me this address. She seems to think Luisa is living with you, or at least staying with you most nights."

The man's eyebrows drew together. "Maria Alvarez? That old bat?" With a laugh, he shook his head. "Oh, *that* Luisa. Maria's daughter. I don't believe this. Maria Alvarez used to live across the road from me, and I saw her daughter come around a couple times. I flirted with her, sure, but we never even went on a date. She said she had a boyfriend."

At last, he took the chain off the door and opened it wide enough to point past her shoulder at a little white house on the other side of the road, kitty-corner from the man's house. In contrast to his place,

Señora Alvarez's old house was in desperate need of a coat of paint and probably a new roof. The driveway was lost in snow the same height as what blanketed the yard, which was high enough to nearly cover the sad brown FOR SALE sign.

"I don't mean to be cruel, but Maria isn't all right in the head, you know? I wouldn't be surprised if she actually did think I 'stole her daughter' from her or whatever. She already thinks I stole her house."

"Stole her house?" When Elle looked back at him, his arms were folded across his chest. The gray hoodie he wore made him look soft, warm; he could be her dad, a man she'd interrupted in the middle of a Monday night football pregame show.

"You see the state of it? Last year, I complained to the council that she wasn't taking care of it. The grass was overgrown, there were more weeds in her garden than flowers, the front of the house looked like it was going to slide right off. Still does, don't you think?" Redness rose in his cheeks. Something about his rage sparked a hint of familiarity, but men's anger wasn't unique — all red, contorted faces and spluttering, affronted tones.

He continued: "Anyway, I registered a couple complaints with the council, like I said. Finally, someone went to check on her and realized she wasn't living well. She was sick, and her house was apparently an even bigger disaster inside than it was outside, so I guess her daughter was called and she took the old broad to live with her."

"You got an old lady kicked out of her home?" she asked, trying to keep the judgment out of her voice.

"I got an old lady the help she needed but was too damn stubborn to ask for." He met her gaze through his tinted lenses. "Why are you looking for her, anyway? You a friend of Luisa's?"

"You could say that." Elle tapped her fingers against her thigh. The guy was being nice enough, but he had nothing for her and this was now officially a waste of time. "So, when you flirted with Luisa, you said she turned you down because she had a boyfriend?"

The man's smile grew. "She didn't turn me down."

"But you said —"

"If I'd wanted her, I could have gotten her. She was obviously interested. I chatted with her outside her mother's house, gave her a few compliments. Turned out to be a bit of a waste." The man stared past Elle at the house across the street, as if remembering the conversation. Then he looked back at Elle. "She was a hairdresser. I'm looking for a little more in a woman, you know?"

Elle kept her expression neutral. She didn't even know Luisa; for all she knew, the other woman was a nightmare — maybe even Leo's killer. But that didn't stop her from wanting to elbow this guy in the throat.

The man tipped his chin up in a smug nod, eyes gleaming. "Right. Okay then, thanks for stopping by. Gotta get back to the game."

When he closed the door, Elle turned to walk toward her car, studying the broken-down house that was apparently still on the market. The man's plan of getting Maria Alvarez kicked out so the place would be better taken care of seemed to have backfired, and she couldn't help but feel a little bit of pleasure in that.

10

Justice Delayed podcast

December 19, 2019

Transcript: Season 5, Episode 3

[SOUND BREAK: Bell chiming as door opens; indistinct radio music playing.]

ELLE:
Hi, are you Simeon Schmidt?

SIMEON:
That's me.

ELLE:
Hi, my name is Elle Castillo. I spoke to you on the phone.

SIMEON:
Ah, right. Hey, Lily! Lil. Can you come take over for a minute?

ELLE VOICE-OVER:
I'm at the gas station off I-94, outside Lakeland, Minnesota. I can see the St. Croix River from where I'm standing, just shy of the Interstate Bridge that would take me over to Wisconsin. After a few minutes of wrangling with his wife, the owner, Simeon, brings me to his

cramped office in the back of the building. Once we're situated, I remind him why I'm here.

ELLE:

So, I'm investigating the murders of the Countdown Killer from the late nineties, and I understand you have a connection to the case. You helped TCK's last victim escape, is that right?

SIMEON:

I don't know about that. By the time she came to me, that little girl had run half a mile in the snow, barefoot. I think she gets full credit for her escape. I just gave her a warm place to wait for the police to arrive.

ELLE:

That's a fair point, but I'm sure she would still be grateful to you for providing a warm refuge and a place to call the police.

SIMEON:

Anyone would have done the same.

ELLE:

You may be right. Now, can you describe what happened that night?

SIMEON:

Sure, well, I've owned this gas station for over twenty-five years, and I work seven days a week, open to close. My wife and I, we live in the little apartment above here, so when I close up, going home is as simple as climbing the stairs. That night was the same as any other. I was about to lock up, I think, turn in for the night, when I seen this little girl running toward the station. She burst through the door, and I knew right away something was wrong. Her hair was a rat's nest, it looked like she hadn't eaten in days, and she was only wearing a nightgown.

It took a few minutes to get her to talk. She seemed terrified, eyes wild, always looking behind her like a monster was chasing her. My wife finally woke up after I yelled for her a few times, and once the girl saw a woman in the room, her shoulders came down from her ears and she talked. While my wife called the police, the girl told me she'd run away from a cabin where a man was keeping her and forcing her to clean his house. She said she climbed out of the window and down a drainpipe and ran to my station in the snow. I wouldn't have believed her, except you could tell she'd been through hell, you know? Plus, we'd seen the stories on the news about that psycho killer who was kidnapping girls. Anyway, she calmed down enough to drink some hot water and put on the pair of sweats my wife got her, and by then the police and ambulance were there. I never saw her again, except for her picture on the news a couple times.

ELLE:
I imagine the police asked you some questions.

SIMEON:
Oh yeah, they were here for an hour or two after, and I had to come into the station one other time, I think. Some detective from the Cities was here, the lead investigator on the TCK case, if I recall correctly. He wanted to ask me some questions about it, but I can't really remember what they were, to be honest with you.

ELLE:
And you got some media attention afterward, too, is that right?

SIMEON:
Ah, I don't know, I guess. The news cameras were around for a few days. I suppose it was a big story. We did good sales for a couple months, I remember that. Wife and I were able to spend a week at the Wisconsin Dells.

ELLE VOICE-OVER:
In the days following Nora's escape, the public and the police were on tenterhooks. On the one hand, everyone was relieved she had survived and would be returned to her parents after recovering in the

hospital. On the other, for the first time, everyone was at a complete loss over what TCK would do. His second victim in a triad had escaped. Would he replace her with another one? Would he move on to the third, the ten-year-old, as if nothing had happened? Would he do the unthinkable and try to recapture Nora? The last, at least, they did everything in their power to prevent. Police put her and her family under twenty-four-hour watch for a month after she escaped. Her father, a moderately wealthy bank manager, hired security for several more months when the law enforcement detail was removed. By July, no new victims that matched TCK's pattern had been taken, and Nora turned twelve years old.

But by that time, most people believed all of those precautions had been unnecessary.

[SOUND BREAK: Snow crunching underfoot; a crow cawing.]

ELLE VOICE-OVER:

I'm here at the site of the two-story cabin where police say Nora Watson was kept. To avoid retraumatizing her, police never brought her back here. But based on pictures of the area and distance from the gas station, it's the most likely location. And there is one other reason to think this is where Nora was held captive. When police found it, it was a pile of ashes and charred wood, still smoldering in the frigid winter air.

There is nothing left of the cabin now, just a small empty clearing in the middle of the woods. Forests don't come thick in these parts, but this cabin is surrounded by about as many trees as you can find here. It's set back a mile from any major highway, accessible only by a narrow gravel road that passes by an even narrower gravel driveway. This land is owned now by the same people who owned it then, a wealthy couple who spent their summers in the five-bedroom cabin near the river and their winters on the beach in Florida. At the time of Nora's escape, they were both confirmed to be at their townhouse in Florida, having escaped the north like they did every year—as soon as the leaves turned.

The place looks equally abandoned now. Drifts of snow gather up against trees, blown by blizzard winds. Wet, dead leaves form patches of brown where the ground peeks through. It should be peaceful, but I get no comfort here. It's a foreboding place. Police were never able to determine how many of TCK's victims were brought here, but it's a place where at least two young girls were held captive—where at least one was killed. And it's a place where Jessica's body, along with those of two adults, was found among the ashes.

ELLE:
What can you tell me about the bodies found in the cabin?

SYKES:
We estimate they were discovered approximately six hours after Eleanor Watson would have escaped, if we calculated the time she spent running correctly. Jessica's body was the only one identified, as you know. Based on the ME's report, we determined she died before the fire was set, thank God. It was the middle of the night on the seventh day, so it's no surprise she succumbed to the poison then. The other two were the bodies of a man and a woman, both between twenty-five and forty-five years old, Caucasian, and unrelated. As of today, November 3, 2019, neither has been identified. While the autopsy determined Jessica succumbed to the effects of ricin poisoning, the adults were killed with a single gunshot wound to the side of the head, and the gun was burned in the cabin with them.

ELLE:
And the cabin fire was definitely started intentionally?

SYKES:
Yes, firefighters found an accelerant and a lighter on-site.

ELLE:
The bodies of these two have caused a considerable amount of controversy in this case, is that fair to say?

SYKES:

That's putting it mildly.

ELLE:

Can you explain why?

SYKES:

As you know, since Nora Watson escaped, we have never been able to tie another murder to the Countdown Killer. Like I said before, even though I'm retired, I still look into cold cases when given the chance. But I haven't been able to find one in the years since that fits TCK's pattern. Most people think that's because he's dead, because he was the man in that cabin and it was a murder-suicide. They say the woman he killed must have either been his partner in the crimes or an unsuspecting wife he killed to prevent her from turning on him.

But there are others, like me, who know that's what he wanted everyone to think. Say he's alive. He would need to go into hiding and regroup, reassess his mission. He would have to decide whether to continue his countdown or run away and try to live a normal life somewhere else. If he did live, if the two people he killed and burned in that cabin were a decoy, we don't know what he decided, what kind of life he chose to live. He could be a retiree in a villa in Arizona. Maybe he got put in prison for another crime later on, and that's why he never returned to killing.

Regardless of where he is or what he's doing now, by burning that cabin down, he got exactly what he wanted. Once it was clear TCK was no longer active, once a year passed and no other girls were killed, they told me to pack the case up and focus on the others. There are more than two hundred thousand unsolved murders in the USA. If we all spent as much time as I did on one case, we'd never get anything else done.

Every few years, I'd open it up again, chase down whatever leads I could, try to get media attention on the anniversary of one of the girls' deaths or the day of Nora's escape, but nothing ever panned out. That's why I agreed to help you with this podcast, because I think the community has become complacent over time. They think the danger has passed, that he is long gone. And I'm not sure that's true. I think it's past time for police to actively look at this case again, to try to get justice for these victims, if nothing else. They won't be happy about me saying it, but hell, I'm retired now. I've done my time. Let them get mad.

ELLE:
What's the one thing you wish people knew about this case? The thing you think would help solve it.

SYKES:
That no matter what anyone online says, no matter what the reporters and the other investigators tell you, there is no proof — none whatsoever — that the Countdown Killer is dead. And if he's not dead, he's not done.

ELLE VOICE-OVER:
Obviously, I know I'm opening myself up to outrage by even suggesting that TCK is still alive. Most people are quite comfortable believing that he is long dead. But for reasons that will come to be apparent, I agree with Detective Sykes. I agree that it's past time the public paid more attention to this case, that we demand it get solved. As he said earlier in this episode, we think a key part of that will be finding who his first victim was, if it wasn't Beverly Anderson. If you know of any unsolved homicides in the area that preceded hers, please get in touch. Links to my website and email are in the show notes. You all know by now that I will listen and at least look into your ideas as much as I can.

This is on us, now — the public. It's time for us to look at what we know about the Countdown Killer. Who he was, what he did, why he did it. And if police aren't interested in looking at the case anymore, then that's what I'm here for.

Next time, on *Justice Delayed* . . .

11

Elle

January 14, 2020

Elle sat in her desk chair and ran her fingers through her hair, examining the Wall of Grief — the name Martin had coined for the massive expanse of corkboard that held her case photos. She had two pictures of each girl in the Countdown Killer's series: one alive, the other dead. A headshot and a crime scene photo. They were grouped together by year: 1996, 1997, 1998, 1999. It wasn't the coldest case she'd solved since she quit her job in social work to do this full-time, but it was close.

That designation belonged to the Duluth Phantom, who terrorized the city in 1991, stealing four babies from their rooms at night over the course of a year. Using an online database of self-submitted results from commercial DNA tests and the services of one of her listeners — a genealogist — Elle tracked down all four. They'd been told they were adopted and had no idea who their birth parents were. During questioning by police, their parents admitted to paying for what they had been led to believe was an elite — although suspiciously covert — adoption agency. Their descriptions and dodgy records led to the kidnapper. It turned out, the police had been close to catching him after he abducted the last baby in 1991, so he had used the money to fade into obscurity rather than risk continuing to build his black-market network.

The Phantom launched Elle's podcast from its modest but loyal following into a cult phenomenon over a year ago, but the TCK case had already topped it. This was the case she wanted to solve more than any other, and she had a new lead. She just needed to crack it.

The hunt for Luisa Toca had taken her all over Minneapolis the last two days, with no luck. Her employer still hadn't heard from her. The woman was in the wind. City council confirmed that several complaints had been filed about the condition of Maria Alvarez's house, so the man's story in Falcon Heights seemed to check out. It had been five days since Leo was killed, and Elle was no closer to finding out who Leo was referring to, or what might have been on the flash drive in his pocket, than when she started.

Her podcast listeners often acted as crowd-sourced investigators once she got through the first few episodes, where she set up the case. Even so, there was a limit to how much information she was willing to put out publicly when it came to persons of interest. If she put Luisa's name on the *Justice Delayed* subreddit, she might be able to track her down faster, but then listeners would assume she had something to do with the case when there was no evidence she was involved at all. It would also be breaking the rules Elle had set for herself and her listeners since the very first episode. Don't dox each other, don't dox suspects, don't be a dick. They were pretty simple, and in general, people stuck with them.

Well, her normal audience did. Since she'd started season five, there had been some nonsense from a few vocal new listeners clogging her feed. Then there were the dozens of red-flagged emails in her inbox to tend to.

Elle opened her laptop and took a deep breath. A season on the Countdown Killer was always going to be big, but even she couldn't believe how fast it had taken off since the first episode launched in December. She went from around a million overall downloads to nearly two million. Armchair detectives and true crime aficionados who had followed TCK's case for years tuned in to *Justice Delayed* for the first time, and it seemed like all of them had something to say about how she ran her investigative podcast. Her social media accounts and podcast forums—normally her places of refuge, where she went to brainstorm with listeners and bounce theories off each other—had become unwieldy. There were great thoughts and questions being shared, but it took a lot longer to find them than it had before.

Before she could tackle her email, she called Tina. Her producer's face lit up the screen.

"Elle, this next episode. Hot damn, it's going to singlehandedly give all of Reddit an orgasm."

Elle's lip curled, but she laughed anyway. "Ew, I hope not."

Tina leaned forward, eyes close to the screen as if she could stare into Elle's very soul. "No, I'm serious. If you're right about this, it's huge. You found TCK's actual first victim."

Elle put her hands on her face, the skin burning underneath her fingertips. She'd been so busy hunting Leo the last couple days, she'd almost forgotten the next episode might be an even bigger reveal than the last. She looked back at the screen between her fingers. "Not me. We. You're the one who did all the legwork, got me the information I needed."

"Psh, fine, we're both badasses, let's just agree and move on." Tina grinned, swiping her straight black hair over her ear. "Now, on a more serious note. I'm glad you called; I want to talk to you about the show account."

Elle pulled up the browser next to the video call box. "Yeah, I see we've got a lot of fire in here."

"Mostly embers, I'd say," Tina said. "But a couple of them imply they know your location, at least the suburb. I've reported them to the local PD, but those guys aren't really equipped to handle cyber cases like this. I tried to help them out by tracking down a couple of the senders' IP addresses, but some of them have been routed through VPNs."

Shivering, Elle took another drink of wine. She opened one of the emails Tina had flagged red.

*You're going to cost innocent people their lives you stupid bitch.
I will come for you if anyone I love gets hurt I will end you. That
pussy handgun won't save you you know.*

Well, they knew she was carrying. That might be a good guess, or
an observed behavior. The email went on for several paragraphs, but
there was no other personal information. She archived it.

After a few more, she felt like someone had poured a bucket of fire
ants on her head.

Tina sat silent, watching her read them. "You okay?" she asked
when Elle started topping up her glass of wine.

"I'm fine. Thanks for going through these. Are you okay?"

Her friend nodded. "Sure." Then she shrugged. "I mean, no, not
really. Like, I'm a business analyst, Elle. I didn't exactly train to deal
with these kinds of creeps. The most heated I get when writing an
email is saying shit like 'per my last email' to my coworkers, and half
the time I delete it because I sound like a bitch. I'm not going to lie, I
had to smoke a joint after reading those this weekend."

Elle licked across her lower lip, tasting the bitter tang of red wine.
Her tongue was purple on the web cam. "I'm sorry. You don't have to
keep reading them if it's too hard. I really do get it."

Tina waved her off. "Don't worry about me. I've got my girlfriend
here, and she likes it when I'm needy." She winked, but her smile
didn't go all the way to her eyes.

"Thanks, Tina. Take a break if you need to, though."

"Will do. And you . . . just, please take care of yourself, okay? You
might want to consider calling Ayaan, letting her know about the
threats."

Elle nodded, but she knew that she wouldn't. For all she knew,
Ayaan's department was still working to make sure she had nothing
to do with Leo's murder. They probably wouldn't look kindly on a
requested favor right now.

When she hung up with Tina, Elle closed out the email. There
were still hundreds of *unread*s, but she had hit her limit on the red-
flagged menaces for tonight. If she had her way, she would shut the
whole thing down and go downstairs to watch a movie with Martin.

But she had been avoiding this for days, and she needed to stay engaged. Her listeners did their best to give her good information; the least she could do was listen to them.

She opened her social media. Her post with the link to episode five, the one from last Thursday, had more than ten thousand comments. Elle took an extra-large gulp of wine and started weeding her way through.

> @truecrimeobsess
> @castillomn love your latest episode—holy shit!
> *mic drop*

> @TCKlives
> @truecrimeobsess @castillomn ikr? Can't believe she
> scored that interview. That's our girl, though. If any-
> one can get people to finally look at this case again,
> it's Elle Castillo.

> @iowafairy
> @castillomn I WAS NOT PREPARED OMG. How
> did you find her???

Elle scrolled through, liking the encouraging and exclamatory tweets, answering questions where she could. But when she swapped over to her direct messages, she saw the *Requests* inbox lit up with notifications from people she didn't follow. She took another sip of wine and clicked them open.

She should have known better. People had gotten more brazen in public comments over the years, but the private messages were always worse, and these were no exception. She'd been part of a panel discussing online harassment at last year's CrimeCon, alongside four other women who ran high-profile investigative podcasts. The moderator had put together a slideshow of comments from their mentions with the usernames blurred out. They were hardly able to guess whether a comment was directed at them or one of the other panelists—they all saw similar fare in their own feeds every day. The only exception was the Black woman, who had to deal with both sexism and racism on her accounts.

To be a vocal woman online was to face constant abuse for the things you said and did, no matter how meaningless or innocent.

Elle started scanning the direct messages. Unlike the show's email inbox, her social media accounts were hers alone; Tina didn't have access, and therefore couldn't filter anything.

It was mostly trolls, the people who thought they knew this case better than she did and were determined to discount everything she said. Most of the messages followed the same theme: she was lying about her sources; she was misleading people about the police investigation; she was fearmongering by implying that TCK was still alive when most experts had concluded that it was him in the burned-out cabin. No one was outright threatening, but there was an ominous undertone to the messages. One person had messaged simply, *Careful what you wish for,* and for some reason it chilled her more than any of the others. Her investigation was being closely watched, and some people weren't impressed.

Her phone buzzed and she jumped, reaching for it with shaky hands. The police station's number flashed on the screen.

"Hello?" she said, sounding drunker than she felt.

"Castillo, are you working my case?"

Knowing it would piss him off, Elle sat back in her chair and said, "Who is this?"

"It's Detective Sam Hyde. I know you're nosing around my case, and I'd like you to come in and explain yourself. This is completely unprofessional, and I could have you charged with obstructing an investigation."

That snapped her into focus. "Detective Hyde, I'm sure you're aware that I've worked closely with Minneapolis PD on a number of recent cases." It was only one, but the red wine had loosened her tongue. "I am confident you're not suggesting that I don't have a right as a private citizen to go talk to other citizens about any topic I so choose."

"You told a woman her son had been murdered."

"I told a woman her ex-son-in-law had been murdered. Several days after the fact, I might add."

For a moment, there was silence on the other end of the line. Then: "I'd like you to come into the station and tell me what you know. Maybe tomorrow, since you obviously shouldn't be driving tonight. And then if you don't mind very much, I'd like you to stay the fuck away from my case."

Part II

THE RESET

12

Elle

January 15, 2020

It was obvious when Elle got to the station that something was in the air. Homicide and Crimes Against Children sat near each other —often, unfortunately, working cases together. She walked through the doors and signed in at the desk, surrendering her handgun before turning toward Ayaan's office out of habit. The commander was sitting at her desk, staring intently at her computer screen. It was the same look she'd had on her face when they were digging into the Jair Brown case together—that don't-talk-to-me-I've-almost-got-it look. Damn. Elle was really hoping she'd get Ayaan on her side before talking to Sam Hyde.

Bracing herself, she turned on her heel and headed toward his office alone.

Sam was waiting there for her, leaning against his doorway with a scowl wrinkling his brow. He gestured for her to come in and take a seat, then closed the door and sat on his side of the neatly organized desk.

"Sixteen weeks," he said when he sat down.

"Sorry?"

"Sixteen weeks. That's how long it takes to get through the police academy. Then you've got about half a year of field training, and boom, you're an officer. If that's the career you're after."

"Thanks for the recruitment info," she said. She was dying for a cup of coffee. The messages she'd gone through last night had kept her awake. She hadn't told Martín, didn't want him to worry. Instead, she'd stayed awake alone, staring at the ceiling in the dark and jumping at every rustle and creak of the house.

Sam looked annoyed. "Do you want to explain what you were thinking, going around and interviewing my witnesses before I even got to them?"

Elle shrugged. "I didn't know you hadn't gotten to them. I mean, the ex-wife seems like a pretty obvious first step. I would have thought you'd talk to her right away."

The pale skin on Sam's neck turned scarlet. "Just because you run some radio show where you like to play detective and it's worked out a couple times doesn't mean you can come in on an active murder investigation and do whatever the hell—"

"All right, you're right. I'm sorry." Elle let out one short, harsh breath. "I swear, I wasn't trying to interfere with your murder investigation. I really wasn't. I was . . . I was trying to figure out if anyone knew Leo well enough to know what he was going to tell me about a case I *am* working. The case I was there to talk to him about when I found his body."

"TCK."

"That's right."

"I don't understand, what could his ex have helped you with?"

"I thought maybe if he really knew who TCK was, he might have told someone. I'd ask his business partner, but I'm guessing he's still on the run?"

Sam shook his head. "No, local PD pulled him over the night of the murder, speeding toward his place. He and Leo were definitely running a chop shop business, and the guys in Robbery have been building a case against him for that. But between the time Leo talked to you on the phone and when you walked in, we have a pretty narrow time of death, and Duane was captured on security footage at the gas station down the block just five minutes before you walked in.

We found no murder weapon at the scene and nothing at his apartment or workplace, but our best guess is the uniforms got him before he even made it home. So, either he ditched the gun on the way or he isn't our guy."

The hair on Elle's arms stood up. "You mean he didn't kill him?"

"Can't say for sure, but we didn't have enough to hold him. He's been out since Friday afternoon."

He was going to tell me who TCK was. Leaning forward, Elle put her elbows on the desk and rested her forehead in her palms. The room was spinning, so she took a deep breath through her nose.

"Are you all right?"

"Shh, I'm thinking."

Closing her eyes, she tried to remember the apartment exactly as it looked when she got there. Leo was on his back on the floor, Duane kneeling next to him. The room had been undisturbed, the bare furnishings worn but tidy. Duane didn't have a weapon on him, not that she could see. There was no one else in the room. Could someone have been hiding by the door, slipped out when she walked in the room? No, one of them would have noticed. They must have just missed the killer. Maybe whoever it was had passed her on the stairs, although she couldn't remember seeing anyone. He might have gone one level up in the stairwell, waited for her to go in. That would imply he knew she was coming, which made her shiver.

She was dying to ask about the flash drive in Leo's pocket, whether the police had gotten access to it yet. Her best guess was it was sitting on some stack of evidence right now, waiting to be processed. Even if it had been, there was no way Sam would tell her, and he seemed just vindictive enough to charge her for rummaging around in a murder victim's pants.

Finally, she looked up at him. "I know you're not a fan of independent investigators." He opened his mouth to respond, but she continued. "I promise to try to stay out of your way, but I can't promise to stay out of this case. If Leo knew something about TCK, I'm going to find out what it was. And if he died because he was going to give me that information, I owe it to him to find out who killed him."

For a moment, Sam stared at her. Then a smile spread across his face, parting his lips in an expression of disbelief. "You think TCK killed him."

Elle could feel her cheeks getting red, but she refused to look down. "I did *not* say that."

"But you do. You think this guy got shot by TCK because he wrote an email to your podcast?"

The way he said it sounded more astonished than mocking, but Elle had had enough. She stood up and walked out of the room, ignoring Sam's half-hearted calls for her to come back.

She was waiting at the elevator when Ayaan poked her head out the door. "Hey, Elle, do you have a minute?" When Elle met her gaze, Ayaan pulled back. "Whoa, are you all right?"

"Hyde," Elle said, too tired to explain more.

Ayaan nodded. "I hear that. He's a new transfer. Does good work, but he's a bit of a prick."

"You don't say."

"Well, maybe this will take your mind off things." Ayaan stepped into the lobby between the elevator and the door to the station, folding her arms across her white blazer. "I've got a missing person, presumed kidnapped yesterday morning while waiting for the school bus. The girl's mom loves your podcast. She's losing her mind with worry, but all she keeps talking about is that she wants you on the case. I've just gotten approval from the brass to bring you on as a consultant, if you're interested."

Elle's eyes widened and she straightened up. She had been certain the police chief didn't trust her, even after everything she had done to try to prove herself. She clarified, "A consultant on an active case?"

Ayaan nodded. "If you want. I'd be happy to have your insights."

It would mean less time to work on the podcast, chasing leads and recording new content. On the other hand, it would take her mind off the garbage in her email inbox. Plus, if she turned Ayaan down now, she might never get an opportunity to help with a Minneapolis PD case again.

Biting the inside of her cheek, Elle looked past Ayaan into the station. She could see Sam's office from here, see the back of his head where he sat at his desk. He would hate it if she was working on an active case. That was an added bonus, but the more she thought about it, the more she wanted to do it anyway. Someone wanted her; someone thought she was a good enough investigator to trust with their own child's case.

Elle locked eyes with Ayaan again and gave her a firm nod. "I'm in."

13

Justice Delayed podcast

January 2, 2020

Transcript: Season 5, Episode 4

ELLE VOICE-OVER:
Minnesota has thousands of log cabins. Family homes dotting the countryside, hunting shacks hidden in clusters of trees. Mansions that belie the diminutive connotation of "cabin" hug the shores of some of our famous ten thousand lakes. They are beautiful, practical structures brought over from Scandinavia in the era of pilgrims and pioneers. But they are also fire hazards.

Fire needs only two things to thrive: fuel and oxygen. By their nature, cabins are constructed of fuel—thick, dry logs notched together tight to keep out the wind and snow. Understandably, many of the people who own log cabins have a nostalgia for the past and forgo more modern heating systems in favor of fireplaces or wood-burning ovens. These families lie in their beds each night, listening to the wind whistle around their sturdy homes, soaking up the heat from the fireplace snapping in the corner. They might feel safe, but it only takes one element to turn their home into a pile of kindling. One small thing could transform this place of safety into a fiery death trap.

A spark.

[THEME MUSIC + INTRO]

ELLE VOICE-OVER:

Police records are confidential, but between my inside view from Detective Sykes and the vague answers I've been able to glean from Minneapolis Police, no one is investigating the Countdown Killer case in any official capacity at this time. The position of investigators is that nothing more can be done until new evidence comes to light. That's why I'm here, digging. Finding new evidence is my specialty. But I'm not the only one. After releasing the first episode of this season, I was contacted by a forensic scientist in the Minnesota Bureau of Criminal Apprehension. She wishes to remain anonymous, although her employer has authorized her to give me the information she is about to reveal. She simply doesn't want to be contacted by anyone in the public or the media about her role in this case, and I respect her wishes. I'll be calling her Anne.

ELLE:

Thanks for agreeing to meet me here. I understand you have some information you want to share about the state of the bodies found in TCK's cabin in 1999?

ANNE:

That's correct. To be clear, I wasn't with the Bureau when the bodies were found. However, as you know, on the twentieth anniversary of Nora's escape last winter, there was a temporary push in the media to solve this case, and I was assigned to review the forensic evidence in the case file. Of course, we'd never found any of TCK's DNA, but they had found a long hair on the fourteen-year-old victim, Carissa Jacobs. This isn't public knowledge—well, I guess now it is. The hair came from an unknown adult female; the mitochondrial DNA was not a match for any of the girls TCK had kidnapped, and at the time, that was the only DNA they were able to extract from a rootless hair.

In my review of the evidence, I was able to use advancements in

DNA extraction to get a better sample from the charred bones of the female victim in the cabin. It was so degraded that in 1999, they weren't able to amplify the genetic markers enough to be confident in making an identification. However, in this recent round of testing, I was able to generate a stronger sample, as well as extract nuclear DNA from the strand found on Carissa's body. Within a reasonable degree of scientific certainty, I can say that the woman whose hair was found on Carissa Jacobs's clothing was the same woman who was found dead in TCK's cabin.

ELLE:

That's a significant discovery. I'm sure there are some people who will wonder why you're sharing it here for the first time, and not in, say, the *Star Tribune* or even a national newspaper.

ANNE:

With all due respect to those publications, your podcast is the reason this story is even back in the papers at all. Everyone else has moved on. They did their duty by putting a feature and a call for information in the papers last year, but that's it. You're the only one who is investigating this thing for real, trying to find the guy who did this. The police got the information first, of course, but there's no match for the woman's DNA in CODIS, the national DNA database. They're working with a forensic genealogist now to trace the family tree and find the woman's relatives. This method has helped solved a lot of high-profile cases recently, but some of the databases used early on have made it harder for law enforcement to access people's DNA results, so that has slowed the process. They may well find a close enough match to locate her relatives and identify her, but it could take months — maybe years. In the meantime, I think progress can be made. That's why I contacted you.

ELLE:

What do you think this means, personally? I know you said it's outside your area of expertise, but if you had to guess.

ANNE:

Well, it lets us know that the woman probably wasn't just a random victim TCK killed to confuse detectives. She was known to him for at least a year, since she had proximity to Carissa before she was killed. Unfortunately, all other potential forensic evidence was burned up along with the house, and there was no male DNA found on any of the victims' bodies, so we have nothing to compare to the man in the cabin with her. I performed the same test on his bones, and the results have been entered into CODIS too. They didn't come up with a match, which means he was likely never arrested before his death. That doesn't rule him out as being TCK, but it doesn't necessarily make him likely to be the killer either.

ELLE:

Because most serial killers start with low-level violent offenses and petty crimes, like stalking or burglary, right?

ANNE:

That's what I understand, although it's not my area of expertise. Now, TCK could have done crimes like that and just never got arrested, but it's something to consider. But for those who are so confident the man in the cabin was TCK, there is one other key piece of evidence that you should be aware of. As best we can tell, the DNA belonged to a man in his forties. This corroborates initial age determinations our office made after examining his skeleton.

ELLE:

That's . . . huge, actually. Every expert profile developed on TCK determined he was late twenties or early thirties. Even if the profilers were wrong, the statistics bear out that most serial killers are in that age range. Why was the age of the man in the cabin never made public?

ANNE:

By the time they provided the age estimation of his skeleton, the media fervor surrounding the TCK case had died down. There were no killings in 2000, and then the eyes of the nation were on New York City and the nightmare surrounding the terror attacks on 9/11. The few papers that did report the findings buried the information in later paragraphs, and even if people did see it, they didn't seem to think it mattered. The consensus among law enforcement was that the profiles must have been wrong. Everyone was more than happy to believe he was dead. It was easier — neater — to imagine that TCK took his own life after killing his partner and setting fire to that cabin. The murders stopped, after all.

ELLE:

The question I always get when I posit that TCK is still alive is, "Well, then who was the man in the cabin?" I have to be honest, it's one question I have a hard time answering. I've imagined dozens of scenarios, but I can't seem to come up with anything I feel confident in. Do you have a theory?

ANNE:

It's pure speculation, of course. Like you said, it's probably something we will never know unless and until they catch the killer. But if I had to guess, I'd say there are two options: one, TCK killed a man — someone known to him or a stranger on the street — or two, he robbed a fresh grave to steal a decoy. Either way, the public and law enforcement have fallen for it for two decades.

[SOUND BREAK: Skype ringtone chiming and then being answered.]

ELLE:

What have you got for me, Tina?

ELLE VOICE-OVER:

After I interviewed Anne, I got in touch with Tina Nguyen, whom you might remember from previous seasons of *Justice Delayed*. She's my intrepid producer-slash-researcher extraordinaire.

TINA:

I looked into all the missing persons records in the Midwest for men in their thirties and forties, like you asked. You wouldn't believe how short the list is. I opened up the timeframe to eighteen months on either side of the cabin-burning incident, but still. I only turned up about a hundred names.

ELLE:

Middle-aged white men don't go missing without explanation very often.

TINA:

Lucky them. I tracked down a few of the guys, even though their case files were still open. Contacted the local departments to make sure they knew where they were. They seemed surprised, so oops. Sorry, fellas. Guess your second families are in for a shock.

ELLE:

Of course, you solved a couple decades-old cold cases while you were researching another one. That's very on-brand for you.

TINA:

What can I say? I don't like it when men ditch their child support payments to start new lives in Florida. Anyway, I managed to narrow it down to three really good possibilities. These guys all went missing within a week of the cabin burning, and they have supposedly never been heard from since. I can't find anyone who resembles them on-line, and their personal information hasn't been used since they were reported missing.

ELLE:

You're amazing. Anyone in particular catching your eye?

TINA:

Yeah, this one guy, not-his-real-name-Stanley. He was reported miss-ing by his secretary three days after Nora escaped. No wife or family of his own to miss him, poor guy. There was suspicion he had run away with a married woman he was having an affair with—someone from his office. Apparently, neither of them showed up for work after that day, and no one ever heard from them again. Rumor was the woman's husband was abusive, so everyone assumed that's why they ran off together and didn't tell anyone where they were going. Her husband seems to have gone AWOL at the same time. I looked into him, but from what I can tell, he used a fake name on their marriage certificate and there are no records of him before 1990. His wife, though, she has a whole history. Her social security number has never been listed on another job or credit card application. She didn't have a passport, so it's unlikely she got on an international flight.

Now, it's possible they really did just run away together. Back then, you could cross the border into Mexico without a passport. Maybe they drove to Central America and are living a life of leisure on the beach, selling hemp bracelets for enough food to get by. But I doubt it.

ELLE:
I doubt it too.

ELLE VOICE-OVER:
As many of you know, I plan as much as I can, but a lot of my investigation happens in real time. I get more information and tips as soon as I start airing episodes, and this case is no exception. This is a lead we've only been working for a couple weeks, but we have already turned up a huge break in the case. It's very possible that this couple Tina uncovered were that couple in the cabin. If that's the case, given his use of a fake name, it seems that TCK was a cuckolded husband who killed his wife and her lover, then burned them in that cabin to cover his tracks. We don't know, but we have shared the information Tina gathered with Minneapolis PD, as well as the Bureau of Criminal Apprehension, and they are looking into it now. We have new evidence. We are breathing life into this case. And TCK, if you're listening, we are going to find you. This time, it's you who's on a clock—and your time is almost up.

14

Elle

January 15, 2020

On the way to the missing girl's house, Ayaan filled Elle in on the case. Yesterday morning, on her way to the bus stop, an eleven-year-old girl named Amanda Jordan disappeared. The police hadn't been able to locate any eyewitnesses, and the bus driver said that Amanda was not at the stop by the time she pulled up. Only one of the five kids waiting for the bus remembered seeing any adults in the area: a young man standing on the sidewalk down the street. She had described him as being tall, Caucasian, with black hair. The girl's parents had been asked yesterday, but they couldn't think of anyone they knew that matched the description.

"But I was having a hard time getting anything useful out of them," Ayaan said as she pulled onto a quiet residential street. "They were both bordering on hysterical. There's an officer with them now, just in case of a ransom call, but apparently they have barely spoken since I left yesterday afternoon." She shook her head. "It never gets easier, cases like these, but her parents seemed particularly unstable. The mother blames herself."

"Why?" Elle asked, shuffling through the notes Ayaan had taken on the case so far.

"She usually watched her daughter until she got on the bus, but yesterday she got a phone call, so she walked away for a moment. When she came back, the bus had come and gone. She just assumed Amanda was on it."

Elle shook her head. It was natural for the mother to feel guilty, but guilt was a useless emotion. More than that, it was detrimental. Paralyzing. They wouldn't get anything from her until they could push her past it.

Ayaan parked behind the squad car on the street, far enough from the curb that Elle could get out without stepping into a snowbank. The commander stood at the foot of the driveway and pointed at a right diagonal across the street. "The bus stop is there. Between five and ten kids get on each day; it varies since a few of their moms work part-time and drive them to school some days. From the Jordans' front door, you can kind of see the spot where the kids wait, but it's partially obscured. Mrs. Jordan says usually there's enough kids waiting in a group there that she can at least see when Amanda joins up with them after crossing the road."

She turned back to the house, and Elle looked with her. "Sandy Jordan was standing inside her porch with the storm door shut, watching through the glass. As soon as Amanda left the house, their landline rang. From the phone records, we know the call came in at eight twenty-seven. The bus driver showed up less than three minutes later, at eight thirty. Somewhere in that time, Amanda was taken."

"And no one actually saw the kidnapping?"

Ayaan looked across the road again. The bright glare from the snow made her brown eyes glow. "Not as far as we could tell. Officers canvassed the neighborhood, but none of the other parents saw anything. Since Amanda's house is around this slight bend, we figure there must have been blind spots from where the parents were watching. We interviewed the parents, the bus driver, and all the kids at the bus stop yesterday. A couple of the kids seemed nervous, of course, but they just wanted to help. The only other information we have is from the bus driver. She said she's sure she saw a van in the area that she didn't recognize. A dark blue van, unmarked, no plates. She keeps an eye out for that kind of thing. Watches too much *SVU*.

We've asked around, but so far no one has claimed it or explained its presence here. We're looking into security footage in the area, but every house we've found that has a camera has it focused on their own driveway, and most of them don't even have systems. It's considered a pretty safe neighborhood."

Elle crossed her arms as the wind kicked up. "They always are." She looked up and down the street. Ayaan's sedan and the squad car were the only vehicles on the street; everyone else either had cars in the driveway or a two-car garage. The front lawns were open, blending into each other without fences. Clean paths were shoveled up to the wooden decks or brick stairs that formed the welcoming entries of Colonial-style homes. These houses would mostly belong to upper-middle-class folks with teenagers or grown children, considering so few elementary students were getting on the bus. By eight thirty, it was a good bet most of them would be at work, but certainly no guarantee. If most of the parents watched their kids until they got on the bus, that meant the kidnapper had to know exactly where to be to remain unseen. And he had to know that Amanda's mom would be distracted.

It was a risky way to kidnap a child—already a fraught mission in itself.

"What are you thinking?" Ayaan asked.

"He must have made that phone call."

"We got the phone records this morning," Ayaan told her. "The call came from a prepaid cell phone, bought two months ago from the Target in Shoreview. A burner phone, basically. The customer paid in cash. We're trying to see if we can get security camera footage, but the store managers aren't sure it has been saved."

Elle nodded. "It probably hasn't, but if they do still have it, I'm betting the guy went in disguised. He planned this carefully. He'd have to know the neighborhood, the behavior of the parents, what time people left for work. Let's say the blue van did belong to him: if he got Amanda to get in it that quickly, you know what that says to me?"

"That she knew him." Ayaan met her gaze. "Maybe you can get

something out of her parents that I couldn't. It's not a very detailed description, and we don't even know if the man that girl saw was our kidnapper, but it's the best lead we have at the moment."

Elle turned toward the house. "Let's go talk to the parents."

\\\\\\\\\\

The Jordans' house was a cozy little two-story with every light on, even in the late morning sun. Like maybe their daughter just got lost and the light would help her find her way home. When Ayaan knocked on the front door, a local patrol officer answered. He let them in after confirming Elle's ID.

The white couple huddled together on the sofa were Dave and Sandy Jordan. Sandy's blond hair was in rumpled knots around her shoulders, and both of their flushed faces were streaked with tears. Sandy stood as soon as she saw Elle, dropping her husband's hand. For a moment, she just stared, tears streaming down her face. Then she launched herself at Elle, hugging her so tightly Elle felt her ribs adjust.

A memory flashed through her head from when she was a child: waking up tangled in urine-soaked sheets and screaming from the terror of a nightmare. Her mother had come running, ready to attack an intruder. Instead, she found her daughter sitting up in bed alone. The only enemy that night was inside Elle's mind, and that was a place her mother could not reach. Elle had grasped for her then, hoping for soft arms wrapped around her like Sandy's were now, but her mother had just looked at her, eyes hot with pain that Elle would never understand.

Elle blinked as Sandy's embrace tightened. Awkwardly, she patted the woman on the back.

"Okay, okay," she said, rubbing a gentle circle between the woman's shoulder blades. Her frail body shook. Elle guessed she hadn't eaten or drunk anything since yesterday morning.

"Thank you for coming," Sandy said when she finally pulled away. Her body hunched forward, as if the act of standing straight was painful. "I just . . . I'm friends with Grace Cunningham's older sister. The girl from your season one case."

Elle nodded. "Right."

"I know what you were able to do for them. I thought maybe you could help. It's not because I don't trust the police." At this, Sandy gave Ayaan a desperate glance, as if to reassure her of her faith in the force. "I felt like I had to do something. We've both been so useless, trying to think of anyone who could have done this. I'm going crazy thinking about what might be happening to . . . I just . . ." She trailed off into a sob and collapsed back on the sofa next to her husband. When Sandy looked up again, Elle made eye contact with her.

"Can you tell me what happened?"

Dave Jordan had yet to say anything, but he put his beefy arm around his wife in a gesture that nearly swallowed her tiny body whole. He gave Elle a doubtful look. "I saw you outside. Wasn't Commander Bishar filling you in?"

"Yes, she told me what happened, but I'd like to hear *your* story. Please."

Dave finally handed a box of tissues to his poor wife. After wiping a few handfuls of them across her face, Sandy spoke again. "I was going to watch Amanda walk to the bus stop, just like every other morning. It's freezing, so I stayed inside like I usually do in the winter. As she was walking down the driveway, I went . . ." She paused, wiping away a fresh flood of tears. "I went into the kitchen because my phone rang. No one ever calls us on the landline, so I thought maybe there was some kind of emergency. I answered, but no one was there. By the time I got back to the window, the bus had come and gone. I just assumed . . . I just assumed she'd gotten on. Didn't think twice about it."

Sandy looked up at Dave and shook her head. "I'm sorry. I'm so sorry."

His jaw clenched, but he reached out and put a hand on her knee. "You didn't do anything I wouldn't have done. This isn't your fault."

Elle tried to catch his eye, keep him present while his wife tried to compose herself. "What happened next? How did you find out she was missing?"

"The school called," Dave said. "They rang us when she didn't show up after first period. We were obviously shocked, so we called 911 right away. When the officers looked around, they found her school bag in the gutter. We couldn't see it from our window because of the snowbank, but it was out there, in front of the house two doors down."

"So, whoever it was that took her didn't mind making it obvious she was gone." Elle said the words more to herself, but when she looked up, she saw that Ayaan was watching her from her position leaning against the door frame. She nodded.

Ayaan said, "Officers found the bag right away when they got here, but nothing else. It was in the same vicinity as the van the bus driver thought was suspicious."

Goose bumps prickled along Elle's arms, even though the heat was blasting in the house. "So, if the van was used to kidnap Amanda, that means she was in the vehicle when the bus arrived?"

Sandy sobbed again, the sound grabbing at Elle's heart. Ayaan simply nodded, her lips pressed together.

Elle leaned forward, hands clasped in front of her. "Mr. Jordan, do you and your wife have any money? Any wealth that you've come into recently that someone might know about?"

"What? No. I'm a building contractor. My wife is a stay-at-home mom." Dave's eyes welled up with tears again, and he knuckled them away. "All we've got is this house and two beautiful kids. I just . . . This can't be happening."

"You can't think of anyone who would want to take Amanda? No relatives, acquaintances who have shown special interest in her? Nobody strange following you recently?"

They both shook their heads, and then Sandy started to cry again. "I don't know! Everyone keeps asking me that. I don't know. I don't know. I don't know who would do this to us." Her last word trailed off into a wail.

Wanting to give the couple a moment, Elle looked around for the patrol officer who had greeted them at the door. He must have gone to the kitchen. "Excuse me," she murmured as she left the room.

The officer was filling the kettle at the kitchen sink and held it up when she walked in. "Thought I'd make them tea. I've tried twice, but they let it go cold without drinking it every time. They've basically been just crying and asking me if I've heard anything." The short Black man cracked his knuckles after he put the burner on under the kettle.

"I gathered that—" Elle broke off. "What's your name?"

"Hamilton. Before he was big." He winked and she smiled.

"I think Alexander Hamilton might be offended by that disclaimer, but okay," she said. "I'm Elle Castillo; I'm a police consultant." The words felt good coming out of her mouth, but she held back her smile. "You're telling me you've been here, what, four hours and they haven't said anything?"

Hamilton looked at his watch. "I'm telling you, I took over from Officer Eastley at eight a.m., and these folks have barely said anything that wasn't an answer to a direct question. The dude has been staring out the window the whole time, and the lady goes back and forth between sleeping and crying. I've never seen people so devastated."

"What have you asked them?"

"Just if they had seen anyone strange in their neighborhood recently, or if anyone had a grudge against either of them. You know, maybe someone at work or something?"

Elle nodded. "And what did they say?"

Hamilton scoffed and shook his head, looking disappointed. "Nothing useful. They can't think of any reason why someone would do this to their daughter." He met her gaze, brown eyes thick with worry. "I've seen some shit, but I've never seen folks messed up like this before. I really hope we can find her."

He stayed in the kitchen when Elle went back into the living room. Dave was standing by the window now, looking outside as if Amanda might walk up the path to the house at any moment. Ayaan sat across from Sandy, ramrod straight and looking more uncomfortable in a recliner than anyone Elle had ever seen. Her face smoothed out with hope when Elle walked through the door, but Elle shook her head. Ayaan gave an almost imperceptible nod.

Rather than sitting in the chair next to Ayaan, Elle took the empty spot on the couch next to Sandy. Her body shifted with the new weight on the cushions, sagging in toward Elle. It was enough to snap Sandy out of whatever trance she was in, and she sat up at last, lifting her head from the back of the couch. She looked at Elle, and her eyes took a second to come into focus.

"Where did you go?" she asked, her voice shredded.

"Just to talk to the officer," Elle said. She looked at the commander. "Ayaan, you mentioned there was a description one of the kids gave of someone they saw in the area, right?"

Ayaan nodded as she pulled out her notebook and flipped several pages over the top. "Yes, a ten-year-old girl told us she saw a man standing next to the street while she was waiting for the bus, although she didn't see him approach Amanda. She said he was really tall with dark hair and pale skin, and he was wearing a tan jacket. She didn't recognize him."

Elle looked at the Jordans. "Does that sound like anyone you know?"

"I don't know. Commander Bishar already asked us this last night. I don't know . . . I can't—" Sandy's face crumpled. She leaned forward, putting her face in her hands and wiping away a fresh batch of tears. "I can't think. It's like . . . it's like my brain keeps going blank."

"I know," Elle said. "I honestly can't imagine how this must feel, or how frustrating it must be to try to answer questions like this, that you never thought you'd have to answer."

Ayaan spoke softly. "No one likes to think of this, Sandy, but sometimes the ones we trust most around our children are the people who put them most at risk. We don't see that our children are scared of them, that they have reason to be. Is there anyone in your life, anyone at all, that Amanda might have demonstrated fear of in the past? An uncle? A cousin? A friend you've had over to the house? Someone who works with you, Dave?"

When neither of them responded, Elle spoke again. "Think about whether you have ever had to encourage Amanda to say hi to someone, to give them a hug, maybe. Someone she didn't want to engage with, and you thought she was just being disobedient. It probably didn't seem weird to you at the time, but kids don't always tell us important information in alarming ways. But there was something about this man—this tall, white man with dark hair—that Amanda didn't like. She didn't like him. Do you know someone like that?"

The redness in Sandy's eyes grew worse, but she didn't blink as two tears streamed down the right side of her face. Dave continued to stare out the window, unresponsive. Elle took a deep breath, clenching her fingernails into her palms.

Hamilton came out with a tray loaded with a teapot, teacups, and cookies. He set it down on the coffee table and smiled at Elle, whispering, "Attempt number three."

This one seemed to be a success. As if on autopilot, Sandy reached out and poured herself a cup of tea, her eyes focused somewhere in the middle of the room. She narrowly avoided sloshing the scalding liquid on her hand, but she didn't spill a drop. Without shifting her gaze, she raised the cup to her lips, blew into the steam, and sipped. Then she took a deep, whistling breath through her nose, and said, "You know, she never seemed to like Graham Wallace."

Elle's body went rigid. Hamilton stopped midstride and turned his head, mouth agape. Ayaan was the first one to move; she reached for her tablet and started typing, likely searching the name in the police database.

"Who is Graham Wallace?" Elle asked.

But before Sandy could answer, Dave sank to the floor with a long, stricken moan. Sandy leapt from the couch and ran to him, cradling his head on her lap as he sobbed. The backs of Elle's hands prickled; she looked at Ayaan, but she was too busy staring at her tablet. Hamilton watched the couple on the floor, as if to make sure they weren't physically hurt.

When Dave sat up, his face was streaked with tears. "If it's Graham Wallace, it's my fault. I hired him three years ago. I knew what he was, and I hired him anyway." His body shuddered, but Sandy only pulled him tighter against her.

"What do you mean, 'what he was'?" Elle asked. "What was he?"

"He's a sex offender," Ayaan answered, turning her tablet to face Elle. "He's a sex offender that lives two miles away."

15

Elle

January 15, 2020

It took Elle a few minutes to convince Ayaan to let her ride along to Graham's house. She promised to stay in the car while the commander and the two officers she'd called for backup went inside.

Now, watching police approach the quiet, unassuming townhouse from the car, Elle shivered even though the heat was blasting. On the way here, Ayaan told her that Graham Wallace had been arrested twice for sexual contact with a minor. His first victim was thirteen years old and he was sixteen. He had agreed to a plea deal without facing prison time, but then he'd offended again, having had sex with a fifteen-year-old—willingly, according to her, although legally she was too young to consent—when he was twenty-two. He had been released four years ago after serving his time.

Since then, he had no record of new offenses, and kidnapping would have been a huge escalation from his previous crimes. Still, he was a solid suspect.

Graham's parents apparently let him squat in one of their rental properties, a little townhouse not far from the Jordan family home. Every other home in the community had their sidewalks and driveways neatly shoveled, so it wasn't hard to spot the one that belonged to a lazy, entitled child of privilege. Drifts four or five feet high swelled in front of the Wallace townhouse, blew over their sidewalk. On the road, in front of Ayaan's car, there was a small hill of snow and ice where someone had clearly left their car parked overnight during a blizzard and became the victim of a passing snowplow. Even with the car now gone, the snow remained frozen in the approximate shape of a sedan.

Elle watched Ayaan assemble the officers she'd called for backup, preparing to knock on the front door. Feeling like she might go mad not doing anything, Elle pulled out her phone and called Martín.

"Bueno," he answered after four rings. In the background, she could hear people talking and laughing. "Everything all right? I'm just in the middle of something."

"Oh, okay." Her shaky voice gave her away. "I can call back."

There was a swishing sound on the line and then the click as a door shut. "It's okay, Elle, it's just a lunchtime poker game. I can talk. What's wrong?"

Elle stared out the windshield as she spoke. "There was a kidnapping yesterday in Bloomington. The parents asked Ayaan if I could help. It's . . . it's a little girl. She's eleven."

Martín knew that Elle understood what the girl was going through, at least mentally.

There was a pause, and then a slow inhale. This was how Martín calmed her—he knew when he took a deep breath, she had to also. It was a reflex, contagious like a yawn. She sucked air in through her nose, closing her eyes. Her fingertips ran over the semicolon tattoo on her wrist.

"Better?"

"Yes. Thank you."

"Are you having panic attacks?"

Rather than answer, she said, "They asked for my help. I don't want to mess it up."

"You won't, love."

"It's already been more than twenty-four hours. If he planned to kill her, she has less than a one percent chance of still being alive."

"You are living proof that there is an exception to every statistic. Please, be careful."

Elle's eyebrows knit together. "I will. I don't know how long this is going to take. I was calling because . . . well, I wanted to hear your voice, but I also wanted to let you know I might not be home for dinner, depending on how things go."

"Elle—" He paused, but then he just said, "Okay. I'll see you when you get home."

"Te amo," she said. "Go kick their asses in poker."

He laughed softly. "Will do. Yo también te amo."

As she put her phone back in her pocket, a flash of color appeared in the corner of her eye. Elle's gaze flicked to the townhouse again. The police had disappeared, but a young man in nothing but pajamas was rolling out of a window on the side of the house. Once he landed, he stood and started bounding through the deep snow in a poor attempt at a run. Elle looked at his open front door, but she didn't see Ayaan or the other officers anywhere. They might not know Graham was fleeing. For a second, she considered how much trouble she'd be in if she chased him, but if this man knew where Amanda was, she couldn't let him get away. She opened the passenger door slowly, trying not to make a sound as she got out of the car, leaving it open behind her. Graham was looking behind him to see if he was being followed when Elle held up her hands and shouted, "Stop!"

Graham obeyed, staring at her as his body trembled from head to foot, the skin on his hands and face bright red with cold. "Who the fuck are you?"

When he saw she wasn't holding a gun, he started to move again. She had her Ruger in a hip holster, but she wasn't allowed to pull it on him except in self-defense, and even she could see he posed no threat to her. He could barely walk as he turned and headed toward his neighbor's lawn.

"Out here!" Elle shouted, hoping Ayaan would hear her. "He's running away!" Then she sped after him and tackled him into the snow. He pushed against her, not quite managing to get her off. Her bulky coat was slippery and made it harder to lock her arms around him, but she was grateful for it. It was below zero outside, and she could see that the temperature was making him more lethargic every second. She needed to get him inside.

A moment later, the two officers were pulling Graham away from her and whisking him to the back of their police-issued SUV, where they had blankets and an old pair of boots to put on his bare feet.

"What were you thinking? Are you okay?" Ayaan asked once she had Graham secured and Elle back in her car.

"He was getting away—came out the window. I called for you." Elle tried to disguise the fact that she was shaking as she held her hands up to the heat vents. "I take it you didn't find Amanda?"

Ayaan shook her head. "He locked the door on us and ran inside as soon as we identified ourselves. We had to break the door down, and he must have sneaked out while we were searching the house. But she's not in there, at least not that we can see."

"You think he's holding her somewhere else?"

The detective's round face was grim. "Maybe. But I don't see why he would. The townhouse isn't exactly secluded, but he lives there alone. He has an attached garage where he could park and move her in and out of a vehicle without being seen. Why would he bring her somewhere else unless—"

Elle's body finally grew still. "Unless he's already killed her."

\\\\\\\\\\

As soon as Ayaan led Graham through the door at the station, a young woman with red hair pulled into a ponytail stood from her seat in the entryway and greeted Graham with a tight smile. Elle wondered which detective had let him make a phone call from the car on the way over here, but she wasn't surprised. White guys getting better treatment by the police was nothing new.

"Mr. Wallace. Have you stayed silent?" the woman asked.

"I encouraged him to reserve his rights," Ayaan said, meeting her iron-gray eyes. "Come with us, Miss—"

"Delaney." The lawyer smirked, probably at the expression on Elle's face. Delaney, Block & Gomez was a relatively new firm in the city, but they'd already developed a reputation for being cutthroat. And for winning. Her gaze flicked to Elle, but she continued speaking to Ayaan. "I heard you had a civilian consultant working with you. I trust she hasn't been allowed to handle any evidence in my client's case?"

"She attacked me!" Graham said.

A smile tugged at Ms. Delaney's lips. "Oh, really?"

Elle crossed her arms. "That was a lawful citizen's arrest. I'm allowed to stop anyone who is committing a crime in my presence, and he was fleeing from police." She might not be a cop, but she had spent years in CPS, and she knew the law. Her work as an independent investigator was no good if everything she touched got thrown out in court; she knew what the rules were, and she chose very carefully which ones were worth breaking.

"We'll see about that." Ms. Delaney took Graham's arm, relieving Ayaan of her grip.

Ayaan's expression stayed neutral. "Right this way, Miss Delaney." She led them toward an interview room, Elle trailing behind.

The lawyer paused outside the door. "I'd like a few minutes alone with my client."

"Certainly." Ayaan let them into the room and shut the door behind them, turning to Elle. "You don't have to stay, you know. But thank you. For all your help. Are you sure you're not hurt from before?"

Elle shook her head. "I'm fine. Sore, but nothing a long bath won't fix." She nodded at the room. "What are you thinking, with this guy?"

Ayaan chewed the corner of her lower lip. It was the first time Elle had ever seen her look uncertain. "I'm not sure. He's a good suspect, but I don't like that we didn't find any sign of Amanda in the townhouse. They're taking samples from his car now, but it'll be at least a few days before we know anything. If he's holding her somewhere else—"

"It'll be too late."

"He's a sex offender with a known relationship to the family and matches the physical description of the man the student said she saw in the area," Ayaan said, as if trying to convince herself. "It almost has to be him."

The phone in her office rang, and Ayaan rushed past Elle to pick it up. While she spoke in hushed tones, Elle went to sit in the dark, empty office next to the commander's. She stared at the clock on the wall. It was nearly three in the afternoon. Amanda had been missing for more than thirty hours. The clock ticked loudly in the shadows, marching forward with no regard for how each second that passed made it less and less likely that Amanda would be found alive. A rush of unexpected panic made Elle light-headed, and she closed her eyes.

Just like that, she was no longer in the police station. She was huddled in a cold, isolated room, alone and terrified. Fear coursed through her body as the sound of the ticking clock was blocked out by a man's footsteps as he came up the stairs. The door opened on soundless, oiled hinges; it shut with a soft click. He walked toward her. She tried to pull away, but her body would not listen to her mind. The nausea, the pain—it threatened to swallow her whole, blacked the vision in her eyes.

Her phone vibrating against her right thigh snapped Elle out of the flashback. She quickly dug it out of her pocket. Martín.

"Hi." Her voice was breathless.

"Hey, I just wanted to check on you. Are you all right?"

Elle stood up and shut the office door. "Yes, I'm fine."

"Are you sure? You sound kind of shaky."

"I will be fine, Martín. I can handle this."

For a moment, he was quiet. Then he said, "I know you can, but you don't have to. You can't help everyone. You were already so focused on the TCK case that you've hardly slept in weeks. Then you started chasing down family for a guy who wrote in to your show and ended up killed. And now you're adding something new? A little girl's kidnapping?"

A sharp headache started in Elle's eye, radiated backward. She leaned forward, elbows on her knees, and rubbed her temple with her free hand. "I can handle it. I've hit a dead end with Leo's case anyway."

"It's just, last time you got involved in an active kidnapping, it didn't go so well."

Elle was suddenly glad she'd gone into a room where no one could see her. The hollow, trembling aftershocks of her flashback gave way to anger that stiffened the muscles in her jaw. "That was a long time ago, Martín. I have a lot more experience with cases like this now."

"Mi vida, I believe in you. I trust you, if this is what you want to do. I just don't want you to feel like you have to . . . to please everyone. I'm only trying to make sure you're okay. I have never seen you like this, taking so many risks."

"I'm fine. I don't need you to protect me." Elle scrubbed her hand across her face. "I'll see you at home, if I can *remember* how to get there without your help."

"Elle—"

She ended the call, turned her phone off, and slipped it back into her pocket. Her breath was coming in short bursts, and she stopped to inhale, long and slow, through her nose. So many people thought they knew what she could handle better than she did. Usually, her husband wasn't one of them, though. The TCK case was always going to be a major one, something that required 110 percent of her time. And there was no way she could have known she'd be asked to help with a kidnapping, but how could she say no? If she could help, she had to be here. Martín was probably trying to call her again, but she resisted the urge to turn her phone back on to check. They'd figure it out when she got home.

The sound of Ayaan's voice at the door made her jump. "We've got the presumed abduction vehicle on security camera footage," she said, her eyes sparking with excitement. "Are you okay?"

"Yep." Elle forced a smile, jumped up, and followed Ayaan into her office. She dragged a chair around to sit next to the commander on her side of the desk, looking at the windows lined up on her monitor.

Ayaan pointed at the screen. "We've got footage from six security cameras at businesses in the area. It's from the hour before through the hour after Amanda was taken."

"Have you watched it?" Elle asked.

"Yes, we think we have the van that was used for the kidnapping. At least, it matches the description the bus driver gave us: plain dark blue, with no license plates."

Ayaan hit a key on her computer, and the videos started at the same time. White digits counted the passing time down to the millisecond in the bottom right corner of the video. After a few seconds, she paused it again and pointed to where a van was driving. "See here, on video number four, there's a dark-colored van at 8:35:21 driving in front of the Super America station, going north on Lyndale."

Elle squinted at the screen. "Is it Graham? I can't see his face at all."

Ayaan shook her head. "Not sure. The windshield is tinted, and there was a glare our techs couldn't edit out."

Elle clicked back on the progress bar under the video and paused. "He's not reckless, that's for sure. If he's got a kidnapped girl in the car, it shows a lot of discipline to drive the same speed as the other cars around him, to not draw attention even in such a high-stress scenario."

"You're right, but still, it seems pretty dangerous," Ayaan said, looking at Elle. "I suppose in his mind, it might be worth the risk of being pulled over for driving without plates rather than the bigger risk of getting caught on camera or by a witness who could track down the plate number."

Elle stared at the image of the van. "He probably only drove a couple miles in that vehicle, during rush-hour traffic on a weekday morning when he knew he wasn't likely to be pulled over for such a minor offense. Not if he's a white man, anyway."

Ayaan smiled wryly, nodding. "It shows a level of criminal sophistication, which matches with how seamlessly he pulled off the kidnapping. It's unlikely to be his first time doing this. Maybe Graham hasn't been as aboveboard the past four years as his record would suggest."

"Do we know whether he has access to a van like that?" Elle asked.

"No, but odds are it's stolen anyway. I've been looking into his alibi. He's got another job, besides working for Dave Jordan. Washing windows for some office cleaning company. They said he was working yesterday until two p.m. Backed up the dad's story." Ayaan met Elle's gaze. "I'm going to have to do some more chasing up for this alibi, but could you see what you can find using your normal investigative methods this afternoon? We can meet up tomorrow and compare notes. I'll let you know if anything changes in the meantime."

"Sure. Yeah, of course. I'll talk to you tomorrow."

She didn't want to go home, where she'd have to talk about the case with Martín, but she didn't have much choice. Elle pushed down the rising swell of panic in her gut as she stood and left the office. Right now, a little girl was depending on her. She couldn't afford to fall apart.

16

Justice Delayed podcast

January 2, 2020

Transcript: Season 5, Episode 4

[SOUND BREAK: A clock ticking.]

ELLE VOICE-OVER:

Dr. Sage works at Mitchell University, a local college in Minneapolis that has one of the top forensic psychology degrees in the state. This interview took place in December 2019, prior to the first episode launching, and obviously well before the revelation about the potential identities of the burnt bodies we have uncovered in this episode. I'm sure Dr. Sage would have much to say about this new information, but while we wait for possible DNA matches to be made, I think it's important we still focus on TCK himself. The more information we have about him — who he is, what made him do what he did — the more chance we have of finding him.

ELLE:

Doctor, you studied the TCK cases a few years after he went dormant, correct? Sometime in the early 2000s?

DR. SAGE:

Yes, that's correct. I'm one of the psychiatrists who spoke with the

FBI about the profile they had put together for him, before they all stopped investigating the case.

ELLE:

Okay, could I ask your expert opinion on what can be interpreted from his killing process? For the sake of background, my husband is a medical examiner, and just candidly, he disagreed with the assessment of the ME who examined Katrina Connelly. Whereas the official report states that TCK likely killed her in a fit of rage because she was fighting back, my husband theorized that TCK killed her in that manner because she wasn't dying from the poison, and in order for him to be fulfilled by her murder, she had to die on the day he designated for her—the seventh day.

DR. SAGE:

It's possible. Based on everything I have seen of the Countdown Killer's work, it is clear he operates on a strict timeline with inflexible criteria for his murders. He is immensely detailed, and it's quite possible he has some sort of compulsive disorder, although I would be remiss if I didn't say that likely had nothing to do with why he murdered. The vast majority of people with a compulsive disorder live successful, full lives and cause no more harm to those around them than someone without one. But based on his obsession with the numbers three, seven, and twenty-one, it seems plausible that those numbers trigger him to kill. If that's the case, they likely have a root in some sort of trauma for him.

ELLE:

Wait, trauma for the killer?

DR. SAGE:

Yes, that's most likely the case.

ELLE:

But . . . isn't that—couldn't some people interpret that as an offensive excuse? A lot of people go through traumatic experiences as kids. If everyone with a violent childhood used that as an excuse to slaughter innocent people, there'd be a lot more murders to investigate.

DR SAGE:

That's true, and you're right; it's not an excuse. But it is a fact. Most of us don't like to think about the people who commit horrific acts of violence as former victims themselves, yet the reality is most of them are. The extensive research on serial killers has shown that almost all of them have instances of severe abuse and neglect in their childhoods. It is important context to be aware of when examining a killer's motives and trying to figure out what kind of person they may be. However, I will say this. There's this FBI behavioral analyst, Jim Clemente, who has a saying: "Genetics load the gun, personality and psychology aim it, and experiences pull the trigger." It takes a perfect, devastating blend of circumstances to create a serial killer. Childhood trauma is only part of it.

ELLE:

Okay, that makes sense. Back to those numbers: I've spent years researching them, as I'm sure many of my listeners have. Do you have any insights on what they might have signified to him?

DR. SAGE:

Short of some sort of personal message or manifesto, which we've seen from other killers many times before, it's impossible to say with absolute certainty. However, the victim who escaped did tell police there were symbols of the Christian religion inside his cabin. Bibles, crosses hanging on the walls, postcards with Scripture on them. This led me to review the significance of the numbers in the Bible. Theologians and biblical scholars have found meaning in all sorts of numbers throughout the centuries—some of them considered more of a reach than others. But the first two numbers in TCK's series are universally found to be important. Three is symbolic of the Trinity: the Father, Son, and Holy Ghost. It's also the number of days that Jesus descended into Hell before he rose again after the Crucifixion, and it's one of what is considered the spiritually perfect numbers—along with seven. Seven signifies completion, perfection. The world was created in six days, and on the seventh, God rested.

ELLE:
And twenty-one?

DR. SAGE:
Well, the first thing to note is that multiplying seven and three results in twenty-one. This might be significant—in fact, it might be the only reason he chose it. But if we're following our theme of biblical symbolism, in II Timothy, Paul lists twenty-one sins that demonstrate the wickedness of self. Twenty-one is seen as the combination of thirteen, the number of depravity and sin, and eight, the number of new beginnings. Added together, it symbolizes a new, active commitment to rebellion and wickedness. If you believe the idea that TCK was motivated by a twisted view of the scriptural meaning of those numbers—which many of the original investigators did, considering the items in the cabin and the conservative religious makeup of the area at the time—then it makes sense why he chose twenty-one as his third number. It implies a conscious decision to rebel, to stray from the Word of God. If we're right about that, though, it is confusing why he would start with a twenty-year-old girl instead of a twenty-one-year-old. Everything else about the numbers in his pattern is consistent, so it's strange he deviated from it with something as significant as the age of his first victim.

ELLE VOICE-OVER:
Dr. Sage brings up a point we've discussed in previous episodes—something that listeners will remember is a bit of an obsession for Detective Sykes as well. My producer and I have been doing a lot of work on this behind the scenes, and I'm excited to let you know that we have a promising lead. It's too early to confirm right now, but I'm hoping we'll be able to tell you more about our findings soon. Stay tuned. Now, back to the interview.

ELLE:

Based on what you've said, it sounds like you believe the pattern is a decision, not a compulsion he couldn't control? Am I correct?

DR. SAGE:

That's my assessment. He's a very calculated killer, and that is evident by every aspect of his crimes, from his choice of victim to the way he leaves their bodies when he's finished. He is fully in control of his faculties, and power actually plays a big part in his crimes. From the meticulous pattern he has established to the way he forces these women to do his bidding, he is demonstrating too much control in his killings for them to be some wild, impulsive action.

ELLE:

Let's talk about that. I understand from my own research that there are different types of serial killers. Can you give my listeners an overview of what they are?

DR. SAGE:

The reason I even have a job is because of John Douglas, the father of criminal behavior analysis. You've seen that show, *Mindhunter*? It's more or less based on his early career. Douglas interviewed hundreds of serial killers all across the country, found out why and how they did what they did. He used that knowledge to help the FBI and other law enforcement catch active killers. After a while, he noticed there were key differences between many of the men he was interviewing, and he started categorizing killers based on various factors: what motivated them, how they killed their victims, how organized they were, et cetera.

There are visionary killers, who are usually experiencing a break from reality and think they are being directed by God or the Devil to commit their murders. Hedonistic killers do it for the sexual thrill, the pleasure of controlling and then destroying someone. If someone enjoys exerting power or authority over his victims and prolonging their deaths, we would call him a power/control killer. And then there are mission-oriented killers, who commit their crimes out of a sense of duty, to rid the world of a specific type of person.

ELLE:

And do serial killers usually fit in only one category? Because a couple of those sound like they could be TCK.

DR. SAGE:

There are some who fit into more than one category, yes. Generally, power/control killers sexually assault their victims as the penultimate exertion of power before killing them, but we don't see that with TCK's victims. However, as I said, control is a key aspect to what he does, so I would say that he is still a power/control killer. He degrades them by not feeding them, makes them clean for him—serve him, essentially—before poisoning them and beating their bodies. The way he abuses girls specifically makes me think he was abused as a child, and that he somehow blames that abuse on a woman in his life—probably his mother—whether she was responsible for it or not. He doesn't seem to get any sexual thrill from killing his victims, so I would rule out a hedonistic killer, and he strikes me as too organized to be a visionary killer. But I would argue his choice of victim, his stringent criteria, also alludes to a mission-oriented killer. Even though he doesn't choose victims from a marginalized group like many mission-oriented killers do, he does select the same type of victim over and over: a white female from an upper-middle-class family. The only thing that changes is the age, and that's obviously intentional too.

This man, whoever he is, is highly intelligent. He would almost certainly be college-educated, perhaps even with a master's or doctorate degree. He is white—Nora Watson described him as such. And he would no doubt be aware of the connotations of choosing a young white female as his prey. They have historically been considered a symbol of innocence, which of course is rooted in harmful tropes of classism, white supremacy, and patriarchy.

It's also worth noting that while the common adage is that killers only kill within their own race, that is not always true. Samuel Little is possibly one of the most prolific serial killers in the country, and he seemed to kill women indiscriminately, paying no mind to their age or race. It was about access. Statistically, people do tend to kill within their own race, but that is usually more a matter of proximity than psychology.

ELLE:

You said he didn't get any thrill from killing his victims, but what about the way he tortured them, tortured the public psychologically?

DR. SAGE:

How do you mean?

ELLE:

Well, after the first few murders, we all knew what his pattern would be. We knew once a girl was kidnapped by him, she had a week to live. There was the way he tortured them, of course—with a slow, painful death and the torment of working for every scrap of food he gave them. The poison. The whipping. But there was also us, the people in the community, observing and preparing ourselves for the inevitable. It was like he was tormenting us too, like he knew we were all sitting at home watching the news on the seventh day, waiting for story to break about a corpse being found. The bodies weren't hidden away; they were made to be found, left exposed in public places. I was only a kid, but I remember what it was like on that seventh day. It was like the siren had gone off and you were bracing yourself for the tornado to touch down.

DR. SAGE:

I suppose you're right.

ELLE:

How do we know that the numbers and the formulas and the patterns were compulsions at all, that it wasn't all designed to throw people off and make detectives chase their tails while he killed more and more girls?

DR. SAGE:
The short answer is, we don't.

ELLE VOICE-OVER:
After everything I've discovered talking to Dr. Sage, Detective Sykes, Tina, and Martín, I have put together my own profile of TCK. It might not be FBI-grade, but it is based on all the evidence we have gathered so far. Remember, criminal profiling does not help investigators identify a singular person. Profiles are not evidence; they are educated guesses based on deductive reasoning and statistics. But on a case this cold, a beam of light pointed in a plausible direction is better than stumbling around in the dark.

I want you to listen carefully and think about everything we've learned. Remember, the people we have investigated and caught for previous seasons of *Justice Delayed* have turned out to be ordinary, everyday people with neighbors and relatives and friends who never suspected them. People who do monstrous things often don't seem like monsters to us.

If you have any questions or theories, I want to hear them. We'll talk about it next time.

The Countdown Killer is smart, college-educated, perhaps with an advanced degree. He likely suffered abuse as a child and would be abusive to women in his everyday life, possibly physically but definitely emotionally. He has an interest in numbers, which means he may have a career in math or science, although as Dr. Sage noted, all the numbers he chose seem to have particular relevance in the Bible. At least at one point in his life, he had a fondness for Darjeeling tea —specifically Majestic Sterling.

He's white, probably between twenty-five and thirty-five when he first killed, so in his late forties or early fifties now. The only physical description we have is that he was strong, well built, and had blue eyes and a deep voice. He wore brightly colored clothing or accessories the very few times he was witnessed close to a victim. Given the extensive time we believe he spent stalking his victims, as well as the fact that most of them were taken in the daytime, he likely works a flexible job where he controls his own hours, or possibly he works the night shift. He has to have a vehicle, perhaps several, and might even be skilled at stealing cars. It's possible he's even been arrested for this without the police knowing what he meant to do with that vehicle.

He seems to have knowledge of law enforcement processes and movements, which has led some to suspect he's a police officer or private investigator of some kind. But he also has a keen sense of the limits of the human body, how to measure his victims' vital signs well enough that he could poison them at just the right rate that they died on the day he wanted. He likes to have control and make people do his bidding, and he lacks empathy when his actions harm other people—in fact, he may enjoy it.

And on this podcast, we are operating on the assumption that he is alive—he's still out there. And we can find him and bring him to justice.

Next time, on *Justice Delayed* . . .

17

Elle

January 15, 2020

The sun was setting and Martín was still at work when Elle got home. She turned her phone back on, and a single text from him popped up on the screen: I'M SORRY. She let out a breath, her shoulders relaxing. After brewing a pot of coffee, she set to work in her studio.

Elle didn't have access to the police databases, but social media was free—and it was where she got most of her big breaks in previous cases. Hashtags, location data, pictures of landmarks—it was all useful for tracking people down if you knew where to look.

It didn't take her long to find Graham's social media profiles. His Facebook was troubling—lots of racist memes and links to misogynistic blogs. His last activity was from two days ago, when he commented on a *New York Times* article about the Clinton Foundation with a doctored meme of Hillary Clinton counting stacks of money, mouth wide open in a greedy grimace. His Instagram wasn't much better, filled with more memes and selfies in various poses, trying to look like a badass in a bandana and sunglasses. He reminded her of every avatar from the slew of trolls in her Twitter mentions after she posted something even slightly liberal.

A message popped up on Elle's screen—from Sash.

HEY! INVESTIGATING OR SCROLLING?

Elle smiled and typed back. GET THIS: WORKING A KIDNAPPING CASE WITH THE POLICE. MARTÍN ISN'T TOO HAPPY ABOUT IT.

The dots bounced for a moment as Sash typed her reply. They disappeared and then reappeared a couple times before a short message came through. WHY DO YOU THINK HE'S NOT HAPPY?

Her smile fading, Elle typed more firmly than was probably necessary. HE JUST WORRIES. I'M FINE. I CAN HANDLE MYSELF.

NO ONE DOUBTS YOU CAN HANDLE YOURSELF. SWEETIE, SOMETIMES YOU JUST SACRIFICE YOUR OWN SAFETY TO HELP OTHERS, THAT'S ALL. I JUST WANT YOU TO BE OKAY — WE BOTH DO.

Elle stared at the screen. DID MARTÍN TELL YOU TO MESSAGE ME?

Two minutes passed before the reply came. JUST BE CAREFUL, PLEASE, ELLE. I DON'T WANT ANYONE TO GET HURT.

Anyone. Meaning not just Elle. The comment was a kick to the gut. Sash had never brought up what Elle had told her about why she left CPS, but this was a not-so-subtle reminder. She had messed up before, and people got hurt.

Exiting out of the chat, she turned back to Graham's social media. It took a few tries to track down his Twitter feed, since he didn't use the same handle as he had on Instagram and Facebook. But when Elle finally started to scroll through his timeline, goose bumps broke out on her arms. She hunched forward to look more closely at the screen.

Graham was a certifiable Twitter troll with a penchant for going on long rants in other people's replies. For a while yesterday morning, he engaged in a vicious argument with a verified account that apparently belonged to a leftist blogger from Montreal.

Elle took screenshots of each tweet and then read through the time stamps, feeling her heart sink.

\\\\\\\\\

It was after nine p.m. when Elle ventured out of her studio and was greeted by the smell of the Castillo family's pollo asado recipe. Entering the kitchen, she watched her husband for a moment as he moved around at the stove.

"You made me dinner," she said.

Martín turned around, stepped forward, and pulled her exhausted body into his arms. She inhaled the scent of aftershave and cumin on his neck, any residual anger from their phone conversation fading away.

"I just got home an hour ago," he said. "I was too keyed up to read, so I thought I'd make us a late dinner."

With her arms still around his waist, she looked up at him. "What has you keyed up?"

He gave her another squeeze and then turned back to the food. "I'm having trouble identifying the cause of death on a body that came in today."

She put a hand between his shoulder blades as he basted the meat with more homemade achiote paste. "Too distracted taking everyone's money in poker?"

A low chuckle rumbled in his chest. "I did do that. Although we don't bet money — just paperwork duties." After flipping the meat, he turned to face her, resting his backside on the edge of the counter next to the stove.

"So, what's the deal with the body?" she asked.

"Young guy, in his thirties. His roommate found him dead after realizing he'd never gotten up on Sunday morning. As far as we can tell, he didn't have any preexisting conditions, nothing that would explain a sudden death. He didn't have a heart attack, stroke, or aneurysm. There's nothing to indicate suicide. His parents are devastated, naturally. I want to be able to give them answers, but I'm not sure there are any."

Elle met his gaze with a rueful smile. "People think it will make them feel better if they have an explanation for why their loved one died. But knowing doesn't really make it any better, does it?"

Martín shook his head. "No, it doesn't. Anyway, don't worry about that. Maybe it'll come to me in my sleep, something I missed. I wasn't exactly focused this afternoon."

Elle's eyes flicked to the pan of sizzling chicken, then to the pot of polenta he had covered to keep warm. "Right, of course." She went to the fridge and pulled out a bottle of white wine. Martín set two glasses out on the island where they usually ate dinner when it was just the two of them.

"Any luck with your case?" he asked as he dished up the plates.

She sat down and poured them each a glass. "We've got a suspect in custody, a real creep, but unfortunately I think I just proved it wasn't him. I left a message for Ayaan, but I'm guessing she's gone home to get some sleep."

Martín set a plate in front of her, then came around the kitchen island and sat down next to her. She tilted her lips up as a peace offering. He leaned in and kissed her, his hand trailing down her cheek when he pulled away. "Tell me about the suspect."

She took a bite of creamy polenta and her eyes rolled back, which made him smile. "The Jordans were sure it was him," she said as she chewed. "That's the parents of the girl who went missing. He's a registered sex offender, worked for the girl's father. But I found evidence on social media that he was in the middle of a conversation at the time of the kidnapping, so now basically the whole day of investigation is down the tubes, and she's already been missing for over thirty-six hours."

"If anyone can help find her, it's you."

She looked up, surprised, but Martín was studying his plate intently. "You're just saying that 'cause you know I was pissed before," she said after moment.

"I'm not just saying it. I was worried earlier." He picked at the chicken with his fork. "I still am. But I also think I get why you need to be on this case. I work with detectives every day, but you're one of the best investigators I know. You know more about child abduction than most, even if you are still new to investigating it. If you think I'm just saying that to make up for before, you're selling yourself short." Finally, he looked back up, meeting her gaze. "I'm not sorry for being concerned about you, but I am sorry I made you feel like I didn't think you could make your own decisions."

A small part of her wanted the decision to be out of her hands, though. Maybe it was the wine or the rich food, but the exhaustion from the last few days was hitting her hard.

"You think better of me than I am," she said at last. The words brought up a surprise knot of emotion, and she had to blink tears away while she looked at him.

"No, Elle." Martín's voice was firm. "I just know you are better than you think."

Halfway through washing the dishes after dinner, Elle saw her phone light up with a message. She wiped her soapy hands on the dish towel and opened it to find a text from Natalie.

MOM SAYS YOU'RE MAD AT HER.

Elle sighed and typed back. I AM NOT.

DOES THIS MEAN YOU WON'T PICK ME UP FROM PIANO FRIDAY?

OF COURSE I'LL PICK YOU UP. AND I'M NOT MAD AT YOUR MOM.

Natalie sent back a girl-shrugging emoji.

I'LL SEE YOU FRIDAY AT FIVE. BE NICE TO MS. TURNER.

NO PROMISES 😜

Elle chuckled and set her phone down. After finishing the dishes, she turned off all the lights and went up to bed, where Martín was already snoring lightly, having failed to wait up for her. Part of being a doctor meant being able to fall asleep whenever, wherever. When he was doing his residency, she'd made him stop driving for a few months after watching him drop off while waiting at a stoplight.

She climbed into bed next to him, wrapped one arm around his body, and drew him close. But when she closed her eyes, she was in a different room. She heard another man's voice saying her name, telling her to come to him. She felt his hands, strong and cold, on her skin.

Elle buried her face between her husband's shoulders, squeezing her whole body tight as if that could shut out the memories.

18

Elle

January 16, 2020

The next morning, Elle arrived at the station just after nine, her eyes gritty with exhaustion. Ayaan waved her in before Elle even had a chance to knock. Holding the folder containing printed screenshots of Graham's tweets, she stepped in and sat down across from the commander.

"Forensics is finished at Wallace's house," Ayaan said, looking disappointed. "Aside from some marijuana, the most suspicious thing was in his streaming record. A few nights ago, he watched an adult film which depicted two teenage girls engaging in sexual acts with each other."

"Child porn?" Elle's lip curled.

Ayaan shook her head. "Two adult women *acting* like they were teenagers. We have found no evidence that Mr. Wallace had any child pornography in his possession." She sighed. "I got your message. What's this about his Twitter account?"

Nodding, Elle put the papers on the desk and pushed them across to Ayaan. "I don't think he could have taken Amanda. Graham was in a full-on Twitter war during the exact window of time that she was kidnapped. I double-checked the times. He sent eight tweets in the five minutes the bus driver says she would have been stopping to pick up at Amanda's corner."

Ayaan looked through the papers and then opened something up on her computer—probably her witness statements about the time of the abduction. Finally, she looked up at Elle. "Is there any chance he scheduled the tweets ahead of time?"

Elle had anticipated that. "I don't think so. You *can* schedule tweets, but you can't schedule a whole, live argument with a person. I checked out the blogger he was talking to. She's verified, lives in Montreal. She has blogs going back to 2012 and more than seven years of pictures on her social media accounts that are clearly taken in different parts of Canada. Seems like a pretty elaborate long-term con, not to mention a huge escalation for someone whose other crimes were committed under the pretense of a romantic relationship."

"You're probably right." Her expression neutral, Ayaan picked up her phone and hit three keys. "Hey, Cruise. Can you look at Wallace's Twitter account for the time of the kidnapping? Handle @wallyg420. If it checks out, please call Miss Delaney and let her know her client is free to go. No, if she wants to speak to me, she can schedule an appointment. Thank you."

After she hung up, Ayaan looked down at the papers on her desk again. "We might be back at square one."

"I guess so. Sorry."

"Don't be. I'm glad you found it now, so we don't waste any more time on him. I am concerned, though. If she was taken for ransom, they should have called by now. Not that that was ever probable, but I did hope."

"Then you think she was killed." The words were metallic in Elle's mouth. So final, so likely.

Ayaan paused, bringing her thumb up to her mouth and running the nail back and forth across her bottom lip. It was a nervous tic of hers, something she did when she was thinking hard. It occurred to Elle how carefully she studied Ayaan, how much she wanted to understand her. The commander was so good at keeping people out— Elle wanted to be a person Ayaan opened up to, someone she let in.

Finally, Ayaan said, "At this point, I'm afraid so. I have never worked a kidnapping case where the child turned up alive three days after being taken unless the kidnapper traded them for money or leniency."

Silence fell between them, bleak as a January night.

"How do you do it?" Elle asked after a moment. "I still lose sleep over some of the cases we worked together when I was in CPS, and I quit almost six years ago. Now I get to choose what I investigate, stay away from the ones that are too disturbing. How do you not lose your mind, seeing the horrible things people do to children every day?"

Ayaan leaned back in her chair, folded her arms over her chest. "My parents didn't want me to become a police officer. They had hoped I would study medicine, like my brother. But I saw the way the world pressured and even forced some women to bear children, only to let them flounder once they were born. I wanted to protect them from that. I am keenly aware of who the system leaves behind. In this country, police have rarely served people who look like me. That's why I'm here—I work for them."

"What do your parents think of you being a detective now?" Elle asked.

"They are supportive, more so now that I'm a commander and not in as much danger as I was when I was on patrol." Ayaan's smile was soft. "They came here to get away from the civil war in Somalia when my mother was pregnant with me. All they ever wanted was to give me a better life, more opportunity than I would have had in their home country. A lot of Somali immigrants came to Minnesota over the years, before the ban."

There was so much injustice summarized in those three words. Elle wondered if Ayaan had family in Somalia still, people who wanted to come to America that were being shut out because of hate and fear. She kept her eyes on the commander, but she stayed silent. There was nothing she could say.

Ayaan met her gaze. "What about you? I know you love your work now, but do you ever think about becoming a detective someday?"

"I don't want to be a cop."

The words were tinged with negativity. She opened her mouth to say more, but then Ayaan's phone rang. She answered and exchanged a few quick words, then pressed a button on the handset.

"Camilla, I've just put you on speakerphone so another investigator can hear. Can you please say that again?"

A woman with a French accent spoke. "Yes, my daughter Danika said she spoke to you yesterday in school, about the missing girl. She said when you asked if any of the kids had seen the person who took Amanda, she didn't say anything, but this morning she told me she had seen the man. Can I put her on the phone?"

"Yes, of course." Ayaan rubbed her forehead, scratching underneath her hijab before adjusting it back over her hairline. Elle could see her fingers were trembling.

"Hi," a little girl's voice said over the phone. "I'm sorry I lied."

"I don't think you lied, Danika," Ayaan said. "I remember you. You were trying to tell me something and got interrupted by that other girl, right? Did that make you feel like what you had to say wasn't important?"

"Yes." She sounded like she might have been crying. "I told Maman it wasn't my fault." Camilla's voice murmured in the background, and then Danika spoke again. "I should have told you that Brooklyn was wrong. But I was scared. Sometimes she can be really mean to me."

"What was she wrong about, Danika?"

"The man who came up to talk to Amanda . . . He wasn't tall, and he didn't have black hair. I don't know if Brooklyn even saw him. She just wanted attention."

Elle grabbed a pen from Ayaan's desk and started writing under the printed screenshot. Ayaan nodded at her and kept talking. "Okay, sweetheart. It's so good of you to call and tell me that. Do you remember what the man looked like?"

There was another murmur between Danika and her mother, and then Danika's voice came back on. "He was the same size as my papa. Maman said to tell you he's five feet" — another whisper — "and ten inches. And he didn't have any hair."

"So, no black hair?" Ayaan clarified.

"No, and he wasn't wearing a hat, just a scarf and these big work boots. I didn't see a lot of his face. He had a shiny white head and red cheeks, and he was wearing the big black sunglasses like my dad has. I saw Amanda at the bottom of her driveway when I was walking to the bus. The man ran up to her and said, 'You have to come with me. I work with your dad and he's been in an accident.' And she just went off with him."

Ayaan met Elle's gaze as she asked, "Did you see where the man came from? Did he get out of a car?"

"I don't know. I didn't really see him until he said Amanda's name."

"Did he see you?"

"I don't think so. I kind of hid behind a tree when I saw him. He didn't look nice."

"And did you watch Amanda go anywhere with him? Did you see her get in a car?"

"He grabbed her hand and started running toward this blue van. But I didn't see her get in. As soon as his back was turned, I ran across the street. I didn't want to be late for the bus."

"It's okay," Ayaan said, her voice gentle. "You didn't do anything wrong, Danika." She looked up at Elle, eyebrows raised to ask whether she had any questions.

Not wanting to surprise the girl with an unfamiliar voice, Elle scribbled on her notes. Next to the word *scarf,* she wrote *color?* and underlined it before turning the paper to face Ayaan.

"Do you remember what color the scarf was, Danika?" Ayaan asked.

"Orange. Bright orange like one of those cones at soccer practice."

Elle wrote the description down, her penmanship sloppy from shaking fingers.

Ayaan looked at her for a moment, as if expecting another question, but Elle shook her head. "That's great, Danika. You've been so helpful. Do you think you might be able to describe what he looks like to someone so they can draw him?"

"I don't know. I'm scared."

"I won't let anything happen to you, okay? I promise."

Elle squeezed her burning eyes shut and rubbed her chest. A pair of eyes flashed in her mind, red-rimmed and so dark blue they were almost black. When she opened her eyes again, Ayaan was still watching her carefully.

"Can I talk to your mom again real quick, honey?" Ayaan asked.

Camilla's voice came through the speaker. "Yes?"

"Camilla, I think your daughter has some really critical information to our investigation. I'm sure you've heard by now that Amanda Jordan is missing, and we are treating her disappearance as a kidnapping."

"Yes. I'm keeping Danika home from school until she's found. I will not let my daughter out of my sight until I know she will be safe."

She will never be safe, Elle wanted to say. *None of us are.*

Ayaan said, "That's fine. Do you think you could bring her in to the station today, if possible? I want to get her to sit with a forensic artist and describe the man she saw."

"Today?"

"I know it's last-minute, but this is critical. Every second Amanda is missing becomes more dangerous for her. If your daughter could help us find her before she gets hurt, it's worth a little inconvenience, don't you think?"

After a moment, Camilla said, "Okay. Oui. I will bring her after lunch."

\\\\\\\\

The results of the composite sketch seemed to be printed on the back of Elle's eyelids whenever she closed her eyes. The man looked to be in his fifties, with a square bald head, big sunglasses, and a neon orange scarf wrapped under his nose. Elle had spent the afternoon comparing the sketch to known sex offenders in the area, only to come up short. Ayaan had shown it to Amanda's parents, but the man was unfamiliar to them. Definitely not someone who worked with Dave. After his Twitter activities were confirmed by the police and Danika failed to pick him out of a photo array, Graham Wallace had been released.

Somehow, another day had passed and there was still no trace of Amanda.

No body, either, though. That, at least, gave Elle hope.

Sash had made them dinner at her house, wanted all the details on what was happening with the podcast, but Elle had barely been able to stay engaged in the conversation. She'd been relieved when Martín changed the subject by asking Natalie about her science class. As much as she'd hoped an evening with the Hunters would take her mind off the case for a moment, it had been a lost cause. When she looked at Natalie, all Elle could think about was Amanda—where she was, who had taken her.

Right now, the composite sketch was probably playing all across the twenty-four-hour news cycle in the area, splashed on local stations and websites and social media. A network of officers was on the lookout across the Twin Cities metro for a blue van with no license plates. All of this stuff was being taken care of without her. Elle had shared it on her channels, boosted it with paid ad space. There was nothing else she could do, not tonight.

But she couldn't sleep.

Elle lay with eyes wide open next to her lightly snoring husband. She couldn't get Danika's description out of her mind. The brightly colored scarf had to be a coincidence. It was just because she was so deeply immersed in the TCK case for her podcast that she couldn't stop thinking about it. She had waited years for a new lead. She was so close it was like a physical ache, a hunger pang. That was the only reason she was drawing connections between him and Amanda's disappearance.

"You need to come with me. Your dad was in an accident."

That excuse had probably been used by thousands of kidnappers throughout the years to get little girls into their vehicles. But she couldn't shake it. Ayaan and her team had come up dry on any reasons why Amanda or her family would be targeted for revenge. Her well-orchestrated kidnapping in broad daylight by a man who knew her name suggested an organized criminal with a fixation on the little girl. No ransom call had come through, which meant that the remaining options were grim for Amanda. If Elle was going to work this case right, it was her job to consider every possibility—even the most outrageous. The problem was, the most outrageous possibility didn't seem so unlikely right now.

Maybe it was because of the podcast, or because of Leo's possible tip and sudden murder. Maybe it was old trauma trying to resolve itself in her brain.

Or maybe it was that stupid orange scarf.

She glanced at Martín, sound asleep. Not even he would believe her about this.

Elle knew TCK's work—knew his signatures and idiosyncrasies like she knew the voice of her favorite singer. It was absurd that he would start killing again after more than twenty years, ridiculous that she was even thinking this way. But she couldn't turn off that voice in her head.

12:05 a.m. glared from the clock next to her bed. It was now the third night since Amanda was taken. If she was kidnapped by TCK, today she would be served food mixed with castor beans, which she would eat because she'd been worked to the bone and slowly starved. She'd start having diarrhea and throwing up and feeling feverish within a few hours. Elle clenched her sheets in her sweaty fingers, bunching them up so tight she worried they would tear.

This was stupid. She could not lose a night of sleep chasing fantasies about Amanda Jordan's kidnapping. They were running out of time, if they weren't out already.

If this was TCK, Amanda Jordan was going to be poisoned. If this was TCK, he'd take another girl today.

This can't be TCK. She squeezed her dry eyes shut, trying to slow her thoughts without success. *He can't have started his countdown again. It's just a coincidence.*

After all, why now? What was so special about Amanda that he came out of hiding and risked discovery after getting away with it for all these years? He would be better off staying wherever he went in 1999, going on about his life. Unless his urge became unbearable.

Or unless it wasn't him.

Frustrated, Elle reached for her phone and opened Twitter.

@justicedelayedfan12
@castillomn Still can't get over Episode 5. TCK is even more of a monster than I thought. Thank you for exposing him! #FryTCK

Elle shuddered at the hashtag, forcing herself not to click on it. Nothing good waited for her there. She flicked down the screen. Most of her notifications were celebrating the new lead they had revealed on today's episode. Elle liked a couple dozen tweets, replied to a few questions she couldn't answer with "more soon . . ."

There were some trolls to block and report, as always. No threatening DMs today, though—that was an improvement. She kept scrolling.

@candlesbyfatimah
@castillomn What these girls went through is obscene. Aren't you worried you're giving the killer a bigger platform by talking about his crimes in such detail, though?

The tweet had a few hundred likes and about twenty replies, most disagreeing with the sentiment, but Elle still felt a tug of unease. Maybe Fatimah had a point. She didn't usually focus on the killer as much as the victims in her cases, but this one was unique. TCK was a special kind of murderer. His crimes were so intricate. Analyzing every detail was the only way she might catch something that other people had missed.

A notification popped up: a text from Tina. CAN'T SLEEP?

NO, YOU?

NEGATIVE. LOOKING INTO SOME OF THESE EMAILS WE'VE BEEN GETTING, TRYING TO TRACK DOWN IPS FOR THE POLICE. NOT GOING TO LIE — A LITTLE CONCERNED.

Teeth worrying at her lower lip, Elle typed: I ARCHIVED SOME

OF THE ONES I REPORTED TODAY. IF IT GETS WORSE, I'LL TALK TO AYAAN.

GOOD. WE ALSO GOT A FEW MESSAGES ABOUT EXPOSING THOSE "MISSING" GUYS TO THEIR FAMILIES, BUT THOSE ARE ALL MINE. 😏

Elle smiled and sent back a thumbs-up. She hadn't told her executive producer about the kidnapping investigation she was working on. They were hitting their stride with TCK, and the podcast network was over the moon. They wouldn't be happy she was sacrificing time working on *Justice Delayed* to help with an outside case. Tina knew more about her than most people, though. It would help to have someone else on her side.

I SEE WE'RE GETTING SOME ATTENTION FOR TODAY'S REVEAL. I LISTENED EARLIER. YOU KILLED IT WITH THE SOUND DESIGN THIS WEEK.

THANKS E. LET'S HOPE WE CAN FIND SOMETHING IN IT SO WE CAN CATCH THIS GUY.

Elle took a deep breath and sat up against her pillows, resting the phone on the comforter covering her lap. YOU SHOULD KNOW I'M WORKING A CASE WITH AYAAN. THAT KIDNAPPING IN BLOOMINGTON. I'M STILL INVESTIGATING TCK, BUT A LISTENER ASKED FOR MY HELP. COULDN'T SAY NO.

A few moments passed with the message on *read*. Elle ran her tongue across her teeth, leaned her head back and closed her eyes. When she opened them again, there was a new message.

GO GET 'EM.

THANKS. LET ME KNOW IF YOU FIND OUT ANYTHING ABOUT THOSE EMAILS.

Now wide awake, Elle turned her phone off and rolled out of bed. The cold wood floors stung her bare feet as she walked over to her slippers, putting them and her bathrobe on before creeping downstairs to make a cup of coffee.

At the bottom of the stairs, she caught her reflection in the entryway mirror. Her hair was swept into a messy ponytail, bangs a puff of frizzy curls framing her exhausted eyes. She looked so much like her mother. She had been a chronic insomniac for the second half of

Elle's childhood, roaming the house at night long after everyone had gone to bed. As long as she was awake, in her mind, she could keep the monsters away. In her own quiet way, it was how she could deal with what had happened to her daughter.

Elle's gaze hardened in the mirror at the thought of her mother stealing around in the dark like a wraith. All she had wanted was for her mom to come and lie with her in bed, hold her until she fell asleep. Instead, the woman's soft footsteps had padded up and down the stairs, patrolling the perimeter around Elle's room while she lay cold and isolated inside.

She turned away from her reflection and walked to her studio.

19

Justice Delayed podcast

Recorded January 16, 2020

Unaired recording: Elle Castillo, monologue

ELLE:

The studio is where I come to think, and I can't stop thinking tonight. When you investigate cases like the ones I cover on this podcast, you get used to them staying with you. When I'm shopping, cooking, having sex, trying to sleep—I see the faces of TCK's victims on the backs of my eyelids whenever I blink. I see them now, and there's a new face.

Edit that last line out.

I'm in my studio now, about one o'clock in the morning, because a new girl has gone missing. And maybe it's just this case, this podcast, that is making me suspect TCK is involved. So here I am, with a cup of coffee in the middle of the night, to record. Because this is how I think.

I am starting to believe that something everyone told me was impossible is happening. I know how unlikely it sounds. I know all the reasons it shouldn't be true. But I believe the Countdown Killer might be back in Minnesota—now, in 2020.

Three days ago, an eleven-year-old girl went missing. She was apparently taken on her way to the bus stop, by a man with a bright orange scarf and a bald head with no hat despite the freezing temperature. The uncovered head could mean a couple of things. He could be stupid or forgetful—maybe he meant to put on a hat and didn't in the end, the fault of some surge of adrenaline due to what he was about to do. Or he could have done it on purpose. An uncovered bald head in winter is memorable, just like a bright orange scarf is memorable. He was taking a girl in front of witnesses—maybe he wanted them to note those parts of his appearance so they wouldn't notice anything else. TCK did the same thing, the few times he was seen near his victims.

The man told Amanda he needed her to come with him because her dad was in an accident. This is similar to the pretense we know he used to get Nora Watson to come with him, and based on the victimology of his other targets, is probably an excuse he had used before.

Amanda is the right age to continue his countdown, if he wants to replace the victim who escaped. And we have found no clues that she was taken by anyone else. The one suspect we had has already been cleared. A dark, unmarked van unfamiliar to the area was seen in the vicinity. There has been no ransom call.

If he has come back, if he has started killing again, the next girl will be taken tomorrow—today, actually. If it really is him, he wouldn't have made the decision to start killing again lightly. He doesn't do anything by accident. In order to figure out where he'll strike next, we need to know why he came back in the first place.

Maybe he came back because of me.

Edit that last line out.

Maybe this is connected to the man who told me he knew who TCK was. I still don't know what he was going to tell me. But I think that could have been the start. If TCK knew he was about to be exposed, maybe that would be enough to get him to kill Leo. And that was enough of a taste of murder to remind him how much he liked the control, how badly he missed his mission.

But that doesn't line up with how he stalked his previous victims, how he carefully chose them and knew everything about their routines. He would have needed to start that months ago, before he ever knew he was at risk. Could that be what Leo saw? A man stalking young girls? Maybe Leo was a neighbor or a coworker, and he saw the man behaving strangely. He did say something about "before it's too late for her." Could *her* be Amanda? Is there evidence on the flash drive that he was going to give me?

Edit that last line out.

It can't be a coincidence, a murdered witness who says he knows the identity of TCK followed by another kidnapped girl who exactly matches his preferred type of victim?

No one will believe me. Or maybe everyone will blame me.

Edit that last line out.

I can't use any of this.

20

Elle

January 17, 2020

At the police station, the sound of the elevator bell made Elle look up from her notes, hoping to see Ayaan step off. But it was just Sam Hyde.

She yawned and looked back down; she had gotten there first thing, leaving the house even before Martín was awake, and her eyes burned from lack of sleep. She had spent the night rambling into her mic, recording absolutely nothing usable. Finally, she'd tried to gather her thoughts and suspicions into something resembling coherent. She had two pages of handwritten bullet points, ready to show the commander.

Sam sauntered up to her. "Heard Bishar's got you on one of her cases. How'd you manage to wrangle that?"

Not in the mood, Elle turned a page in her notebook. It didn't seem to be enough to convince him to leave her alone, though.

"So, are you doing this case for your radio show too?" he asked, thumbing her notebook.

She jerked it away from him and looked up. "How's that murder case going? Any leads on the person who shot Leo Toca in cold blood a week ago?"

A slow smile tugged at the corners of Sam's mouth. "In fact, there has been some progress. We're still looking into Duane Grove, but Leo's ex has apparently been dating someone new, and her coworkers say he had a jealous streak. We haven't been able to get ahold of her, but her phone last pinged a cell tower in Stillwater. We figure she's laying low with her new man there."

Well, that confirmed for sure that Maria Alvarez's suspicions about who her daughter was dating were wrong. She didn't even get the city right. The more Elle thought about it, the more she felt Luisa was a dead end. If she was seeing someone who lived thirty minutes away and working full-time, she probably didn't have time to keep tabs on her ex-husband—if they were even still on speaking terms. It was weird that she wasn't answering her phone, but if her boyfriend killed Leo out of some stupid jealousy, that would explain why she vanished.

With Amanda's case looming and another episode to record next week, Elle just didn't have time to keep chasing Leo's family around. Which reminded her: there was at least one other element to this case that she knew about, although Sam didn't know she did.

Trying to appear casual, she looked away from him as she asked, "Did you ever find anything on Leo—anything that looked like a clue he might have been about to give me? I'm guessing it would be something he printed, or maybe something on his computer."

Suspicion flashed in Sam's eyes, but the smirk didn't leave his lips. "Sorry, that's privileged information. Couldn't give it to you even if I wanted to." He turned on his heel and walked through the security doors into the main police office.

Elle watched him, temper flaring. If they had gotten access to the flash drive and there was something important on it, she had no way of knowing. And if Sam talked to Luisa first, she was sure he would tell her not to talk to Elle if she ever came sniffing around. She groaned, glaring at her notebook again. A long yawn made her eyes water. The day stretched out, endless and exhausting, in front of her. If she could convince Ayaan to look at her theory, they'd have several hours to investigate it before she had to pick up Natalie from piano lessons this afternoon. But the commander had to get to the station first.

Fifteen minutes later, Ayaan finally stepped off the elevator into the lobby. She wore a rose gold hijab and matching hoop earrings, with a navy blazer and slacks. Her outfit was sharp, but her eyes betrayed her—she looked as exhausted as Elle felt. There wasn't a lot of sleep involved when you were on a missing child case. Elle clasped her notebook and stood, saying the commander's name a little too loudly.

Ayaan looked surprised to see her. "Elle, how long have you been here?"

"Not long," Elle lied. "I wanted to talk to you before you got busy."

She searched Elle's face for a moment before nodding. "Come on in. I want to see if we got any tips on the sketch overnight, and then we can talk."

While Ayaan spoke to the night squad lieutenant, Elle made herself a coffee in the staff kitchen and then sat in the commander's office, antsy and buzzing from lack of sleep and too much caffeine. After a few minutes, she opened her bag and pulled out all her papers. In addition to her handwritten notes, she had transcripts from her podcast with portions highlighted, crime scene photos, witness statements about TCK's penchant for wearing bright clothes. All of this she spread out over Ayaan's desk, as if to cover it with enough evidence that she might be believed.

"Well, we got about sixty tips, but nothing that sounds promising," Ayaan said as she walked into the office. When she saw her desk, she paused, studying what was on it.

Elle held her breath as she watched Ayaan's expression, waiting for the light of realization in her eyes. It never came. A couple minutes passed, and then Ayaan met Elle's gaze. She looked concerned. Elle hated that.

"I'm fine," Elle said, taking a drink of coffee.

"You think Amanda Jordan was taken by the Countdown Killer?" Ayaan sounded baffled.

Elle stood up and walked around the desk to stand next to Ayaan. She pointed to a picture of the thirteen-year-old girl. "Katrina Connelly. She was abducted from a bus stop by a man in a van. Witnesses said a man told Katrina that her mom was sick and he had been sent to pick her up. He was wearing a bright paisley scarf and a neon green hat."

Ayaan did not look up from her desk. "That was twenty-two years ago, Elle."

"He did the same thing with Jessica Elerson." The name caught in Elle's throat as tears ached behind her eyes. "Then Nora Watson said he convinced her to get in his car because he said her mom had been in an accident and was in the hospital. It's such a vulnerable position to put a young girl in, to worry about her mother."

When Ayaan didn't say anything, Elle continued. "He didn't die, Ayaan. I have never believed he died, and my podcast has uncovered that the body everyone said was TCK's probably belonged to a man at least a decade older. Maybe he's been in prison for something else all this time, and he just got out. Maybe he was married, and whatever it was that made him a murderer went dormant for a while. Maybe he's pissed about the progress I'm making in my investigation, so he intentionally took someone in Minneapolis to get to me."

Elle stopped for a breath, realizing her hands were shaking around her coffee cup. She turned away from Ayaan to stare at the desk, at all the ashen faces of those ruined girls.

After another moment, Ayaan's hands came to rest on Elle's shoulders. Her body jumped at the touch, so unexpected. She gently turned Elle around, and Elle raised her gaze to look into the commander's dark brown eyes.

"Elle, you need sleep."

"It's been almost seventy-two hours since Amanda was taken."

"I can hold down the fort for a few hours. You go home and rest for a little while. You're no good to Amanda if you're exhausted."

Tears sprang up, and Elle blinked them away, looking at the floor. She couldn't cry here; she didn't need another reason for anyone to think she couldn't handle herself. But soon tears were spilling over and dripping down her cheeks. After a few minutes, Elle regained control and pulled away from Ayaan's comforting grasp. She opened her bag and pulled out a tissue. Wiping under her eyes, she straightened her shoulders and looked at Ayaan.

"You don't believe me."

Ayaan's head tilted to the side, and her gaze was obnoxiously full of pity. "Elle, come on."

"I know TCK's work, Ayaan. I know his methods. This *feels* like him; I don't know how else to say it. I know you're an experienced detective, and I know I'm just on this case to make Amanda's family happy, but I thought you were starting to trust me." Fingernails of doubt scraped inside her.

"That's not fair, Elle. When you're in your element, you are one of the most natural investigators I've ever seen. But this is different. This case does something to you, clouds your instincts."

Elle threw her hands up. "Okay, then, what's *your* grand theory? Who do you think took Amanda? Some neighbor that none of the kids recognized, somehow? Because it's been three days, which means if I'm right, he's going to start poisoning her, and if I'm wrong, statistically, she's dead already."

"Even if she hasn't been killed yet, that doesn't mean it was TCK." Ayaan's voice did not rise to match hers, which just made Elle feel worse. "Leads have been coming in since they aired that little girl's sketch on the news last night. We might not have a slam dunk yet, but we will find her."

Elle shook her head, looking at the papers on her desk. "I can't get him out of my head."

"Maybe that's the problem."

"No, you don't understand. I haven't had a feeling like this, ever. It's like . . . it's like he's taunting me with this, showing me he's back, reminding me what he can do."

"That's not entirely true."

"What?"

Ayaan sat back against her desk and folded her arms. "You've done this before. You've felt this before."

Elle's mouth went dry. She looked away, but Ayaan kept talking.

"Five and a half years ago. Maddie Black's case, before you quit CPS? You were sure of it then."

Elle stared at the notes and pictures, pulse hammering. "That was different. That was a long time ago."

"You were convinced it was TCK. I even believed you for a while —you almost cost that girl her life."

Clenching her hands into fists, Elle whispered, "I did not."

Ayaan shook her head. "Why do you think it took me so long to get back to you about Jair Brown two years ago, Elle? I had to get clearance from the chief himself to be allowed to work with you. Even after your help, he was still hesitant to let you on another case. Maybe he was right."

"I made one mistake."

"You tried to convince us to ignore the witnesses who came forward about her father."

"Stop."

"We only just made it in time. She would have died."

"I wasn't as sure then as I am now." Even as she said it, Elle wasn't convinced that was true.

"I'm calling Martín to come get you," Ayaan said. "You can't drive like this." She pushed away from the desk and stood between Elle and the pictures and notes until Elle met her gaze. Ayaan's eyes were kind, but determined. "I'm not sure this is a good idea anymore."

〰〰〰〰

When Elle got in his car, Martín asked only one question: "Do you want to talk about it?"

"No."

They rode home in silence.

She had never been very good at talking about what was bothering her. She should be, after years of therapy, but historically, things hadn't gone well for her when she spilled her guts. Her parents could never accept what had happened to Elle when she was a child. After a while, she started to believe them—that it wasn't as bad as she had built up in her head, that the things she remembered weren't true. By the time she became a teenager, she had pushed all the memories of that incident down so far that it would take more than a decade for them to resurface.

Then she met Martín.

Elle glanced at him; his eyes were trained on the road, and he leaned slightly forward as if he was watching for something to jump out at him. Martín hated driving in Minnesota winters, even though he should have gotten used to them by now. He was born in Mexico, but he'd lived in the land of ten thousand lakes for seventeen years, since he moved here at eighteen to go to college. Still, he had never gotten used to all the snow and ice.

The Castillos were the opposite of Elle's family in every possible way. He had four siblings, each of them married, and eleven nieces and nephews. Every other year, Elle and Martín rented a big van, picked up Angelica's family in Wisconsin, and drove down to meet up with their brothers at his parents' place in Mexico. There was not a moment's silence for two weeks. Crying babies and screams of laughter and dishes of food passed around and around until you felt like you would burst. Elle absorbed their potent energy and un-guarded love like parched soil in the rain. His mother had taught her to cook — a skill she'd never learned from her own mom, who worked every day of her life and relied on food that came from a box. In some ways, that was one of the things Elle respected most about her mom: she refused to give up hours every day to put food on the table just because her husband wouldn't.

It had been more than a decade since Elle cut her parents out of her life, but sometimes she imagined her mom the way she must look now: a bit grayer, the hollows of her cheeks more pronounced, still standing over the stove with a box of Hamburger Helper in one hand and a glass of Cabernet in the other. Maybe now that she was retired, she'd learned to cook for real. Elle doubted it.

At a stoplight, Martín turned the dial on the car stereo until his favorite talk radio show came on. He wasn't a music guy, not while he was driving, anyway. Comedic drive-time kept him alert. He met her gaze for a minute, offering a small smile. Too exhausted to force a smile of her own, she looked back out the passenger window. Soon the light turned green again, and he moved forward.

The Maddie Black case Ayaan had referred to was a complex sort of salvation. On the one hand, Elle wouldn't have been doing the *Justice Delayed* podcast without it. On the other, she had nearly cost the girl her life and shown she could have blinders on when look-ing at certain kinds of cases. But that was more than five years ago, and even though she had recorded a monologue about it, Elle hadn't found the right episode of the TCK case to include it in yet. If she was being honest with herself, she probably never would. It didn't fit the narrative.

She put her elbow up on the car door and rested her forehead in her hand, squeezing her temples with thumb and middle finger. Her pulse throbbed against her fingertips.

"Are you okay?" Martín asked as he pulled into their driveway. Once the car was in park, he reached across the center console and put his gloved hand on hers. "Hey, Elle? What's wrong?"

She shook her head, blinking again. "Nothing. Let's just go inside. I need to sleep."

"What happened at the station, querida? Tell me."

"Nothing." Opening the door, she stepped out onto the icy driveway and made her way to the front door.

Once inside, Elle hung up her scarf and coat, knocking her boots on the rug before taking them off.

Martín kept his on but handed her the keys to his car. "I'll get a taxi in so you can have the car. We'll pick yours up later."

"Thanks. Sorry for making you late," she said.

"It's okay, I told them I would be. I knew it must be serious if Ayaan called me." He reached up and cupped her face with his warm hands. "Your eyes are red."

"I haven't slept."

He looked like he wanted to say more, but after a moment, he nodded. "Okay. Go to bed, amor. The case will still be here after a few hours of rest, and you can't help that little girl if you can't think."

She blinked away a fresh batch of tears. "Are we good?"

Rather than answer, he tilted his head and pressed his mouth softly against hers.

"Good," she murmured, too exhausted to say anything more. She started up the stairs to their bedroom.

"Elle," he said.

"What?" She looked down at him.

Martín folded his arms across his chest, gazing up at her with the crease between his eyes that he got when he was stressed. "I believe you."

"What?" she said again, this time in a whisper.

"I can tell there's something you're not telling me, and I don't know why. But I need you to know that I have your back, no matter what." Martin took two steps up to get closer to her. "No matter how outrageous it sounds, remember that I will always believe you first." He leaned in, kissed her cheek, and then walked back down the stairs and out the door.

21

Elle

January 17, 2020

She was in the room again. The gray sheets were rough under her fingertips as she lay flat on her back, blinking at the mold patches on the ceiling. He hadn't come to get her for more than a day. All her water was gone, and her stomach cramped with hunger. It made her . . . want to see him. Even though she knew what he'd make her do when he came back.

She closed her eyes, and when she opened them again, it was getting dark, the scrap of weak sunlight that came through her one small window disappearing like a dying flashlight. She could barely see the ceiling anymore.

Then he was in the room with her, thick arms and torso making a striking silhouette in the fading light.

The man sat on the bed, but her limbs were pinned down, frozen, as he leaned over her. He moved the thin blanket off her, examined her scabbed knees. She wanted to tell him to stop. She wanted to beg him for a drink of water. She wanted him to leave her alone.

She didn't want to be alone.

In the gloaming, his face was a blur of indistinguishable features.

His fingers trailed up from her navel, across her sternum, and then landed on her throat. He pressed down, and this was new, this *pain, this force he hadn't used before that made it hard to breathe. She gasped, and it was tight against his palms, limited in a way her breathing had never been, and her chest clenched painfully.*

"Please." Her whisper was ragged in the cold air of the room. "Please."

Elle jerked awake and sat up, her fingers throbbing against a pillow she had in a stranglehold. She dropped it as if it was on fire, pushing herself out of bed onto unsteady feet. The room was dark, and it took a moment to place where she was in time. She didn't know how long she'd been asleep, but something felt off. Something had happened.

And then it hit her with a sudden shiver of anxiety: she was supposed to pick up Natalie from piano lessons today. The black clock with big red numbers on Martin's nightstand told her it was 5:22.

"Shit!" Her phone was nowhere to be seen. She ran down and rifled through her purse—sure enough, she'd missed seven calls from various numbers and had three texts from Natalie asking where she was. Even though Elle was only twenty minutes late, the first message from Natalie was from nearly an hour ago, just after she would have gotten off the bus in front of Ms. Turner's house.

Something was wrong.

After shoving her feet into her boots and grabbing the nearest winter coat, Elle ran out to Martin's car. She didn't have time to let the engine warm up, and the car screeched in protest as she reversed out of the driveway. As she drove toward Ms. Turner's house and the setting sun, Elle called Natalie's phone. It went straight to voicemail. Once she got to a stoplight, she sent her a text.

ON MY WAY. I'M SO SORRY.

The light turned green, and she gunned the engine, tires skidding on the road salt and ice.

Ms. Turner's house was only ten blocks away, and every time Elle had been there to pick Natalie up before, the whole two-story had been ablaze with light. The elderly woman lived alone and was afraid of the dark, so she kept all the lights on, no matter which room she was in. When Elle pulled up outside, a stab of foreboding knocked the breath out of her. The house was gray in the fading sun, the shades drawn, as if the place was abandoned. She ran up the path and knocked anyway, but she wasn't surprised when no one came to the door. The phone rang inside the house when Elle called from her cell, but no one answered. After ten rings, she finally gave up.

She tried to imagine what had happened. Maybe Ms. Turner went out of town and forgot to tell Sash. Then Natalie came for her lesson and called Elle when she realized Ms. Turner wasn't home, which was why the missed calls and texts started sooner than they should have. Maybe Ms. Turner had taken Natalie someplace special, and the calls were just to let her know about the change of plans. But that didn't explain Natalie's frantic where-are-you messages.

Elle growled in frustration and ran back down the icy sidewalk, forgetting to be careful and nearly falling twice on her way to the car. She forced herself to drive toward home at a crawl as her eyes searched the sidewalks for any sign of movement. If Natalie left an hour ago, she should have gotten home way before now, but maybe she was still walking, playing in the snow or something. She liked to climb the large drifts piled up in the gas station parking lot that sat about halfway between Ms. Turner's house and the Castillos'. Maybe she had stopped there and Elle had just missed her on the drive. Her eyes were so focused out the window as she passed the station, she almost rear-ended a car at the stop sign. She hit the brakes just in time and craned her neck to study the mountains of snow, but Natalie was nowhere to be seen.

"You're being paranoid," she said aloud. A long, deep breath did nothing to calm the nerves ricocheting around her body. She remembered the first time she got angry with Natalie. It was about a year ago, and the nine-year-old had been in one of her passion-project modes about homelessness in Minnesota. Without telling anyone, she took the bus to downtown Minneapolis and visited a group of people who camped near the bridge over the Mississippi. Sash had used an app on her phone to track Natalie's phone's GPS, and they'd finally found her an hour later. While Sash had been frustrated and concerned, Elle had gone from panicked to irate. She'd screamed at Natalie for the first and only time, and it had taken the girl three weeks to speak to her again.

That was when Elle realized how attached to Natalie she had become—when she started to panic about all the hypothetical scenarios that could play out to take her away. Little things that used to be inconsequential now felt rife with danger. Going to birthday parties. Attending field trips. Walking home.

When Elle was a kid, she and her friends used to roam the neighborhood together, doing stupid things like rollerblading down giant hills and riding their bicycles "no hands." Growing up, she usually left the house with a couple of the neighbor kids after breakfast in the summer, came back for a quick lunch, and then didn't return again until the sun went down. She didn't even remember what they did to pass all that time. Goof around, mostly. Head over to the local park, swing and slide for hours. Climb the jungle gym. Try to be acrobatic on the monkey bars. That was back when playgrounds were a risky adventure, constructed of metal and rubber. Swings were held up by chains that could pinch your fingers, and monkey bars gave you bright red calluses on your palms. Whatever they did, wherever they went, they always knew exactly where those invisible boundary lines were between their neighborhood and Too Far to Hear Mom. Their parents left them alone, and no one cared.

They just couldn't do that anymore.

It didn't matter that the danger was no greater now than it was then; the societal pressure was different. People expected you to know where your kids were at all times, to be able to reach them at the push of a button.

Sash gave Natalie a cell phone to use between school and home, and she was always, always supposed to answer when an adult called. Still driving at a crawl, Elle called the number again. No answer.

Her phone lit up and Elle looked at it eagerly. Martín. She answered, but her greeting came out too breathless to be a word.

"Hello, dormilón."

"Did you pick up Natalie?" Her voice sounded very high.

"Uh, no. I thought you were picking her up."

"I did." Elle's hands were trembling, numb. A sob burst from her lips. "I mean, I tried. I fell asleep, and I was late, Martín. She wasn't at Ms. Turner's. No one was. And she's not answering her phone."

There was silence on the other end. They had both seen too much to not immediately imagine the worst.

"Where are you?"

Elle wanted the release of crying, but no tears would come. "I'm just about home. I drove back slowly, but she wasn't walking next to the road. I didn't see her on the way to Ms. Turner's either. It's only ten blocks. Where could she be?"

"All right, mi vida, cálmate."

"Do not tell me to calm down. You know how much I hate that."

"Right. Sorry. Just . . . I don't know." There was a shuffling sound on Martín's end, and then he spoke again. "I'll come home. Have you gone to her house? Maybe Sash got home early or something."

"She's not supposed to—"

"I know, okay? I know. But try anyway. I need to take care of this body and then figure out how to get home."

When he hung up, she swiped to get to Sash's name. The call went straight to voicemail. Sash was probably in court.

No one was here when she needed them. Anger coursed through her, however unjustified. Martín was trying to get home to her; Sash would call her back as soon as she could. She knew that, but the rage and fear persisted.

Elle had been freezing two seconds ago, but now felt like she was boiling alive. She parked outside Sash's house and jumped out of the car with her coat open. The only way past the sheer, blind panic was to be angry with Natalie. She tried to work up the motherly fury because even if she wasn't a mom, damn it, she could have motherly fury. Because of course, Natalie just walked home when Elle didn't answer her phone to come pick her up. It was only ten blocks. No big deal.

Except she was nowhere to be seen. The lights were off in her house, but Elle walked up the slippery path and knocked on the door anyway. "Natalie?" she called, fishing in her purse for the spare key. As soon as she found it and opened the door, she knew Natalie wasn't home. The house was cold, set to the daytime temperature that was just high enough to keep the pipes from freezing.

Elle stumbled back outside, tears finally flooding her eyes as she looked up and down the sidewalk on their block. The evening sky glowed pale orange from the freshly fallen snow. The streetlights illuminated sparkling tree branches, parked cars, and a couple abandoned plastic sleds. But there was nobody in sight.

Natalie was gone.

22

Justice Delayed podcast

Recorded November 28, 2019

Unaired recording: Elle Castillo, monologue

ELLE:

Every investigation has flaws. Every investigator makes mistakes. Over the decades since he officially became inactive, detectives and even a couple investigative journalists have blamed cases on the elusive TCK. Sometimes they did so with compelling evidence: a case of ricin poisoning, eleven-year-old girls who went missing or were killed at various times, another couple found dead in a cabin fifty miles north of the one TCK's last victim escaped. Even Detective Sykes admitted to being fooled once, in 2008, by a series of four murders in Fargo that seemed to revolve around an obsession with numbers.

But they have all been wrong. We have all been wrong.

Longtime listeners might remember that I actually knew Ayaan Bishar, Commander of Crimes Against Children at Minneapolis Police Department, before we worked together on the Jair Brown case. We met when I worked in CPS, when I was put on a case that involved a missing child.

I responded to a call from neighbors concerned about a young girl named Maddie Black. They hadn't seen her in several days, which was unusual as she often played on the swing set outside their apartment building. Her mother was separated from her father and lived with a man that the neighbors said was often verbally abusive. The mother and the boyfriend both claimed to have no idea where Maddie was, and based on witness statements from the girl's friends, it seemed the last time she had been seen was when she got off the school bus to walk the two blocks to her house. No one saw her get taken, but she never arrived home.

We looked into the girl's father, which was routine procedure. He lived two hours away and seemed to be shocked about Maddie's disappearance, although a couple of her friends mentioned that Maddie had seemed afraid the last time she was supposed to spend the weekend at his house.

I . . . I should have listened. Those are the kinds of clues that make a good social worker's senses fire up, but I ignored them.

The circumstances of her kidnapping were eerily familiar to me. Even at that time, I knew the TCK case inside and out. Maddie was eleven years old, and although her family was in much more turmoil than those of the other TCK victims, it seemed possible to me that he was responsible. Once I started looking at the similarities, it seemed obvious. She was the right age, from the right background. She had disappeared the same way most of his victims had — walking alone in the course of her normal daily routine. So when I spoke to Ayaan Bishar, who was the detective assigned to the case, I told her I was certain that TCK had decided to start killing again. By the time two days had passed and there was no ransom call or sign of a body, I thought I had her convinced. Not only had Maddie been taken by TCK, but another girl was due to be snatched the next day. Other clues came in, a couple of family friends saying we should really take a closer look at Maddie's father, but TCK was so clever, I wouldn't have even put it past him to choose a victim that would have us pointing the finger at someone else. Maybe it was an improvement, a sophistication of his technique that he had added over the years.

It was not. Four days after Maddie disappeared, Ayaan pursued a tip about an alias Maddie's father used, and she tracked down an apartment he'd rented under the fake name. Having heard police busting down the door, the man decided that if he couldn't have his daughter, no one could. They broke in just before he could shoot her. She was saved, but the next day when I went in to work, I had a resignation letter with me.

I was burned out at my job. I feared my mistake had nearly cost a girl her life. At the same time, in my personal life, I had my first and only taste of what it was like to be a parent through a burgeoning friendship with my neighbor and her daughter.

I spent a few weeks on my couch, mourning what felt like the end of my career and binge-listening to every true crime podcast I could find. Finally, late one night, drunk on sleep deprivation and half a bottle of Shiraz, I decided I could do one myself. Despite my failure with Maddie's case, I hadn't lost my passion for helping children who were victims of crime. Maybe I just needed to go about it a different way.

The thought of a predator going after my neighbor's daughter — this perfect, tiny, bright-eyed girl with the stubborn chin and unfair dimple in her cheek — made me queasy with rage. But I knew it was a reality. There were men who preyed on girls like her. I had known too many of them in my life, seen too many get away with their crimes, and I knew I could do something to stop it. That night, I recorded the first episode of what would become *Justice Delayed*. A few months later, I released season one.

As it is with so many things in life, it wasn't one event that led me to this work — it was a confluence of them coming together at the right time. We are a product of not just the experiences we have, but our reactions to them. If I had to point to one thing, though — one thing that started it all — it was Maddie Black's case. Everyone has a catalyst, a person or event or message that sets them on their path. Something that when you look back at their history, you can see how everything that happened later all flowed out from this one thing.

Their origin story.

Part III

THE FUSE

23

DJ

1971 to 1978

The first woman DJ killed was his mother. She died in childbirth, screaming as she expelled his writhing body along with too much of her own blood.

It was God's will that she died; that was what his father reminded him whenever one of his schoolmates teased him for not having a mother. The Lord had made DJ for a purpose, and it was the last act of God's plan for his mother to bring him into this world. Once he was born, her purpose was fulfilled and the Lord called her home. There was some comfort in that, knowing he must be special since God was willing to sacrifice his mother to put him on this earth.

DJ never felt like he lacked anything by not having a mom. The men in his family were strong stock. His father, Josiah, was a plumber who worked six days a week and never went to a doctor as far back as DJ could remember. His brothers were football players and part-time farmhands once they entered their teenage years. They had dinner together every night that Charles and Thomas didn't have practice. They went to Mass every Sunday, and Josiah read to DJ from the Bible each night before bed. It wasn't a remarkable life, but the familiarity of each day wrapped around him like a warm blanket.

Everything changed on a Tuesday in the middle of summer when DJ was seven years old. Charles and Thomas were off at Bible camp for a week, and DJ was alone with his father. They were playing chess on their front porch, listening to the cicadas scream. As the muggy afternoon slowly melted into cool evening, the phone rang and Josiah went to answer it. DJ was planning his next move when a loud, violent sound came from inside the house.

He ran to the kitchen, where his father was on the floor, holding the phone to his ear with the cord wrapped around his forearm. There were tears on his face. DJ had never seen him cry before. It took him several tries to get the news out of Josiah.

Charles and Thomas had sneaked a boat out onto Lake Superior the night before, and they had never come back. Josiah packed him up in the truck and they drove to the summer camp in Duluth, five hours in the car with DJ sitting quiet and numb. His father alternated between shouting denials and whispering prayers.

Nothing had changed when they arrived. The boat was still missing, lost on the great lake that stretched farther than any body of water DJ had ever seen. He wondered if this was what the ocean looked like. Surely, it couldn't be any bigger than this. He scanned the horizon, as if somehow everyone had just missed it, and there his brothers would be, waving for help or laughing in their natural carefree way, surprised that everyone was so worried while they were just out for an adventure.

The hours dragged by, and more search parties were dispatched. A helicopter beat the air over DJ's head.

"Charles and Thomas will be back soon," he told his father. His brothers were just making trouble. It was summer. They probably found some girls and went out with them for what Charles called a "night squeeze."

As they waited, DJ noted down the number of police officers, vehicles, camp counselors, and other searchers that crawled the shore. He couldn't believe the quantity of them. He liked numbers. He was no good at writing, and he was never an athlete like his older brothers, but when he was given his first math worksheet at six years old, it was like seeing a language he'd always spoken written down for the first time. Numbers formed the foundation of the world. Every angle, every atom, every cell could be defined by an equation. Learning this had allowed him to grip on to a world that usually slipped through his fingers. He tried to calculate the odds of the boys returning safely as the hours went by, but there were too many variables — too many unknowns.

Twenty-one hours. That was how long it took the police to find his brothers' bodies. They washed up on the shore of Manitou Island, one of the Apostle Islands off the coast of Wisconsin. A storm had brought them there, thrashing their boat and their bodies against the rocks. DJ was never allowed to see them, which made it worse. He imagined his brothers' broken bones, torn skin, crushed heads. He pictured their last moments, when they knew they would die. He later found out they had drowned, had already been dead before their bodies were broken, but the images still remained.

The night after they were found, his father brought DJ home. He said nothing in the car, spoke no words when they arrived at their stuffy, empty house. People came over every few hours during that first week, neighbors and church friends filling their refrigerator with lasagna and weird hot dishes. Then came the funeral and, after that, silence.

For days after, Josiah didn't speak. DJ tried asking him questions. He tried pretending to fall and hurt himself. He did the things he knew annoyed his father the most: played Charles's drum kit in the barn, whistled loudly while he peed, drank from the orange juice carton. None of it made a difference.

Then he remembered the plant. It was in his mother's sunroom, the special sanctuary his father had built for her when they bought the house. The leaves were a bright, eye-catching red; she had planted it herself using seeds from the bigger version growing wild on the farm. He had brought it to school for show and tell once, without asking his father, and when Josiah found out, he had screamed at DJ until the vein in his jaw turned purple. He told him the seeds on the plant would make him sick and it was too dangerous to bring to school.

Maybe the plant would wake his father up.

DJ brought it out to the dining room table and set it in the center, pushing aside a week's worth of dirty dishes to make room. He left it there and went up to his room when he heard Josiah coming. He expected to hear his father's feet stamping up the stairs any second, but they never came.

When he went down for breakfast the next morning, his father was sitting there, drinking his coffee with the plant in front of him. It was like he didn't even see it.

The anger swirled in DJ like a funnel cloud. His brothers were gone, but he was still here, and if his father didn't even notice the bright colorful buds on this sacred plant, then what hope did he have? Then it came to him: if he got sick, his father would have to take care of him.

When Josiah left for work, DJ plucked one of the pods from the plant, cracked it open, and popped the brown seed in his mouth. It was oily, but not bitter.

DJ picked up his backpack and went to school.

\\\\\\\\\

At lunch, DJ's stomach started cramping when he ate his peanut butter sandwich. His mouth and throat burned like he had swallowed a lit match. By the end of the day, his body was radiating fever. He stumbled home holding his gut and collapsed on the sofa with a glass of lukewarm water on the coffee table. He awoke to a sensation he'd never felt before: the pressure of father's rough palm on his forehead. Josiah picked him up and brought him to his own bed, laying him down on what DJ knew was his mother's side, even though he'd never had the chance to see her resting there.

He drifted back to sleep.

The next day, his father stayed home from work and cared for him, leaving cool compresses on his forehead and feeding him tepid broth. He sat by DJ's bed and read from the Bible, just like he had every night before Thomas and Charles died. There was a warm comfort to it, the sound of his father's voice wrapped around the poetry of Psalms and the wisdom of Proverbs. Those were his two favorite books; all the advice you needed in the world was right there—that's what Josiah always said.

DJ shifted between sleep and wakefulness without being conscious of the transition. Once he opened his eyes and his father was lying down next to him, eyes closed and tears streaming down his face. "Please," he was whispering. "Please, not him. You promised me."

Each time that he woke, he only felt worse. A doctor friend of Josiah's came and scanned his body, and DJ thought about telling him, but his father refused to leave the room, and he couldn't bear the idea of the wrath he knew his confession would inspire.

But when the doctor came back the next day, DJ couldn't even move, his entire body a mass of sore, dried-out muscle from days of vomiting and diarrhea. When he saw the grim expression on the doctor's face, the childlike expectation that he would soon feel better was finally replaced with a spark of terror. "Can I talk to you alone?" he whispered to the doctor. The man looked at DJ's father, who hesitated before leaving the room.

As soon as DJ whispered what he'd done, the doctor picked him up and rushed him out of the house. Josiah followed along, barking questions as the boy was shoved in the backseat of the doctor's car. Both men got in the front, and the doctor gunned the engine.

The time at the hospital came and went in flashes. There was the needle in DJ's arm and the beeping of machines and the concerned faces hovering over his as he opened and closed his heavy eyes. Then suddenly he was awake and remembered what it was like not to be in constant pain, not to feel like someone was turning his stomach inside out. His father was next to him, but when he saw DJ's eyes open, his face did not look relieved. There was something else there instead, a darkness DJ had never seen before.

Three days later, he was allowed to leave the hospital.

Josiah said nothing to him when they walked into the house. DJ went to the kitchen, his body still shaky and weak from days of sickness and lack of movement. He poured a glass of water and sat at the table. The plant was still there, in the center of the table, as if that was where it had always been. He sipped his water and stared at the strange, colorful blossoms. When his father came in, DJ didn't look away from the plant. He didn't want to see the expression of anger and disappointment that he knew now might never go away.

"Is this what you want?" Josiah asked at last.

DJ continued to stare at the plant. The picture of his father's face, twisted in agony when the police officers finally came to their hotel door in Duluth, wouldn't stop flashing in his mind.

"Answer me, boy. You want to throw away the life God gave you? You want to torture me? You want all the attention, me and the doctors hovering over your bed?" DJ looked up in time to see Josiah's eyes flash. "Go ahead, then. Eat some more." He shoved the plant across the table. DJ moved out of the way and it crashed to the floor. The pot exploded on the gray tiles, dirt and spiky red blossoms scattering like globs of blood.

"You spoiled shit," his father hissed. He stormed around the table and grabbed the back of DJ's neck, pulling him out the kitchen door and into the backyard. The summer evening was muggy and thick with gnats. They swarmed DJ's mouth and eyes as he cried. His father had never touched him like this before, holding on to his neck like he was a misbehaving dog. Josiah half carried, half dragged DJ to the tall grass that had grown up behind their old shed, the one he and his cousins used to play cops and robbers in. The seat of an ancient tractor separated the blades of waist-high grass, a relic from when his father's grandfather owned the house. It was DJ's favorite thing to play on, and now his father put his hands on it and told him to stand still. He pulled down his pants, and DJ felt a slap of cold air on his naked skin even though it was over a hundred degrees outside.

"'Train up a child in the way he should go, and when he is old he will not depart from it.'" Josiah's voice boomed over the sound of cicadas. "'Spare the rod, spoil the child.' I knew I was too soft on you boys. First your brothers go out on that boat, and now you—" He didn't finish.

The first strike came down with such force DJ was sure his back had been ripped open. He locked his knees, trying to stay standing.

"My daddy used to whup me here. I swore I'd never be like him, but maybe he got this one thing right."

He landed the belt a second time, followed by another, and another. His father gasped in between, words popping from his mouth like grease in a hot pan.

"You . . . did . . . this . . ." One word for each strike, repeated over and over.

The belt fell on DJ's bare legs, lighting his calves and thighs on fire. He tried to count the seconds between them, but the numbers started blurring together. This made him panic, made his breaths come shorter and tighter as his hands trembled on the tarnished metal seat of the old tractor. Numbers were the only thing that mattered to him, the only thing that made sense. If he couldn't think about numbers, he would never be able to escape this.

Instead of counting seconds, he tried counting the strikes, reminding himself what the numbers meant, what they signified. *Seven, the number of oceans, the number of continents, the number of dwarfs in* Snow White, *the number of completeness and perfection. Eight, the largest single-digit even number, divisible by two and four, the smallest prime numbers cube, the number of new beginnings.*

He felt his mind start to churn, to lift him away.

Thirteen, unlucky, the sixth prime number, a Fibonacci number, the number of depravity and sinfulness.

Seventeen, the only prime number which is the sum of four consecutive prime numbers, the number of complete victory.

Twenty-one, a triangular number, the sum of the first six natural numbers, the number of rebelliousness and sin.

At last, the beating stopped.

DJ stood for what seemed like hours, metal digging into the joints under his knuckles, his knees trembling. Finally, Josiah placed his hand on his shoulder. The boy jerked and nearly cried out at the fresh rush of pain, even though he'd not made a sound yet.

"'Blows that hurt cleanse away evil.'" It was a Bible verse Josiah had read a few days ago, one of the proverbs. When DJ looked up, his father's eyes and cheeks were red, tears streaming down his face. Panic overcame the rage from a few moments before. The man turned his son's body, staring at the lashes he had left behind. "I'm sorry, son. I'm sorry. I'm sorry."

DJ pulled away, the sight of his father's shame somehow more unbearable than the beating. Maybe this was part of what would make him clean—pure and holy. Maybe now he could be forgiven for lying to his father, causing him so much grief when he already had more than enough. This was a new beginning. He would be everything his father wanted from his boys. He would be the best at everything he put his hand to.

He would be enough for three sons.

24

Elle

January 17, 2020

The first officers arrived at her house less than ten minutes after Elle
called Ayaan. Martín was next, rushing through the front door in a
blaze of concern; he swept Elle into his arms for a strong, disinfec-
tant-scented hug. Then Sash was there, a statue with the life sucked
out of her, barely capable of saying anything except, *Where is she?*
Where is she? Where is she?

They combed the neighborhood, walking in pairs—Martín and
Elle with an officer on one side of the street and another officer with
Sash on the other—and knocking on every door. No one had seen
her. They walked all the way back to Ms. Turner's and checked there
again, but the place still seemed abandoned. The only thing they
found was a cold hunk of glass and plastic that Martín spotted on
the icy street.

Natalie's phone. Police collected it into evidence and scoured the
area around it, but nothing further was found. It had been crushed,
driven over by someone's tire.

Finally, they went back to the Castillos' house and waited. Waiting, in this case, involved a lot of crying and pacing and looking out
the window over and over and over.

Everything blurred together as Elle huddled on her couch with her eyes on the floor until suddenly Ayaan was kneeling in front of her, a clear voice breaking through the haze.

"Elle, tell me what you know."

She recounted the story again, every detail she could remember. Falling asleep, waking up feeling that something was wrong, the missed calls and texts from Natalie. She told Ayaan everything, down to the cold emptiness of the Hunter household and how she knew Natalie had never made it home.

Only when she finished everything did the sudden thought flicker to life in her mind, and she finally brought her eyes up to meet Ayaan's serious gaze. "It's been three nights since Amanda was taken, Ayaan."

Ayaan's full lips pressed into a tight, straight line. "Elle."

"Don't you see? This is . . ." She trailed off, horrified tears filling her eyes. "This is exactly his pattern. Natalie is ten years old. She's next in the countdown."

Martín walked through the door from the kitchen with a mug of tea, but he stopped short when he heard Elle. A pitying look passed between him and Ayaan, and Elle was about to open her mouth to say something when Sash stunned them all by shouting.

"Are you serious right now, Elle?" she spat, standing up from where she'd been slumped in Martín's favorite recliner. "You're really making *this* about your podcast? My daughter's . . . disappeared . . . and you're talking about fucking TCK right now?"

Setting the mug down in front of Elle, Martín turned to face Sash and held his hands up in a calming gesture. "Sash, I'm so sorry. This is a traumatic time. Please give Elle a chance to—"

"To what?" Elle cut in, jumping to her feet. Ayaan rose after her, taking a step to the side. "You said you believe me, always. Well, believe me now, Martín. This is TCK. It all fits—this is exactly what he does."

With a growl of rage, Sash threw her cup of tea across the room. It shattered against the wall near Elle, hot amber liquid splattering on her clothes and down the wall. She flinched at the drops that splashed across her skin. An officer came rushing into the room, but Ayaan waved him away. Sash stood with her legs planted firmly apart, her shoulders heaving with anger as she glared at Elle. "Shut. Up." Her friend's face was contorted in a way Elle had never seen it before, her chest and neck flushed, her eyes gleaming. "TCK is dead, Elle. He killed himself in that cabin twenty years ago, and you *know* it. Everyone knows it, and they only indulge this stupid fantasy you have about catching him because they feel sorry for you."

Elle drew back, her face stinging. "That's not true."

But Sash wasn't finished. She took a step toward Elle and pointed her finger. "Stop deflecting. It's your fault that Natalie left that house by herself. You promised me you would always be there to pick her up. You promised me, and I trusted you like you were my own sister."

All the strength vanished from Elle's legs, and she sat back down abruptly. Sash's furious words beat on her eardrums like fists, the cold accuracy of them. It *was* her fault. She shouldn't have fallen asleep. She should have been there the second Natalie realized Ms. Turner wasn't home.

"Miss Hunter, we're going to do everything we can to find your daughter," Ayaan said, her voice a calming force that none of them could fight. Then, to Elle's surprise, Ayaan sat down next to her and put one soft, comforting arm around her back. "I've seen relationships torn apart when something like this happens, but I promise you, it's so much more bearable when you stick together. Blaming each other won't help us find Natalie faster. Try not to turn on each other, okay?"

Sash looked back and forth between the two of them for a moment and then, without a word, she picked up her coat and stormed out of the house.

Elle wiped her eyes as her friend left and looked at Ayaan. "Do you believe me?"

Ayaan looked away, a small gesture that was crushing nonetheless. "I think you should take a step back from this, Elle. We don't even know if these kidnappings are connected, and you are already convinced you know who's responsible. You're too close to be objective, especially now that Natalie is missing too."

"Ayaan—" A sob cut Elle off. Through her tears, she could see that Martin was still standing in the corner of the room, but she couldn't bring herself to look at him. Shame burned her neck, coiled in her shoulders.

"I know you're hurting, Elle." Ayaan's brown eyes were troubled when she met Elle's gaze. "I hope you get some help."

\\\\\\\\\\

A few minutes passed in silence after Ayaan left. Elle sat on the sofa and stared at the wall, letting the tears fall down her face unobstructed. Finally, Martín crossed the room and sat next to her. Slowly, his hand came up to rest in the center of her back as if to keep her from falling.

"What happened?" he murmured. "What can I do?"

Stiffening, Elle sat up and pulled out of his reach. "You can't do anything, Martín." When she looked at him, the pain in his eyes took her breath away. She felt a surge of guilt. He had lost Natalie too.

"I have to," he murmured, voice hoarse. "There must be something we can do."

"Do you believe me?" she asked. She stood up and strode to the window overlooking their street. It was pitch-dark outside; if anyone was out there, they would be able to see her perfectly, but on her side, the window was so opaque it might as well have been a mirror. Her dark hair was frizzy, mussed, strands falling out of her ponytail. She couldn't see her eyes, but her forehead looked creased with worry. Behind her, the reflection of her husband sitting on the sofa where she had left him. His head was resting in his hands, and she knew he was probably praying for strength.

"I believe that this case is affecting you even more than you initially thought," Martín said. "I believe that you are seeing clues here that you might not have seen if you hadn't been immersed in this case so deeply for the past few months."

"I've been immersed in this case for years."

"That is true." He lifted his head, and she imagined they could meet each other's gaze in the dark blue reflection of the window. "But this is different. You haven't been sleeping. You lied to me about going to speak with a witness. You agreed to work an active case without even talking to me, and you of all people know how dangerous that could be. I'm just worried about you."

Elle turned around to face him. "I don't want you to worry about me. I want you to believe me."

"And I do, Elle. I told you that I do. But believing you and agreeing with you are not the same thing. I believe you have reasons to think this is TCK, but you can't ask me to tell you that you're right when I'm not sure that you are."

Her vision blurred again, and she shook her head. "Everything matches up with TCK's pattern, though: the ages, the brightly colored accessories, the careful planning. The only thing I can't figure out is where Ms. Turner is, how he knew she wouldn't be there for Natalie's lesson. Maybe TCK lured the woman away from her house so Natalie would have no choice but to walk home alone."

"But how could he have known you wouldn't answer your phone when Natalie called?" Martín asked gently.

She pinched the bridge of her nose between her fingers. "I don't know."

"Everything I know about TCK indicates he is abundantly cautious. Meticulous, like you said on the podcast. He would have every last detail planned out."

Elle met his gaze. "So maybe he didn't know I wouldn't answer my phone. Maybe he just had a plan for if I did." Martín's lips pursed in an expression of disbelief, but she pressed on. "They think he did that before, you know. Planned for every outcome."

For a moment, he watched her, tapping his fingers on one knee. "Does this have anything to do with your last couple of episodes?" he asked at last.

Her gaze flicked to his. "What?"

"I've seen the response to them. Your fans are supporting you, but some of the comments are horrible. It would be completely understandable if this set off something for you, mi vida. The things people have been saying, calling you a liar. If they only knew—"

"I'm fine, Martín. This has nothing to do with that." Elle closed her eyes. Right now, the online threats seemed distant, pretend. What could anyone do to her that was worse than what was happening right now?

When she opened her eyes again, he was walking toward her. He put his hands on her shoulders and met her gaze, eyes wet. It struck her again, that Natalie had disappeared. The fresh wave of grief might have knocked her over if it wasn't for her husband's gentle grip.

He held her close, and she felt one of his tears land on her head. "I know you don't want to make this about you, but you should tell Ayaan about those emails, Elle."

She pulled away and looked up at him in surprise. Martín's expression was grim. "How did you know about the emails?" she asked.

"Tina. When you didn't answer your phone while you were napping this afternoon, she called me to say she'd tracked down some of the people who'd been sending threats. She wanted you to know that none of the ones she'd found so far were local."

Elle looked down, played with the buttons on his shirt. "I'm sorry I didn't say anything. I just didn't want you to worry."

"You're always saying I should trust you, Elle. Well, you can trust me too. Trust me to handle my own feelings. No more keeping big stuff like this from me."

"No more, okay."

He put a hand over hers to still it, brought the other to her chin and tilted it up until she met his eyes again. "I just want you to be safe."

"I will never be safe, doing what I do." The words sounded harsh, but they were true, and sometimes the truth was the cruelest thing of all.

"Astucia, then. If you can't be safe, be able to outsmart anyone who wants to do you harm. Can you do that?"

After considering for a moment, she nodded. "I can try."

25

Justice Delayed podcast

January 9, 2020

Transcript: Season 5, Episode 5

UNIDENTIFIED VOICE-OVER:

You're trapped in a room with another girl. She's only been with you for a day, but you've been here longer. At least three or four days —you can't keep track anymore. You've barely been allowed to eat more than a few scraps of food, and you have worked yourself to the bone just for those. Cleaned the walls with a sponge, dusted every inch of the blinds, scrubbed the floor so hard your knuckles are raw. Your skin smells like bleach, constantly, and has the chemical burns to prove it.

Your body is weak, broken, and you can barely move for fear when you hear your captor approaching the door. This time, though, he's bringing food. It's a thick porridge that you would have turned your nose up at a couple weeks ago, but now you nearly knock the other girl over to get to it. He watches you eat. When you're more than halfway through, you realize he hasn't brought any for the other girl. Reluctantly, you offer to share, but he shakes his head. No, it's only for you. He watches you finish it, every last spoonful, and then he takes the bowl away.

For a few hours, you lie on the dirty mattress, stomach full for the first time in what feels like forever. You drift off to sleep.

You awake when the burning starts. It hits your throat first, a stinging sensation like the time you had the flu and vomited six times in one day. Another hour, and your stomach has gone from satisfied to twisting with nausea and cramps. The other girl checks on you after you throw up the first time, but you can't even speak, your throat hurts so badly.

The next day it's worse, but he makes you work anyway. You clean the bathroom so you have easy access to the toilet, and you spend half the time bent over it in one way or another. Then it's back to bed, where you collapse. You can barely move when you wake up and he comes for you again. The day after that, you can't move at all. Not long ago, you would have done anything to get out of this tiny gray room. Even the hours spent in the rest of the house were a relief. Now you don't have the strength to hope for escape.

You can feel your body shutting down, and you know that's what he wanted. He wanted to watch all the strength drain out of you. He wanted you to fade, so it would be easier to wipe you out completely.

[THEME MUSIC + INTRO]

ELLE VOICE-OVER:
This week's podcast format is a little different. Rather than the usual blend of interviews, back-story, and monologue, I am dedicating the full episode to a special interview. I've got a stack of newspapers in front of me, all the words I could collect that were written about her the first time she entered the public consciousness. Although her name is now recognized by true crime aficionados the world over, when she first went missing, the *Tribune*'s headline didn't even mention it. She was simply:

ANOTHER GIRL, 11, TAKEN BY TCK?

After much time, consideration, and gentle persuasion, Nora Watson has agreed to tell her story on *Justice Delayed*. As those familiar with the case may know, Nora is living under a new name and has avoided public interviews since she was a teenager. However, she has agreed to break her decades-long silence in the hopes that her memories will help contribute to finding the elusive serial killer who stole her childhood—and very nearly her life.

I have disguised her voice for this episode. The interview is unedited, but she also had a say in which questions she wanted to answer. Mostly, though, I wanted to let her tell her story without encumbering it with a bunch of interruptions and questions. Now, on to the interview.

ELLE:
So, why don't we start with this. What happened when you were kidnapped?

NORA:
You have already told the story about how I was tricked into TCK's car at my friend's house. That was all accurate. When I realized he wasn't driving toward my house, I started screaming and kicking the back of his seat. He told me to shut up and threatened to smack me, but as soon as he slowed at a stoplight, I jumped out of the car and tried to run. I didn't make it far. He caught me within seconds and threw me back in the car, then he jabbed something in my leg. It must have been some kind of sedative, because the next thing I remember, I was waking up in that room in the cabin. And Jessica was there.

She was fiercely protective right away, acting like my big sister. She yelled at the man while I cried until he left the room. She warned me how to behave with him, but I didn't listen right away. When he came back later and called me to the door, I ignored him. Jessica hissed at me to get up and go to him, but I just closed my eyes and turned my head away. That's when he opened the door and walked in. He sat on the bed next to me and looked down into my eyes. I don't remember his face now, but I remember those hard, hateful eyes. He didn't say anything for a while, which was worse than if he'd yelled. The silence while I waited to hear my punishment almost made me wet the bed. And then he slapped me hard across the face, just once. My parents never hit me, so I was too stunned to cry at first. He said, "Next time, come when I call you," and then he got up and walked back out. I never ignored him again after that.

ELLE:
What happened the next time he came for you?

NORA:
Jessica tried to convince him to take her, but she was vomiting almost constantly. Even though she said she thought the food he gave her had made her sick, by that point I had been there for more than a day with no food, and I felt like I was starving. He didn't seem to mind letting me see everything when I walked out into the hallway. It was a nice place: big and airy, even though the room he kept us in was tiny. Looking back, I think it must have been a study. The rest of the place was nothing like it. I remember four bedrooms, two living rooms, a big fireplace. There was a Bible on the coffee table in one of the living rooms, a few crosses on the walls. Other than that, the rest of the stuff was all hunting themed: taxidermied ducks in flight, a dozen antler plaques, a full buck's head. It gave me the creeps.

He brought me downstairs to his kitchen and told me he would make me something to eat after I cleaned the whole room. "If you're going to eat my food, you need to earn your keep," he said. "The Bible says, 'If anyone will not work, neither shall he eat.'"

I had learned dozens of verses from memory by the time I was eleven, but I had never heard someone recite them with as much spite as that man did. Our pastor used to say the Bible was like a hammer; it can be used as a tool or a weapon—it just depends on who's holding it. Evil men use it as an instrument of control, and it seemed like he liked to control us.

He didn't look evil, though. I remember thinking that; I never would have gotten in the car with him otherwise. It's been a huge source of frustration that I can't remember anything specific about his face, but I think that's partly because he looked so normal. Like he should have been nicer than he was.

ELLE:
So, you don't remember anything about his appearance?

NORA:
Not beyond what I was able to tell police when I was eleven. They tried a lot of things to help me remember more: hypnosis, therapy, forensic interviewing. But I just couldn't. The psychiatrist who analyzed me said that I had repressed the memories of him, that my mind had been wiped clean by anxiety to protect itself. Sometimes I wonder if I would recognize him if I saw him on the street, but I'm not sure that I would. I've never had a good memory for faces; I don't know if that's because of what happened, or if I'm just one of those people. It's not unusual for me to "meet" someone three or four times because I've forgotten our previous interactions.

ELLE:
I see. What happened next?

NORA:
When he left the room, I searched for a way to escape, but there was no outside door from the kitchen and the windows wouldn't open from the inside. It was getting dark, and all I could see was a thick cluster of trees and snow on the ground. Because I was unconscious when he drove me there, I had no idea how far away from home I was. I was desperate for food, but I had the feeling that he was watching me and would know if I stole any crackers from the pantry. So, I pulled the cleaning supplies from under the kitchen sink and got to work.

I had cleaned before. My mother never spoiled me, even though she wasn't the typical housewife herself. If cleaning was what I had to do to get a meal, I intended to make sure the kitchen was clean enough that I could eat that food off the floor. I washed the cabinets from top to bottom with soapy water, cleaned the crumbs out of the toaster, scrubbed at the grease in the oven, pulled all of the food out of the refrigerator and wiped down the inside. That was a special kind of torture, moving all that food without eating any of it. But I knew Jessica was hungry, too, and I thought if I did a good job, he might give me enough to share with her.

There were more Bible-ish things in the kitchen: cheesy quotes about faith and overcoming typed in cursive on floral postcards. The only thing that stood out was a handwritten card stuck with a magnet to the fridge. Exodus 34:21. "Six days you shall work, but on the seventh day you shall rest."

That was when I knew. I was young, but I had heard rumors about the Countdown Killer at school. We knew he would be coming for girls our age then, and the boys in school used to joke about it—that TCK would come for us if we didn't kiss them behind the bleachers, like he was some kind of boogeyman. Jessica had told me she was twelve. I was eleven. I kept cleaning, but from then on, all I could think about was how we could get away.

It took me more than three hours to finish. After I mopped, I sat on the counter while the floor dried around me, and for a second, just a moment, I felt proud of what I'd done. Then the fear and longing for my mother came crashing back down, and I started to sob. I don't know how long I cried before I heard the man come back in the room. I looked at him and said, "Why are you doing this to me?"

He reached out, and I knew better than to pull away, so I let him touch me, play with my hair. "Oh, Nora," he said. "Nora, I chose you. You're special. You should feel lucky."

Then he told me to bring my cleaning supplies, and he took me down the hall to the bathroom. He had changed the rules; now, while I was waiting for him to cook, I needed to clean the bathroom too. I was furious, but I would have done anything to eat by that point. It didn't take long, and when I finished, I could smell the tomato and basil coming down the hall. He was making me spaghetti. I still don't know if he knew it was my favorite, or if it was just a coincidence. Either way, I had to force myself to walk at a normal pace to the kitchen. When I opened the door, I think I whimpered out loud at what I saw.

There was red sauce everywhere—streaking the counters, splattered across the cabinets, even dotted on the eggshell-colored ceiling.

Dirty pots and pans were piled in the sink. The man was sitting on a stool at the island, twisting his fork in a plate of pasta. He lifted it and closed his mouth around the food while he looked at me. I still remember those emotionless blue eyes, like a lizard's.

After swallowing his food, he smiled at me and said, "Look what a mess you've caused. I'm afraid I didn't save you any. The effort of cooking made me quite hungry." I will never forget the way he looked at me, like I was pathetic, like he hoped I would cry. Then he told me to clean up the mess, and maybe after, he would give me something to eat.

But he didn't. When I finished cleaning again, he grabbed my arm and dragged me back to the room where he was keeping me with Jessica. I was so angry that I tried to pull out of his grasp and run back to the kitchen, but when I saw the state she was in, I forgot all about my hunger. She was obviously incredibly sick, but he didn't seem to care. I screamed at him that she needed a doctor, and he looked at me like I was an idiot. Because of course, he was trying to kill her, and he was going to kill me too.

ELLE:

Was Jessica able to help you at all?

NORA:

No, she was very sick. It was perfect, really — his system. Break the first girl down and make her paralyzed with fear before you bring in the next one and start the process all over. It makes surviving, fighting back, feel impossible. You're watching the life drain out of a person, knowing this is going to happen to you next. If TCK is good at anything, it's knowing how to cause and intensify terror until it's excruciating.

I kept trying to convince her she had to come with me, we had to find a way out, but she could barely move. He came and got her once, I think on my second morning there, but he brought her back only twenty minutes later. She was barely able to move. She told me he left really early in the morning for about an hour every day, drove off into the countryside. That was our chance, but the only way out of the room was through a window. It was so small and two stories up, so it didn't have a lock. He had told us there were vicious dogs guarding the property, that we were thirty miles from the nearest town. During winter in Minnesota, with no coat or shoes, that was a death sentence itself. He made escape seem impossible. I think he'd also gotten a little cocky. No one had gotten away from him before—he assumed he had such a hold on us that we wouldn't try.

On my third day, I knew we had run out of time. I didn't know if he would kill Jessica before kidnapping another girl, or if the reason he left that morning was to stalk and abduct his next victim. Either way, I told Jessica, we had to go then or we never would. The girls before us had probably been too big, but both of us were small enough that we could squeeze through the window if we went headfirst. I thought if we stretched, we could reach the drainpipe and shimmy down. I had no idea if it would hold our weight, and once we got down, we would have to contend with dogs and snow in nothing but the pajamas he had given us, but it was the only way.

[Through tears.] I was wrong. I tried reaching for the drainpipe, but I couldn't get hold of it before I lost my balance on the floor inside the room. There wasn't enough space for me to get one leg over the windowsill to hold myself steady. Then, when I was reaching for about the tenth time, just as I started to fall forward, I felt a hand grab on to my clothes. Jessica was behind me, keeping me from falling onto the frozen ground below. I told her no, that we both had to go, but she just shook her head. She didn't even say anything. All she did was hold my hand and nod toward the window.

With her holding me steady, I was able to reach far enough to grasp the drainpipe without losing my balance. She leaned out the window, bracing her shaking legs by putting her feet against the wall inside the cabin. She held me until I was able to grip the drainpipe with my feet, and then she let go.

I didn't have time to think, time to cry. That would come later. I was already freezing when I hit the ground. As far as I know, the dogs were just another lie he told. I never saw or heard them, but I didn't stick around. I ran as fast as I could in the early morning dark. Looking back, I think that's the only reason I survived. If the sun had been up, I wouldn't have seen the gas station lights. There was enough of a glow in the sky that I knew which direction to go, and it was only half a mile away. Just another one of TCK's lies—and it saved my life.

ELLE:

Why have you never appeared in the media before? Surely you could make a fortune by telling your story.

NORA:

I don't want to *profit* off what happened to me. I want TCK to be caught. I want him to be punished for what he did to me, to Jessica —to all those other girls.

ELLE:

What do you think people should know about TCK, based on your personal experience?

NORA:

There were two things that seemed to be important to him: control and fear. Everything he did, every move he made with the girls he kidnapped and every word he spoke to me when I was trembling in his cabin, fed those two needs. The lore that surrounds him now, the mythical status he has created for himself, I think that has fed his need for the last twenty years. I think that's why he hasn't killed again. Not because I escaped and ruined everything, but because he was already getting what he wanted even though he wasn't killing anymore. By never being caught, he has controlled the narrative, and he is still feared.

But if that ever stops, if he ever feels like his work or his legacy is being challenged, he will come back. And if he does, it will get so, so much worse.

26

DJ

1978

Every part of the house was spotless.

It was a Saturday in late September, more than two months since his brothers had died, and the layers of grief and grime spread throughout the house had been visible in every room he entered. While his father was away fishing, DJ threw open the windows to let in the mulch-laced autumn breeze while he swept and vacuumed the floors. He filled a bucket with hot, soapy water and got down on his knees to scrub the linoleum. DJ even used an old toothbrush to clean out all the grooves and dents that filled with extra dirt. It took six hours to wash every item of clothing and bedding in the house and hang it out to snap on the clothesline.

Now the house was clean, filled with the scent of sun-kissed linen and glossy wood. He sat on the front steps, waiting for Josiah to come home. His fingers were red, slightly burnt from the harsh chemicals he'd used to strip the bathtub of months of soap scum and mildew. There had been no rubber gloves under the sink when he looked, so he'd borne the pain, dipping his hands into the bucket over and over to refresh his sponge. His body throbbed, but the tub sparkled.

It was nearly dark by the time Josiah pulled into the driveway, his red truck jolting to a stop at a sloppy angle. The parking brake screeched in protest when he set it. DJ stood, pressing the front of his pants down to get rid of any creases from sitting so long. He had even dressed up, putting on his nice church slacks and a button-up shirt—a "child choker" his brother used to call it, tugging at the collar when he was forced to do up the top button for Easter Mass.

Josiah flung open the door of his truck and heaved himself out onto the driveway. DJ watched as he shuffled around to the back and retrieved a large white pail. It was only when Josiah was halfway up the sidewalk that he noticed his son on the steps, waiting for him.

"What're you doing here?" Josiah asked, his voice slurring. His gaze focused somewhere to the right of DJ's face. He hadn't looked his son in the eye since that night two months ago when he had beaten him. He hadn't touched DJ since, either in affection or anger.

After a moment, he held the pail out to his son. "Never mind. Take these to the shed and clean 'em, like I taught you."

DJ took the pail, the thin metal handle biting into his sore fingers as he carried it back to the shed. When he got to the table his father had set up specifically for fish cleaning, DJ looked down at his shirt. He couldn't risk getting fish guts and scales on this, but he couldn't go inside empty-handed. It was still warm, even more so in the shed away from the cool night breeze. Not knowing what else to do, he stripped off his shirt and trousers and hung them over a hook on the door. Then he opened the pail and pulled out the first fish.

He put his index finger slightly inside the walleye's mouth to hold it steady before poking the pointy end of the knife in just at the edge of the cheeks. The glassy dead eye stared up at him. His father had taught him to always remove the cheeks first, the best part of the walleye, to make sure he wouldn't forget later. DJ traced the circumference of the cheek with the blade until he had gone all the way around it. Then he pushed his finger under the broken skin and peeled the meat away, setting it aside. Moving the fin, DJ sliced into the side and then up next to the backbone, his knife vibrating against the bone as he slid it under the flesh from head to tail. Once he had a good fillet, he flipped it over and repeated on the other side before pulling the chunks of meat off both. He discarded the first fish car-cass in the garbage can by the workstation and pulled out another, blinking away the exhaustion in his eyes.

By the time he was finished with all seven fish, DJ's chest, arms, and hands were flecked with scales and blood. He had a few nicks and cuts on his fingers, but he had a plate full of the most beauti-ful fillets he'd ever cut, so he walked into the kitchen through the back door with his head high. Finally, he'd get to see how his dad felt about the clean house.

When he got inside, Josiah was sitting at the kitchen table, beer in hand and hair wet from a shower. DJ put the fillets in the fridge and went to the sink, where he splashed water and soap up his arms. He dried himself off with a towel before turning around to see his father regarding him with the bottle raised to his lips.

Josiah took a long drink. After he set the bottle on the table, he looked DJ up and down. "Happened to your clothes?"

"Didn't want them to get dirty."

"So, you just left your Sunday best on the floor of the shed?"

DJ shook his head. "No, sir. I hung them on the hook."

"Don't sass me, boy."

"I'll go get them."

"Nah, don't bother. They're already full of dust anyway. You'll have to wash them tomorrow."

DJ sucked his bottom lip into his mouth and looked around the kitchen. It still made his chest swell a little when he saw how good everything looked. He couldn't remember the house ever being this clean. Charles and Thomas definitely never made things look this good. But Josiah didn't seem to care.

After a moment, his father looked at him again. "Well, what are you waiting for? Go get cleaned up."

With a nod, DJ walked up the stairs to the bathroom. His mouth fell open when he flicked on the light. The bathroom was splattered with mud; blades of grass and small pebbles littered the floor. The bathtub was empty, but there was a fine layer of sand and dirt sit-ting in puddles of water at the bottom. There were spots of shaving cream and fingerprints on the mirror above the sink. Josiah had left his wet towel in a heap on the floor.

The injustice built up inside him like a storm, but he bit the insides of his cheeks to force his mouth to stay shut. Josiah had lost everything. He was doing the best he could, and DJ was all he had left.

DJ pulled a cloth out of the linen closet, wet it down, and got on his knees to scrub up the mess.

27

Elle

January 18, 2020

The street in front of Sash's house was lined with cars. Elle blinked at them in the glare of the early morning sunlight, seeing if she recognized any of the license plates. It was odd, thinking of Sash spending time with anyone other than her and Martín. Besides her and Tina, Elle didn't really have other friends—sometimes she forgot that made her the strange one.

Her best friend hadn't answered the phone last night after everything happened. Knowing Sash probably didn't want to see her, Elle had sent Martín to check on her, but even he got turned away by a police officer at her front door. Elle had sat up on the couch all night, alternating between sobbing and staring at the wall, hoping for a call that would let her know Natalie had been found.

None came.

Conversation rumbled inside Sash's house, as though a meeting or a cocktail party was underway. A peek through the sliver between the window and the curtain indoors showed a room full of people wearing formal clothing and grim expressions. It looked like a wake.

Raising her hand, Elle knocked on the front door. A moment later, someone answered—a young man with thick dark hair slicked in a cresting wave on top of his head. "Are you here for the prayer service?" he asked.

Interesting. As far as Elle knew, Sash never put much stock in religion, but maybe she had started getting into it to support Natalie's interest in the Bible. Of course, if there was ever a time to pray, it was now.

Without a word, Elle nodded. The man gestured her inside, and she followed, unsettled at being led by a stranger into a house she knew so well. When they rounded the corner into the living room, Elle's eyes widened at the sight of her best friend surrounded by at least twenty people. They all had their heads bowed, and one woman wearing a pink sweater was praying out loud, her left hand raised and extended toward Sash. The man who had answered the door grabbed a chair from the kitchen and set it down in a silent offer. Elle smiled at him and sat, joining the staggered circle.

"What are you doing here?"

Sash's voice cut through the middle of the pink-sweater woman's prayer. Everyone's head seemed to lift and turn toward Elle in one fluid susurration of movement.

"I . . . I came to see how you're doing."

"You shouldn't be here."

Elle flinched but did not look away from her friend's burning gaze. She ignored the murmurs and awkward shifting of the other people around them. "I'm sorry for what happened, Sash."

"You're *sorry?* My daughter called you. You were supposed to be there for her. You promised you would be there for her. But you were too busy investigating your stupid serial killer." A bitter laugh bubbled from her lips. "In fact, you're *still* too busy investigating him to do what's best for Natalie."

This time, Elle did look away, staring at the green carpet with its worn pink flowers—left over from the previous owner. Natalie used to call it their "jungle floor" when she was little. Maybe Sash was right. Maybe she had let herself get sucked into this case, despite the years of preparation and practice it took to get here. If her obsession with finding TCK had caused Natalie harm, she would never forgive herself.

"What do you want me to do?" Elle asked.

Sash reached out to a woman sitting next to her, clasped her hand tightly, and looked at Elle. Her nostrils flared and tears welled up in her eyes. "I want you to find her. And I want you to bring her home to me like you promised you always would. Until then, I don't want to see you."

Elle licked her lower lip and nodded, forcing down her own tears. Unable to think of anything else to say, she stood up and walked out of the room.

Outside, the sun bounced off the snow with a blinding glare. Elle zipped her coat and looked up and down the street. She half expected to find officers searching for more clues, but they must have been satisfied there was nothing else to find. Slowly, she walked home, eyes on the icy ground as she went, just in case she saw something the others had missed. There was nothing of Natalie left behind, though— only grit and ice and salt.

When she got to her front door, Elle put the key in and paused. She couldn't face the idea of sitting in an empty house all day. Martín had gone to work, hoping to keep his mind occupied. All that awaited her inside was a studio full of notes and tasks she had no interest in sorting through.

If she was going to fulfill her promise and bring Natalie home, her best bet was to work with Ayaan. If she could convince the commander her suspicions about TCK were a momentary lapse in judgment, brought on by fatigue and heightened emotions, maybe Ayaan would let her keep helping with the investigation. There must be something she could do, even if Ayaan wouldn't allow her in the field. She'd do paperwork, review security camera footage—anything so long as it wasn't sitting here in this house.

Taking her key from the lock, she turned around and went to her car, grateful Ayaan had gotten one of the officers to drive it back from the station last night.

The station was as hectic as Elle had ever seen it. Several officers milled around the kitchen, pouring cups of coffee and trading stories over a box of muffins. Probably from Ronny, the receptionist. His husband owned a bakery down the road. A few of them offered her a polite nod, one extending a paper plate with a pastry on it, which she waved away. She couldn't remember the last time she'd eaten, but she wasn't hungry. Sam Hyde stood by the sink, stirring milk into a cup of coffee, and his gaze was curious when he looked at her. She ducked her head, hating herself for looking like a dog with its tail between its legs.

Through the glass walls of Ayaan's office, Elle could see the commander leaned over a stack of papers. Ayaan raised her head when Elle knocked. For a moment, she just stared at her; then she tipped her chin to the side, a faint gesture to come in. Elle opened the door and stepped inside.

"Elle, how can I help you?"

Ayaan didn't invite her to sit, so Elle stood behind the chair and shifted her weight from one foot to the other.

"I wanted to talk to you about the cases. I know you have reservations about me right now, but I really think I can offer some insights as to who the kidnapper might be."

"Kidnappers."

Elle froze. "What?"

"As far as we know, these are two separate incidents."

"Ayaan—"

"The victimology is completely different. Amanda is a child of a dual-parent household. She went missing in the early morning performing her normal routine—waiting at the bus stop. The event was orchestrated so that her mother would be distracted at the precise time Amanda was taken, which shows careful planning. A witness saw the abductor, but whoever kidnapped her was obviously brave enough to do so anyway."

Elle clenched her fists.

Ayaan continued. "Conversely, Natalie is from a single-parent home. She went missing late in the afternoon when doing something out of character that made her vulnerable—walking home alone. Nobody apparently saw or heard anything, which suggests she didn't scream or make any loud noise. It was likely a crime of opportunity. She was in the wrong place at the wrong time, and someone took advantage of her vulnerability."

Elle shook her head, but Ayaan lifted her hand. "Elle, you're blending your podcast investigation with these kidnappings, but there is just no evidence they're connected. It's understandable, though; I've gotten confused and seen connections between my own cases before. It happens. But Natalie is like your own child. There's no way you could be involved in her case. I think it's best if you take a step back for now. I spoke to the Jordans, and they have agreed. Sam's caseload is light at the moment, so he is assisting me."

Somehow, the idea of Sam taking her place was an extra twist of the knife. Elle bit back her arguments and tried to force down the panic rising inside her. "But, Ayaan, I . . . I have to do something."

Ayaan's eyes were wide, gleaming with pity as she said, "I know you want to help."

"I do."

"But you clearly have blinders on when it comes to TCK, and it stops you from thinking clearly. I can't work with you anymore. I'm sorry; it's too risky."

With that, the last bit of hope flickering inside Elle vanished, a burning wick drowned in hot wax.

\\\\\\\\\\

While she was waiting at the elevator doors, a man's voice called Elle's name. She turned to see Sam walking toward her from the other side of the security doors, one hand out.

"Hold up," he said.

The bell dinged, and she was tempted to just get on and leave. The last thing she needed was another rant about how she was an armchair detective who got in the way of real police work. But she paused with her hand on the open door, knowing he would just follow her downstairs if she fled.

He came through the lobby and nodded at the elevator. "Can I ride with you?"

She looked between him and the open doors, confused. Then she shrugged. "Sure, why not." They got on together, and she pressed the button for the first floor before turning to face him, arms crossed. "What do you want?"

He glanced away from her. It was the first time she'd ever seen him look anything but cocky and smug, and it was a disconcerting shift. "I know you've been working that kidnapping case with Ayaan, but I was just wondering if you had found anything further on Leo Toca. You know, about what he was going to give you on TCK."

She studied him, waiting for the punch line, but his expression didn't change. He was actually asking. He must be really stuck. "I don't know, I've been pretty busy doing my fake master's degree and talking to all my fake witnesses while doing my job as a fake detective."

He crossed his arms. "Come on, give me a break."

"Why should I?" They arrived at the first floor and the doors opened. She stepped out into the building lobby. "You can't suddenly decide you want my help after telling me to butt out of your case."

Sam scratched the back of his head, eyes flashing. "I'm sorry, okay? I just . . . I'm at a dead end right now. I've interviewed the people he worked with, looked into his phone records, even called his parents in Mexico. I went to Stillwater and tried to track down Luisa, but I didn't have any luck. I'm not even sure who she was seeing there. Duane is still looking good for the murder, but I don't like that I can't find Leo's ex. I've got a BOLO on her car, but so far no hits. Then Ayaan basically handed me the Amanda Jordan case because she's treating it like a homicide, so I've been reviewing the notes and tips all night."

"Wait, what?" Elle's stomach sank the way it did when she looked down from a tall building. "Did you say Ayaan is treating Amanda's case like a homicide? Like, officially?"

For a moment, Sam blinked at her. Then he swore and looked around, as if checking to see whether there were any witnesses. They were alone in the lobby, though. "I thought you knew. She's been missing for four days, with no sign of life. There's a very good chance she is dead. That's why I'm assisting her now."

Elle shook her head, pushing down a wave of anger. It was understandable that Ayaan would hold information back from her, but it still felt like a betrayal. She had never been a part of this investigation, not really. Then she realized something. If Sam was following her, asking for help with his murder investigation, he probably didn't know yet that Ayaan had removed her from the Jordan case. This might be her only chance to get some more details on its progress before he found out she was persona non grata at Minneapolis PD.

"Were any of the tips from the composite sketch promising?" she asked.

Sam let out a frustrated breath. "Not really. One person thought they saw a van matching the getaway vehicle's description heading north on Snelling a few days ago, but that's it. Now, can you help me with the Toca case or not?"

"Not." She thought for a moment, then her gaze flicked to Sam's face. "Or maybe so. You know what's on Snelling, don't you?"

He stared at her for a moment before his eyes lit up. "The auto shop. Let's go."

"Me too?" she asked, trying not to sound excited.

"You gonna wait until I change my mind?"

"Nope."

While Sam drove, she scrolled through the news on her phone. All the local papers had an article about Natalie, although they barely gave her name a cursory mention. To everyone else, she was simply *another young girl goes missing in the southern suburbs of Minneapolis.* Elle blinked tears away, pushed her worry for Natalie into the dusty compartment in her mind she had developed when she worked at CPS. That was where she put all the rage and terror and pain until she could breathe again, focus again. It had been the only thing that made the job bearable. She knew Martin had one too—as did everyone who worked in jobs that dealt with the worst of humanity.

At Simple Mechanic, Duane Grove stood outside in front of the massive garage door that looked like it could accommodate a semi-truck. His bristled cheeks were flushed, and he had a scowl on his face when he saw Sam and Elle step out of the car. No smile necessary. Not customers.

"Hiya, Duane," Sam said, his tone chipper.

"What are you doing here?" Duane looked back and forth between her and Sam. "Hey, aren't you the lady who—"

"Yeah, I'm the one who found you with Leo's body."

His face reddened further. "Detective, me and my guys answered all your questions last week. You had our shop closed for almost a whole day, made us lose a few grand in business. I told y'all, I had nothing to do with his murder, and I don't know who does."

"I'm not here about Leo." Sam looked at Elle and then back at Duane. "*We* are here about a car. A van, actually."

Duane sighed with a little growl behind it, looked over his shoulder, and then gestured them toward the inside area attached to the garage. They followed him, and Elle relished the blast of heat as they entered his little fun-size office. There was barely enough space to walk around the desk, but Duane squeezed past with a practiced ease. Elle sat in the only other available chair, letting Sam watch the door.

Plastic storage drawers and containers were stacked floor to ceiling against the wall to Elle's right, so close one brushed her elbow when she set it on the armrest. The small patches of carpet she could see were gray with years of ground-in dirt and sand. Smudges of motor oil streaked the surface of the light brown desk where Duane rested his clenched hands.

"All right, what's this van?" Duane asked. He pulled his beanie off, rubbing a hand over his shaved head.

"I'm working on a case," Sam said. "We have a blue 2001 Dodge Ram 1500 van, no plates, fleeing the scene. Seen anything like that around here lately?" Sam took out his phone and showed it to Leo. Elle could see the same security footage she and Ayaan had reviewed a couple days ago on the screen.

Pushing his lower lip out pensively, Duane shrugged. He barely glanced at the photo. "Do you mean, have I changed oil for a car like that lately? Probably. I see about thirty cars a day in here, sometimes more."

Sam laughed. "Oh, Duane, you might not be a murderer, but you and I both know you're not a mechanic either. Or at least, that's not all you are. I've looked into you the past week. Talked to some of your friends locked up in Hennepin County, and it seems like you run a pretty lucrative 'car part repurposing' business in here."

Duane's expression did not change, but he said nothing to argue. Sam continued: "I might not be able to get you for Leo's murder, but

I've heard some interesting stories. Now, I'm happy to bring my findings to the Robbery Unit and see what they might have to say about it, or I could write your buddies off as jailhouse snitches that would say anything to get a deal. It's really up to you."

After a moment, Duane licked across his teeth and jerked his head toward Elle. "Seriously, man, what the hell is she doing here?"

Elle's teeth came together as Sam said, "Never mind that. What can you tell me about this van?"

"What do you want to know?"

Sam smiled. "I would like to know if anyone drove a blue 2001 Dodge Ram 1500 van into your shop in the last four days, and if they did, I would like you to take me to it right now."

Duane looked at Elle again, but she just glared back. He sighed. "Okay, yeah. Someone brought a van like that in here the other night."

"Which night?" Sam asked.

"I don't know? Like, three nights ago, I guess."

Elle jumped in. "Which night? Monday or Tuesday? Where is it?"

"I don't know! It's . . . it's not here anymore."

She slammed her hands down on the armrests and slid to the edge of the chair, ready to strangle him. "What do you mean, it's not here anymore?" Then she paused, horrified. "You . . . you stripped it already, didn't you?"

Duane didn't even have the sense to look ashamed. He jutted his chin out and crossed his arms. "What are you going to do?" he asked. "Arrest me?"

"Not us." Sam crossed his arms to match Duane's. "We'll let the Robbery Unit take care of that."

"Whoa, whoa, whoa, hold on." Duane held up his hands, palms out. "I might not have the van anymore, but I can tell you who brought it in." He waggled his eyebrows.

Elle scoffed and cut her eyes to Sam. "And he's not going to tell us without some kind of deal. Guess this is what we get, asking a sleazebag like him for help."

Duane shrugged, a cocky smile slicing through his ruddy face. "You know what they say: careful what you wish for."

"You know the guy who brought it in? You're sure?" Elle asked.

"Don't even bother trying to lie your way out of this, either," Sam cut in. "You're not that hard to find if your lead ends up being a dud."

"Are you kidding? I'd never lie to a fine, upstanding detective." Duane's eyes flicked to Elle's face and he gestured at her. "And the nosy armchair detective with a radio show."

Before Elle could respond, Duane continued. "That's right, I knew I recognized your voice. Leo used to play your shit all the time in the shop. Fake, bleeding-heart crap. Maybe if you hadn't gotten him all riled up, thinking he could play detective, he wouldn't have gone and got himself killed. You're no investigator; you're just a cocky bitch with a microphone and nobody to tell you when to shut your mouth."

For a moment, Elle stared at him. Everything he said was what she had been worrying about for days, since she walked in and found Leo lying dead on the floor. But the constant buzz of terror in her mind when she thought of Amanda and Natalie, the thought that he could know more than what he was saying—that made her brave. It made her fearless.

Her face stretched into a wide grin, teeth bared. "Don't you see, Duane? That's the best part. I'm not a cop. I'm just a citizen who cares about finding that van. I'm just the host of a podcast with hundreds of thousands of listeners who would happily give your name and place of work to the whole internet and let them know you not only got rid of evidence in a little girl's kidnapping, but then gave us the runaround when we asked for your help finding the guy who brought it in. But don't worry. People on the internet are notoriously happy to hear both sides of the story when it comes to crimes against children."

Duane's face drained of color. "What the fuck?" He turned to Sam. "You're just going to let her threaten me like that?"

Sam's brow wrinkled in feigned confusion. "I'm sorry? I wasn't listening."

"His name's Eduardo, okay? I don't know his last name." Duane's eyes skittered between Elle and Sam. Drops of sweat broke out across his forehead, among the dark stubble on his scalp. "Don't talk about me on your podcast, okay? I know the kind of thing you do, taking clips of what people say out of context and analyzing them so it sounds like they meant something different. I'm telling you the truth —that's all I know. And you didn't tell me this was about a fucking kid getting kidnapped. I would have told you everything right away. Geez."

Elle ignored the insults. Men who took issue with her voice and theories on the cases she investigated were old news at this point.

"Seriously? That's all you have for us?" Sam walked around the desk to face Duane. His voice was casual, friendly. It made him even more frightening. "We came all this way, man. I'm sure you have more information about the guy than that. You probably know everyone who comes in and out of here, don't you?"

"Uh, yeah, I guess."

"Course you do! Smooth businessman like yourself. You can't afford to forget a face. Sure you can't remember anything more about this guy?"

Duane's expression changed, the color returning to his cheeks. He managed to stare up at Sam in both fear and admiration. "H-his name's Eduardo. He's about your height and Mexican. Or Central American—I don't know. He works at Mitchell University, cleaning the floors and shit. That's all I got, I swear."

Sam stood up with a wide, genuine-looking smile, and clapped Duane on the shoulder. Duane flinched, and Elle smirked, knowing Sam was squeezing hard. "Great, thanks, man." He turned to her, teeth still showing, and lifted his hand in a wrap-it-up motion. "Let's go."

28

Justice Delayed podcast

January 16, 2020

Transcript: Season 5, Episode 6

ELLE VOICE-OVER:
Twenty-one.

Seven.

Three.

These are the numbers that run through my brain, every moment of every day. Turning them over, pushing them together and apart — dividing, multiplying, adding, subtracting. They repeat over and over in the Countdown Killer's series, so much that it's noticeable when they don't. The 1996 TCK murders don't fit with the pattern the way he established it in 1997, but I am confident they belong to him nonetheless. So, it must mean something that they were different. Killing does not come naturally to us, no matter what anyone might tell you. Even those who seem to have been born with the desire to end people's lives have to learn the craft of murder. And they make mistakes — sometimes throughout their careers, sometimes just at the beginning.

It never made sense that TCK started with a twenty-year-old victim when we know his obsession with the number twenty-one. For the past two months, my producer Tina and I have been looking into every missing person and murder we could find in the area, hoping to find something we might have missed. Hoping to find the start of the countdown.

[SOUND BREAK: A phone ringing.]

SYKES:
Hello?

ELLE:
Detective Sykes. You asked me to call?

SYKES:
Elle, I think you did it. I . . . I really think it's him.

[THEME MUSIC + INTRO]

ELLE VOICE-OVER:
Sometimes people ask me why I do this podcast. They accuse me of acting like I am capable of something police are not. But replacing police has never been my goal with *Justice Delayed*. My goal has always been to bring attention to stories that have faded into obscurity, to focus new resources and ideas on investigations that have long gone cold. A couple weeks ago, just such a case was brought to my attention by a listener. Formerly a resident of Eden Prairie, Christina Presley now lives in rural North Dakota. She kindly met me halfway, in a little roadside truck stop outside Fargo. Apologies if you hear more background noise than normal; we've done our best to cut it down, but it was a game day, so there will be a few cheers now and then. Skol, Vikings.

Christina is a white woman in her mid-sixties. Having spent her early adult life staying home as a mom of four, she now works part-time for the local library in her town. She is a kind-looking woman, but there are deep lines around her mouth that appear when she tells me her story. We talked for nearly two hours, and despite all that she had to say, I never once saw her cry. Grief can be like chronic pain— what is so sharp at first becomes a part of you until you forget what it was like to live without it. When the ache is constant for years, shedding tears over it feels excessive.

[SOUND BREAK: Distant referee's whistle; a low rumble of conversation.]

ELLE:
Thank you for agreeing to meet me here. Like I told you over the phone, my police contact, Detective Sykes, was able to get ahold of the case file. But before we go through that, can you please tell me about Kerry.

CHRISTINA:
Of course. Kerry was a senior in 1996, studying physics. It was the start of spring semester, just four months until graduation. All our kids made us proud, but we knew Kerry had something special. All the professors seemed to agree, and doctoral programs around the country were offering fellowships. But then . . . only a couple weeks after returning to campus, he disappeared.

ELLE:
When did you find out?

CHRISTINA:
It took a few days. That was back before everyone had cell phones, you know, and Kerry would usually call us just once or twice a week. The first indication we got that anything was wrong was a call from one of his housemates. None of them had seen him, so they wanted to check if he had come to visit us. Of course, we were immediately worried. It wasn't like him to disappear without telling us. I called his girlfriend to see if he was with her, but she said they had broken up four days before. They had been very close, and I knew Kerry was thinking about marriage, so this made me even more concerned. My husband and I thought . . . We thought maybe he had gone somewhere to blow off steam, maybe did something silly like fly to Vegas for a few days. But it still didn't explain why he wouldn't contact us.

ELLE:

[Over the sound of cheering in the background.] When did you report him missing?

CHRISTINA:

We never filed an official report. We talked to police, of course, but they said Kerry was a low-risk victim and was probably just taking a few days to himself. Dealing with the stress of being a senior, getting dumped, you know. And then . . . then they called us a few days later to say they'd found his body.

ELLE VOICE-OVER:

Kerry Presley was found half-buried in a snowdrift on the banks of the Mississippi, just a few miles from the house he rented with four guys from his university. At first, police believed it to be a suicide. There was a rope around his neck, tied to a tree behind him, and his body was slumped forward as if he had used its weight to hang himself.

ELLE:

Can you go through the autopsy results for us, Martín?

MARTÍN:

Sure. First, let me clarify something. As a medical examiner, I am asked to determine two things in the autopsy room: the cause of death and the manner of death. Essentially, what killed the person and how they died—whether it was homicide, suicide, natural causes, et cetera. Like you said, the scene was set up to make it look like Kerry had taken his own life. Preliminary MOD was suicide, but once the ME cut their case, things got more complicated.

ELLE:

Just for listeners who haven't heard that term before, when you talk about the medical examiner cutting their case, you mean performing an autopsy, right?

MARTÍN:

Yes, that's right. Without going into the gory details, the ME confirmed that Kerry's hyoid bone was fractured, a classic sign of strangulation. However, there was no indication that a rope or similar ligature was used to effect his death. The marks you would expect to see around the throat of a hanging victim—bruises, hemorrhaging—were not present. In fact, the autopsy report states that based on the lack of abrasions on the skin, it's likely the rope was not put around his neck until long after he was dead.

ELLE:

So, it was staged to look like a suicide.

MARTÍN:

Correct. At least, that's how it appears to me. However, when the ME examined the victim's stomach, he found dark red and brown spots covering the lining.

ELLE:

What does that mean?

MARTÍN:

It happens when the body's temperature is dropping, as the blood supply redirects, trying to save essential organs. Despite the strangulation injuries, Kerry did not die of asphyxiation. His cause of death was officially hypothermia, and based on my review of the autopsy results, I would have to agree with that. Which brings us to the manner of death. The investigation determined that the suicide was staged, which automatically makes the average person assume it was a murder. But the ME on the case could not definitively prove whether this was a homicide or an accident that was later covered up to look like Kerry took his own life. Hypothermia is an extremely rare method of homicide, so it's understandable why the ME was loathe to make that determination, despite pressure from the family. At the same time, it makes sense why they would want homicide to be the manner of death, as it would force police to investigate it more seriously.

ELLE VOICE-OVER:
Unfortunately, the official manner of death on Kerry's death certificate was listed as "undetermined," and the family's fears soon came true: with no real leads on who had staged the suicide and no proof that foul play had occurred, police soon moved on to more pressing cases. And the Presley family has been left without answers for more than twenty years.

ELLE:
Thank you for sharing your son's story with me. I'm so sorry about what you have gone through. Not getting any real answers, having your son's death just fade into the background. It's gut-wrenching.

CHRISTINA:
It is. No one seemed to care why or how he froze to death, or who would make it look like he'd killed himself. It never made sense to me. How could they just not care? Anyway, when I was listening to your podcast the other day, you said something about trying to find TCK's first victim. You wanted to know about any unexplained or unsolved deaths around the same time as Beverly Anderson's, and so I emailed you about Kerry. I figured it wasn't connected, but I don't know . . . I just needed someone to listen to me, you know?

ELLE:
I do. And you're right, it does seem unrelated. Nothing about Kerry's death looks like a TCK murder. But your email caught my eye, mostly because you sound like so many of the other mothers I talk to for these cases. Women who have waited years, decades, for answers that never came. So, we looked into it. And Mrs. Presley, we think you might be right.

CHRISTINA:
[Inaudible.]

ELLE:

Take your time.

CHRISTINA:

You . . . are you sure?

ELLE:

Detective Sykes got me a copy of the case file, and we've gone through it together. Based on statements from you and his friends, it appears Kerry went missing on the first of February, 1996. That's three days before TCK's first confirmed victim, Beverly Anderson.

CHRISTINA:

Oh. I . . . Is there more?

ELLE:

Yes. There were multiple witnesses who walked the same trail along that part of the river who said they hadn't seen Kerry there the day before he was discovered. Because of that, police thought he was probably placed there the day he was found. The medical examiner could not determine time of death because his body was frozen, but the contents of his stomach were only partially digested and appeared to contain pineapple and some pork substance. His girlfriend said they'd had Hawaiian pizza the last time she saw him, the night they broke up. If that's what it was, then he would have been dead within hours of that.

CHRISTINA:

So, you're saying he was killed the night he went missing and just . . . just kept somewhere?

ELLE:

I'm sorry, I truly hate having to tell you this. But I can promise you one thing, Mrs. Presley. If your son really was killed by TCK, I just got one step closer to finding him. But no matter what, I'm going to do everything in my power to get justice for your son.

ELLE VOICE-OVER:

Kerry was twenty-one years old. Like the other two victims in 1996, he was a college student in the Minneapolis area. Even though he died in a different way from the young women, other aspects fit the pattern. He went missing three days before Beverly. His body was found seven days after he vanished. The reason he's never popped up as a potential victim is because he was killed in such a different way, and of course, because he's a man and the rest of TCK's victims are women. As I looked into Christina Presley's eyes, though, I couldn't help but think of the irony. Even when his victim was a man, TCK still found a way to destroy a woman's life.

Everything about the 1996 murders seems to indicate TCK was finding his feet, and I actually think it makes perfect sense that his first victim would be so different. It explains why he changed. He obviously didn't intend to kill Kerry, at least not the way he did. The murder is sloppy, unplanned—nothing like the deliberate poisoning we see with the girls.

Maybe he strangled Kerry in a moment of passion, and—thinking he'd killed him—he panicked and brought the body to wherever he kept the others later on. If he dumped Kerry in a barn or some type of outbuilding and left him for days, TCK would never know that he really died of hypothermia. I can only hope that Kerry never regained consciousness before it happened.

The first victim being a man tells us something about the profile, too, I think. It tells us that TCK's initial instinct to kill was probably not born out of his hatred of women, but that—finding no satisfaction in murdering a young man—he switched to young women and girls after. If Kerry is the first TCK victim, and I believe he is, that means that the numbers have always mattered to him. The medical evidence proves Kerry was killed within hours of his disappearance, but he was not found until seven days later.

Even if TCK did not enjoy killing a man, he found a way to be fulfilled by it. He found a way to include his signature—by waiting until the seventh day to let his body be discovered. I keep thinking about that Bible verse Nora saw in TCK's cabin: "Six days you shall work, but on the seventh day you shall rest." There are many meanings I could infer from this, but here's what I think. I think that producing a body on the seventh day, making sure it is found, that is what gives TCK fulfillment. That is how he finds rest.

Staging Kerry's death to look like a suicide, though, that also tells me something. It tells me that TCK did not want credit for that murder, and the only reason a killer would spend so much time staging a body and risk discovery is if he had some sort of known relationship or connection to him. And that is what I'm going to find.

Next time, on *Justice Delayed* . . .

29

DJ

1989 to 1992

It wasn't enough for DJ's father when he excelled in school. It wasn't enough when he was specially chosen to serve as an altar boy at their church's midnight Mass on Christmas. It wasn't enough when he received scholarships to summer math programs.

Nothing he did made his father look at him the way he had looked at his older sons — the pride, the love that had shone in his eyes. His father remained a husk of the man he used to be; the shape of Josiah was there for everyone to see, but inside he was hollow.

DJ left home when he was sixteen, after graduating high school early. He took all the money he'd saved mowing lawns for the last two summers and bought a bus ticket to New York City. He did not say goodbye.

New York was beyond anything he could have imagined, despite watching every movie and TV show set in the city that he could get his hands on. Nothing prepared him for the noise, for the constant light, for the lack of space or privacy. He shared a studio apartment with three other young men, contributing cash to the bowl for shared groceries for several weeks until he realized he was the only one doing so. After that, he bought his own instant noodles, which he hid under his mattress to keep them from the others' sticky fingers, and fresh vegetables, which everyone else seemed to leave alone.

DJ worked several odd jobs, lying about his age to get cash in hand as a bartender at night and carrying parcels on a messenger bike by day. Living with his nightmare roommates and saving every extra cent paid off when his acceptance letter finally arrived eighteen months later—he was going to Harvard, with just enough money in his account for the first year's tuition and board. He left the apartment without notice, taking nothing but a duffel bag with his best clothes.

Harvard was another new world. After nearly two years of being surrounded by cheap beer, marijuana smoke, and strung-out slackers, the academic community was like a salve that soothed a persistent itch. There were people who had the same passion for numbers that he did. People who knew equations and formulas he'd never heard of. Philosophy professors who would not deride his references to religion, but instead engaged him on them.

After excelling in his first year, he qualified for scholarships and was able to drop to three work shifts a week. Every semester, he posted his perfect grades to Josiah. It was the only communication between them. DJ never received a response.

He was well into his second year at Harvard when he met Loretta. She was doing the same degree as he, a joint concentration in math and physics—one of the few women doing so in 1990. DJ had never had much luck with women, having grown up in a house with only males and attending an all-boys Catholic school. The few times he'd allowed himself to be dragged out to a club in New York, his roommates had scoffed at his inability to score. He never drank, never tried to pick up women—simply watched as his roommates made fools of themselves on the prowl, bolstered by the liquor running through their veins. When they brought their conquests home, he lay in bed awake, listening to them move and groan in the dark of their apartment.

But Loretta was different. As her name suggested, she had grown up old-fashioned, in a house with values and morals. She wore high-collared shirts buttoned to the top, skirts below the knee, and thick-heeled plain black shoes. Her reddish-brown hair fell around slender shoulders, thick bangs framing her blue eyes. The most intimidating thing about her was her brain, and DJ knew he was a match for it. So, he asked her to dinner one night, ready to blow his whole week's worth of food budget to take her to the nicest restaurant within walking distance of the campus.

He met her at her dorm and held his breath when she walked out the door. A pale pink blouse floated around her thin frame, her long black skirt swishing against her calves. She had her hair pinned back, exposing her neck and just the edge of her collarbone. She looked stunning, prepared, innocent—all for him. DJ held out his arm like he'd seen men do in movies, and Loretta linked hers through it with a shy smile.

The dinner passed with an animated discussion about their classes and classmates, debates about the merits of string theory, and the necessary overview of their individual histories—which for DJ's part, was heavily edited. By the time he walked her home, he was convinced she was the One.

They began spending every spare moment together, preparing for exams and quizzing each other with flash cards. After a few months, he convinced her to quit her job at one of the college cafés so they could have more time together. That gave them several more hours each week, outside of classes and DJ's after-hours security job on campus.

By the time they entered their third year at Harvard, DJ was saving for a modest ring and looking for a place for them to live together. He sat down one night in October and wrote a letter to his father, the first in a long time. Fueled by half a bottle of scotch, he laid out all the ways Josiah had wronged him, everything DJ had done to prove himself. He told his father he had found a woman who loved him, a woman who was smart and pure and beautiful. Then he selected two photos to send with it: one of him and Loretta together, and another of just her—a yearbook photo that highlighted her gorgeous features and soft eyes.

When she visited him for their date the next day, DJ left her for a moment to retrieve his coat, and when he turned around, she was standing by his desk with his letter in her hand.

"What is this?" she asked, turning to him.

"It's nothing! What are you doing reading my private letters?"

She drew back as if slapped, glaring at him. "I saw my picture, so I looked to see why it was there. Your letter was so . . . mean, DJ. I've never known you to be so cruel."

He took a step toward her, getting close enough to see the tiny muscles around her lips tremble. "You have no idea what you're talking about. You have no idea what my life has been like. Now, let's go."

But instead of going with him to the movies as planned, Loretta whirled around on her short heel and stalked out of his apartment.

It was the biggest fight they'd ever had. His friends advised him to let her cool off and she would come to him, but after three days, he couldn't stand it anymore. He went to her dorm with a dozen roses and told her he'd thrown away the letter, which wasn't completely true. He had "thrown" it in the mailbox. Eventually, she relented and let him inside.

Their relationship changed after that. When he saw her, DJ's stomach dipped and rolled, but not from infatuation the way it had when they first met. Now it was pure anxiety. He found himself following her on campus, hiding behind trees and buildings to observe the way she interacted with other men. Was she being unfaithful? Why did she look at him that way? Was she getting ready to leave him? He tried to talk to her about it, but when he told her he felt that things had changed between them, she dismissed it.

Like him, Loretta was planning to go to graduate school and was researching programs at the same time as doing her coursework. She started to put off dates, claiming to be swamped with assignments. Every time he asked which universities she was looking at for grad study, she avoided the question. DJ could see her whole life formulating in front of her, and he was becoming less and less sure that he would be a part of it.

On Loretta's twenty-first birthday, DJ stood outside a restaurant on the Charles River that her parents had booked for the celebration, with sweat trickling between his shoulder blades and the lump of a ring box in his pocket. Through the glass, golden light illuminated thirty or so people milling about with drinks in hand. Serving staff weaved between them, balancing trays laden with finger food. Loretta's mother had organized everything, but DJ had advised on her favorite foods. Apparently, her tastes had changed since she left her parents' home in South Boston nearly four years before, and he was proud that he knew things about their daughter that they did not.

With a swipe across his upper lip to clear away the sweat, DJ reached out and opened the restaurant door. Loretta greeted him in a vivid red dress. It was so unlike her, so much more alluring than her usual clothing, that the air left his lungs for a moment.

"New dress?" he murmured, placing a kiss on her cheek.

"Yes, you like it?" Her fingers pressed into his shoulder as they embraced.

"It's a bit . . . much," he said, before he could think better of it. Loretta blinked, stunned, and then he was swept away by her father.

"Does she know?" Loretta's father asked. He'd given DJ permission to ask for his daughter's hand only two days ago, on the condition that he would support whatever graduate school she chose to attend. DJ had been nervous asking, not just for the obvious reasons but because he suspected Loretta had been planning to break up with him. Obviously, she hadn't expressed any such plans to her parents—a fact which made him wonder if he was imagining her distance in recent weeks.

DJ shook his head. "It's a surprise. I was thinking I would ask her when the cake is served, after we've all sung but before she blows out the candles. I want a photograph of the light dancing in her eyes when she says yes."

Loretta's father chuckled. "You really are something, aren't you?"

Not knowing whether that was a compliment or an insult, DJ could only nod. "Sir."

The next hour passed in a blur of food, wine, and pointless conversation. Every single member of Loretta's family who lived within a hundred miles seemed to have come out for her birthday, and he spoke to each of them. They were to be his family soon too, so it was just as well they got to know him.

Then, at last, his moment arrived, and suddenly DJ felt like he was unprepared. He hadn't had a chance to speak to Loretta since she'd walked away hurt by his comment on her dress, and now he was unsure whether she would welcome a proposal when they were in the middle of a tiff. Although, what better way to say *I'm sorry* than with a diamond engagement ring, however quaint the stone might be? DJ threw his shoulders back, straightening up as the cake was wheeled out. It was a six-layer masterpiece, and Loretta's mother looked even more excited than her daughter as the group of partygoers began to sing.

When the song was done and Loretta stepped up to blow out the candles, DJ raised his wineglass with a trembling hand and tapped his fork on the side, drawing everyone's attention. Loretta paused and turned to look at him, her expression unreadable.

Every eye in the room on him, DJ cleared his throat. This was the largest group of people he'd ever spoken to, outside of presentations in class, and it occurred to him that he should have prepared note cards. Or would that have been too impersonal? No matter—it was too late now.

"Hello, everyone. Um, as you may know, I'm DJ, Loretta's boyfriend." After his eyes swept the crowd, he looked back at Loretta again. Her cheeks were flaming red. She didn't like being the center of attention any more than he did. "Um, I met Loretta outside our quantum mechanics class over a year and a half ago, and I knew there was something special about her." The audience murmured pleasantly, spurring DJ on. "I've never met someone before who seems to understand the way my mind works, and who so deeply engages with the things that interest me too. Loretta is pure and wholesome from the inside out, and I'm lucky to call her my girl."

He paused and looked at her again. Her eyes glowed like dark embers in the candlelight.

"Loretta, I knew from the moment I met you that I would be a fool to let you get away. We spend every moment we can spare together, but for me, it's still not enough." DJ put his hand in his pocket and pulled out the ring box.

A few gasps and scattered squeals of delight echoed around the room. Loretta's lips parted as DJ crossed the floor to stand in front of her, and then dropped to one knee.

"Loretta, will you marry me?" He opened the box and held it up to her, a humble offering.

For a moment, her mouth stayed open in shock. *It's okay*, he thought. *This just caught her off guard. Could it be she didn't want a public proposal?* He pushed that thought away. Women loved big romantic gestures, and besides, he wanted everyone to know how much he loved her, how proud he was to be with her.

Then Loretta bit her bottom lip, and he realized tears had gathered in her eyes. Tears of sadness, not excitement. DJ's stomach dropped, as if yanked by a new gravitational force.

"DJ, I'm sorry," she whispered. Her eyes darted around the room, looking at all the people gathered behind him. DJ felt their eyes burning into his back, felt the pain of their embarrassment for him, the same way he'd felt it from his friends when his father showed up to school drunk and screamed for him until he came outside. "I . . . I don't think we should get married."

The hand holding the ring box slowly sank until it rested by his side. Unable to meet her gaze, he looked at the ground. "W—why? I thought we were happy."

"Can we talk about this outside?"

Rage welled up in his chest, giving him the energy to face her. "Outside? You didn't seem to mind humiliating me in front of everyone; why take me outside now?"

Loretta's chin lifted in that defiant way it always did when they argued, and the light from the almost melted candles danced across her cheeks. "Fine! You want to know why I don't want to marry you? Because I don't want to spend the rest of my life being another *accomplishment* of yours. You don't think I know how you talk about me to your friends? In your letters to your father? Like I'm some prize you won. 'Smart, pure, and beautiful'—like I'm a figurine of a person, not a real woman. But I am real, and I'm more than just a trophy for your wall."

"I never thought of you that way!" he protested, reaching out and grabbing her shoulders. He was rougher than he intended, and Loretta cried out, backing away from him with an emotion he'd never seen in her eyes before: fear. Then her father was there, along with her brother and several other male friends, pushing him away and out the door. In a haze of shouts and clumsy shoves, DJ was deposited on the sidewalk on his hands and knees.

After catching his breath, he sat back on his haunches and looked at the ring box still in his hand. He lifted his eyes to see through the windows, watching as Loretta's family and friends surrounded her crying form, offering her hugs and cake and drinks. Then he tilted his head back and screamed.

30

Elle

January 18, 2020

It didn't take much convincing to get Mitchell University's weekend security team to confirm they knew a janitor named Eduardo Mendez. They gave Sam a phone number and he called it several times, but there was no answer. Sam left a few voicemails, but Elle wasn't holding her breath that they would hear back. Eduardo was supposed to start his shift at six that evening, so they agreed to kill a few hours until they could pay him a visit.

Rather than driving across town to get back to the station, Elle suggested they set up shop in a diner while they waited. She was relieved when Sam agreed, although Ayaan could call him at any moment to check in and realize what Elle was doing. Once they settled in a booth with two black coffees, Sam pulled his laptop out and started looking into Eduardo's background — low-level criminal record, mostly petty crimes and a few misdemeanor robberies — but he'd avoided trouble for the last six months, at least.

After a while, Sam pushed his stuff to the side and they ordered an early dinner. Grief and guilt turned Elle's stomach when she thought about Natalie, but she picked at her sandwich anyway. It was the first thing she'd eaten since the day before.

She was halfway through her food when Sam set his fork down, spine straightening. "Leo Toca was a janitor at Mitchell University."

"Wha—?" Elle asked around a mouthful of turkey club.

"Leo Toca. I knew there was a reason that job sounded familiar. He and Eduardo must have worked together."

Elle wiped her greasy fingers on a napkin and picked up her phone. "That's right, I remember seeing that when I was looking at Leo's social media." She went to his profile, turning the screen to show Sam. "He and Eduardo are Facebook friends."

"Maybe that's why Eduardo knew to bring the van to Duane's shop."

"Maybe." Elle studied his profile picture—a young Latino man with a soft smile and glittering brown eyes, laughing at the camera with one hand out, like he was trying to stop the photographer from capturing the moment.

Sam took a long drink of coffee. "So, you think Eduardo is the guy who took Amanda?"

Elle shook her head. "He doesn't fit the description, if he looks anything like his Facebook photo. If nothing else, Danika said the man was pale, and Eduardo has medium-brown skin. And it doesn't look like he's bald. But if that van he brought in was used to abduct Amanda, then he has to know something about it. And if he knows Leo, maybe he has information on who might have killed him."

"Even more reason to visit him, then," Sam said, shoving the last bite of food in his mouth.

"Definitely." Elle stared out the window, trying to think about what the connection between the two cases might mean. It wasn't just a possible tie between Amanda's kidnapping and the chop shop —Leo himself might have known the guy who brought the van in. But he was already dead before Amanda was kidnapped. As much as she hated coincidences, this might just be one.

She tried to focus, make the pieces form together in her head, but something kept bothering her. Finally, she asked, "Hey, Sam? What made you change your mind? About me?"

His full lips pursed in thought, and then one corner of his mouth lifted in a small smile. "I listened to your podcast."

She opened her mouth to say something, but nothing came out. Even though she had thousands of listeners, it embarrassed her to know that this detective was one of them. It felt intimate.

"You have good instincts. You ask good questions. And it seems like you actually are helping people. Ayaan is the best commander in the precinct. Don't tell my commander I said that. But if she trusts you, then I guess I trust you too."

Shame heated Elle's face and snatched the breath from her chest. After a moment, all she could mumble was, "Thanks." His respect felt good, but it wouldn't last. Soon enough, he would find out that Ayaan had kicked her off the case. He would know she lied, even if it was just a lie of omission, and he would look back on this moment as a betrayal.

Unless . . . unless they could come up with a lead big enough to make it all worth it. She was the one who had realized the van was headed for Duane's shop, after all.

After the darkness descended outside, they got back in Sam's vehicle and drove toward Mitchell. Red brake lights lit up Elle's face as cars inched by, threading through the city streets. People passed them on the sidewalks, hustling in tight, quick strides with their coats zipped to the throat. A horn beeped, and the sound of a young woman's laughter pierced the night. Elle glanced down the block at a line of young people waiting for a theater to open its doors, no doubt after rush seats for the seven o'clock show. Even on the coldest weekends, Minneapolis had an active night life. It was impossible not to think about Beverly Anderson, leaving her friends behind on a night like this twenty-four years ago. The man responsible for ending her life was still free.

Twenty minutes later, they pulled into the parking lot abutting a stately brick building and got out of the car.

"The woman I talked to in security said the janitor would be cleaning in the administration building tonight. Apparently, there was some big conference today." Sam led her through the unlocked main doors. "How about we split up? Call me if you find him, and I'll do the same." They exchanged cell numbers, and then they each picked a direction and started off.

The halls looked like Elle's old university. Beige walls occasionally hung with mismatched artwork and poetry created by students. Message boards covered with flyers calling for roommates or experiment volunteers or new members for the Christian union, tabs of paper with phone numbers and web addresses hanging off like confetti. Closed, dark blue office doors with a large square of glass that allowed you to see the rooms lit only by computer monitors inside.

It was creepy being in a university after hours, when all the buzz and life of students was gone.

Her phone vibrated. "Where is he?" she asked, by way of greeting.

"By the registrar's office. Same floor, down the hall and to the left."

She speed-walked back down the hall, hoping Sam wouldn't ask him too many questions before she got there. She was the reason they even found out about Eduardo. She didn't want to miss a single thing he had to say.

She shouldn't have worried. When she found them, Eduardo was leaning back against the wall, large arms folded across his sculpted chest, jaw clenched in a silent refusal to talk. Eduardo had put on at least fifty pounds of muscle since his social media profile picture was taken, and he had a fresh cross tattoo on his left forearm. No wonder he'd been trying to get straight. Must have found Jesus.

"Hi, Eduardo," she said, her heart racing—from the rush down the hall or the excitement of talking to a possible witness, she wasn't sure. She didn't think he was Amanda's kidnapper, but he was the closest thing she'd had to a suspect since they let Graham Wallace go. "My name is Elle Castillo. I'm an investigative—"

"I know who you are," he said, his deep voice annoyed. "This guy already told me. Why are you here, ambushing me at work? What did I do?"

"I'm really sorry, but Sam did try to call you several times." She put on a what-a-bummer expression. "I'm sure you just haven't had time to check your messages. I totally get that. I hate having to interrupt people at their jobs, but unfortunately, we just couldn't wait any more."

Eduardo looked at his cart full of cleaning supplies. "I'm supposed to be working, here. We're shorthanded right now, so I'm already killing myself to get everything done on time."

"Of course! Actually, since you mentioned it, can I ask you about that? I understand that you knew a guy who worked here until recently. Leo Toca. And possibly his friend Duane Grove. Do those names ring a bell?"

Understanding flicked on in Eduardo's eyes like a switch. For a second, she thought he might run, but instead he just slid down the wall until he slumped in a heap on the floor, his face buried in his knees. "I knew this wouldn't work. I knew it was pointless to try."

Sam knelt next to him, clapping a hand on his shoulder. "It's never pointless to try to do the right thing. We know about the van you brought to Duane's shop a couple nights ago, a blue Dodge Ram 1500. Can we ask where you got it?"

Eduardo lifted his head. His green eyes were tinged with red, but there were no tears. He just looked exhausted. "I'm not saying anything else. Arrest me, if that's what you're going to do."

Like Sam, Elle got down on his level, but instead of kneeling, she sat cross-legged in front of him, like they were at a summer camp trading stories by the fire. "Where did you get the van, Eduardo? It's really important you tell us the truth."

He didn't flinch, keeping his lips pursed shut and his eyes focused at some spot on the floor.

"See, the reason it's important you tell us the truth is that the van was used to kidnap a little girl four days ago."

His eyes snapped up to hers, wide with fear. "What?"

"That's right," Sam said. "Amanda Jordan. She's eleven years old. She was taken from her bus stop on Tuesday morning by a man driving a dark blue Dodge Ram 1500."

Energy seemed to return to Eduardo in an instant. He pushed himself up to stand and pointed his finger at Sam. "I didn't kidnap a little girl. I'm no pervert!"

"So, tell us who did take her, Eduardo. If it wasn't you. Where did you get the van from? Did you steal it?" Sam asked.

Eduardo shook his head. "Someone gave it to me."

"Who?"

"I don't know. I don't know his name. He . . . he came up to me when I was walking out to the parking lot after work."

"What did he look like?" Elle asked.

Eduardo gestured around his head. "He was all wrapped up in a big coat, hat—you know, the kind with fur on the inside and those flaps that go over the ears—and a scarf. I couldn't really see his face. He was white . . . maybe fifty or something? About my height. He gave me a set of keys and said he'd pay me two thousand dollars to get rid of the van. Said he knew I had connections to a local chop shop. I don't know how he knew that. I only knew about it because of Leo." He laughed humorlessly, shaking his head as he looked up at the ceiling. "I thought, two thousand bucks. If I can get that, plus the money I knew my guy would give me for the vehicle, I could pay off my credit card and be out of the game for good. Live aboveboard, pay my taxes, raise my kids. All the stuff I'm supposed to do, the right way."

Elle looked over at Sam, expecting his expression to be unimpressed, but instead he looked like he felt sorry for the guy. She kind of did, too.

"And you'd never seen him before?" Sam asked.

"I don't know. I don't think so."

Pulling her phone out of her pocket, Elle opened her photos to get the sketch that Danika helped the police artist put together. She held it out to Eduardo. "Did he look like this at all?"

Eduardo took the phone and squinted at it for a moment. "It's . . . it's hard to tell. Like I said, he was all bundled up. But maybe. The nose—the nose looks kind of right." He handed it back to her.

"This guy came up to you in the parking lot . . . here? Outside this building?" she asked.

"No," Eduardo said. He pointed down the hall through double doors leading outside. "Two over, Building J. That's the physics building. They have a small lot out back, maybe thirty spots or so."

"Were there any other cars in the parking lot besides the van?" Sam asked. His arms were folded, weight resting on the balls of his feet like he was ready to jump out of his skin.

"I don't know."

"Think! This is really important, man. Don't you get it? A little girl's life is at risk here."

"Okay, okay!" Eduardo shut his eyes, his eyebrows drawn together in a harsh V. He put his hands out, gesturing with his left. "The van was over here, right in front of the door. He was parked in the disabled parking spot; I remember that. Then my car was in the back of the lot, in the corner." He pointed to the left. "I think there was another car there. On the right. I remember because I didn't think there would be anyone left by the time I finished my shift. This was at, like, one a.m. But there was another car there, besides the van. Yeah." He opened his eyes, meeting Elle's gaze.

"Do you remember what it looked like? Color? Make?"

He shook his head. "All I know is that it was a dark sedan; I couldn't make out the color. And I don't even know if it belonged to the guy. He went inside once he gave me the keys to the van. How would he have driven the van there if he'd brought the car too?"

"There's a bus that goes between the campus and the city center," Sam said. "He could have caught that, especially if he lives near the city. Or he could have taken a taxi. Do you remember anything else?"

"No, sorry. I . . . I never would have gotten involved in this if I knew—"

"We know," Elle said. She couldn't speak for Sam, but if anything was going to, this case would probably be the thing that scared Eduardo off crime for good.

"Thanks for your time," Sam said, reaching his hand out. Looking surprised, Eduardo took it for a firm shake. "If you think of anything else, please call us right away. Day or night." He handed the man a card.

Taking it, Eduardo looked up at him. "Is that really it? You're not going to arrest me?"

"You're not the one we're interested in, Eduardo. Consider this a late Christmas present."

Sam and Elle turned and started down the hall, toward the parking lot where Eduardo said he got the van. It probably wouldn't do any good, but it would be useful to get an idea of how big the parking lot was, at least.

"Hang on, I just thought of something," Sam said when they'd almost reached the exit.

"What?"

But he ignored Elle, turning back around. "Eduardo?" he called out.

Eduardo paused in the act of putting his headphones on and looked at them.

"Did you say the guy went into the building after he gave you the van?"

"Yeah."

"You saw him go in?"

Again, Eduardo nodded.

"Do you think he works here?"

Eduardo thought for a second. "Yeah, I guess he would have to."

"Why?" Elle asked, taking a few steps back to him.

"Because he'd need a key to get into that building after hours."

31

Justice Delayed podcast

Recorded January 18, 2020

Unaired recording: Elle Castillo, monologue

ELLE:

I was right. Everything is adding up to show that I was right. There are too many coincidences for me to write off, but still no one sees it.

When I was a kid, my father used to read me stories of Greek mythology. Something always drew me to Cassandra, the priestess given the power to accurately predict the future, and then doomed to never be believed. Her gift of prophecy was bestowed by Apollo as a seduction, and when she refused to love him, he turned the gift into a curse. Cassandra's story is a familiar one. She's no different from all the women whose lives are destroyed by the spite of a jilted man—women who speak their truths and are never believed.

I don't think I'm always right, but I know I am right about this.

Another girl was taken yesterday. The world might not know who she is, but she is special to me—the perfect target to isolate in order to break me. Natalie Hunter was taken from the side of the road walking the ten blocks from her piano lessons to my house. I was . . . I was supposed to be there for her, and I failed.

As long as I live, I will never forgive myself for that.

Natalie is the kind of kid that sticks with you once you know her. You can't not notice her. Maybe it's because her mom is fierce and independent, or because she had to deal with kids bullying her for not having a father. Or maybe it's just who she is—but Natalie is the toughest, strongest, most passionate kid, and I can't . . .

I can't believe she's gone.

I remember the day we met. I was watching TV when the doorbell rang, and this little kid—barely four years old—with messy curls and three different colors of marker on her skin was standing on my doorstep. That was back when I was working at CPS, and for half a second, I thought it was someone from one of my cases. I was trying hard to get pregnant at the time, but I rarely spent time with kids outside of work. There was no one else around that I could see, but she was way too young to be out on her own. Before I could even open my mouth to ask where her mother was, she held up a mixing bowl and said, "You have an egg? Mom's in the shower. I dropped the last one."

Apparently, mine was the fourth door she had knocked on, and the first one that answered. She was obviously fine, but I'd seen enough in my work to be alarmed—anyone behind those prior doors could have put her in danger. We had lived in the area six months by that point and hadn't really met any of the neighbors. For all I know, if it wasn't for that moment, I never would have met the Hunters at all.

Of course, I gave her the egg and walked back across the street with her to make sure she got home safely. By that time, her mom had gotten out of the shower and noticed her daughter was missing. She ran into the yard when she saw us walking up the sidewalk, and we nearly lost the other egg when Sash swept her daughter off the ground.

When things settled down, she invited me in. In some ways, I never really left.

Turns out, the egg had been for a surprise birthday cake. Natalie, four years old going on fourteen, managed to mix up a halfway decent chocolate Bundt with very little supervision. Her mom poured the batter into the tin and put it in the oven, but that was it.

I don't know why I'm saying all this. None of this is usable, I guess. I just . . . I want it on the record somewhere that Natalie is a good kid. She is special to people—to me, to Martín. To her mother,

Sash, most of all. Natalie has a pure heart and a strong will, and I will kill anyone who tries to take those things away from her. I will—

I know they are connected. No one wants to believe that TCK is back, but two girls have gone missing three days apart and they're the right ages and that's more than enough information for me. We don't need to wait until Amanda turns up dead at the end of the week. We can stop this before the worst happens.

We are closing in. Sam and I, we have a good lead, and we're going to solve this. We are going to find these girls and stop this man before they get hurt.

We have to.

32

Elle

January 19, 2020

"I can tell you're still awake."

Martín's voice sliced through the silence in their dark bedroom. He took off his clothes and climbed under the sheets with a shiver. Elle flipped over to face him. She could just make out his profile in the shadows.

"Murder?" she asked.

He'd been called out to a suspicious death scene, which meant Elle had come home to a dark house, an apple for dinner, and a long night of recording thoughts she couldn't share publicly on the podcast yet, if ever. She had tried to look into the faculty pages on the Mitchell University website, searching for the bundled-up man Eduardo saw, but the thing was a mess, and half the stuff she followed led to broken links. After a while, she had just given up, hoping Sam would have better luck at the police station.

Martín turned onto his side, putting one arm across her body. "Suicide, looks like. I'll know more after the autopsy tomorrow. Are you all right?"

"I can't stop thinking about Natalie. Have you talked to Sash? Do you know if they've found anything?"

"A detective interviewed me this morning at the morgue. I get the feeling they're eliminating all the men in her life first, which can't be that many." He squeezed her hip, moved his face closer until his forehead brushed hers. His breath was warm and smelled like toothpaste. "How are you? I know you must be frustrated, not being able to help."

She kissed him and then shuffled down the bed, burying her face in his chest. Then she told him about everything that had happened since that morning: getting dismissed by Ayaan, the surprise request from Sam, talking to Duane and realizing how much he hated her, catching Eduardo at the university. By the end, her mind was racing.

"I keep trying to think of all the reasons why Leo's murder and Amanda's kidnapping might be connected. It just doesn't seem like a coincidence." At last, she paused, taking a deep breath as Martín pulled her tightly to him.

Tracking down Eduardo had felt like such a huge discovery, but nothing had really changed. Natalie and Amanda were still missing. Elle was still technically barred from the case, and Sam would probably find out about it when he saw Ayaan again tomorrow. She felt like TCK was taunting her, giving her enough evidence to convince her while holding back anything that could help her persuade others.

"I was thinking," Martín started, then went quiet again.

"Yeah?"

"When the detective talked to me this morning, it seemed clear they think Amanda's kidnapping and Natalie's were done by two different people. But you still think it's connected, right?"

She pressed her nose into the warm skin of his neck, unsure if she wanted to confirm it out loud even after everything she had just said. Because although it was the truth that she still suspected TCK, she wanted to hide from it. Every time she let herself think about it, she saw Ayaan's doubt and Sash's fury. If she admitted that to Martín and he still didn't believe her, she wasn't sure how she'd cope with that.

"Why do you ask?" she finally said.

"Well, you're looking for the connection between Leo's case and Amanda's, but there's one thing you haven't suggested." Martín pulled back and tilted her chin up. Even in the dark, they were close enough that she could see his expression. "What about you?"

She froze. "What?"

"What if the connection is you? Leo emailed you and ended up dead. And Natalie is . . . Natalie is ours. What if this is about getting revenge on you?"

The skin on her neck burned where his breath landed. "Are you saying you believe me now, that this is TCK?"

"I'm not saying it's definite, but Leo's chop shop being used to get rid of the abduction vehicle adds another thread that wasn't there before. The connection between the three cases shouldn't be disregarded. If we're going to convince the police it's TCK, we need to have an answer for why he has suddenly struck again."

Elle chewed the corner of her lip, fingers wrapped in Martín's T-shirt. "What about Amanda, though? She wasn't connected to me, not really. There's no way he could have known her parents would ask me to consult on the case."

"I was thinking about that earlier. What if Natalie was his target all along, but she was too young? He had to take Amanda first, because she was the right age, but Natalie was the one he wanted."

Hearing the words made her feel sick. "But why now?" she asked, feeling as though she was echoing the questions Ayaan or Sam would ask if she told them Martín's idea. "Why not wait another year until Natalie turned eleven? TCK is nothing if not patient. He's waited twenty years—what's one more? Plus, like you said, Ayaan doesn't even think the cases are connected. She said Amanda's seems planned and perfectly orchestrated, while Natalie's looks like it was just a crime of opportunity."

"Maybe it's like you said before, then. That he planned for her to walk home."

She sat up and turned on the lamp next to her side of the bed. They squinted at each other in the golden light. "But how?"

"I don't know. Something out of the ordinary *did* happen. Her piano teacher wasn't home. As far as I know, police still don't know where Ms. Turner went. If TCK knew she wouldn't be there, if he planned it somehow, he might have known Natalie would leave on her own to go home."

"But he couldn't have known that she would, or that I wouldn't answer my phone when she called."

Martín was quiet again while her mind darted around, trying to string the story together. He could be right. If TCK was watching carefully, he could have done everything Martín just said.

"Again, though, why now?" she asked.

Her husband looked up at her, his eyes burning. "Something happened, something that triggered him to act sooner than he'd planned."

She stared at him, afraid of what he would say next.

"You."

Tears flooded her eyes.

"You're working to expose him, Elle. You have made more progress on this case than anyone in the last twenty years. Your podcast is reaching hundreds of thousands of new people with this story. He's coming after you because, otherwise, he knows you're going to catch him."

She'd opened her mouth to respond when the sound of their doorbell shattered the stillness of the house. His eyes widened, and she leapt out of bed. A glance at the digital clock showed it was 1:13 a.m. Elle reached into her nightstand, pulled out her handgun, and slid the cartridge in. Martín followed her out the bedroom door.

They crept down the stairs. The window above the front door was glowing with the light of the motion-sensor bulb outside. She took a deep breath, trying to imagine who would come to their house this time of night. Maybe it was Sash, seeking comfort after two days of trying to deal with her missing daughter alone. Elle hoped so. She looked out the small window at the top of the door but couldn't see anyone.

Reaching for the door handle, she glanced back at Martín. He nodded, having grabbed an umbrella from their front closet. Not a great weapon, but better than nothing. She pointed the gun at the door and pulled down the handle, yanking it open.

Fresh snow swirled into the house on an icy breeze. No one was standing there. But a small figure was slumped on their front step against the railing. Her hands and feet were bound together, not to keep her from moving, but as if to make her easier to carry, like a package. At the sight of Natalie's bright yellow winter coat and furry brown boots, Elle clapped her hand over her mouth. The girl's eyes were glassed over, staring up at them.

Elle didn't have her husband's expertise, but she could tell Amanda Jordan hadn't been dead for long.

Part IV

THE SACRIFICE

33

DJ

1996

Parties weren't his thing, but DJ decided to attend Mitchell University's mixer for "PhDs under 30" after being promised there'd be at least a few eligible young women there. He had dated on and off in the years since Loretta, but nothing lasted longer than a few weeks. Now that his free time was mostly spent with a bitter old man who only bothered to speak when he had something insulting to say, DJ was eager to get out of the house whenever possible. His father's disability check helped pay for a part-time nurse, but other than that, DJ was responsible for his care in addition to his studies and the two jobs he needed to pay the medical bills. He was ready for a full night out for the first time since he'd moved back to Minnesota six months ago.

He was disappointed to give up his place in Yale's doctorate program to care for his father after the old man's stroke, but there were benefits to finishing his degree at Mitchell. Here, at least, he was a big fish in a very small pond. People recognized him. The mixer was at a venue in downtown Minneapolis and open to all the local universities, but within five minutes of entering the room, he was greeted by no fewer than ten people. DJ smiled, shook hands speckled with pen ink, brushed his lips past rouged cheeks, inhaled the cheap colognes and perfumes favored by lifelong academics.

"DJ, how are you?" A PhD candidate he recognized leaned in for an embrace, a smile stretched across her round face. DJ obliged, pressing his lips to her cheek. What did it say about him, he wondered, that this was the closest he'd come to intimacy with a woman in weeks? The last relationship he had was short, meaningless. Easily ended when he left Yale. He didn't so much miss the companionship, but he could do with a warm body in his bed on a cold winter's night.

He pulled back with a smile to match hers, gave a shake of his head that he hoped looked adorably clueless. "I'm so sorry, I've just gone blank. Remind me of your name?"

She giggled and shook her head too, a mutual agreement that he really was *such* an airhead. "Maggie Henderson! Remember, from the laundromat?"

DJ smacked his forehead. "Of course! I remember now." He did not, but it hardly mattered. "With the . . ."

"Quarter that wouldn't work, yes," she nodded, edging closer. "You were so sweet to give me yours. I owe you." Her eyebrows lifted in a way that stirred something in his gut.

Now he could place her. The incident happened maybe six weeks ago, though he'd barely noticed her. He had his own washer and dryer at home, but the campus laundromat provided a good source of white noise when the library became too crowded. All the machines whirring and students silently waiting for the endless cycles to finish. It was a supremely underrated study space.

"I was actually hoping to run into you here," she continued.

This brought a genuine smile to DJ's face. As Maggie leaned against the wall behind her, he moved in closer, tilting his head slightly. "Oh, really? Why's that?" Out of the corner of his eye, he saw a flash of bright red. He glanced in that direction and froze.

There she was, like a vision from his nightmares.

Loretta.

Momentarily, DJ lost his balance and pitched forward, catching himself on the wall behind Maggie just in time. She shrank away from him, as if she saw something dangerous flicker in his eyes.

"I'm sorry," he whispered, glancing at her before his eyes returned to Loretta. Without another word to Maggie, DJ straightened up and adjusted his tie. He watched as Loretta spoke to one of the faculty directors from Mitchell who had helped organize the event. The past four years had been kind to her, fleshing out the hollows in her cheeks, although she had shadows under her eyes. The marks of an academic. She had cut her auburn hair into a short, edgy bob—something he never would have expected from the girl he fell in love with. But it suited her.

Nerves buzzed across his skin, skittered around inside his ribs. Maybe this was his chance. He could show her how far he'd come, how much he'd accomplished since she left him. Regardless of her intent, her rejection had woken him up, focused his ambitions. Now he could prove she had made a mistake. If she was here, it must mean she had also gone on to do her doctoral studies, was also single.

Shoulders back, DJ approached her. She was still wearing her bulky red coat, a testament to the frigid winter weather outside. When he was a few yards away, Loretta looked away from the man she was talking to, and her eyes lit up with an emotion DJ couldn't decipher. He smiled, reached out his arms in what he hoped was a casual, friendly invitation for embrace. She let out a short, astonished laugh but stepped in for a hug. When she was pressed close to him, he felt it and stepped back, shocked.

With his hands on her shoulders, DJ stared at her midsection. He hadn't noticed with her coat on, but it seemed obvious now how much it stuck out. Heat flooded his neck and cheeks as his mouth dropped open. "I . . . Hi," was all he could manage.

Loretta offered a small smile. "DJ, hello. How are you?"

"I'm fine," he said, finally ripping his gaze away from her pregnant belly and back to her flushed face. "I'm sorry. This is a surprise."

"It was to me too," Loretta said with a laugh. "Obviously I didn't plan to have a baby while doing my PhD, but sometimes things happen, I suppose."

They do, he thought, *if you are irresponsible.* But it would do no good to tell her what she must already know. They had always been chaste with each other, never sharing more than a passionate kiss, due to their religious upbringings. Even though he had done plenty more since, the thought of her going farther with another man sent a flash of jealousy through him.

Loretta shifted in front of him, scratched behind her right ear. "So, what are you doing here in Minnesota? Jenny told me you were at Yale."

DJ briefly filled her in on starting his program back East and the subsequent move to Minnesota after his father fell sick. She then explained that she had moved to Minneapolis shortly after graduation, having accepted a fellowship at the University of Minnesota. When she held up her left hand, a gold ring sparkled there. DJ's heart clenched.

"My husband is from here originally and wanted to be closer to family. It was a small sacrifice to make. The U of M has a great—"

"You're married?"

Loretta blinked, her hand moving to cover her stomach. "Yes, of course."

"Why are you here, then?" Fury zipped through DJ's veins like the aftershock of drinking strong coffee. "This is a singles event."

Lips tightening, Loretta leaned in and lowered her voice, as if to balance the sudden loudness of DJ's. "This is a networking event, DJ."

"It's disingenuous for you to take the space of a person who actually needs to meet people," DJ said. "Some of us are actually here to meet fellow PhDs, not flirt with faculty representatives to get ahead."

For a moment, neither of them spoke. He wasn't sure if everyone had frozen around them to watch the show, or if he just felt like the noise and motion in the room had stopped. He couldn't look away from her pink cheeks, her obscene belly, her stupid whorish haircut.

"You know, I had hoped you might change over time, but I can see that isn't the case," Loretta said, her voice even but firm. Her hands rested at her sides, opening and closing into fists. "What we had was good at the beginning, DJ. But after a while, I didn't feel like you really saw me. You didn't have any interest in me as a person, not really. Then I read that letter you wrote to your father, and everything became clear. I started noticing the way you spoke to your friends, and I got it. For you, people are either obstacles to your success or a means of achieving your goals. I was not going to be either."

"That is utter nonsense." He hated how his jaw stiffened at her words, how they made his heart race with anger and embarrassment. "And I cannot believe you are doing this again. Humiliating me in front of dozens of people, again."

Loretta glanced around, as if just remembering they had an audience. His eyes followed hers. People stood in clusters around them, pretending to talk as glasses clinked and the jazz band played, but he could tell they were watching. Listening.

Looking back at him, she drew her coat around her swollen stomach and folded her arms like a barrier. "I'm not sorry I left you. But I'm sorry I humiliated you. It was not my intention."

"'It is better to dwell in a corner of a housetop, than in a house shared with a contentious woman.'" DJ clenched his jaw. "I pity your husband." Avoiding the gaze of his colleagues, he left the room and ran out into the cold winter night.

He stalked down the sidewalk, sucking in deep breaths of frosty air until his chest burned. His coat had been left behind, but the rage coursing through his blood dulled the cold. After walking aimlessly for a while, he finally turned and headed in the direction of his car. The night was overcast, the dark sky heavy with clouds ready to burst with snow. A storm was coming, and he wanted to be home before it hit. The first flakes were starting to come down by the time he reached his station wagon and got the engine running. DJ pulled out of his parking space and onto the road.

A slight figure passed in front of his car, and he slammed on the brakes as the person jumped back, hands flying to their chest. Pulse skyrocketing yet again, DJ leapt out of the driver's seat and opened his mouth to start yelling when he saw the person's pale face, stained with tears above his scarf. It was one of the boys from a class he TA'd for.

"DJ?" the young man asked, drawing out the vowel sound. "Whoa, you almost hit me. I didn't see you coming at all."

DJ took a step toward him. "Sorry about that. I pulled out of my space pretty fast there. Are you all right? It's Kerry, isn't it?"

Kerry nodded, body shivering. "Yes. And yeah, I'm fine." He turned and started to walk again.

"Wait!" The word left DJ's mouth before he had time to think about it. When Kerry looked back at him, he pointed to his car, the driver's side door still hanging open. "Do you want a ride? It's way too cold to be walking."

Kerry glanced at his car, then shrugged. "Sure, thanks. Freezing my nuts off out here."

Once they were both buckled in, Kerry gave DJ directions to his apartment, and they were off into the night again.

Several moments passed in silence. Kerry adjusted himself in the passenger's seat, pulled his scarf down, wiped an ungloved hand across his face.

Finally, DJ said, "So, why were you out walking? Cold night for a stroll."

Kerry's laugh was bitter. "You could say that. Uh, my girlfriend dumped me, actually."

Hands tightening on the steering wheel, DJ slowed the car. "Really?"

"Yeah." Kerry cleared his throat—a deep, guttural sound. "It's fine. I'm fine. She'll come around, I'm sure. Just overreacting to a stupid fight."

"Right." DJ licked his lower lip. At a stoplight, he turned to look at the younger man. "You're better off without her, trust me."

Kerry met his gaze in the dim, reddish glow. His eyes were wet, but no more tears were falling. DJ could count on one hand the number of men he'd seen weep in his lifetime, and the sight made him uncomfortable.

"I love her."

"She obviously doesn't love you."

The light turned green, and DJ pressed down on the accelerator. Kerry turned away from him, looking out the window.

"I'm sorry if that's harsh, and I know it's none of my business, but trust me. I've been where you are, and it's not worth it." DJ thought of Loretta tonight, defiant and swollen with another man's child. She would have given him nothing but trouble.

"This is it," Kerry said when they rounded the corner, but DJ did not slow down. "Hello? You passed my apartment."

DJ stared out the windshield, speeding up.

"Hey, man, what are you doing? Take me back there." When DJ didn't listen, Kerry grasped the door handle and opened it.

The car swerved as DJ tried to pull over, but Kerry was already out the door by the time his station wagon slid into the curb. Rage zipping through him, DJ jumped out of the driver's seat and followed him.

Kerry was clearly hurt from the fall, limping as he tried to run across the icy sidewalk back toward his apartment. DJ stalked after him, unsure what he planned to do. He had to find a way to stop this, get through to him. He couldn't watch another man make the same mistakes he did, let a stupid woman who didn't know his worth tear his life apart.

Within a few seconds, DJ had caught up and run around to stand in front of Kerry on the sidewalk. He was taller than the boy, stronger too. Even with the bulky coat, Kerry was slender — weak. It was no surprise this girl had left him, hurtful as it might be.

"Seriously, what the fuck is going on?" Kerry was breathing hard, hunched over to rub his right leg where he'd rolled out of the moving car. "Why are you being so weird?"

"I'm just trying to get through to you, Kerry!" DJ took a step forward. If he could just get the boy to look up at him, look up to him, maybe he would understand. "You're in your last year, and I've seen you in class. You have so much potential. Let that stupid bitch go and live your life."

In a second, Kerry had straightened up and then there was a fist swinging toward him. DJ blocked it easily and shoved the boy, who fell backwards. DJ stood over him and then crouched down, pinning his arms on the ground and sitting on his chest, the way his brothers had done to him when he was a child. To get him to stop, to get him to *listen*.

But Kerry wasn't listening. He was shouting, cursing, screaming, and any minute someone was going to come walking out or call the police. So DJ grabbed the boy's throat, cutting the vile words off midstream. Kerry's eyes went wide, hot with terror, and DJ felt something shoot through his abdomen — pleasure, power. He could fix this.

"Now, listen to me, Kerry," he said, pressing down on the man's throat. "Listen. Kerry, stop." But the young man kept struggling, bucking his chest, kicking his legs, so DJ pressed harder, letting his anger take over. No one ever listened to him.

DJ brought his face close to Kerry's, saw it turning red even in the shadows cast by the streetlight. At last, the younger man grew still. "There, see? You're going to have to trust me, Kerry." DJ's arms shook as the tension fell out of Kerry's body, his eyes closing. DJ closed his own, breathing deep. "Trust me, it's better this way."

For a moment, everything was still. The distant sound of cars passing in the night, a rustle of wind in the dead branches above. DJ opened his eyes, staring at the boy. Then he looked around. The opposite side of the street was lined with parked cars, forming a barrier between him and the unlit houses beyond. As far as he could tell, no one had seen a thing. Still, every moment they were out in the open was a risk.

Snapping into motion, DJ rolled Kerry's body over his shoulder and rose slowly to his feet. He walked carefully to the passenger's side of his car, door hanging open like an invitation. With Kerry slumped and buckled into the seat, he ran to the other side and got back in with one more glance around the neighborhood.

He needed to buy himself time to think, time to plan. No one knew Kerry had gotten in the car with him. If he could get the boy out of the way, there would be time to make sure he didn't have any evidence on him, and DJ could decide what to do next.

The barn. DJ could dump Kerry's body in the barn—one of the many places on the property his father couldn't get to anymore, since his stroke. Forcing his eyes to stare straight ahead, DJ started the engine and drove toward home.

34

Elle

January 19, 2020

Five days. It had only been five days since Amanda was taken, and now she was dead.

In the interview room at the police station, Elle stared at the chipped wooden table under her arms until her eyes burned.

Every time she blinked, she saw the girl's face again: purplish bruising on her lips, bursts of red flecking the skin around her eyes. Smothered, Martín had guessed while waiting for the first responders to arrive. He was in the room next to hers, answering questions for Sam. They weren't suspects, she knew, but it made her anxious nonetheless.

Five days, not seven.

She wasn't Cassandra, after all—not some omniscient prophet, doomed to be disbelieved. She was no better than a cheap psychic, making baseless predictions and hoping one would land. Amanda and Natalie's cases were connected; she had gotten that right. But they hadn't been taken by the Countdown Killer. No matter how the deaths varied over the years, he never broke his signature. The bodies were always found on the seventh day.

The door handle turned, and Elle looked up to see Ayaan enter. Exhaustion made her usually glowing skin dull, darkening under her eyes. Her somber navy hijab had been put on in haste, slightly askew across her forehead.

"Elle, were you offered a drink?" she asked.

"Yes." The word croaked out of her. "Ronny's bringing me a tea."

"Good." Ayaan sat across from her, opened a folder. Inside were freshly printed crime scene photos.

Elle closed her eyes, but the images were already branded on her mind from seeing them in person hours before. At this moment, Amanda was probably being cut open by someone in her husband's office, dissected for secrets. Maybe they would find the killer's DNA. Maybe this would give them a lead, an opportunity to save Natalie. But that wouldn't change the fact that an eleven-year-old girl was dead.

She thought of Dave and Sandy Jordan, wondered if the police had told them yet. Ayaan would have been the one to do the job. Would the police wait until a reasonable hour to wake the Jordans up with the worst news they'd ever received, or had Ayaan already been to their house and returned? Elle opened her mouth to ask, but the words stuck in her throat. It didn't matter whether they knew yet or not; the result would be the same. The couple would be destroyed.

Ronny came in with a mug of peppermint tea, set it down in front of Elle with a sad smile. The crisp smell cleared her sinuses, stuffy from crying, as she wrapped her hands around the mug. After a moment, she lifted her eyes to meet Ayaan's.

The commander's gaze was steady, her pen poised to take notes. "Tell me what happened."

Between sips of tea, Elle explained about Martín coming home after being called to a crime scene, talking to him in bed, the doorbell ringing, the discovery of Amanda's body. She had no idea when she had last slept, but the peppermint and adrenaline shot through her, making the words come out fast and unfiltered. She finished with the text she had sent to Ayaan, after they had called 911.

For a few moments, Ayaan let the silence rest between them. She finished a note and met Elle's gaze again. "I noticed you didn't talk about what you did earlier in the day. The time you spent with Detective Hyde."

Elle froze with the mug lifted halfway to her lips. Slowly, she set it back on the table. "Oh."

"Yes, oh. He and I had an interesting chat. Seems you didn't tell him I had asked you to take a step back from Amanda's case?" Ayaan's head tilted to the side as she held Elle's gaze.

Elle took a bigger drink than she intended, scalding her throat. Her eyes watered as she tried to keep from coughing. "I'm sorry. We got to talking in the lobby, and he asked if I'd found anything on Leo, and then I had an idea about where the van was headed on the security footage that came through . . . I just wanted to help. I'm sorry. There's no excuse."

For a moment, they looked at each other in silence. Finally, Ayaan nodded. "Probably not the time to bring it up, I suppose. But you must have known I would find out; I wish you had told me yourself."

"You know me, Ayaan. I've always been more of the better-to-ask-forgiveness-than-permission sort of person."

Frustration sparked in Ayaan's eyes. "If we're going to be able to work together in the future, you can't be that way with me. I consider you a friend, Elle, not just a colleague. I'd like us to trust each other."

Elle looked at the pale green liquid in her mug, fiddled with the string hanging over the rim. "You're right. It won't happen again." She wanted that to be true, but the promise rang hollow. There was so much Ayaan didn't know about her. Maybe if Elle had trusted her sooner, Amanda would still be alive. As soon as the thought tried to burrow into her head, she pushed it away. She had done the best she could with the information she had. Shouldering the blame wouldn't bring Amanda back, wouldn't help her find Natalie.

Ayaan cleared her throat. "Now, can you think of any reason why Amanda's body was left on your doorstep?"

"I . . . Martin and I were talking about this right before it happened. That maybe TCK was attacking me for covering him on the podcast. But I was wrong about him, Ayaan. I'm sorry. I was so sure, but this isn't TCK. The victim showing up five days later, with no marks from whipping and killed by asphyxiation? It doesn't make sense."

"How do you know she was asphyxiated?"

"Martín. At least, that was his guess." Elle's fingers shook on the tea mug.

Ayaan nodded, wrote something down.

Elle continued: "So, I don't know. If it's not TCK, then I don't know why the person seems to be coming after me. The only other thing I can think is—" She paused, shaking her head. The thought had been prodding at her for the last few hours, too horrible to allow in.

"What?" Ayaan leaned forward. "What do you think?"

"I'm sure I'm overreacting." Elle looked away, focusing on the window behind Ayaan. She wondered if Sam was in there, watching her, and then she kicked the idea away. This was not an interrogation. Finally, she said, "I've been getting threatening emails lately. Some private messages on social media. Tina reported a few to our local PD, but last I checked, most of the IP addresses showed they came from out of state—some even from overseas."

"Why didn't you mention this before?"

Elle looked at her, surprised to see the commander's eyes glowing with concern. "I get harassed all the time for the work I do. I thought the spike in messages was just because the podcast had gotten more popular, was reaching more people. Plus, conversations about TCK always bring out the trolls. I didn't think it was relevant to our investigation, and like I said, Tina had the locals looking into the ones that seemed to know my address."

"But you were concerned about your safety. Didn't you think I should know about that?"

"A little girl was missing, Ayaan. Compared to that, my concerns seemed small. Still do." Elle cleared her throat, trying to rid it of the tightness brought on by another wave of emotion. "If someone took Natalie as a way of tormenting me because of this podcast . . ." The depravity of people shouldn't surprise her anymore, but sometimes shock still broke through.

"Okay, Elle. When you get home, please send me everything you and Tina have flagged, including the stuff you sent to the local department. I'll get in touch to let them know we're taking over."

Ayaan folded her hands on top of her notepad. Her expression tensed, and Elle felt her shoulders bunch. It was one of the few times she'd ever seen Ayaan look hesitant.

"What is it?" Elle asked.

"Well, we didn't know about the online harassment. So, that's a possibility. But Sam and I have developed another theory I want to run past you. In fact, the two might fit together."

Elle nodded for Ayaan to continue.

"We're thinking along the same lines now in terms of this being related to your podcast. The second victim being so close to you and the first victim showing up dead at your house, wearing the coat of the second victim, make that almost undeniable. But we came at it from a different angle. We think it's possible that someone has been inspired to copy TCK's methods, carry the mantle of his countdown, so to speak."

Elle stared at her, unsure what to say. The thought had crossed her mind before, but up until today every part of the kidnappings was so perfectly aligned with TCK's methods that it seemed obvious it was him. A huge mistake like this, though — displaying a body two days early when TCK had never done so before — that had the marks of a sloppy mimic.

Ayaan pressed on. "You said yourself that the man who took Amanda and Natalie couldn't be TCK, because he never reveals his victims early. Even if he accidentally killed one early, he would always put them in a public place on the seventh day. That is the one part of his pattern that has never varied, not once."

"That's right." Elle's mind raced, trying to put together everything that this would mean. Ayaan was right; it still fit with her concerns about the online harassment. If the copycat hated the podcast and wanted to hurt her, what better way than to emulate the most horrific things her featured villain had done?

"But there's no denying the killer did copy some of TCK's methods," Ayaan said. "You were right about the similarities: taking the girls three days apart, continuing with the ages TCK left off on twenty years ago. So, he's a copycat. He wants what all copycat criminals want: the fame and notoriety of their idols. What better way to get it than using his supposed return to work to target the very woman that is making the case go viral in 2020? He's got all the information he needs on how to be TCK right there."

That jolted Elle out of her thoughts. "Right there . . . as in on *Justice Delayed*? Are you saying the killer learned how to copy TCK's murders by listening to my podcast?"

Ayaan's expression was grim. "It's possible, don't you think? Law enforcement has always worried that shows like *Criminal Minds* give bad people too many ideas for how to kill. Why wouldn't murderers also take inspiration from true crime podcasts?"

"But I'm not putting out any information about his methods or patterns that isn't publicly available." Her breathing picked up, and she could hear the panic in her voice, but she was too exhausted to restrain it. "Besides, I don't glorify the killers like a lot of the shows out there. I'm trying to get justice for the victims, not tell some lurid story about a serial killer."

Ayaan pulled her lower lip into her mouth for a moment, then nodded. "I'm sure that's true. I haven't listened to all of this season, but you've always done a good job of focusing on the victims rather than the perpetrators."

"That's all I want to do," Elle said. She ran her fingers through her hair, giving it a subtle yank; the sharp pain helped her brain to focus. Despite Ayaan's placating words, fury still rocketed through her body. Every word she had spoken on her podcast, every detail she had provided her hundreds of thousands of listeners, seemed to gather in her mind like a noisy crowd. She was wrong. This case was different, and she knew it. It was only a few days ago that a Twitter user had suggested that very thing.

"That bastard," she spat. "I am going to destroy him."

35

Justice Delayed podcast

January 19, 2020

Transcript: Season 5, Bonus Episode

ELLE:

The body of Amanda Jordan was left on my doorstep in the early hours of this morning. The evidence now shows without a doubt that she was taken by the same man who kidnapped Natalie Hunter.

When I took on this role, hunting monsters who hurt children, I knew that it came with risks. I knew that I was putting myself in danger. But I never could have guessed that it might cause two families to lose their precious daughters—one of them, at least, for good. I will never be able to express how truly, deeply sorry I am for their loss.

Amanda's body being left on my doorstep is all the proof that I need. The man who kidnapped these girls is coming after me. He listens to this podcast, of that I'm sure. I don't know if you're one of the trolls harassing my accounts, sending death threats to my email, or if you're smart enough to stay away from anything that could be traced back to you. I don't know if you were inspired by the details on this podcast, but I suspect that no matter why you kidnapped these girls, you wanted me to blame myself.

You planned this out. You made it look like the Countdown Killer had returned, just to torment me and undermine my credibility. You wanted me to make a fool of myself, to raise the alarm and start spreading panic that TCK was back. But you broke the structure, killing Amanda early. You couldn't stick to the control, the calculated patterns of TCK. You like chaos, don't you?

But you don't know who you're messing with. You don't know who I am.

I have enjoyed living the past two decades with hardly anyone knowing my real identity, but the time for secrets is over. Because I want you to know that you will lose. You might have the most important girl in the world to me, but you underestimate just what I'll do to get her back. You can't possibly know what I will endure to find you until you know who I am.

I am Eleanor Watson.

Twenty-one years ago, I was playing at a friend's house when a man came to the door and asked for me. He told me that he needed to take me home, that my mother needed me. He said he was friends with my dad, so it was okay. I went with him. Instead of bringing me home, he drugged me, and I woke up in a cabin with another young girl who had already been there for several days. Jessica Elerson—the last girl to be killed by the *real* TCK. The man's features are a blank in my mind, but I remember Jessica—every curve and dimple of her face. I'm doing this for her, for all of the ones before her who weren't as lucky as I was. For what possible reason did I survive if it wasn't to stop men like you, men who think they have a right to our bodies and our lives?

That's why I started this podcast—and I'll be damned if a monster like you scares me into stopping.

I am the one who beat the real TCK. You think I can't defeat a cheap copycat like you?

36

Elle

January 19, 2020

As soon as she was done recording her episode, she emailed the audio file link to Tina with a one-sentence subject line: *for immediate release*. It didn't need editing or sound design beyond the basic, but her producer had been doing the episode uploads for the past two years, so it would definitely go faster in her capable hands.

That done, Elle set about downloading all of the red-flagged emails, as well as taking some screenshots of the worst tweets and private messages in the bunch. The one she'd opened a few days ago, *Careful what you wish for*, stuck out once again. It was sinister in its simplicity, but something else nagged her about it — she couldn't figure out what. She dragged everything to a folder titled *FILTH* and sent an email to Ayaan with the link, copying Tina in so she knew it was being taken care of. If there was even a chance the copycat killer had been stupid enough to contact her, the police's computer analysts would hopefully be able to track him.

It was just past noon. Elle stood up, turned around to stare at her Wall of Grief. She had added Kerry's pictures next to Beverly's only a couple weeks ago. His freshman college photo smiled down at her, young and full of promise that he would never get to fulfill. Someone had really leveraged the stories of these victims, these young lives snuffed out, to torment her—to achieve some twisted sense of noto-riety for themselves. They had killed Amanda and taken Natalie, and they knew how to do it because of her.

Elle pulled her phone out of her pocket. Martin had texted while she was interviewing with Ayaan to say that he'd gone to the morgue to watch Amanda's autopsy. Other than that, there were no mes-sages. After responding to him, she sent Sash a quick text.

MISS YOU. I'M SORRY. YOU WERE RIGHT. I'M DOING EVERYTHING I CAN TO BRING NAT HOME.

As she pressed send, her computer chimed. A call was coming in from Tina.

"So, you're finally ready to tell the world," Tina said as soon as Elle accepted the call.

Elle studied her friend on the screen. Tina looked serious, but not upset. "How . . . how did you listen so fast?"

Tina waved her hand. "Please. I live for my emails from you." She smiled and met Elle's gaze through the camera. "Does it feel good? Being honest about who you are, I mean."

"Not really. I kind of want to throw up."

"Why? That monologue was dope. I added some epic close-out music."

Elle shook her head but couldn't stop a nervous laugh from escap-ing. She quickly sobered. "Ayaan thinks maybe the guy started killing because he listened to the podcast. Like . . . like my episodes trained him how to be like TCK."

Tina's expression hardened. "That is bullshit, and you know it. If someone wanted to learn how to do crimes like TCK, all they'd have to do is look at Reddit or Wikipedia. You are not going to take on the blame for this, Elle. You have done nothing but try to solve this case from day one."

"And look how that's gone. I keep screwing it up. People who get close to me keep dying or disappearing. Are you sure you don't want to hang up?"

In response, Tina rolled her eyes. "Okay, but seriously. I called be-cause I wanted to make sure before I hit go. You definitely want me to put this up? You've thought about it? Because I can tell just from looking at you that you probably don't even know the last time you slept, and you are coming off a pretty horrific night."

Elle stared at the screen. For some reason, Tina's words made her want to break down and cry. Instead, she just nodded. "Yes. Put it up."

"Okey-dokey." With the video call still running, Tina clicked a few things around on her screen. Elle watched the windows dance and change in the reflection on her glasses. "And done."

Elle let out a long breath. "Okay, then. Good." Holy shit. She'd really done it. She might have just blown up her whole life, but right now in this moment, she felt ecstatic.

"Congrats, Nora." Tina leaned forward, trademark mischievous glint in her eyes. "By the way, I have some news for you. On the down-low. I have a friend who works in the Minnesota Bureau of Criminal Apprehension, and apparently tomorrow they're issuing a press release to say they got a DNA result back on the male in the cabin."

"What? Did they tell you who it is?"

"It was Bob Jensen: not-his-real-name-Stanley. The guy who disappeared along with his office lover."

Elle sat back in her chair. "Do they . . . do they think he was TCK?"

Tina shook her head. "Can't be. He was the VP of sales for his company. Lived overseas for all of 1997 and didn't come back to Minnesota until late 1998. There's no way he could be TCK."

"That means, if the office rumors about the affair between him and his coworker were true, the woman was probably married to the Countdown Killer. Remember how they said Jensen was sleeping with a married woman?"

"I remember."

"Holy shit." Any other time, she would have sat down now and slapped together another unscheduled podcast episode. Those ones were the best—got the highest ratings in her other seasons—when she found a piece of evidence that changed everything about a case. But she couldn't stomach the idea of releasing another episode right now. She had to focus on finding Natalie.

Tina looked straight into the lens. "So, are you still helping with the investigation?"

"No, Ayaan basically kicked me out of the station." Elle summarized the last six days, including all the details they had found about Amanda and how she had been booted off the case by Ayaan. She told Tina about talking to Eduardo and the possibility that the killer worked at Mitchell University.

At the end, Tina whistled. "Well, what are we waiting for? Have you searched their staff records?"

"I tried for a little while last night, but their website is a mess."

Tina scoffed. Something flickered on the screen and a moment later, her desktop popped up. She shared it with Elle as she went to the Mitchell University website and navigated to their staff section. As Elle had found last night, several hundred profiles were there, and it was impossible to know if it was even up to date. A subpoena for the university's records would give police better information, but that could take weeks.

"What do you know about the person you're looking for?" Tina asked.

Elle thought back to Eduardo's testimony. "Just that he's probably a middle-aged white man."

She snorted. "Good thing those are hard to come by in academia."

Despite everything that had happened that day, Elle smiled. "Tell me about it. Oh, I know that he had a key to the physics building. Building J. But I don't know for sure whether he's a student or a janitor or a professor or something else. The witness told us only staff were allowed access after ten p.m., and it was apparently around one a.m. when the man approached our witness."

"So that rules out students, at least," Tina said.

Elle nodded. "It should. Unless a student got someone else's pass."

"If we go down that hypothetical, though, then it could literally be anyone. Is it only the staff who work in the building that can access it after hours, or can any staff member access the building?"

"I don't know."

On the small square of video that was embedded next to the shared screen, Tina's face was focused. "So, this is the course page for the math and physics degrees."

"Yeah, I found that last night, but that's where I got stuck. Each course has the professor's name next to it, but I couldn't find any links to the full faculty, and I didn't have the energy to comb through dozens of courses."

"Hmm, they must have . . ." Tina typed a few more things, clicked a couple times.

"Oh, what's that?" Elle sat forward. "Where it says 'meet our team'?" There was a link lost in a chunk of text on the main physics course page.

Tina clicked and then sat back with a victorious smile. On the screen was a page filled with pictures, names, and profiles of about thirty men and women.

Elle read the headline at the top. "Physics and Mathematics Faculty. Well, that took you all of two seconds."

"It would have taken you two seconds too if you'd slept in the last week."

"Hush," Elle said, already scanning the list of names. At least two-thirds of the people fit the description Eduardo gave them. Tina scrolled again and a new face popped onto the screen.

"Didn't you say the girl who saw the man talking to Amanda said he was bald? There are, like, ten bald guys here."

"Wait . . ." Elle whispered.

Tina stopped scrolling. "See something?"

Elle pointed at the screen. "I know that guy. Third from the bottom, in the white collared shirt. Dr. Stevens. That's the guy I went to see last week. The one Luisa Toca's mother said her daughter was dating."

"Luisa Toca. Leo's ex?"

"Yeah," Elle said, staring at the photo. The man was clean-shaven and not wearing a baseball cap like he had been the day they met, but she recognized him anyway. "He told me he and Luisa's mom were neighbors and he just flirted with her daughter one time. I figured her mom just misunderstood. His story checked out."

"Hmm, weird. But you know, Minneapolis is one of those big small towns. And there are a few guys here that match the description."

"True." Nevertheless, Elle pulled out her phone and got the sketch

Danika helped put together up on her screen, holding it up next to the man's picture on the computer. She shook her head as her stomach sank. "Looks nothing like the sketch. The guy three above him does, though, at least a little. Dominic Jackman."

"Cool. Why don't you head over to Stevens's house again and see if he has an alibi. I'll check out Jackman and the other baldies."

37

Natalie

January 19, 2020

Natalie was alone now.

She shivered in the dark as she watched the slot on the door. It had been hours since it last opened. Upstairs was silent. She heard no footsteps. This might be her only chance.

Until yesterday, she and Amanda had agreed they would wait to be rescued. Natalie had read a lot of true crime books she sneaked out of Elle's studio, so she knew their chances of escaping on their own were low. She warned Amanda over and over not to make the man angry. Elle would never stop looking for her. She would find a way, use her podcast to find the man that had taken them. Help was on the way; they just had to wait.

But that was yesterday.

Time had blended together, but she was pretty sure a full night had passed since the man killed Amanda. The two of them had been locked in the basement for what felt like days, with no windows letting in light or dark that would indicate the passage of time. Amanda was sick, vomiting and crying into the gross toilet that was the only piece of furniture in the room besides the bed. They had no food, and the single bottle of water he'd left them was almost drained from Amanda trying to get her fluids back up.

After ignoring them for hours, the man had finally opened the door. He brought a bowl for each of them, which held just a few spoonfuls of some boiled, brown mash. Amanda took a couple bites, and then she lost it. She threw the hot dish at him and screamed her head off and thrashed around on the bed while the man tried to calm her and Natalie cowered, weak with fear and hunger. Then, when Natalie was sure the neighbors would hear the girl even though they never had before, he leapt across the bed, straddled her body, and tried to cover her mouth with his hands. She bit him, and he yelled, then grabbed the pillow both girls shared and shoved it down on her whole face. She kicked and writhed and screamed with a kind of intensity Natalie had never heard before. Finally, after several long minutes, she was still.

The man left her in the basement and ran up the stairs. Natalie could hear him pacing back and forth, footsteps creaking the boards above her head. When he came back, he did not look at her. Natalie stayed where she had sat since Amanda threw the bowl, face buried in her knees, until he was gone. Amanda was no longer on the bed when she finally opened her eyes again.

Natalie was alone now.

She sat up in bed and listened closely again, waiting for the tell-tale clomps of his feet. Nothing. He was so angry when he stormed away yesterday, and he hadn't been back with food or water. She was pretty sure he wasn't even in the house. If he didn't come back, if Elle didn't show up soon, she would die here.

Now was her chance. There were no windows and the door to the basement was firmly locked, but there was a vent up high near the ceiling.

Natalie shoved the bed across the room, metal screeching against the concrete floor. She picked up the large bucket Amanda had used to throw up in when she was too weak to get out of bed and tipped it into the toilet. There was no sink to rinse it out, so she turned it upside down on top of the mattress. She wouldn't be sleeping here again anyway.

The bucket wobbled when she stood on top of it, but if she held her palms flat against the wall, she could balance. One of the bedposts was broken, its sharp, splintered point jabbing at the ceiling just to her right. If she fell on that, she'd be dead. Once she was stable, Natalie reached up and pulled at the grate over the air vent. At first, it didn't budge. She banged her fist against it, sharp pain shooting into her skin. It had to come loose.

Then, with one final smack, the metal sprang free and fell, bouncing off the mattress before clattering to the floor.

Natalie held her breath, eyes trained on the ceiling. No footsteps sounded above her.

Again, she reached up, this time to grip the inside of the vent. It felt dusty and slippery under her sweaty hands, but she managed to get a good grip. But how could she hoist herself up? She didn't have any leverage, any footholds in the smooth surface of the wall.

The wall.

Heart crashing in her chest, Natalie jumped down and picked up the bucket, doing her best to keep her hands dry as she swung it toward the wall. It thunked uselessly three times before finally taking a chunk out of the plaster. She hit it twice more before a decent divot was formed, enough for a couple of toes to squeeze in. Setting the bucket down on the bed again, she climbed back up. This time, when she got a grip inside the vent, she swung her left leg up and put the tip of her foot in the divot. Then she tensed her muscles and tried to pull her body weight up the wall.

She slipped, holding in a scream even though she had already been making a racket. She'd been practicing holding in her screams for days. Her feet landed back on the bucket. The scent of urine filled the room, and at first she thought it was coming from the bucket before she realized she'd just wet herself. Tears blurred her already dim vision. She felt like a baby, or an animal, or both. She should be stronger than this. She had an advantage Amanda didn't have. She'd read the books. She'd learned about monsters. She should be braver than she was.

After saying a quick prayer, Natalie took a deep breath, reached up again, and this time didn't stop to think. She scrambled like a kid climbing a fence to get away from a bully, and it worked. The muscles in her left calf and her shoulders twinged as she shot herself up into the vent, but she was there. She landed on her belly and panted for a moment. Only a moment.

This vent wasn't for heating. The ones in the floors did that. She hoped that meant it was for ventilation and would take her outside, to the cold winter air and freedom.

Crawling through the vent proved much easier than getting into it was. Using her elbows and knees, she wriggled her body along the bottom, stopping every now and then to listen for any sounds besides her own harsh breath. The vent came to an abrupt stop, and panic surged through her, but she realized it had changed to a right angle leading upward. She stood up and waved her hands around in the dark until she felt the edge of another bend around chest height. She pulled herself up and into the next tunnel.

A few moments later, she felt icy fingers of air dance across her sweaty face. She was getting closer. The first smell of snow made her crawl faster, whimpers escaping her mouth beyond her control as the air got colder and colder.

And then she was there, banging against the grate on the outside of the house, whatever house this was, and she had forgotten about the noise, about keeping quiet, because the air was here, and it was fresh and clean and better than the death and sewage and vomit that had been stuck in her lungs for days. She launched through the broken grate and tumbled into the snow, lying still for a moment as the brightness of the outside world burned her retinas. Snowflakes drifted around her pajama-clad body.

Then, a crunching sound, unmistakable. A sound that should remind her of sledding and snowball fights and drizzling maple syrup over freshly scooped snow in a bowl, but instead sent knives of fear slicing down her skin. Before she could even scramble to her feet, he had her by the back of her neck, his hand a hot clamp on her skin.

"Very clever," he whispered. He swung her into his arms like a baby, like she'd fainted and he was helping her. Her eyes darted around in the gray morning light, but she only saw suburban houses with closed doors and curtained windows, just like every other house in her neighborhood and probably every neighborhood in Minnesota. Nothing stuck out. She had no idea where she was, and no one knew she needed help.

She opened her mouth to scream, but his voice cut her off, low and threatening. "If you even so much as squeak, I will pull every tooth out of your mouth and save your tongue for last."

Her teeth clicked together as tears flooded her eyes. He opened the front door with his hands still underneath her body and began to walk through the house. The smell of bleach and broccoli made her stomach churn.

She was still frozen, unable to move or protest, when he threw her back on the filthy mattress. In the dim light, he looked down at her as if she was a misbehaving dog.

"'You shall rise before the gray headed and honor the presence of an old man, and fear your God.'" His voice boomed in the cramped basement room. "You will not run from your purpose. You will not defy me. No one will defy me again."

Then he left, locking the door behind him. A few moments later, she heard a loud crash outside, followed by the sound of the drill.

He was sealing the only exit shut.

38

Elle

January 19, 2020

When she finally set off for the drive to Falcon Heights, Elle was feeling foggy, thick-headed after taking a nap for a few hours at Tina's insistence. Her body was crying out for more sleep, but she could only answer with the large travel cup of coffee in her hand.

As she took another drink, Elle's phone buzzed in the console. Missed calls and texts were coming through every few minutes. At a stoplight, she glanced at it; notifications from journalists and bloggers she'd interviewed in the past filled her screen. There were emails from her podcast network, from Detective Sykes, from about a thousand listeners. Her old name, her real name, was trending on Twitter. A text from Angelica, Martín's sister, was the only one she opened.

PROUD OF YOU. REPORTERS AT MY HOUSE BUT I'M NOT SAYING ANYTHING UNTIL WE TALK.

"Shit," Elle murmured. She typed back a quick thanks and promise to tell her sister-in-law more soon. Putting that episode up had been so clearly the right decision this morning, but she hadn't even paused to consider that it wasn't just her life that would be affected when she told the world who she was. There were no texts from Martín, but he was probably being inundated too.

She powered the phone down and put it back in the console. At some point, she'd have to face the questions—but there would be time for that later.

When she arrived at Dr. Stevens's house, the curtains were drawn and there were no cars in the driveway. Elle walked up and tried to peer through the windows in the garage door, but it was too dark to see whether there was a car inside.

She started up the path to the house, but then stopped, looking down at the ground. Leading away from the front door, there were footprints in the snow, slightly covered by drifts. With another glance at the front door, she turned and followed them around the house, thankful she had worn boots.

On the side of the house, the footprints stopped next to the indentation of a snow angel. She remembered being young, before TCK, before her childhood stopped, when she would rush outside after a blizzard and sink into the flakes, eagerly swiping her arms and legs up and down to create angelic shapes in her backyard.

Dr. Stevens had a child—or maybe a grandchild, considering his age. That shifted something in Elle's brain, and doubt swept through her. Maybe she shouldn't be here. It looked like Dr. Stevens wasn't even home, and she wasn't sure what she would ask him if he was. He might loosely fit Danika's description, but so did a bunch of the other men in the faculty. He wasn't even fully bald; his picture showed a dark ring of hair around his head. A power donut, as Tina had called it, making Elle laugh until she cried.

Still, it had to mean something that both Leo's murder and Amanda's kidnapping investigations had now led her here. She had to at least knock on his door. Otherwise, it would always be an incomplete task in her head.

"It's just ticking a box," she murmured to herself, walking back around the house. She knocked on the front door.

After a minute, a woman about Elle's age answered. She opened the main door, leaving the screen shut, and stared at Elle through it. "Yes?" she asked.

Her hair was a wild mess of wispy blond. Shadows carved gray spaces underneath her watery eyes. She wore only a T-shirt and cotton shorts, despite the freezing weather.

"Um, hi. My name is Elle Castillo. I'm wondering if I can talk to Dr. Stevens."

"He's not here."

Elle's eyebrows drew together. Strange that he hadn't mentioned this woman when Elle came here before, asking about Luisa. They must have already been together by that time, if the man trusted her to be in his house alone. Then again, if he was having an affair with one of his graduate students, it was understandable he'd want to keep that quiet.

The woman started to shut the door.

"No wait!" Elle held out her hand. "Please, just give me a minute of your time. Can I come in?"

The blonde shook her head, eyes wide. "No, he won't like that. I really can't talk to you."

Something crept along the back of Elle's neck when she saw the fear in the other woman's eyes. It was something she had seen far too many times, doing follow-ups for CPS after police informed them of a domestic violence report in a house with children. Not abject terror, but guarded, like self-defense.

This was a woman protecting herself from even the prospect of her partner's anger.

Elle put her gloved fingers against the screen, hoping she'd take it for the gesture of empathy that it was. "Are you okay?" she asked.

Whatever emotion Elle had seen in her expression quickly shut down. "I'm fine." She tacked a smile on her face.

"Are you . . . are you safe, in this house?" Elle looked at her arms, her thighs, her wrists—all the places she would expect bruises if there were any to see. There were none. He might not hold on to her physically, but he had a grip on her.

"What kind of question is that?" the woman asked. She crossed her arms against the cold wind blowing through the screen, her body tense and leaning away from the door. "Of course I'm safe."

Elle tried to recalibrate. "How long have you been seeing Dr. Stevens?"

"That's none of your business."

"When will he be home?"

"When he gets here. He's a college professor; he doesn't exactly get weekends off."

"And you?" Elle tilted her head to catch the woman's gaze. "It looks like I woke you up. Do you work nights?"

"I'm a PhD candidate," she snapped. "I was up all night working on my dissertation. What's your excuse for looking like you haven't slept in a week?"

The woman started to close the door.

"Wait, wait!" Elle dug into her purse, pulled out a business card and stuck it in the crack between the screen door and the frame. "I'm sorry to have bothered you. If you ever have anything you want to tell me, please contact that number. I'm not a police officer or anything, but I'll help you in whatever way I can."

With a sneer, she took the card and slammed the door in Elle's face.

When Elle got back to the car, she started the engine and shivered as she waited for the vents to produce heat. Picking up her phone, she turned it back on and gasped when she saw the screen. She had missed nine calls from Martín. Ignoring the other messages that popped up, she called him back. He answered on the first ring.

"Elle, there's something you need to know about Amanda's autopsy."

"What? What's happened?"

"She was smothered, but we found something in her stomach. It looks like castor beans."

\\\\\\\\\\

At the morgue, Martín paced back and forth in his office. When he saw Elle, he rushed over and threw his arms around her, burying his face in her neck. She sank into his body, absorbing the relief of him for a few selfish seconds. It felt like a hundred years had passed since they found Amanda Jordan's body in the wee hours of that morning.

"I'm so glad you're safe. I've been going out of my mind trying to reach you." He put his hands on her shoulders and held her at arm's distance, as if to be certain she was really there. "I thought . . . I thought he might have come after you."

"You really found castor beans in her stomach?"

Martín turned and picked up an evidence bag from his desk. Inside, there was a sealed plastic container with some wet, brownish material. She swallowed the buildup of bile in her throat. It had *Jordan, Amanda: Stomach contents* written on the side.

"I'm ninety percent sure," he said. "We've been doing tests here all afternoon, and from what we can tell, that's what it is. And, she showed signs of gastrointestinal distress and dehydration that we'd expect to see from ricin poisoning. We've sent a sample to another lab with more expertise than ours. They should have results later next week."

"By next week it won't matter."

Martín closed his eyes and pressed a thumb and finger into the corners, rubbing the sleep away. "I understand, but we have to confirm before we can put anything in the official report. I'm too close to this case—our office can't afford to make any mistakes."

"I know, you're right. I don't want this to come back on you." Then she shook her head. "I told Ayaan about the harassment we've been getting when she interviewed me this morning. I sent her all the information, but I haven't had any time to check my messages to see if they've found anything. Did Sam tell you their theory? That it's a copycat?"

A shadow passed over Martín's eyes. "No, he didn't. So, you don't think it's the real TCK anymore? I hoped the castor beans would help you prove it was."

Elle looked at the bag of stomach contents again, tears blurring her vision. "The copycat theory makes sense, even with the castor beans in her stomach. He had copied TCK's countdown patterns, why not try his method of killing too? The smothering could have been a mistake, or maybe whoever it is just lost his temper."

Martín nodded. "Maybe. But we know TCK lost his temper and killed before. It's not outside the realm of possibility, but you're right; this does feel messy, considering what we know about him."

Elle tore her eyes away from the plastic container to look at him again. "Ayaan thinks that my podcast inspired him. That he got the idea to copy TCK by listening to me detail his methods on *Justice Delayed*."

"That's—"

"Don't." Elle cut him off, meeting his gaze. "Maybe I have sensationalized this case too much. I have been focusing on the villain more than the victims this season. I let my personal connection to this case cloud my mission, and now we're paying for it. Amanda's parents have paid the ultimate price for it."

"But that's just a theory, Elle," Martín said, hands on her shoulders. "It could still be the real TCK; it could be that he always intended to target you, to get revenge for your escape."

"It doesn't matter!" Elle shouted. Then she laughed, feeling on the edge of hysteria. "Really, it doesn't matter who he is. Whoever has Natalie, we need to find him and stop him before he kills her, and I have no idea when he will. Amanda died early, so there's no reason to believe he will stick with the pattern now. I have turned this over in my head from every possible direction, and I still have too many questions and no answers."

Tears ran down Elle's cheeks. "I failed her. I've been weak, fragile." A memory leapt into her mind like a deer running onto the road. *He* had called her fragile, while he wiped her brow and pretended to nurse her back to health. He seemed so caring then, so far from the man who had ordered her to polish his shoes with her tears.

Martín's deep brown eyes were glassy as he took her hands in his. "Okay, you're right. But you're not fragile, mi vida. You have not failed her. You know everything there is to know about TCK, and even if this guy is just an imitator, you can beat him. You have beaten the real deal. Isn't that what you said on your podcast today?"

Blinking, Elle looked up to meet his gaze. Martín gave her a wry smile and held up his phone. "I know you were probably going to tell me tonight, but I'm afraid about a thousand people beat you to it. I've been getting calls and visits from reporters at reception all day."

"I'm . . . I'm sorry. I should have called."

"You know, I've always encouraged you to tell people who you really are," he said. "I understood that you thought it would make other people think you were weak or damaged, but for me it's the opposite. When you first told me what you had been through, I saw clearly how strong you really were. I was only surprised you put it out there like that."

She squeezed his hand. "After Ayaan told me the killer might have been inspired by me, I just snapped. As soon as I saw the news was reporting Amanda's death, I recorded it and told Tina to publish it right away."

"Can you understand why I'm not thrilled about you going on your podcast to challenge a serial killer in front of hundreds of thousands of listeners?"

Elle bit the inside of her cheek. "I see your point, but it's not like he doesn't know where we live already. I wanted him to know that I'm not afraid of him."

Martín sighed and shook his head. Then he put a hand on the back of her head, drawing her in for a kiss. "You're very brave—no one could deny that. But there is a difference between being brave and being reckless."

"How would you classify this?" she asked.

"I'm not sure yet." He paused for a moment, studying her face. Then he asked, "So, do Ayaan and Sam know about you now?"

Elle shifted on the desk, looking at the floor. "I haven't told them directly."

"They're going to find out eventually. Even if they don't get a chance to listen to the episode, it's already everywhere online."

"I know. I'll cross that bridge when I come to it."

In her coat pocket, Elle felt her phone vibrate. Tina's name flashed on the screen, and she swiped to answer it. "What's up? Did something shake loose with one of the guys from Mitchell?"

Tina's voice sounded strained. "No, nothing that I could see. But I thought you should know . . . Elle, I finally tracked down the IP where a bunch of the threatening emails came from." She took a breath. "It belongs to Simple Mechanic. Duane and Leo's auto shop."

Elle's eyes flicked to Martín, who could clearly hear through the phone. His face paled. The memory struck her then, the reason the words in that message she'd sent to Ayaan nagged at her so much.

Careful what you wish for.

Duane had said the same thing when she and Sam interviewed him in the shop.

"I think Duane might be your copycat."

39

Elle

January 19, 2020

When Elle got to the station, Sam's office was empty. Ayaan's wasn't. The commander was leaning over her desk with her head in her hands when Elle walked up to her open door. She hesitated. Ayaan's fingers rubbed slow circles on her temples, as if she had a headache. Her black blazer was rumpled, flecked with white cat hairs. It was jarring, seeing her anything but perfectly put together. Finally, Elle knocked on the door frame, and Ayaan looked up with a start.

"Oh, Elle. Hi." The commander waved her in, and Elle took a seat across from her. "Did you call me? Sorry, I haven't checked my messages."

"I tried, just to make sure you were still here. Glad I caught you."

"What's going on?"

Elle fidgeted in her seat. The list she and Martín had put together back at the morgue grew damp in her hands. It was all the evidence they could think of linking Duane Grove to Leo's and Amanda's murders, as well as Natalie's kidnapping. Tina had promised to forward the IP information she had found to Ayaan.

"I think I know who the copycat is." Elle put the paper on the desk, slid it across to Ayaan. "Duane Grove. He was the main person of interest in Leo Toca's murder, the guy I saw standing over the body. Sam said they never had enough to hold him on, and that he was captured on a gas station security camera a few minutes before the murder, but I think that can be explained. He's criminally sophisticated enough to have gotten away with running a chop shop for years without getting arrested, so I'm sure he knows how to fake an alibi. If he knew Leo had called me and I was coming over, he could have committed the murder, gone to the gas station so he would be on the camera, and then returned to the crime scene to be 'discovered' by me."

Ayaan studied the paper. "And the kidnappings?"

Elle pressed on, ignoring the doubtful expression on the commander's face. "You already know that the chop shop got rid of the van that we think was used to kidnap Amanda. Eduardo was friends with Duane and Leo—he could easily have made up the story about the person at the university giving the van to him as cover for Duane. Plus, Duane matches the physical description given by Danika: a bald white man. But the biggest thing is this, Ayaan. Tina, my producer, found out a bunch of the threatening emails we've gotten came from the IP address used by Duane's auto shop. I looked back; he's been sending a few a day since I found Leo's body."

Ayaan's gaze flicked to hers. "Where's that information?"

"She said she'd forward it to you."

The commander turned to her computer, swiping the mouse to wake up the screen. She scrolled and clicked. After reading for a minute, she looked at Elle again. "See, the thing is, Elle, we already suspected Duane. The connection between the likely abduction vehicle and his chop shop makes him an even stronger suspect. Sam has been interrogating him about this all day, but he insists he doesn't know anything about the kidnappings. We searched his property, both his apartment and the auto shop. There's nothing there. No evidence of Natalie or Amanda."

"Then he must be hiding her somewhere else," Elle said. She looked at her notes on the desk, all the clear thoughts she and Martin were so sure pointed to Duane. "It has to be him, Ayaan. He hates me, hates the podcast. Leo said the person he suspected had the Majestic Sterling tea in his house. Did you look for that?"

Ayaan shook her head. "No, but even if he did, that wouldn't prove anything."

A rush of nerves blew over Elle, like a drift of snow covering the highway. She held steady. "It would be more evidence he was obsessed with the Countdown Killer. He has to be the person Leo suspected, and that's why he was killed. Leo saw all the warning signs and assumed he was the real TCK, not just someone who idolized him. So, he wrote in to the show. Duane found out somehow and went over to kill him, because he wanted to start killing like TCK did and he knew Leo would mess up his plans."

"That's a good theory, but it's all circumstantial. And there's another problem. We recovered a long black hair at the crime scene for the Toca murder, and the DNA results came back today." Ayaan turned her screen to face Elle and pulled up a report, alongside a mug shot. "Luisa Toca, his ex-wife, whom he supposedly hadn't seen in months. She's in the system because of a DUI a few years back. We haven't been able to track her down, but her car was found last night at an abandoned house outside Shoreview. We think she must have ditched it there and left with someone, probably the new boyfriend her coworkers told us about."

Elle stared at the woman's picture, brown eyes glowing with defiance. "It wasn't her. I don't know where she is, but Leo was killed because he wrote in to the podcast about TCK, I'm sure of it."

"Elle . . ." Ayaan looked over Elle's head.

Sam stood in the doorway of Ayaan's office, his cheeks blotchy and red. "You really think you know better than everyone else, don't you, Elle?" he said, taking a step toward her. There were gray circles under his bloodshot eyes, and exhaustion made his voice hoarse. "We have actual DNA evidence pointing to a suspect who's on the run, and you're still thinking about your stupid podcast?"

"I'm sorry, but not twelve hours ago, you were the ones telling *me* this was about my fucking podcast!" she snapped. "I don't know why Luisa's hair was in Leo's house, but it seems like there could be a whole host of reasons. Like, it could have stuck in something he moved from their old house. Or maybe she went to his house to make up with him. Or *maybe* Duane planted it there to throw you off the track."

Sam shook his head, letting out a sharp laugh. "Not everyone has a master plan, no matter how much you seem to think they do. I guess that makes sense, seeing how you've spent all this time lying about who you really are."

Elle bit down on her tongue, eyes fluttering closed. It had only been a matter of time. When she opened them again, his chin was lifted, smug with victory.

"That's right. I just finished listening to your most recent podcast, *Eleanor*," Sam said. He looked from her to Ayaan. "You've got no idea who you're really working with, do you? Elle is *Nora Watson*. The reason she's so obsessed with TCK is because she was one of his victims."

Elle's face stung as she stared at the table, unable to look at the commander. Ayaan said nothing.

"Did you know about this?" Sam demanded.

Of course she didn't know. Of course not. Tears blurred Elle's vision.

"You were working with an unstable, traumatized woman who's obsessed with catching her own kidnapper, and you didn't even know!"

"Hey!" Elle glared at him, ignoring the panic that rose in her gut. "I am not *unstable*, and I am not *obsessed*. The whole reason I didn't tell anyone about who I am is because I knew that would be the first thing everyone would assume about me. I know the TCK case inside and out because of what he did to me, yes, but also because I'm a damn good investigator. Just because I have been through trauma does not mean I'm useless."

"Elle, you have lied to Ayaan and to me the entire time you've been here," Sam said, not quite managing to cover the hurt in his voice with anger. "Can you imagine how damaging it will be when Amanda's parents find out? They're going to hear you admit on the podcast that the person who killed their daughter did it to target you. We will get raked over the coals and blamed for her death, and it will be because of you."

"Enough, Sam."

His eyes blazed, but he closed his mouth.

Ayaan met her gaze, face drawn with some emotion Elle couldn't decipher. "Maddie Black . . . I should have known. This is why the TCK case has consumed you since I've known you."

"Ayaan, I'm sorry. I don't . . . I don't tell anyone about what happened to me." Heat flashed across Elle's skin, dampness growing under her arms. She couldn't stand the way the commander was looking at her. Like she'd been betrayed.

"You thought I would judge you for being a victim? For wanting to find the man who destroyed your childhood?" Ayaan asked, her voice husky.

Elle sat forward. "I don't want to be a victim. I don't want that to be the first thing people know about me, and that's how it was all through high school, through college. Until I married Martin and changed my name. CPS knew my history, of course, but my boss was kind enough not to tell other people on the job. It shouldn't matter —it didn't matter."

"It matters to me." The power was back in Ayaan's voice, ringing in her small office. Both Elle and Sam were silent as she gathered herself, put her hands on the desk. When her gaze flicked back to Elle's, her brown eyes were serious. "I warned you several times that you were overstepping your bounds on this case. I even looked the other way when I found out you misled Detective Hyde in order to keep investigating after I had told you not to. But Sam's right: your impulsive actions over the past week have put multiple people in danger, including yourself. I think it's best you go home."

Elle wanted to defend herself, but she could barely even bring herself to keep looking at the commander. This was worse than if she was angry, if she threw Elle out of her office with Sam cackling as she went. Elle had let Ayaan down. She hadn't trusted her enough to tell her everything, and now it was too late.

Without another word, she left the office and walked outside. The wind dried the tears in her eyes, sent a shiver to her core. She started the car, unsure what to do next.

Ayaan said they hadn't been able to find any trace of Natalie at

Duane's house, so he had to be keeping her someplace separate, someplace the police didn't know about. Every second she was gone, her life was in danger. Amanda had been killed two days early, so who knew what would happen tomorrow, on the day the countdown said she was supposed to die? Duane had already broken his idol's pattern. What was to stop him from killing Natalie early too?

Police didn't have any evidence to arrest Duane, but that wasn't going to stop her from talking to him. She was going to have to get a confession.

40

Justice Delayed podcast

Recorded January 20, 2020

Unaired recording: Duane Grove interview

ELLE:
Hello, Duane.

DUANE:
What do you want? It's the middle of the night, and I've been talking to police all fucking day.

ELLE:
This'll just take a few minutes. Wanna let me in?

DUANE:
[After a pause.] Fine. Wipe your feet.

ELLE:
I know you don't like me. You've made that clear. But I'm hoping you can answer some questions about Leo.

DUANE:
For fuck's sake, I already told them everything I know. You recording

this for the cops? Think I'm stupid enough to confess to something I didn't do on your microphone there?

ELLE:

Duane, I swear I'm not here to get you in trouble. I'm not trying to manipulate you. Leo called me the day he died with some information about a case I've been working on for over a decade. You know anything about that?

DUANE:

[Loud sigh.] No, I don't.

ELLE:

I think you do.

DUANE:

I told you, Leo was obsessed with your stupid podcast. He started seeing things that weren't there, getting all agitated about how he thought he knew who TCK was.

ELLE:

He told you this?

DUANE:

Yeah, he wouldn't shut up about it. You got him all riled up and then look what happened. The day he writes to your show, he gets popped.

ELLE:

So, you knew that he wrote to me.

DUANE:

Yeah, he told me he was. Said he thought he had enough evidence to actually show you.

ELLE:

And did you know who he was collecting the evidence on?

DUANE:

Nah, I asked, but he wouldn't tell me.

ELLE:

Did you ever suspect it was you?

DUANE:

[After a long pause.] You're a crazy bitch, you know that?

ELLE:

Thank you.

DUANE:

You really came here all alone to accuse me of being a serial killer? You think that microphone is going to protect you?

ELLE:

I can protect myself.

DUANE:

Whoa, shit, what are you doing? You can't do that. Don't you work for the cops?

ELLE:

Answer the question, Duane. Did you suspect that Leo thought you were the Countdown Killer?

DUANE:

I . . . no! Fuck, don't point that thing at me, chill out. No. I'm not the freaking Countdown Killer, okay? I was, like, fifteen when he was killing girls.

ELLE:

That's just the thing, Duane. We're not so sure it's the real Count-down Killer who kidnapped Amanda and Natalie. More than likely, it's just a cheap copycat. A copycat who was inspired by my podcast to start emulating TCK's methods and to target me by coming after a girl I love. Because they hate me. And I think you make a pretty good candidate for that, you know why? Because I have these. Dozens of emails from the last week, threatening my life and making it clear you know where I live. They all came from your auto shop.

DUANE:

I . . . you think . . .

ELLE:

Yes, I think.

DUANE:

I didn't—I sent those emails because I was mad at you for getting Leo killed, not because I was actually going to hurt you.

ELLE:

Keep talking.

DUANE:

That's all it is, okay? Leo died because he was giving you informa-tion on TCK . . . or someone he thought was TCK, I don't know. All I know is my best friend emailed you about your stupid case, and an hour later he ended up dead. I thought you should face consequences for getting people involved in cases like this, that's all. I just thought you shouldn't get away with it.

ELLE:

So, you threatened me.

DUANE:

I never planned to do anything, I swear. I just thought maybe you'd take things more seriously, stop messing with people's lives. Now, can you put the gun away?

ELLE:

Okay, Duane. Say I believe you, here. I could still press charges. But I'd be willing to let this go if you can stop and think. Think really hard about everything Leo said and did in the last few days before he died. Police say that Luisa's hair was in his apartment. They think she had something to do with his murder.

DUANE:

No, no, that doesn't make sense. She started seeing this new guy a few months ago, and Leo was pissed about it, but they were cool. She would never hurt him.

ELLE:

If she was with someone new, why would she have been in his apartment?

DUANE:

I don't know. He didn't seem to like her new boyfriend much, but I guess that's no surprise. I got the feeling he thought the dude was dangerous. He was really high-strung about it, though. Like I think Leo followed him around a little, trying to catch him doing something shady so he could convince Luisa to dump the guy. I don't know, I kind of wrote it off that he was just jealous.

ELLE:

That sounds like something police should know about. Did you tell them?

DUANE:

I'm not a snitch. As far as I know, Luisa and the guy were happy. Leo was just being paranoid. He thought everyone was out to get people because of podcasts like yours.

ELLE:

Okay, Duane, fine. Do you know where Luisa is now?

DUANE:

Her man lives somewhere in Falcon Heights. She's probably with him.

ELLE:

What was that?

DUANE:

In Falcon Heights. Some dude her mom used to live across from. Luisa met him when he and her ma got in some fight. Leo already knew the guy; that's why he got so mad about Luisa dating him. I think he met him at work or something.

ELLE:

Work? At Mitchell University?

DUANE:

Yeah, he was a janitor there. I guess her boyfriend was some professor. Now, will you fucking leave me alone? I could report you for threatening me, you know. Pointing a gun at someone is assault.

ELLE:

Go ahead, Duane. I'm sure the police would love to have you visit the station again, make a statement.

DUANE:

Fuck you. Get out of my apartment.

ELLE:

You've been very helpful. Thank you.

41

Elle

January 20, 2020

When Elle got home from Duane's, the house was eerily silent. It was after two in the morning. An officer sat in his marked car outside, watching, as Ayaan had promised. Even though she didn't really feel that her life was in danger, she was grateful for his presence.

As soon as she was inside, she turned up the thermostat and unwound the scarf from her neck. Unbuttoning her coat, she stared at herself in the hallway mirror. Deep shadows under her eyes gave away how little she had been sleeping.

"You're home." Martín stood at the top of the stairs, wavy hair rumpled from a day of stressed-out fingers running through it.

She grasped the banister, looking up at him. "What are you doing up?"

"I couldn't sleep without you home." He walked down the stairs until he was standing just above her, his warm hand on top of hers. "What did Ayaan say?"

Elle sighed, fighting back a wave of exhaustion. "It's a long story. She doesn't believe me, but I'm not so sure it's Duane now, anyway."

Martín sat down on the step so they were eye to eye. He reached out and caressed her cheek, thumb brushing across the bags under her eyes. "Why do you think it's not Duane?"

She closed her eyes, knowing he would see the lie in them otherwise. She didn't have the energy to explain her reasoning behind going to Duane's apartment alone, gun or not. It would turn into an argument about her being impulsive again, which she probably deserved, but she didn't have time. "Just a hunch. Go to bed, Martín. I promise I'll come once I have what I need."

He was silent for a moment, his gaze probing her for the truth. Then he said, "If it helps, I finally got ahold of Ms. Turner this evening. Or her daughter, actually. Apparently, she was rushed to the hospital after suffering a heart attack about an hour before Natalie's piano lesson was supposed to happen. An anonymous caller phoned 911 and gave them her address, but she was alone when the paramedics arrived."

Elle's knees felt like they'd give out any second. She clutched the banister more tightly. "Will she be okay?"

"Her daughter thinks so. She didn't have any known heart issues, so it came as a surprise."

"Do you . . . do you think she was dosed with something?"

He rubbed his chin for a moment before sliding his hand around to the back of his neck, staring at something over her shoulder.

"You're the one who said he might have set it up, that he would have to have known she was going to walk home alone. Well, maybe that's how he knew. He made sure of it." Elle rubbed her eyes.

"Possibly." Martín watched her movements, looking concerned. "You need sleep, amor."

"I'm not going to sleep tonight," she said. "I've got some research to do."

He let out a long gust of air before clapping his hands on his knees and standing. "Okay. I know better than to argue. Just please . . . please let me know if you need help."

She looked up at him, hoping her smile disguised the guilt swelling inside her. There would be time to tell him everything later, after Natalie was safely home. She watched as he walked back up the stairs and disappeared down the hall.

Armed with a fresh pot of coffee and two slices of peanut butter toast, Elle settled in her studio. She sent a text to Sam, letting him know what Duane had told her about Luisa. He might not be her biggest fan right now, but the detective still deserved to know when she had found a lead on his case.

Then she turned on her computer. Dr. Douglas Stevens had been dating Luisa Toca. Luisa Toca had been missing since shortly before her ex-husband was murdered. He'd been killed within an hour of telling Elle that he knew who TCK was. Even though she wasn't a cop, Elle knew what it took to put together a case for murder against a person. At best, this made Stevens a person of interest.

Elle had already proved to Ayaan that she couldn't be trusted. She had suggested theory after theory and been wrong every time. If she was going to present Stevens as a viable suspect, she needed an airtight case—not a series of uncanny connections. Still, something about the visit to his house that morning nagged at her—the fear in his girlfriend's eyes, the familiar body language of a battered woman. Elle had gotten an ominous feeling the first time she'd been to his house too.

But intuition wasn't evidence.

It took a few searches to find an article about Dr. Douglas Stevens that included a short biography. He grew up in southeastern Minnesota, graduated top of his class from Harvard in 1992 with a joint concentration in math and physics. He then pursued a doctorate in applied mathematics, first at Yale and then finishing at Mitchell University in Minneapolis.

It was a strange move, going to two of the best universities in the country and then coming back to his home state to finish his degree at a midlevel university. She could only think of two reasons someone might do that: a family issue or a romance. Maybe one of his parents died or fell ill and he needed to care for them. Maybe he rekindled a relationship with his childhood sweetheart, giving up the Ivy Leagues to be with her. There were infinite possibilities, but whatever brought him back here, he had stayed.

Douglas Stevens did not fit the profile of a copycat. He was too old, too intelligent, too mature to be consumed with the desire for another man's fame. That left only one option.

The biography included a photo from a few years ago, and she stared at it for a while. She wanted so badly to remember his face, to be hit with the realization of him. But there was nothing; a chalky blur where her memory of him should be. Once again, she pulled up the sketch Danika had helped develop and held it next to his face on her screen. She squinted at it, tilted her head to the side. It *could* work. He wasn't completely dissimilar to the sketch, although she would never have picked him out of a lineup based on it. But Danika was just a little girl. Elle pictured the first grader—baby hairs laid against hazelnut brown skin, tight pigtails held in place by blue and purple baubles. She had sat next to her mother, describing the man to the sketch artist with a quiet, trembling voice. How accurate could she have really been?

Stevens didn't have social media accounts, but he did have a full profile on the university's website. It was pretty dry, full of abstracts from papers he'd written or cowritten, with equations and language that went over her head. But it also provided a more detailed overview of his résumé. When she got to the dates of his PhD, she paused: 1995–99.

If his PhD started in August 1995, he had moved back to Minnesota six months before the first Countdown Killer victim was killed.

The air in the room felt thin.

Swiveling in her desk chair, Elle looked at the Wall of Grief, at the victims carefully pasted in two rows of five.

Kerry Presley. Beverly Anderson. Jillian Thompson. They were all college students.

Taking shallow breaths through her nose, Elle looked at the notes she had under each victim. Kerry and Beverly were University of Minnesota students, Jillian from Bethel. Despite Minneapolis's wealth of colleges and universities, the academic communities weren't insular. There were plenty of reasons why students from different universities might meet one another: sporting events, musicals, debates, math clubs.

The first victim often told you the most about a serial killer. That was where he was learning, honing his craft, and most likely to make mistakes. It was also often the person who sent him over the edge, the one who triggered an instinct that had been dormant for years.

Elle opened her file on Kerry. He was studying physics, getting ready to graduate in just a few months. He had just broken up with his girlfriend the night he disappeared. Walked out of the restaurant where they were eating together, leaving her with the car to get home. He would have been upset, wandering. Cold. Police were confident he accepted a ride from someone. Men were more likely than women to get into a car with a stranger, but Kerry's mom had seemed confident he wouldn't have. He was cautious and small compared with the towering Nordic types that made up most of the men in the area.

Then Elle saw it, the simple dot point on the young man's résumé she'd rushed past so many times before.

- *Audited thermodynamics class at Mitchell University—1996*

She covered her mouth with both hands, staring at the screen. Stevens would have been in the graduate program at Mitchell the same semester Kerry audited a class in the physics department. Like most doctoral students, he was probably assisting professors as part of his funding agreement with the university. Acting as a teaching assistant for undergraduate classes. This was it, the reason TCK didn't want credit for Kerry's murder. He had made a mistake, killing someone he had a connection to.

With shaking hands, Elle picked up her phone and left the studio.

42

DJ

January 20, 2020

Douglas sat at his window in the gray light of an early morning, drinking a cup of tea.

He still remembered the first time his father taught him about sacrifices. The Bible outlined the practice, the way they were to pray and bestow all of their sins and failures and shortcomings onto something else before cutting it open, offering it up to God. Every blemish wiped clean with the blood of another. More than half the years in his life had been reclaimed this way, every second he had wasted controlled by Loretta, by his father, since the moment his brothers had died.

And then, so close to completion, the clock froze. The girl escaped.

For twenty years, he had waited. One day, Eleanor would have a child, and that child would replace her. A lamb instead of a goat. Just when he was losing hope, Natalie appeared, and he watched their bond grow. Today, she would fulfill her purpose, dying on the day Amanda was meant to. He could not wait another moment.

Amanda was not the first girl to die too early, but she was the first he had revealed before her time. Douglas tapped his teacup with a fingernail. He had brought her to the abandoned house, prepared to leave her in the cold garage until the seventh day. But police had been outside, taking pictures of a car he'd thought would go ignored in the driveway. It was too risky to bring her back to his house, and the only other option was nearly an hour away—too far to drive with a dead body.

That left one location, only minutes away. It provided a mild satisfaction, like trying to quench a deep thirst with a single drop of water.

He had planned to wait until Natalie's six days of work were complete, but when he awoke this morning, the need was too strong. It was the seventh day since he took Amanda, and he could not let it pass. The girl would get her day of rest early. Today, he would continue what he had started more than two decades ago with Kerry Presley.

After strangling Kerry, Douglas had driven to his father's house —the only place he knew would be safe. He brought the body to the barn, locked the door behind him. A few days later, he saw a girl challenging her boyfriend out in the street. No regard for his pride. He followed her, offered a ride, showing his university ID. The rest was easy.

When he learned her age, everything fell into place. There was a reason killing that boy, destroying the naive and lovestruck version of himself, had not been enough. The numbers sorted themselves into a formula; the Scriptures came alive for him again. He knew what he needed to do. After that, the hunger to finish the countdown was insatiable.

Now, after years of patience, he would get satisfaction. His world would right itself. He had waited long enough.

On his phone, Douglas swiped to the camera footage from the basement. Natalie was still bent over the side of the bed, her bare back gleaming bluish white in the dim light. Her body tensed and shuddered as she vomited into the bucket he had left for her. The poison was taking hold fast. He had only started feeding it to her last night, but there were ways to make sure she died today.

Douglas went to see her. He slid the lock back and walked down the stairs, ignoring the sour smells of her bodily waste. She was on the bed, hunched into a tight ball with her back to him. He sat next to her and began to stroke her back like a father would his daughter, but she heaved herself off the bed, collapsing in the farthest corner of the room. Her attempt at a scream came out a harsh croak. With her knees pulled to cover her chest, she wrapped her arms around her shins and tried to make herself as small as possible.

"You're sick, Natalie." He made his voice sound kind, a gentle lie. "You should be in bed."

"My bed is covered in shit." She spat the last word out.

Wicked girl. He stood and took a step toward her, but she lifted her chin and did not look away. She was so like Eleanor; the Lord had clearly brought them together for a reason, ordained her for this purpose.

"A mouth like that is unbecoming of a young woman," he said. "'Do not withhold correction from a child. For if you beat him with a rod, he will not die. You shall beat him with a rod and deliver his soul from hell.'"

She glared at him in the dark. "That's not what that verse means. I know the Bible too, asshole."

Rage exploded through him, and in one long stride, he was close enough to grab her shoulders, lifting her off the ground. Natalie cried out, all her bravado lost as he slammed her back against the wall. "Yours is not the first sharp tongue that I have threatened to cut out, but the others had the good sense to keep their mouths shut after a warning." His face pressed closer to hers. "Do you need more than a warning?"

She dropped her gaze at last, hands coming to cover her chest as the fight leached from her body like sweat. After another moment, he set her down on her feet. Still looking at the ground, she whispered, "I'm sick. Please"—she swallowed—"please take me to the hospital. I'll say whatever you want. I just . . . I don't want to die."

How quickly she could be humbled by him. Douglas laughed, one shoulder leaning against the wall as he watched her. "You really are a stupid child."

Natalie stared at him for a moment. Then, straightening up with her hands still covering herself, she said, "'But whoever causes one of these little ones who believe in Me to stumble, it would be better for him to have a heavy millstone hung around his neck, and to be drowned in the depth of the sea.'"

Douglas froze, staring at her.

She spoke again. "'Do not provoke your children to anger.'"

"Shut up."

She moved around him until her back was to the bed frame, and his body shifted with her, keeping her in his sight. She reached down to grab her shirt off the floor and pulled it over her head, then held her arms out wide, as if challenging him to run at her. Douglas's pulse ticked with anger and excitement. Such fire in this girl, even after everything he had done to break her.

"You think I'm scared of you?" she asked, inching backward. *Yes,* he thought, even as she kept talking. "You're using the Bible to justify torturing little girls, you monster. You can only kill me, but you—" She let out a loud laugh, on the edge of wildness, and pointed a finger at him. "You will burn in hell for what you've done."

A switch flicked inside him for the second time in as many days. First with Amanda, and now her. His vision turned red, narrowed in on only her small, panting body. He lunged for her, leapt to tackle. At the last minute, she moved out of the way and he saw the sharp metal pole jutting up from the bed frame.

43

Elle

January 20, 2020

The shades on Douglas Stevens's house were drawn, blocking out the first rays of sunlight. It was impossible to tell if anyone was home. Elle watched the house for a moment, waiting for a sign of movement or life. None came.

Martín would be waking up any minute, wondering where she was. She had turned off her phone as soon as she sent the information she found to Ayaan. Elle couldn't remember making a decision to come here, but in the moments since finding the connection between Douglas and Kerry, she had gotten in her car and arrived at his door.

All that mattered was getting Natalie out. Douglas had evaded police capture for decades; he would have a plan in place if they showed up at his door. The girl was next on his list to kill. Elle couldn't afford to wait.

When another minute passed with no movements in the house, Elle checked her handgun was loaded, got out of the car, and rushed up the sidewalk.

There was no answer to her knock, and she could hear nothing inside. The door was locked with a deadbolt. Douglas had made it a habit to leave the house early every morning back when Elle was his captive; perhaps he did the same thing even now. If she could get Natalie when the girl was in the house alone, no one would have to get hurt at all.

In search of a back door, Elle went down the front steps and started around the side of the house. A quick glance around the neighborhood revealed no nosy onlookers, but there was every chance some old crank would see what was going on and call the police. It was the kind of place that housed a lot of retirees fighting the inevitable move to an assisted living home—folks with nothing better to do than stand at the window and watch the world go by. She had to hurry.

She jogged gingerly through the backyard until she reached the spot where she'd seen the snow angel. It was mostly covered after the snowfall overnight, but Elle could still see its outline. It wasn't as clean as she remembered it being, but that didn't necessarily mean anything. Kids were unpredictable in the winter. Back when Natalie was six or seven, they used to play outside after every blizzard. She remembered the girl waddling around in thick snow pants and oversized boots that tripped her up every third step—how she would collapse in the drifts and giggle at the soft *poof* of a landing that sent fresh powder floating into the sky.

It could be that Douglas did have a child of his own, someone who'd come out here to play and simply fallen or been clumsy while trying to make a snow angel. But the more she stared at it, the less it looked like an intentional design. It looked like the results of a struggle. An icy gust of wind stole her breath.

Elle glanced to her left and right. The footsteps she had walked in were large, the size of a grown man's. Had he carried Natalie here, dumped her in the snow? That made no sense. She looked up, wondering if the girl had climbed down from an upstairs window, just as Elle had done in a different house more than twenty years ago. But there was nothing for her to hold on to, no drainpipe or nearby tree branch.

When Elle looked back at the house, she noticed something she'd missed before. A smooth piece of wood was poorly blended into the siding with a fresh coat of paint. She reached out and ran her fingertips over it. The wood stuck out half an inch from the side of the house, as if it was covering something. She put her head as close to the wall as possible, looking down into the crack between the wood and the siding. It was difficult to see, but she could just make out the black grate underneath.

Her hands shook as she stepped back, looking around again to see if anyone was watching her. She wanted to cry out, call Natalie's name, but if Douglas was inside she couldn't afford to give herself away. She reached into her pocket and pulled out her father's Swiss Army knife, the one he'd given her for protection after she was brought home from the hospital in 1999. It was the only thing she had kept of her parents' after she left home at eighteen. Unfolding the Phillips head screwdriver, she set about unscrewing the plywood. It was tedious work; the screws were wound in tight by an electric drill, and she was sweating by the time she quietly pulled the wood away and placed it in the snow. Cringing in anticipation of the noise, she wrapped her fingers around the grate and yanked it loose from the frame. It came out with a metallic sound that seemed to reverberate around the neighborhood.

Heart racing, Elle crawled into the ventilation system. It was pitch-dark, but she could feel her way easily enough for a while. She hesitated only when she felt blank nothingness in front of her, realizing she would have to go headfirst into a drop with no idea how far it was to the floor. She took a few deep breaths, whispered Natalie's name, and dove. The landing jolted up her wrists and forearms. She crawled forward another few feet before her hands came up against another grate. She had to punch it a few times before it finally fell inside the house.

If Douglas was here, he definitely knew she was too. She crawled to the edge of the vent and looked inside.

It was a small, dingy room with a hard-packed dirt floor, a single bed frame and dirty mattress, on top of which was the huddled outline of a person. Elle's whole body ignited, and a sob escaped her lips. "Natalie!"

Before she could think, she scrambled forward and made the eight-foot drop into the room, somersaulting when she got to the bottom. Her right shoulder screamed with pain, but she shook it off and ran to the bed.

Douglas's girlfriend stared up at Elle, eyes dull but alive.

Elle's legs buckled, and she gave in, letting herself fall to the floor. She pulled her knees in and buried her face between them. She was too late.

Natalie was gone.

∿∿∿∿∿

Activity happened in a blur around Elle.

She had called 911 as soon as she realized it was Douglas's girlfriend on the bed, and they were there within ten minutes. The woman was loaded onto a stretcher and rushed to the ambulance. Crime scene technicians started to fill the tiny basement room, trying to kick everyone else out. One of the first responding officers helped Elle to her feet and the next thing she knew, she was sitting on Douglas Stevens's perfectly neat sofa with a bottle of water in her hands that she couldn't bring herself to drink. The thought of anything touching her mouth turned her stomach.

One of the paramedics tried to check her over; Elle waved him off. Her right shoulder throbbed, but the pain was keeping her mind focused. She'd deal with it later.

After the ambulance took off, she looked around the room in a daze. The wood floors were buffed and waxed, covered in a clean, richly colored Oriental rug. Every cushion on the sofa was plush, corners snapped tight. The lamps, shelves, tables, and books didn't have a speck of dust. It looked like a midrange hotel room—soulless and cold. Natalie and Amanda had cleaned these rooms, worked themselves into exhaustion around this sofa. It made bile sting the back of Elle's throat.

She was out of time. She should have gotten here sooner. There was no trace of Douglas or Natalie, and the one person who might have information for them was drugged, nearly catatonic when they rushed her to the hospital. Elle had felt hopelessness on this case before, but never at this level, this crushing weight.

Her brain churned as she stared at the bottle in her hands, working at the corner of the label with her thumbnail. It was a picture of a spring flowing from the top of a wooded mountain. Nestled among the evergreen trees was a tiny, raisin-sized sketch of a cabin. It was peaceful, a remote refuge. There might not be mountains and springs, but Minnesota had dozens of cabins like that. Maybe when all this was over, she and Martín could go away to one together.

Martín. She looked at her phone, and sure enough, there were half a dozen missed calls from him. She sent a quick text, promising to explain everything later. The thought of even trying to talk about it made her feel sick with exhaustion.

Elle heard Ayaan's voice before she saw her burst into the room, a bright orange hijab framing her fiery eyes. The woman dropped her bag and ran to Elle, gathering her in her arms. Elle froze in shock before surrendering to the commander's embrace, ignoring the pain in her shoulder. She had expected a furious lecture, possibly even a breaking-and-entering charge—not the first hug of their entire friendship.

After a moment, she pulled away and met Ayaan's gaze. "What are you doing here?"

Ayaan laughed in disbelief and swiped at a single tear that threatened to fall. "I could ask you the same question, but I shouldn't be surprised you came here on your own instead of waiting for me. I'll add it to the list."

"What list?"

"Of the ways you could have gotten yourself killed the last ten days."

Elle's face heated. "Every time I told you my theories, you didn't believe me. I didn't want you to try to talk me out of it. When I knew he was the one, I just came here. I couldn't stand the thought of Natalie being here another second."

Ayaan put her hand on Elle's. "I know. I know that I haven't always believed you, but you have been wrong before. You go with your gut, which is great, but that doesn't mean you shouldn't stop to think about the consequences. To yourself, and to the people you love."

Elle looked back down at the water bottle wrapper, picking at the corner.

"I think I know why you're doing it, though. Now that I know who you are."

"Why?" The picture of the cabin tore away in Elle's fingers.

"You have spent the last twenty years feeling that you cheated death. That would make anyone bolder. But I also think that you feel guilty for surviving, like it's your fault you were the girl who got away from TCK." Ayaan squeezed Elle's hand until she met her gaze again. "Elle, you deserve to live, okay? You have fought for your life, and you've earned it. Don't let anyone make you feel otherwise, not even yourself."

Tears welled up in Elle's eyes. Unable to speak, she just nodded.

"I want you to feel like you can trust me. You can always come to me, and I think you know that, or you wouldn't have texted me once you made the connection to Stevens. I'm only sorry I didn't get it until you had already Mission-Impossibled your way into his base-ment."

"So, you believe me now?" Elle whispered.

Standing, Ayaan retrieved her bag from the floor and brought it back over to Elle. She took out her laptop, opened it, and set it on Elle's lap. "Sam got your text about what Duane told you. That Luisa and Douglas were dating, and Leo was stalking him, taking pictures. Once he got that, he was able to push a piece of evidence up the pri-ority list for analysis: a flash drive found in Leo's pocket when he was murdered. He wasn't sure if it was connected to the murder, and it was password-protected, so Sam had been waiting for the techs to get into it. They finally did today."

Elle looked at the screen, hoping her expression was casual enough not to give away that she already knew about the flash drive.

Ayaan continued: "Leo had two-hundred-fifty-six-bit encryption set up on the files, but the cyber team finally cracked the password and got access this morning."

Ayaan double-clicked on the first file, and Elle dropped her water bottle. It landed with a thud on the floor.

"Oh, my God."

There were scans on the screen of diary entries, written in Spanish with perfect handwriting.

"I assume you can read these?" Ayaan asked.

Elle nodded, staring at the screen. It felt wrong, reading someone's diary, but she pulled the laptop closer anyway, skimming the entries as fast as she could.

Luisa had been infatuated with Douglas from the moment she saw him, that much was clear. They met when she worked part-time in the university's salon, providing cheap cuts to poor college students and harried professors. He pursued her, called on her regularly, made her feel wise and insightful and unique. Then there were drinks after work, flirtatious jokes about her going home with him, which both thrilled and frightened her until she finally gave in weeks later. A darkness started to tinge her entries within days of their first night together. He started breaking her down, little digs and prods and twists of a knife that she came to miss whenever she tried to remove herself from the situation, like a runner longing for the ache of muscle after days without a run. She thought of leaving, but it was unbearable. And then her negative language stopped. Elle could almost see the exact moment she decided he was right about her, that she should be grateful for his advice, his instruction on how to live her life.

When she got to the last page, she looked up. "How . . . how did Leo get these?"

Ayaan shook her head. "I don't know. The files were created three weeks ago. He must have found her diary somewhere, scanned it, and returned it before she realized it was gone."

"Or maybe she stopped writing in it because he never returned it." Elle scrolled down more, but there was nothing else in the document. "This diary wouldn't make Leo think her boyfriend is TCK, though. What else did you find?"

"Blueprints of this house, showing there was no access to the basement from the inside. Which you've obviously discovered is wrong?"

Elle nodded and stood, leading Ayaan to the kitchen. The pantry door was already open for the forensics team, revealing the section of shelves that opened out into a narrow doorway. "I got in from the outside, through the vent, but the first responders were able to follow the sound of my voice when they came in."

"Very clever," Ayaan said, her voice bitter. She turned and scanned the kitchen for a moment before crossing to the electric kettle on the counter by the sink. The countertops were like the rest of the house: clear of clutter and debris. More hard work by Amanda and Natalie, no doubt. Ayaan opened the cabinet above the kettle and stepped back. Elle went to stand next to her, and her breath caught in her throat. Inside the white cabinet was a tin of Majestic Sterling tea.

"He got a picture of this too," Ayaan said. "He must have broken in; that's how he found the tea, and that's how he knew there was no clear access to the basement."

Elle shook her head. "He found all of this, just on a hunch."

"That's not all." They went back to the living room, to the laptop. Ayaan's fingers moved around on the track pad, and she typed a few things in before giving it back to Elle. "He also added this."

It was a picture of the exterior of a house. It looked ancient, broken down, but it must have once been impressive. She had no idea what the house meant. Why would this be important to Leo? There was no address, and the file name wasn't helpful. The only clue to its location was a dirty white 213 hanging on the gray siding.

"What's this?"

Ayaan shook her head. "I don't know. I've tried doing reverse image searches, scouring Google Earth, but I haven't found anything. As far as I can tell, Douglas didn't own any other houses, and he doesn't have any close living family. His mother died in childbirth with him, and he had two brothers that were killed in some freak accident when he was seven years old. His father died a couple years ago."

Elle stared at the photo of the old house. "All the other files are named. I wonder why this is just the auto-generated file number from his phone?"

"The photo was uploaded to the folder five minutes before . . .

well before the ME's best guess on when Leo died, factoring in the window of time between talking to you on the phone and when you found his body."

That had to mean it was important. This was the last thing Leo found, something he figured out even after he called her, believing he had enough. The bits of evidence collected in the folder made her smile. Leo reminded her so much of herself, the many wild goose chases she spent years following, sure she had the right person so many times. But Leo *did* have him, and that wiped the smile off her face, because he'd never know that he solved a case that had baffled hundreds of others for so long. He had the distinction of being the one who lost his life for it, though, and for that she would make sure he was remembered.

Finally, she looked at Ayaan. "What do we do now? Douglas has Natalie, and I'm sure he knows we're after him. He'll kill her as soon as possible. And we have no idea where he's gone."

Before she could answer, Ayaan's phone rang. She dug it out of her coat pocket and answered. Whatever she heard on the other end made her instantly alert. "What? Where?"

"What's happening?" Elle whispered, leaning forward.

"Okay, one second, I'm putting you on speaker for Elle." Ayaan pressed a button and held it up. "Sam found Luisa's body."

Elle's eyes were glued to the phone screen as Sam spoke. "After I got your voicemail, I drove to the abandoned house where we found Luisa's car. We initially thought she'd run off with her boyfriend, but knowing she was with Stevens, the picture of why she disappeared changed. We got cadaver dogs in the woods near the house an hour ago and found her. In a shallow grave, buried underneath a fallen tree."

Tears filled Elle's eyes as she thought about Maria Alvarez learning her daughter had been murdered. "How long?"

"It's still early, and it'll be hard to tell, since it's so cold. The body is pretty well preserved. But given how long neighbors said her car has been here, I'd say she's been dead over a week. With her hair at Leo's house, I'd guess she was with Douglas when he killed him, and he killed her afterward to keep her quiet."

Ayaan met Elle's gaze, her eyes reflecting the same devastation. "Does she have anything on her?"

"There's a diary buried underneath her, but it's . . . well, it's unreadable now. But her phone was in her car. I'm just charging it up to see if I can get anything off it."

After updating Sam about the situation at the Stevens house, Ayaan said, "Sam, I need you to look at her phone and see if you can find anything in her maps app. Anything that would show places she visits often, addresses she's entered recently. It's our best shot for finding out where Douglas might have taken Natalie."

He was quiet for a moment and then there was a shuffling sound. He read off a list of her most recent trips, mostly for local department stores and restaurants. But one address made Elle sit up straighter.

"What was that last one?"

"Two thirteen Forest Drive, Stillwater. She went there the day before she was last seen at work."

Ayaan's eyes locked on hers. "Did you say two thirteen?"

Elle stood up, vibrating with excitement.

"Yes," Sam said.

"That was the house number on one of the pictures Leo had on his laptop, the last thing he saved." Elle rubbed her chest with shaking fingers. "Sam, do you have your tablet? Can you find out who owns that property?"

"Sure, let me check." There was another brief silence. "The owners are Mark and Betty Miller. They're in their sixties; I'm guessing it's a summer home. Looks like they bought it from the bank about six months ago. It was an escheatment, forfeited to the state after the previous owner died, so it went cheap."

"Who owned it before the state?" Ayaan asked. From the look in her eyes, Elle guessed that the commander already suspected the same thing she did.

"Hold on. Ah, got it. Shit. The previous owner was Douglas Josiah Stevens, our college professor's father."

44

Elle

January 20, 2020

It took almost a half an hour to get to Stillwater, even blasting the speed limit with the siren on. After Ayaan called for more backup to the house, Elle couldn't stand the silence, trying to push through the panic as they sped along Highway 36.

"Why do you think Douglas gave up his dad's property? Even if the guy died without a will, his son still had a right to it, didn't he?"

Ayaan nodded. "State law would automatically hand over the house to any living children or other relatives, if there was no spouse. It's rare for property to escheat to the state. So, either the lawyers couldn't find Douglas Jr. to hand over the assets, or they found him and he relinquished his rights."

"It doesn't make sense. If this is his kill site and he planned to start taking girls again, why wouldn't he claim the house?"

As she took the next exit, Ayaan cut the lights and sirens. "Maybe this wasn't his planned kill site. We know he used the cabin where you were kept back in the nineties; his father was alive, so it would have been too risky to use his house then. If he murdered Luisa and dumped her body at that abandoned place in Shoreview, maybe that's where he planned to take Amanda and Natalie too."

Elle fidgeted in her seat, shaking with adrenaline. "That must be what made him break his pattern. He accidentally killed Amanda early, and then when he tried to bring her to the house to store her someplace safe, he saw the cops and had to change his plans." Her place wasn't far from there. Maybe knowing the pain and dread he would cause her was a suitable substitute since he couldn't follow his normal pattern.

Silence fell between them. Elle stared out the window, a constant prayer chanting in her brain. *Please stay alive. Please stay alive, Natalie.*

After a few turns, they were on a leafy country road just outside of town, driving past giant summer houses for people who could only stand Minnesota from June to September. Their windows were shuttered like eyes screwed up tight against the winter chill. When they came to the house in the picture, Elle struggled to breathe.

Natalie was in there. She could feel it.

"Sam should be right behind us," Ayaan said. "I want you to wait in the car."

"Ayaan, you said you want me to trust you, and I do. So, I'm going to trust you with this truth: if you leave me here, I will just jump out and follow you the second you're out of sight."

The commander was silent for a moment, jaw tight. Elle knew she was pushing it, but her hand shook on the door handle. They were wasting time.

Finally, Ayaan glanced at Elle's handgun. "That stays in your holster unless I give the word or you have a gun pointed at your head, got it?"

Elle nodded her agreement but looked away from Ayaan's gaze. If she had a clear shot at TCK, she was going to take it. Death was the only thing that would stop him.

They got out of the car at the same time, and Ayaan threw her a bulletproof vest from the backseat.

Sam drove up as they were jogging toward the house, and he ran over, strapping on his own vest. "What's the plan?" he asked.

Ayaan pointed at them. "You two go around the back. I'll take the front."

They started toward the back door, the snow in the yard coming up almost to Elle's hips. She trudged as quickly as she could, following Sam's lead and ducking out of sight underneath the windows.

Sam looked over his shoulder, his eyes tinged red with fatigue. "I'm sorry I didn't believe you, Elle."

Unable to think about anything but where Natalie might be, she simply nodded, and they continued on.

The silence was immense. She heard no sounds from the inside of the house, no cars driving by, no birds singing or planes flying overhead. Nothing to suggest they were not out in the middle of nowhere, even though they were only about ten minutes from the main drag of Stillwater. Once Sam got to the end of the house, he peered around the corner. Elle stepped up behind him, following his gaze. There was a well-shoveled path leading from the back door to a shed about thirty yards away. A drooping, snow-dusted clothesline stretched between two metal poles. Other than that, the yard was mostly bare—or whatever was there was covered by several feet of white powder.

The coast looked clear; Sam nodded at her, and they rushed to the back door. He checked the handle. It was unlocked. No surprise, out in the country, but still stupid. As quietly as possible, he opened the door. She looked inside and saw straight down a narrow hallway to the front, where Ayaan was silently entering. Their eyes met, and she lifted her chin at Elle. Sam stepped in first, and Elle followed close behind, shielding herself behind his bulky frame.

The mudroom was dirty, everything coated in a layer of grime. There were a few old coats hanging on hooks, a pair of dusty rain boots slumped in the corner, and several stacks of old newspapers lined up against the opposite wall. It looked like nothing in this room had been touched in decades.

Exiting the mudroom door, Sam went right and Elle turned left into an old, seventies-style kitchen. The white tiles were decorated with orange and brown patterns. Wood paneling lined the walls. An old teakettle sat on top of the cold black stove rings. She tiptoed through, her legs trembling from the combination of tense muscles and melting snow soaking through to her skin.

Back out in the hallway, there was no Ayaan in sight. The glimpse through the doorway across from the kitchen revealed a sitting room. Elle walked in, gaze darting around for any sign of Natalie. There was barely any furniture here, as if part of the house had been cleared out before the new buyers gave up until next summer. A battered wheelchair sat in the corner, waiting for its owner to return. The grimy window let in a weak ray of light. When Elle looked out through the glass, a flash of movement caught her eye.

Out in the distance, just past the shed, there was a large figure looming dark against the snow. Her stomach plummeted when she saw him lift his arm.

"Natalie!" she screamed. Then she ran — out of the room, through the back door, and as fast as she could down the path. The only sound aside from the pounding in her ears was boots slapping the ground behind her. They were not being subtle in their approach, and it occurred to her when it was already too late that this was a problem. By the time she was close enough to see that Douglas was looming over Natalie's little body, tied to an old tractor, she could see he had heard them coming. And he was not the least bit concerned. Rage seared her skin when she saw the red welts raised on the girl's pale, shivering back.

"Stop right there," he commanded.

"Gun!" Ayaan shouted.

Elle froze and heard no movements behind her, but she knew Ayaan and Sam were there, staring at the same thing she was.

Douglas wasn't brandishing the belt anymore. He was holding the end of a pistol right underneath Natalie's left ear. Elle lifted her own gun to aim it at his chest, but then cried out and dropped her arm. Her shoulder spasmed with pain from her fall inside Douglas's basement. She could switch the weapon to her left hand, but there was no way she could trust her aim with it — not with Natalie only inches away from him.

Terror grew white hot inside her. She couldn't see Natalie's face, but the little girl's body was tense and trembling, and she had vomited into the snow.

The poison. She was dying.

The thought almost kicked the back out of Elle's knees, but she forced herself to stay standing as Douglas finally turned to face her.

He was transformed from the man she saw last week: granite face ruddy with effort, blue eyes free of lenses and glowing from the bright sunlight glaring off the snow. His balding head was covered by a black wool stocking cap. He was unsurprised, unmoved—panting from the lashes he had laid against Natalie's skin. His brown leather belt lay in the snow next to his feet, coiled like a dead snake. He must not have been able to find a switch under such heavy snowfall. On his right cheek, drying blood shone sticky and thick around a fresh wound, suggesting he'd been grazed by a sharp object. She wondered if it had come from Natalie and felt a wild combination of pride and terror at the thought of the little girl fighting back against him.

"Ah, Eleanor."

The sound of her old name on his lips made her tremble. He used to say it so often—sometimes like a curse, sometimes like a prayer. He called her by name every time he gave her an instruction, every time he punished her, every time she pleased him. He made her dread it as much as he made her long for it, all in just a few short days. She would never understand how.

She was desperate to look at Ayaan or Sam, to figure out whether they had a plan, but she didn't dare break eye contact with Douglas now that he was looking at her, his gun still snug against Natalie's head.

"Elle, I'm sorry," Natalie wailed. "I tried to get away." Elle resisted the urge to run to her. Natalie would only live if Elle was in control, if she did not make another mistake. She had made enough of them where TCK was concerned, enough for a lifetime.

"It's okay, sweetheart." Her voice was shrill in the cold, country air. She swallowed, trying to steady herself. "It's going to be okay."

"You'd be proud, Eleanor. She tried to kill me, just a few hours ago. Almost succeeded too," Douglas said. "Uh-uh, I wouldn't do that if I were you." He looked next to her at Sam, who was trying to inch closer.

Elle put her arm out, stopping him. "Do not mess with him."

Ayaan spoke from a few feet behind them. "Douglas Stevens, you are under arrest for the kidnapping and murder of Amanda Jordan, as well as the kidnapping and aggravated assault of Natalie Hunter."

She used the same voice she always did, clear and precise. "Drop your weapon and come with us peacefully. We will not harm you."

While Douglas was looking at Ayaan, Sam broke into a run. Before Elle could even blink, Douglas lifted the gun away from Natalie, pointed it at Sam, and shot.

"No!" Elle screamed, lunging forward, but Douglas had already returned the end of his pistol to Natalie's head. She shrieked at the hot metal burning her flesh, her body contorting, and then she slumped over the tractor. Elle prayed she had gone unconscious. There was nothing she could do unless he dropped that gun. Elle chanced a look to her left. Sam was sprawled in the snow, some of the drifts soft enough to close around his body. He didn't make a sound.

When Elle looked back at Ayaan, the commander was standing resolute, pursing her lips with eyes wide and dry. They had missed the opportunity Sam had tried to give them—that brief second where Douglas's gun was not directed at Natalie. It had passed so suddenly, shattering like an icicle on pavement.

Elle faced Douglas again. She was a few feet closer to him now, close enough to see the hardness in his eyes. He was angry because this was not going to plan. Nothing, so far, had gone according to his plan. She could use that.

"You stopped for all these years." She shook her head as if in disbelief. "What made you lose the urge to kill? Did you finally meet a woman who you actually loved?"

Douglas laughed. "You think that's what this is about? That I was some isolated, involuntary celibate who could have been cured with a regular woman in my bed? Oh, Eleanor, I expected better of you by now. I have no trouble with women. They believe everything I tell them, including my dead wife. You remember her, don't you? I told her you and Jessica were my nieces when she came home early one day and caught you scrubbing the floor."

The way he said "Jessica" brought a memory slicing through her consciousness like a hot knife. He said it the exact same way as he had twenty-one years ago. She sorted through the haze, trying to recall a woman catching her cleaning. She didn't remember ever seeing her. She'd been so hungry and scared that, afterward, it felt like each memory of the place was a card in a deck, and someone had thrown it into the air and scattered them all.

Then she remembered the bodies in the burnt cabin. "I know you killed her."

"My wife killed *herself*. I just cremated her in an unconventional way."

"She was shot."

"She knew what the consequences were for betraying me. In that way, she caused her own death." He smiled. "Conveniently, her lover made an excellent body double."

Elle blinked, thinking of the two charred bodies, buried without names. She pictured Luisa, dumped in a lonely grave behind an abandoned house, her mother distraught and left with nothing but questions. Then there was the woman in Douglas's basement, dosed with some kind of tranquilizer he must have had on hand for his kidnapped girls. Maybe it was the same drug he'd used on her, all those years ago, when she wouldn't stop kicking the back of his seat as he drove her away from her life, from her childhood. How easily this man extinguished lives to find fulfillment in his own. He had probably been doing this for years: finding vulnerable women who looked up to him, who craved his approval, and slowly dismantling their lives until there was nothing left. Maybe that was how he was able to stop killing for so long—temporarily satisfied by the control he was able to exercise over them.

A gust of wind kicked up, slapping the exposed skin on her face. Pushing through the ache in her shoulder, Elle raised her gun again, but only got it to a forty-five-degree angle before the stabbing pain became too much. She tried to take a step forward, but Douglas shook his head.

"No, no. You stay just there."

"Why now?" she asked, doing as he said and planting her feet on the ground. Natalie was still limp and unmoving. Her body must have been half frozen; she was terribly still. *Please, God. Don't let her be dead. Not now.* "You could have come for me anytime. Taken your revenge in a thousand ways. Why do this? Why resume the countdown after so much time has passed and people have basically forgotten about you?"

The comment had the desired effect. Douglas's jaw clenched and the arm holding his gun wavered. Then he laughed again. "Let's not forget who you're talking to here, Eleanor. The story of my work has made you famous. No one has forgotten about me."

She pushed her lower lip out and shrugged her shoulders. "Still, this isn't your best work. I mean, you've only had Natalie a few days. You already screwed up with Amanda. How can they fulfill their purpose in the countdown if they don't even do their full six days of work before they rest?"

His face paled. She had been right; that verse in his house wasn't a coincidence. It was his driving force. She looked at the end of his pistol pressed into Natalie's head. He was only holding it with one hand, so if she knocked him off balance with her bullet, it might be enough to keep her from being hit. But Ayaan was a better shot, so if she hadn't taken it, that meant it wasn't worth the risk. Even if he died, his finger could still reflexively pull the trigger, and Natalie would be gone.

She was going to have to make him come after her. If he turned his gun away from Natalie again, Ayaan would not miss a second chance. Elle put every ounce of fury and frustration from the last two decades into her voice when she said, "So, how does this end, then? You kill Natalie, out of sequence, because you fucked up and killed Amanda before you meant to? That's sloppy, Douglas. You'll never get what you need that way."

"Is that so?" he asked.

"The countdown is ruined. You're not fulfilling some grand design; you're just like any other old monster, caving to instinct and anger. All it took was some security camera footage and a nosy janitor to bring you down."

"Shut your mouth, stupid woman. You have no idea what you're dealing with here."

She let out a single, harsh laugh at his words. Her desire to kill this sad, small man dissipated like car exhaust. Elle took another step toward him, daring him to move his gun away from Natalie's head, to shoot her instead. Four more steps, and she'd be on him. In the distance, sirens wailed.

"Make me shut my mouth, you pathetic old man. You don't have control over me anymore. We caught you. Two women captured the brilliant, uncatchable Countdown Killer. You are finished, and I can't wait to stand in front of a jury and tell them exactly who you are."

Douglas's arm jerked, the tip of the gun moving off the back of Natalie's head. Elle braced herself for the bullet she knew was coming her way.

A shot rang out. Douglas froze, let out a gasping cough. The hairs on the back of Elle's neck stood up as Ayaan stepped forward into her peripheral vision, handgun extended. Two more shots exploded, forming a perfect triangle of holes on his chest. He stumbled, staring down at himself in shock as the gun fell from his hand.

Elle didn't wait for him to fall. Unzipping her coat, she raced across the snowy ground. She dropped to her knees and fell across Natalie's still body, covering her with whatever warmth she had left to give.

45

Justice Delayed podcast

February 18, 2020

Transcript: Season 5, Episode 11

[THEME MUSIC + INTRO]

ELLE VOICE-OVER:

I am an investigator. I am a survivor. I am a storyteller.

This month, I have had to learn what to do when a chapter ends before I know how the next one will start. Over the past few weeks, I have released episodes detailing what happened in this case. I have told you about the two victims in the cabin, trying to give them back their identities after decades languishing in unmarked graves. I covered what we have been able to learn about Luisa Toca, how her ex-husband tried to convince her the man she was dating was a killer. We may never know why Luisa visited her boyfriend's childhood home the day before she died or what made her text Leo a picture of it, but it was the last activity on either of their phones before they were killed.

I have described what his newest girlfriend experienced after she heard Natalie screaming and came to investigate, finding the two of them in his basement dungeon. He drugged her and left her for dead, but like us, she survived. So many women have written in since we aired her episode about the abuse and controlling behavior she endured at his hand. They all tell a similar story: how TCK found them when they were at their most vulnerable, made them believe he was in love with them, and then dug his claws in—not letting go until their confidence was shredded. That episode also inspired his almost-fiancée, Loretta, to tell her story on the podcast last week. I remain incredibly grateful to these women for coming forward and reliving some of the worst moments in their lives.

I have also shared what it was like in that final standoff, facing the man who destroyed so many lives. I have made sure you all know the names of the detectives who helped rescue Natalie. Without investigators accessing Leo's files, we never would have known where to look for TCK. Without Sam Hyde finding Luisa Toca, we would have been too late to save Natalie. I'm glad to report he is out of the hospital and recovering well. And without Ayaan's careful shooting, there is no doubt in my mind that both Natalie and I would be dead.

But one thing I have not done, which several of you have asked about, is say the killer's real name. And I never will. I will get to that in a minute.

Over the past few weeks, I have been grateful for your notes of encouragement and support. I have been grateful that most of you have respected the privacy of my friend and her daughter, and the Jordan family, as they work their way through the trauma. I spoke to Sash yesterday, and she agreed to be recorded for this podcast.

SASH:

I just wanted to let everyone know that Natalie is doing well. This kid is stronger than I ever could have hoped, and she has taken to her physical and psychological therapy without complaint. I want to thank everyone for the money you raised so that I could take an extended leave of absence to be with her and pay the medical bills. And I understand you put together a funeral fund for Amanda Jordan's family—that's amazing. Elle, the community you created around this podcast is something special, and we are incredibly grateful.

ELLE:

Does Natalie have anything she wanted to say?

SASH:

Yes, she recorded a message on my phone.

ELLE:

Okay, go ahead.

[SOUND BREAK: A click, then a shuffle as a recorder is set down.]

SASH:

Do you have anything you want Elle to play on her podcast?

NATALIE:

Um, yeah. Don't give him attention.

SASH:

What do you mean?

NATALIE:

Just that he would want everyone to be talking about him, and I don't think you should. He killed a bunch of people who never got to be famous for anything other than being dead. I don't think he should get the attention because he did that to them.

ELLE VOICE-OVER:

When I was investigating these kidnapping cases, we thought for a time that the person who had done this was copying TCK's methods. We thought he was inspired to do so by this podcast. And while we now know that isn't true, I realize that I have not been completely honest with myself here. I have strayed from my mission of focusing on the victims of crime and bringing them justice. I never intended to make another podcast that glorified the lives and minds of serial killers, but I can see now that in some ways, I did that with this case.

That is why I have decided to take down this season of *Justice Delayed*. All the episodes covering TCK have been removed, but my back catalog will remain, and I will leave this final episode up so that new listeners will know why I've made this decision. I have to be honest, it hasn't been a popular one with my podcast network or our advertisers, but—with all due respect to them—I don't care.

Natalie is right. The man we knew as the Countdown Killer wanted nothing more than to have every one of you looking into his background, holding up the terrible things we've uncovered about his childhood and jilted romance as some evidence for why he was the way he was. He wanted to control the narrative around himself. I'm sure he would have loved for you to dissect his every thought and motivation. So, I'm not going to give him what he wants, and I hope you won't either.

Don't share every moment of his life on your blogs and Reddit posts. Don't delve into the gruesome way he controlled and murdered girls, the unverifiable theories about what he may have done in the twenty years between his triad killings. Don't give him the satisfaction of a legacy, even if it is the worst kind of legacy a person can have. Talk instead about the lives he stole, the futures of the women he wiped out before they could make a name for themselves on this planet. Talk about Amanda Jordan and the impact she had in her eleven short years. Focus on the girls whose lives he ended, not the pitiful life he used as a reason for doing so.

Now that this season is officially concluded, I'll be going on a brief hiatus as I look for a new case where I can focus on the people who are waiting for justice—the victims, their families, their loved ones. That's what this podcast is all about, and yes, it will continue. I'll keep searching for answers for people who have been forgotten and ignored. I'll keep hunting the monsters that got away. And with your help, I will keep bringing them to justice.

Acknowledgments

Writing a novel is a solitary act, but bringing it into the world cannot be done alone.

I'm beyond grateful for my agent, Sharon Pelletier, whose brilliant editorial notes made this manuscript stronger. You are the best advocate and champion I could ask for—I'm glad you're in my corner. Lauren Abramo, my indomitable foreign rights agent, worked with countless coagents and book scouts to make this book even more well-traveled than I am. Special thanks to Kemi Faderin for all you do. The whole team at DG&B is unrivalled in its awesomeness, really.

The first time I talked on the phone with my editor, Jaime Levine, I knew she just *got* this book. The story would not be where it is now without your incisive feedback, your refusal to let me get away with weak character choices, and your deep understanding of what I was trying to say. Also, thank you for introducing me to the phrase "power donut" and knowing a remarkable amount about Darjeeling tea.

The enthusiasm of everyone at HMH for this book has continued to blow me away. Helen Atsma provided early support, and Millicent Bennett and Deb Brody carried it on. Ana Deboo, copyeditor extraordinaire, caught a hundred tiny mistakes that would have kept me awake at night—bless you. Romanie Rout combed every word and punctuation mark with an eagle eye. The design team—Jessica Handelman, Mark Robinson, and Margaret Rosewitz—made this book look gorgeous inside and out. Johannes Wiebel provided a truly stunning illustration for the cover that made me gasp the first time I saw it. The marvelous production editor Laura Brady and editorial assistant Fariza Hawke offered invaluable help along the way. My publicist Marissa Page, marketing genius Liz Anderson, and everyone in sales have worked tirelessly to put it in the hands of readers all over the country. Thank you to each and every one of you.

I am also indebted to the editors throughout the world who saw something in this book and are helping Elle's story cross borders and language divides. Special thanks to Harriet Wade and the team at Pushkin Vertigo in the UK for providing a home for my novel in the country where I learned I was a writer. And I'm thrilled to be published by Text in Australia—my second home. Thanks to Alaina Gougoulis, Madeleine Rebbechi, Julia Kathro, Kate Lloyd, Michael Heyward, and the entire team for taking such good care of this book.

Many experts across dozens of disciplines helped me be as accurate as I could. Any blurred lines between fact and fiction are my choices, not their mistakes! Dr. Annalisa Durdle was generous with her guidance on how one might forensically identify a tea stain. The *Sultan Qaboos University Medical Journal* made their study on a case of castor-bean poisoning openly accessible. Dr. Judy Melinek and T. J. Mitchell cowrote the most fascinating memoir on being a medical examiner, which inspired Martín's character and provided some of the autopsy information in this book. Forensic toxicologist Justin Brower answered my burning questions about ricin poison and how it's detected in autopsy. Hennepin County Library provided a lightning-fast answer on business records from 1996, proving yet again that librarians are superheroes.

Thank you to my fellow writer Rogelio Juarez, who provided diligent attention to detail, insights, and suggestions for the Latinx characters in this text. Candice Montgomery, your generosity and encouragement with the early review of this book and Ayaan's character meant everything to me. Any inaccuracies in the portrayal of these characters are my fault alone.

The road to getting published is paved with rejection, and I'm convinced that friendships with other writers are the only way to survive. Bethany C. Morrow, you are the best friend, confidante, and critique partner in existence. Tap, tap, tap—case ended. Marjorie Brimer, your enthusiasm and excitement rivaled my own throughout the whole publishing process and is such a blessing. Libby Hubscher, I'm thrilled you got your book deal at almost exactly the same time and shared every up and down publishing has to offer with me.

Anna Newallo, Megan Collins, Katherine Locke, Amy Gentry, Rena Olsen, Kosoko Jackson, Kiki Nguyen, Denise Williams, Ryan Licata, Candice Fox, Halley Sutton, and dozens of other authors offered inspiration, support, and essential insights over the years. Crime and thriller authors I have admired for years read this book early and told others to read it too. I cannot thank you enough: it means the world to me to see your name anywhere near my book.

Kingston Writing School in London is where I started to take writing seriously, and I'm incredibly thankful for the lecturers and writers in residence who took my writing seriously too. James Miller, Adam Baron, Paul Bailey, and many others helped me hone my voice and strike my flowery prose.

Coworkers at every job I've had in the past five years have been very cool about my writing, but I'm especially indebted to Clare, who has always encouraged me to take time off for my author career when I need it.

I am extremely lucky to have unflinching support from my family, both in the US and Australia, who cheered me on while I was writing and celebrated this achievement with me. Thanks especially to my siblings—Joel, Erin, and Deborah—for giving me a rich, hilarious, and often infuriating childhood that I can now draw on for an endless number of stories.

My mom was the first big believer in my writing and always encouraged me to work at it, helping me shape my craft and style from an early age. Late-night conversations with my dad led me to discover what I really believe in, and he pushed me to share those ideas with the world. I'm so glad neither of you ever made me feel like being an author was a long shot (even though it was!)

Finally to my husband, Peter, who knew he was marrying a writer and did it anyway. Thank you for not letting me quit, for bringing me snacks, for sending me on writing retreats, and for popping champagne at 6 a.m. when I got my offer. I love you.